ZOTOV

MOSKAU

MAGIC DOME BOOKS

Moskau
Published by Magic Dome Books, 2018

ISBN: 978-80-88231-71-4

TABLE OF CONTENTS:

Part One. The King of Dwarves

Part Two. The Black Sun

Part Three. Gjallarhorn Thunders

Part Four. The Carnival of Phantoms

PART ONE

THE KING OF DWARVES

Valhalla, the Gods await me,
Open wide Thy gates, embrace me,
Great hall of the battle slain
With swords in hand!

Manowar, *Gates of Valhalla*

PROLOGUE

"YOU CAN'T POSSIBLY THINK all those things exist, surely?"

She smiles — not a grin but a small smile, just baring her little white teeth as if she's about to sink them into you. Her eyes glisten; her fingers clench the stem of her wine glass.

She loves to argue. Not because she wants to get to the truth but out of sheer stubbornness: she hates to admit defeat. I bet she feels aroused at moments like these.

I take a theatrical pause, pretending her question has caught me unprepared. The black curtain embossed with a runic pattern quivers in the little current of air from the aircon. The silence is absolute. The closed windows block out the groaning of cars stuck in the traffic. The candles flicker like wolves' eyes in the dimmed light.

You might mistake my room for a hunter's abode. Wherever you look, its walls are lined with the twisted horns of wild ox and deer skulls bleached with time. The dinner table rests on a bear hide of a deliberately crude tanning. A boulder I brought from the Norwegian marshes sits at the center of the room. It's a gorgeous item: a monolith chunk of granite.

"Absolutely," I reply calmly. "I don't doubt it for one single moment."

She sips red wine from her glass. Her cheeks begin to glow. She's about to launch an offensive.

"Very well... I agree, to a point," she says. "Let's presume that our planet was formed in place of the primordial chasm of Ginnungagap that used to divide the two realms of ice and fire. For millennia the two kingdoms drifted toward each other until they finally united, producing the athletic giant Ymir and Audumbla the cow. Personally, I tend not to agree with what was supposed to happen next but... I might just suspend my disbelief that much. The first man and woman emerged from Ymir's sweat while his two legs copulated with each other, giving birth to a son, which was how the ice giants were born into the Earth's stormy night. I'm not laughing at you, oh no. If our historians still argue over the intricacies of the Great Battle, who would take it upon themselves to claim the knowledge of what happened a million years ago? How did humanity come about? Did it emerge from the ocean, drop from the sky or crawl out of underground tunnels? All this is guesswork."

She sets her glass down. Flirtatiously she rearranges a feathery strand of hair. She casts a quick glance around the room — apparently in search of a mirror — but predictably finds none. Well, tough luck, lady.

"But as for the rest... you'll excuse me if I interrogate you extensively," she continues. "Let's examine it all in every detail. So, high in the sky we have the hovering Asgard, the heavenly dwelling of the gods, which is perfectly normal. All cultures place their gods up high. The Christians billet their God among the clouds; the Greek gods used to dwell on top of Mount Olympus, and the Hinduist God Shani actually impersonates the planet of Saturn, or all places. Deities are obliged to live in cloudland: if they dwelled amongst us, they'd lose their wits within a week. Now let's make an effort and imagine one of Asgard's buildings — namely, Valhalla. Odin's banquet hall, a place of unending orgies of bingeing and lovemaking. There, dead soldiers gorge nightly on the meat of Sæhrímnir the boar and drink themselves senseless on the mead produced by the udder of Heiðrún the goat. And once they've eaten, the dead enjoy the services of beautiful maidens. Five hundred and forty doors — and a roof thatched with gold shields supported by a colonnade of spears. You have to agree that an unwashed medieval Viking warrior must have taken this idea of heaven quite for granted in the wilds of their fiords. But what about us? Us, living in our cynical age of e-funks and the world wide Shogunet network? Us who can't watch television without our 3D goggles? We can't even shift our backsides without being assisted by a machine! The office rat responsible for the invention of remote controls must have made a fortune! Do you still think that the Vikings' heaven is any good for the men of today? Well, I don't. You, just you personally — do you believe in Valhalla?"

I reach for a slice of pork and chew on it, slowly and neatly. The wheat beer in a misted glass cheers my eye; I watch it weep. I don't drink wine. I don't consider it patriotic. She? Well, she... she can do whatever she wants. It's all peanuts compared to what she's already done.

"I'd rather believe in Valhalla than in the Biblical heaven," I answer in a syrupy voice just when she's about to lose her patience. "It's much better organized. Every person in the Reichskommissariat, from babies to old women, has a military rank. This is perfectly logical, considering that only an *Einherjar* can enter Valhalla: a warrior who has died in combat, sword still in hand. Admittedly these rules can sometime have the funniest consequences. Even bus conductors are considered a military unit and have their own system of ranks. A bakery manager receives the rank of a Subaltern of Baked Products and wears special black collar insignia shaped as ears of wheat. Even gynecologists have been made into a Sonderkommando unit complete with a coat of arms depicting a naked Valkyrie revealing her heart in her hands."

"This is something I could never understand," she interrupts me. "Why heart?"

"What else should she reveal?" I reply meekly.

She turns red, pretending to play with her wine.

"Everyone wants to go to heaven. This is a prerequisite for our existence," I press the napkin to my lips. "Behave, and you'll be rewarded. Valhalla makes it so much simpler. No need to fast and pray. All you need to do is kill and die in battle. This isn't just what the Vikings think. Muslims believe this too. Or are you uncomfortable about Heiðrún the goat? She doesn't need to be there after all. I'm quite prepared to allow the existence of a modified version of Valhalla. In this day and age it can be refurbished and turned into anything. Even a sushi bar."

She empties her glass in one gulp. The twinkle in her eyes expires. "In any case, the Führer isn't in Valhalla!" she enunciates. "If he's anywhere, then he's in hell!"

Unhurriedly I dunk the meat into sweet mustard and drag it around my plate. "Our whole life is hell," I explain with a polite smile. "And the only way to escape it is by dying. If our priests are to be believed, the Führer is busy enjoying Sæhrímnir steaks even as we speak. I know, I know. He didn't die sword in hand. But what difference does it make? At the moment, the Führer is a trademark, not the nation's leader. His pictures on mobile phones, lighters and condoms — all this is a marketing ploy. No one's going to sacrifice their lives for him these days. They might do so if the price is right, provided it's in yen. Or even Reichsmarks. Alas! All these office rats are unlikely to ever see Valhalla."

I give the wurstsalat its due: the good old combination of sausages, potatoes and a dash of mayonnaise. I increasingly get the impression that there's something perverse about our dinner — indecent even. Still I like it. And so, I believe, does she. The Führer? It's not so simple, either. Even the wisest of our priests admit it, those who were interned in Norwegian caves.

The Führer died on October 20 1942 during a parade at the Nibelung Square celebrating the first anniversary of his armies' victorious entry into the capital of Russland. A lone terrorist driving a truckful of explosives smashed it into the stands by the walls of the Kremlin. Instead of a sword, the Führer was holding a small stack of paper as he delivered one of his fiery speeches. Within a split second, the entire upper echelon of the Third Reich disintegrated in the blast. There wasn't as much as a single molecule left of them. The Führer took a fast train to Valhalla in the company of Himmler, Bormann, Muller, Goebbels and Goering.

I remember a little blond guy in the Higher Theological College ask simple-heartedly, “Do office workers like Reichsleiter Bormann go to Valhalla too?” They kicked the kid out of school on the spot. From what I heard, he became a street sausage vendor.

“Had I not believed in Valhalla, I’d have never become Odin’s priest,” I continue, looking her in the eye. “Spirituality is unpopular there days. It’s easier to put the Führer’s portraits on lighters — Japanese tourists buy them like they’re going out of style. Or get a job at the Institute for the Research of Aryan Origins, that’s something quite popular with girls your age. You spend five years as a hermit at the Mount Kailash archeological digs in Tibet searching for the first Aryan sites. Barley cakes, yak butter tea and tons of enlightment. But personally, I wholeheartedly believe in Viking rituals — and not just because they make part of the Reich’s official religion. Go see Trondheim, it’s no less impressive than Jerusalem. The goat is nothing, after all. Not when you think of all Christianity’s goofs.”

She doesn’t say anything. She doesn’t even look my way. She must have taken offence. How are you supposed to talk about anything with the Schwarzkopfs? They’re not open to discussion.

The moment you say something that contradicts their point of view, they sulk and pout their lips.

The girl reaches for the remote she's so passionately condemned just a moment ago and thoughtlessly clicks the TV on.

A commercial break. Whenever you switch it on, it's always advertisements.

"Want to be sure you're part of the master race?" a juicy kimono-clad blonde inquires from the screen. "Our Sony computers know if you're an Aryan. They require a DNA sample to boot up. Our Sakura Operating System is now available in Russisch. *Konnichiwa!*"

Unfortunately, the only two things the Reich is good at making are sausages and missiles. All the rest is made in Japan. White goods, brown goods, fountain pens even. *The Nippon koku* is so popular that every Fräulein worth her salt has already had an eyelid job done to give her gaze an Asian slant.

Japanese food is everywhere. You get served wasabi even with your beer and sausages. Outdoor advertising has more fancy Japanese characters than normal Gothic letters.

Slowly and smoothly, the Reich is being devoured by the *Teikoku* — the Empire. I wouldn't be surprised if one day we began addressing the Führer as the Mikado!

I sense it's time to break the silence. "You need some rest. Allow me to accompany you."

She lays the napkin on the table.

We head for the bedroom. A black color scheme. The wallpaper pattern is that of crossed battleaxes. The interior designer sought inspiration in Viking caves. Well, admittedly he succeeded. I can even sense a whiff of dampness in the air — but most likely, I have the aircon to thank for that.

This room too is devoid of mirrors. As is my entire place. I have an aversion to the wretched things.

The girl doesn't like it here, I know. The Schwarzkopfs don't appreciate living in style. Well, I'm sorry. She has no choice.

I tactfully turn away from the king-size bed while she removes her dress and dons pajamas. I'm sure she wants me to turn round; but I can control myself.

"Good night," she whispers listlessly and slides under the quilt.

"Sleep tight," I say as I cuff her wrist to the headrest.

She doesn't react. Her eyelashes are lowered.

"You need to understand," I heave a sad sigh. "This is for your own good."

Quietly I close the door, lock it and place the key in my pocket. A camera eye glows in the room. I may not be there but I can see everything my prisoner is up to. I'm not talking about masturbation. Whenever this happens, I switch off the monitor — you can't even imagine what a woman can do with only one free hand — and listen to her groans in the speakers. Sometimes I get the impression that she does it not so much for her own pleasure but in order to seduce me. Which woman would refuse to spend a night with a priest — even a pagan priest? At first, when her two shoulder wounds were still raw, the girl tried to free herself but only managed to scrape her handcuffed wrist. Now she's okay but still I shouldn't be too lax. She's wrapped herself in the quilt — asleep, hopefully.

Excellent. I have terrible vertigo.

It takes me a quarter of an hour to heat up the Norse boulder with red-hot embers. It's so hot I feel like a kitchen cook. I reach for the knife. Its steel is cool against my skin. I ran it across the flat of my hand. Blood drips onto the granite, sizzling and bubbling, streaking the runes brown. My nostrils quiver, taking in the pungent smell of a slaughterhouse.

Pain enters my head. My skin prickles with electric discharges. My eyes fill with white flashes. I can see something but I can't quite make out what it is. Just some spine-chilling outlines.

It's all right. I have these fits sometimes. It'll be over in a couple of minutes.

CHAPTER ONE

THE CITY OF *Soci*

THE AIRSPACE OF RUSSLAND
NEAR THE CITY OF SOCHI

PAVEL DIDN'T KNOW what to do with himself. The old Junkers airliner on a LuftStern flight from Hong Kong to Moskau was packed solid and shuddered in the air like a streetcar. The threadbare economy class seats; the stomach-wrenching stench of microwaved meals; the air hostesses with martyr's smiles on their faces, their unyielding legs swollen from long hours of flight... he'd seen it all on his business trips.

He leafed through a magazine, then listened to the music in his earphones. Doing nothing for ten hours on end could be really exhausting. He couldn't sleep: the seat was too hard and uncomfortable.

Come to think of it, this time he was really unlucky with his seat.

He'd got to sit in the middle. The window seat (to his left) and the one by the aisle (to his right) were taken by two elderly Japanese. An old man and an equally old lady. Both wore floral-pattern shirts, matching pants and those panama hats so beloved by Japanese tourists worldwide.

For some reason, the couple reminded him of two lapdogs, useless and goofy. Plus the cameras, of course. They had even managed to take a picture of themselves in the plane's bathroom.

The old boy absent-mindedly opened a colorful leaflet and peered at its title through his glasses,

Visit Lake Baikal, gem of the Reich!

Tourism operations to Moskau had shrunk 50% over the last couple of years, and so had the reichsmark in comparison to the yen. Japanese tourists were the only hope the Kommissariat had left. Where else was it supposed to get the money from? Industry was on its last legs. St. Petersburg (or should we call it Peterstadt now?) was flooded every summer with groups from the Nippon koku, complete with their panama hats. Tourist guides were run off their feet taking them from Salvador Dali's statue of the Führer all the way to Peterhof and street markets offering swastika-decorated Easter eggs. No one really cared that Operation Barbarossa of July 22 1940 had initially intended to raze St. Petersburg to the ground. There had even been some sort of blueprint detailing the whole procedure. Never mind St. Petersburg! The same Operation Barbarossa had planned to flood Moscow and turn it into a water reserve. They'd had some sick imagination, really. No one would admit this but in fact it felt like half the Führer's entourage had been high on LSD.

The Japanese guy turned the page to the next picture. Palm trees and seaside. A girl in a swimsuit stood on a sandy beach, cocktail in hand.

He turned to Pavel."*Gomen kudasai,*" he grinned, baring a mouthful of teeth. "Excuse me. Do you speak *Russisch*?"

At any other time Pavel might have pretended not to understand the question. Still, the flight to Moskau was going to be a long one. What difference would it make anyway, if you were stuck in a confined space at thirty thousand feet with two old farts for company? Even they were a Godsend to while away the time.

He smiled. "*Konnichiwa, Sensei.* How can I help you?"

The old boy pointed at the girl on the picture, burying his fingernail in her ample chest.

"Excuse me," he said, butchering the language. "My wife and I will be staying two days in Moscow. And after that we'd like to go to the seaside. I can't decide on a destination. Is the city of Sochi (he pronounced it as *Soci*) good?"

The plane hit a turbulent patch. The passengers clenched their armrests. *Soci!* Pavel chuckled to himself. *This guy knows what he wants. Very well, then...*

He pressed an armrest button. His seat slid backwards.

"If the truth were known, Sochi isn't a place I'd recommend," he said with a deadpan face, glancing at the old man. "It's part of the Reichskommissariat Caucasus. That area suffered a lot during the Twenty-Year War. Service is rubbish. Hotels are refurbished barracks. The sea is still full of drifting mines. Kidnappings of tourists are not uncommon. The local tribesmen often leave their mountains to ambush tourist buses and blow up funiculars. And food is too expensive for what it is. Even corn ears sold by beach vendors — former members of SS Turkic legions — might cost you a good hundred reichsmarks apiece."

The old man nodded. Apparently, he hadn't understood half of it. Still, Pavel wasn't going to switch to German. From his experience, few of the Nippon koku's denizens knew any *Hochdeutsch*.

He cast a sideways glance at the booklet.

The blue sea, the palm trees, the cocktail glasses and the girl, laughing out loud, in her Peenemünde swimsuit. This was a paste-up if ever he'd seen one.

...ONCE AGAIN, THE STENCH of burning flesh filled his nostrils. Pavel saw the dead cities; the black skeletons of the buildings. The smoke drifted low over rivers overflowing with dead bodies. Oh, yes. He still remembered it all.

By the summer 1984, when the Reich's flags were finally flying over the Urals' defenses as well as both African and South American jungles, the ruling elite of Greater Germany had split. Nobody wanted to acquiesce. The SS wanted to have control over the oil wells, the Wehrmacht wanted to lay its hands on the diamond fields while the Gestapo claimed the U-mines. That would have made any history scholar laugh. Money and luxury: this was every empire's undoing. The hordes of Genghis Khan had crossed the continent from the Chinese steppes to the spires of Polish churches, but the Mongols' imperium had crumbled to nothing. When a warrior is loaded with gold like a donkey, why would he go into battle? All he can dream of is wine and female affections. Similarly, the Reich's military elite had mutated, becoming a financial oligarchy. All of them had joined in the carving up of world resources, even the Navy's Chief Karl Dönitz in his wheelchair, shaking with old age. It was a miracle that the Twenty-Year War hadn't ended in nuclear attacks: the Reich had tested its first A-bomb already in 1944 on the island of Peenemünde. Unfortunately, the air raids had seriously damaged the nuclear power stations. The air there was still buzzing with radiation and Geiger counters were just as commonplace as aircons.

THE OLD GUY JUST WOULDN'T give it a rest. "I wonder if fishing is good in Soci?"

Pavel didn't hear him. The roaring of the plane's turbines had nothing to do with it. He was far away, reminiscing.

The Twenty-Year War had flattened each and every one of the Reichskommissariats: East, Ukraine, Caucasus and Turkestan. Some cities had been luckier than others, emerging relatively unscathed. But Moskau, Kiev and Minsk had turned into battlegrounds. The Reich was devouring itself from the inside while the Nippon koku was getting richer, offering loans to both sides.

And what was the result? The empire's economy was on its last legs. Moskau alone was still braving it out while in the Caucasus, from what he'd heard, local highlanders were swapping lynx pelts for butter. Japan, however, had ballooned like bread dough, its skyscrapers bayoneting the sky, their walls covered in neon signs. Not just in Tokyo but also in Shanghai,

Manila and Sydney. The post-war accord had granted Japan half the world. They'd received China and Australia, clipped off Alaska, Seattle and Nevada, and invaded Russland's Far East and Siberia.

Oil, gold and gas — the Japs had jumped at their chance then and they had it all now. In 1970s, the Emperor Hirohito had issued a decree gifting Lake Baikal to the Reich. Moskau girls had wrapped themselves in kimonos; TV screens were absolutely flooded with manga and anime.

This was the real enslavement of the planet, creepy and inconspicuous — no need for tanks or airplanes, only fashion statements. Now the Nippon koku was brimming with money while the only thing the Reich still produced was weapons.

But who were they supposed to sell them to if the world was already conquered?

"Fishing?" Pavel resurfaced from his musings. "Plenty of fish there, Sensei. The sea's seething with them. Take my advice: forget the fishing rod. A machine gun is the thing. Did you watch TV last week? About that mutant shark that attacked a speedboat near Adler, just next to Sochi? Lots of victims that day. And the killer crabs... too much radiation, you see."

The two tourists' panama hats rustled as they exchanged anxious whispers. The fact that they had to lean over him to do so didn't seem to bother them. They hadn't even thought of asking him to swap places. He watched their wrinkled faces: they looked like two Shar-Pei dogs sniffing each other.

Oh, well. They were the master race. As simple as that.

"*Arigato gozaimasu,*" the old man finally managed. "Thank you very much for your help, Sir."

His wife nodded enthusiastically. It didn't look as if she'd understood what the conversation had been about. She sneezed and reached into her handbag — apparently, to get a handkerchief. She rummaged through it, rattling its contents, but never produced anything. Her husband exploded in a bout of dry coughing and pressed a hand to his mouth.

Old age ailments! Now they would start taking pills by the handful. Time to bid his *Auf Wiedersehen.*

"You're very welcome," he sighed. "Excuse me, may I squeeze past?"

He walked down the aisle. It felt like being stuck inside a giant bee: a buzzing in your head, a stuffed feeling in your ears. The economy class bathroom was as comfortable as a coffin. He'd have liked to know how porn actors ever managed to make out in places like these. It was too small for two guinea pigs to fornicate.

The tap produced a weak trickle of hot water. Pavel splashed some onto his face puffy from lack of sleep. He glanced into the mirror and cringed. Not the best version of him. On the other hand, how are you supposed to look like when you live, eat and sleep your job while the top office is too stingy to afford a business class seat for their expert?

Sunken cheeks, receding temples, a hooked hawk nose and eyes transparent like jelly. Pavel still remembered what he used to look like while a little kid. He'd never been beauty pageant material, and as for his height... never mind. The Führer had made short men popular. All things considered, not too bad.

Pavel reached into his pocket for a disposable razor and gave himself a good shave.

When he returned to his place, the plane was descending. A viscous lump of nausea blocked his throat. The Japanese's seats were empty. They were off on some business of their own.

"Ladies and gentlemen, please fasten your seatbelts," the metallic voice of the air hostess resounded throughout the cabin. "Our flight will land in half an hour. The weather is fine. The air temperature is 95 degrees. According to the local weather report, radiation levels are within safe limits. No need to wear face masks on leaving the airport."

Pavel didn't look in the window. He was fed up with cookie-cutter views.

Two men awaited him on the ground. Despite the heat, they were wearing gray raincoats.

"Welcome to Moskau, Sturmbannführer," the first of them clicked his heels.

The other one reached out to take Pavel's suitcase. Pavel didn't mind.

"Once again, our apologies for having to summon you all the way from Hong Kong," the first one continued. "It must have been a long flight. You need to get some sleep. We'll take you to the hotel."

Pavel shook his head. "Oh, no. Plenty of time at night to do that. Let's go directly to the Gestapo."

A MIDDLE-AGED AIR HOSTESS — a peroxide blonde with the LuftStern logo on her beret — sprang to attention, watching the three men climb into an executive-class Opel Admiral. She struggled to suppress the desire to shoot her arm out in the party salute. The *Sieg Heil!* had been abolished as the result of the Twenty-Year War. Together with the party, that is.

CHAPTER TWO

SAKURA HOTEL

A SIXTH FLOOR OFFICE, THREE HOURS LATER

FROM A CLASSIFIED AUDIO TRANSCRIPT

"I'M HIGHLY DISAPPOINTED IN YOU, Itiro-san," a male voice said bitterly.

"And so am I, Onoda-san. Allow me to write a poem on the subject, followed by my performing *seppuku*. I will be very careful in ripping my belly; I won't soil the floors. I've brought a waterproof cloak and twenty feet of plastic film specifically for the purpose."

"And what am I supposed to do with your body? Cut it into pieces and burn them in the fireplace? Thank you very much! As far as I know, you and your wife received two million yen for the job. The imperial *Kommandatur* in Hong Kong made sure you boarded the plane without being checked. No, don't start. I've heard all your excuses. But somehow I doubt they'll convince the others."

A heavy sigh. "I understand. What am I looking at?"

"Nothing good, really. The Mikado Bank account where you placed the money has been frozen. Your family isn't getting it until the job is complete. Excuse my being so blatant, Itiro-san, but how much time have you got left until your meeting with Amaterasu, the solar goddess?"

The other voice paused. "About a week, according to the doctors. I appreciate your concern."

An expiring cigarette hissed against the ashtray. "In this case, I have the displeasure to state that you have seven days to complete your mission. In any case, the government will pay for your funeral. Out of pure respect of your past services, Itiro-san."

"I do not deserve a single crumb of respect, Onoda-san."

"Excellent. In this case, try to retrieve some of it, as well as your money. This is the only way to secure adequate living standards for your children. I'll make sure that you have everything you need this week, including reichsmarks. The reichsmark isn't as stable as the yen, but at least you can use this Monopoly money all over Europe

— both in Moskau and in the Reichskommissariats of Norway, Ukraine and Netherlands. Italy is the only country now not accepting the reichsmark. They prefer their hand-soiled liras. What a joke of a nation! They still exploit the bygone glory of Cesar's legions while in fact they struggled to conquer those barefoot Abyssinian savages. War just isn't their thing. They should stay at home and eat spaghetti. All those weekly *Hello Duce!* TV shows! Romano Mussolini is just as eccentric as his father was. He's eighty, for crissakes, and he's prancing around like a college student. All that drunken sax playing of his at the Axis countries summit; his courting the ancient Sophie Loren... the man is a joke. You should rent an apartment by the day. Hotels are crawling with Gestapo agents. You know, don't you, that this so-called empire of theirs is a rather loose structure? It's not a single state but some sort of hostile competing Reichskommissariats. Even their capital is alternating. Last year it was Amsterdam. This year it's Moskau."

"I thank you, Onoda-san. The diamonds of your thoughts enrich the poverty of my mind."

A lighter clicked. "I swear by the Mikado, you won't find it easy. Yes, you do speak a bit of Russisch, that was part of your profession... still, theory and practice aren't the same thing. The Russlanders are a very peculiar nation. They're terribly xenophobic — but they love all things foreign, especially with some well-targeted promotion. You know, don't you, that Japanese food is all the rage here? In less than ten years it has become a sensation."

The other man coughed. "Please accept my admiration for your work, Onoda-san. I always found it strange they eat so much sushi in the Third Reich, considering them a national Japanese dish and the ultimate in health foods. If this is the work of the promotional department at the Mikado's court, they deserve being immortalized. Turning Japanese cat food into the local jetset hors-d'oeuvres!"

"Oh, yes! Thanks to this idea, the Nippon koku has no problem getting rid of raw fish leftovers. As for the rest, it's all the same. Did you notice the abundance of blond people in Moskau?"

The voice paused again. "I did. Everybody's either blond or a redhead. Not a single dark-haired person."

"Exactly. Itiro-san, this is something you need to understand. In Moskau, being Aryan is considered *cool.* The Führer's initial doctrine considered the inhabitants of Russland as an inferior nation of *untermenschen,* as they called them. Substandard people. But closer to September 1945 the Reich's generals realized they weren't going to defeat the guerrilla movement. Which was when the opposite idea prevailed. Reluctantly they recognized the

Russlanders as an Aryan nation which allowed them to recruit them into the SS. Moreover, the Berlin Racial Department officially recognized *all* Slavs as Aryans, including the Bulgarians. Everyone but the Poles, that is. From that moment on, Russland women could claim alimony for the children born from German soldiers[1]. It's been half a century ago. The European nations have all cross-bred since: it's a true melting pot here. These days you'd be hard pressed to guess the origins of anyone. But here, Aryans are obliged to dye their hair blond. It's not a trend even. More of a necessity."

"You don't want to say there're no dark-haired Russlanders left, do you, Onoda-san?"

"Oh, yes. Plenty of those around. But they either wear wigs of shave their heads. Those who have the guts to be seen with their natural hair are called the *Schwarzkopfs* — Black Heads. It's the slang word for dissidents. I told you already that Russland is a very peculiar area. It eagerly soaks up any foreign filth — but by the same token, it resists any foreign invaders. The guerrilla movement is still going strong all over

---

[1] In March 1943 Adolf Hamann, the commandant of Orel — the Russian city occupied by the Germans — issued this little-known order about "alimony payments to children born of Wehrmacht fathers". The reason for the Slavs' recognition as Aryan was simple: Germany needed to replenish its troops after its Stalingrad losses.

the Reichskommissariat of Moskau. They control entire areas in the Urals, in St. Petersburg suburbs and around Yekaterinodar. You won't want to go picnicking in the woods, oh no! Even in Moskau, Resistance is quite active. Two months ago they killed the city's Oberkommandant Gruppenführer von Travinsky."

"This is crazy," the other voice burst out coughing. "Overzealous fanatics."

"You would think so, wouldn't you? But this is simply a local tradition. The Russlanders have lots of habits they inherited from the Mongols. Corruption, for one. An Oriental love of creature comforts. Sucking up to the authorities. Cronyism. And with all this, they resisted the Yoke for two hundred years until the Golden Horde gave up and left them well alone. The Russlanders' ties with the Germans are much stronger than you might think. They were ruled by *Kaiserins*, Empresses of German blood, like Katharina I and Katharina II who is also known as Catherine the Great, the best queen in Russland's history. Every Emperor of Russland starting with Peter the Great married a German princess. The very first Royal Russian dynasty was the Rurik, descendants of Danish princes. They were followed by the Mongols followed by the Germans. After the Bolsheviks had seized power, Jews came — followed by the Georgians followed by the Germans again. Basically,

Russland has always been controlled by a foreign power. So there'll always be some who hate it. Unfortunately, neither the government of Russland nor the Schwarzkopfs have noticed that the Wehrmacht is long gone. They're at war with themselves."

"How can I express my gratitude to you, Onoda-san? All this is highly informative."

"Don't mention it. What a shame that Amaterasu is in such a hurry to summon you. You won't have time to get a feeling for Russland. I've been working here for ten years already. You can't imagine some things I've seen — even in the Siberian cities of Uradziosutoku and Habarosito which are thriving in the Mikado's care. You can make the locals take Japanese names but they'll still drink moonshine instead of sake!"

"How truly awful..." the other voice trembled.

"I haven't told you half of it. No one wants to study Japanese. Women are the only ones who agree to wear geta sandals and kimonos. No one makes rock gardens over here. They prefer to dig the ground up and grow those wretched cucumbers, of all things! The only things that took were *yakitori* and right-hand drive cars. Oh, they love them in Uradziosutoku! This is something they won't let you take away from them! I completely agree with the Mikado's position: in order to ensure our empire's world leadership we do need natural resources. And still sometimes I wish that our acquisitions didn't go beyond taking the second half of Karafuto Island."

"I completely agree with you, Onoda-san."

"Sorry for keeping you so long, my dear Itiro-san. Here, take these reichsmarks," the voice said, accompanied by the rustling sound of paper notes. "I'll give you the address in a minute. Go to the first street kiosk and buy yourself an oxygen mask and a Geiger counter. Do you have the Hong Kong equipment with you? Excellent. But be careful. Don't use it unless it's absolutely necessary."

"If you don't mind me asking..." the other voice shook with anxiety, "could you issue me a handgun, please?"

"You don't need it. Whatever you do, you can't shoot him."

CHAPTER THREE

TEMPLE OF ODIN

ARYAN ST. 46
OPPOSITE THE KOMMANDATUR

I LEAVE THE CAR at a remote parking lot. Even though I have the clearance, no one's allowed to park their cars by the walls of the Kommandatur. The place is wallowing in paranoia; they see terrorists everywhere.

I receive a token made of hard cardboard and head for the turnpike. A fat bespectacled middle-aged guy in a brown uniform with an Obergefreiter lapel badges is manning the booth by the barrier. With his tongue hanging out from the effort, he's studying a fresh issue of *Völkischer Beobachter* plastered with glossy pictures of scantily clad girls.

That's crisis for you. The party press was obliged to adopt the tabloid format in order to survive in the free market.

I knock at the glass of the booth. We've known each other for ages.

"Heiley heil," he mumbles unceremoniously, turning a page.

I wave a greeting. "And heiley to you too."

I know every inch of the Aryan Street which stretches from Berlin Station all the way up to the Reichstag. I can walk the whole length of it blindfolded. Its sidewalks are lined with the blackened skeletons of tanks fenced off with strap barriers: a reminder of the street fighting of the Twenty-Year War. Half a dozen charred Tigers are grouped together opposite the Luftwaffe Heroes Boulevard like a small herd of droopy-trunked elephants. The walls of the state-of-the-art office buildings touch the rotting ruins of bombed-out houses. From what I heard, in Bolshevik times there used to be a monument to the Russian poet Alexander Pushkin here. He's long been removed both from the square and from the school curriculum. He was of African descent, wasn't he?

Actually, the Ministry of Education did a great job. They banned Tchaikovsky's music — apparently, the composer was a closet homosexual. They destroyed some of the most popular old movies which had featured Jewish actors, no matter how minor the part.

The center of the boulevard gapes with black holes edged with fire-licked scabs. These are bonfire sites. On weekends, the Aryan Street becomes a scene of multiple book burnings. They confiscate books from the Schwarzkopfs like they used to do at the Opernplatz in Berlin. The books by Herbert Wells, Feodor Dostoevsky and Stanislaw Lem squirm as they reduce to ashes.

When I was still a young Führerjugend activist, I brought here a copy of *The Three Musketeers* that the school janitor had been hiding in his cubicle. I threw it in the fire. Its author Alexander Dumas wasn't Aryan. There was African blood in his veins too. Have you heard this ripping noise made by burning paper? It sounds like a heart being ripped apart.

In place of the old Pushkin monument, they've got Nietzsche standing now. At first, lots of people confused him with Gorky (another banned author) because of his fat moustache. The Führer used to love Nietzsche's *Thus Spoke Zarathustra.* Unfortunately, he didn't know something that Nietzsche had also said, "Germany is a great nation only because its people have so much Polish blood in their veins." Having said that, it's probably just slander spread by the Shogunet forum trolls. Trust them to post all sorts of sick nonsense.

The government buildings on the Aryan Street are a sorry sight. Most of them are just copies of Berlin's gloomy edifices. Take a look: the Moskau Ministry of Propaganda and Public Education is perfectly in keeping with Dr. Goebbels' old office with its gray columns, its colorful mosaics depicting young Aryan people flashing white smiles as they applaud National Socialism.

A piercing wind invigorates the fluttering Reichskommissariat flags: the scarlet-red banners with a black eagle clenching a wreath of oak leaves. The swastika is long gone. Only souvenir vendors at the Richard Wagner pedestrian zone still sell merchandise featuring *Die Hakenkreuz*, the "angled cross". The swastika on the flag was banned soon after the Twenty-Year War. Regardless of how much everyone worships the Führer, not all of the Reichskommissariats were happy with his legacy, especially those where constant uprisings of the "Forest Brothers" were the norm.

Next, the dilapidated office of the Labor Front. A long time ago, this trade union organization used to be headed by Robert Ley. Reichsleiter Ley was killed in 1968 by some guerrilla fighters during his visit to Kiev. They sent him a messenger pigeon carrying a miniature grenade.

A blood-curdling screech of car brakes shakes the air.

"Where do you think you're going, you motherf- Or, sorry, Priest. My mistake."

I was so busy staring at the Labor Front windows that I didn't even notice myself stepping out into the traffic and very nearly being hit by a green Nissan. Nissan, what a funny name. One of those words you can't help but tweak to make them sound more lewd, if you know what I mean.

Most of Moskau cars are Japanese. The Mercedes, Opels and Volkswagens are reserved for official missions. Their production just isn't viable anymore. Even street buses are all Mitsubishis. Not to mention the Tokyo-imported pushbikes.

I flash him a benign smile. "It's all right! *Alles in ordnung*!"

I didn't even notice saying it. We use Germanic words and phrases mechanically. Nobody refers to an "ID card" anymore: it's an *ausweis*. Russlanders soak up foreign words naturally, me being no exception. Still, I can only think in the local tongue.

I wipe my forehead. The sun is blazing.

Odin's priests don't have it easy. Sacrificial rites call for a special uniform: chainmail, a pair of fur-lined high boots, a wolf pelt thrown over your shoulders and a fifteen-pound ritual sword hanging from your belt. It does take some stamina, I tell you.

I can't walk any faster but I've almost arrived at my destination. I go past a Hashi sushi bar – *hashi* means chopsticks in Japanese — and there I am, entering Odin's Temple.

If the truth were known, I'm not a hundred percent happy with my workplace. The building is far too large and ponderous, shaped as a medieval cave with a central grotto and several branching tunnels. Admittedly, it's quite comfortable. There's a hot water source inside: very convenient when one needs to clean blood from swords. By the entrance, there's a sculpture: Tyr the God laying his hand into the mouth of Fenrir the wolf. The year 1947 saw Norse mythology being adopted as the official religion of the Third Reich, in compliance with Reichsführer Himmler's last will and testament[2]. No one was going to destroy the existing churches or cathedrals: their congregations were free to worship whoever they pleased.

But what is the popularity-driving engine these days? Exactly. Publicity. Billions of reichsmarks were channeled into the promotion of new ideas. TV, radio, even the leading movie stars including the-then star Marika Rökk and the publicly repentant Marlene Dietrich. It

---

[2] In the real world, in 1943 the Reichsführer of the SS Heinrich Himmler prepared a plan to adopt Scandinavian mythology as the country's official religion. The plan provided for the building of Viking temples as well as the execution of the Pope. However, he never proposed the plan to Hitler.

worked. It took less than ten years for half the Reich's population to reject their religions and start worshipping at the altars of Greater Germany.

A sensation? Not at all. The entire history of humanity is proof of the fact that people find it very easy to denounce their religion, provided the publicity is right. The two thousand years of Christianity had left a bad taste in their mouths. The new version of the same old (or a *remake*, as they call it in the California Republic) was extremely timely. Everyone was already bored to death with the four riders of the Apocalypse. Now the story of Fenrir the wolf devouring the sun — that was fresh and original. After all, why shouldn't religion be fun?

I use my magnet key to open the door and barge into the lobby, panting and sweating like a pig. Nobody inside. The black sacrificial goat bleats plaintively.

Of course. Trust my assistants to go on vacation. This is Russland, after all. Even a nuclear war won't stop them from retiring to their summer cottages.

A written prompt shaped as an axe hangs over the altar. I know it by heart:

Monday: Moon's day
Tuesday: Tiu's day
Wednesday: Woden's day
Thursday: Thor's day
Friday: Freya's day

Saturday: Saturn's day

Sunday: Sun's day

Moskauers aren't particularly attentive. They still use the old week names, out of habit. But an experienced priest like myself who was interned in Norway and Tibet can't let his tongue slip.

I walk over to the goat. He stinks and tries to gore me with his horns. He has the right not to like me: he'll be slaughtered soon.

My to-do list, the one in the altar box, renders me speechless. How am I supposed to find time for all this? The very first item on the list is a funeral. This isn't what it used to be: do a bit of singing and incense-burning, bury the poor beggar, end of story. Oh, no. It's not just having to load the stiffs onto disposable plywood Mitsubishi boats to be burned on the Moskva River. It's the priests' duty to cut the dead men's nails! Oh yes. When Ragnarök — the world's end — comes, the earth will disgorge Naglfar, the ship fashioned entirely from dead people's nails. The ocean will freeze over and the ship will slide over the ice, taking an army of *jötunns* — mythical giants — to their last battle. To prevent Ragnarök from happening, dead people's nails should be cut short: this way Naglfar can't form, you see. My scissors are always here. What's a quick manicure? Surely not a big deal.

You really think no one believes it?

Not the Schwarzkopfs, no. They're either

Bolshies or Orthodox Christians or just plain good pagans. But the rest... there's no zealot like a convert, you know. You won't believe the extent of it. Old ladies gossip on boulevard benches about the Goddess Angrboda: were her children begotten by Loki or by Thor? The mind boggles.

I walk over to the statue of Rübezahl, the forest sprite and the king of dwarves. A tiny, hunched old man with a large beard. I mustn't forget to lay a bunch of mushrooms at his feet.

A new bout of pain pierces my head like a red-hot needle.

I clench my teeth. My fingers squeeze the dead head of a goat lying on the altar. Great gods...

The haze before my eyes refuses to dissolve. I gasp. My mouth fills with blood.

Darkness devours everything around me. Rübezahl explodes in a cascade of tiny little stars.

Vision One

The Black Skies

THE WIND SCREAMS. Icy cold, it reaches under my clothes, its skeletal fingers clenching my throat, constricting my movements. My eyelashes have frozen together. I sniffle, wary of opening my mouth. The wind's not screaming anymore: it's howling like a fatally wounded animal, making me colder still.

I scramble through the darkness. There's not a single light here. The flashes of submachine gun fire slice through the pitch black night.

Human hands poke out of the ice. People stagger through the city, sinking knee deep into the snow. Not people: rambling shadows, lice-ridden, in filthy trench coats. There's nothing human left about them. Their frost-burned cheeks are wrapped in women's shawls, their boot legs are stuffed with rags against the cold. Some of them seek warmth by bonfires, wrapping bundles of blankets around themselves.

This is crazy. I turn a corner of a collapsed building. A group of soldiers is swarming around a dead horse. They're delirious with starvation. One of them has crawled toward the horse's head and is busy nibbling at its stiff frozen ear.

Not a star in the sky. Its blackness merges with that of the earth. They're one now. There's not a single house around still intact. Nothing but ruins, their jagged walls like the tooth marks of a mysterious monster.

The earth begins to shake. The starving lunatics duck into the snow, choking on horse meat. An air raid. The howling of bombers adds to the screaming of the wind, growing into a symphony of the Apocalypse. Orange flashes rip through the darkness.

Death.

It's everywhere here.

Each of us knows what they would feed on, once all the horses are dead and all the cats have been trapped. We'll feed on each other. Warmth and food: this is what these ragged people hunt for. A tin of canned meat goes for a gold signet ring. Only who might need it here?

Barbed wire-wound stakes are hung with frozen bodies. Nobody buries them. They're just *too many*. Those still alive have gotten used to the dead men's company. I see shell cases scattered amongst the collapsed brickwork. Tank crews are still alive inside their white machines but they have no gas left. The tanks turn their turrets this way and that, unable to move. They're dying like broken-legged mammoths.

I can see a deluded soldier rip his trench coat open baring his chest, yelling at an Oberleutnant. The soldier is young and drunk as a skunk. The Oberleutnant is older, his face covered with stubble, a bloodied bandage on his forehead. He has a semicircular shrapnel scar on his cheek.

"Why did they send us here?" the soldier screams. "We're all gonna die!"

Alcohol is never in short supply. Without it, all wars would have ended before they even started. Facing death is scary. Alcohol dissolves the panicky fear. Not for very long, but still.

The soldier hurls his submachine gun at the Oberleutnant's feet. His face is distorted.

"This isn't my country! Let me go! I want to leave!"

The Oberleutnant shakes his head. The falling snow is reflected in his pale blue eyes. The soldier collapses into a deep drift and struggles to scramble back to his feet, then tries to crawl away.

The officer pulls his right hand out of his trench coat's pocket. His hand looks so funny in a women's fingerless glove. His index and little fingers are black, septic with frostbite.

He clenches the handle of his eight-round Walther and takes aim in the snowstorm, mumbling something through clenched teeth. The soldier has already made it to the trenches.

He fires.

The soldier drops on his back. The helmet flies off his head. His blond hair is covered in blood.

Immediately another shot resonates through the air: the heavy sound of a far-off rifle. An enemy sniper, shooting blindly. The officer's muzzle flash had betrayed his position.

The Oberleutnant sinks to his knees, drops his Walther and lies down on his side as if to have a nap. It takes the snowstorm but a few seconds to bury the two new corpses.

How strange. Only a moment ago, two men were alive. And now they're not. Every man who goes to war thinks he's going to survive. Human history might have been completely war-free had we known that we were going to be killed. Yes, *killed*.

A new swarm of bombers dives. Explosions. More explosions. And yet more.

I rub my cheeks with snow. I don't sense the cold. It's frostbite.

I know very well why I'm seeing it all. The dead cities. The dead bodies. The ice desert.

She makes me see it.

CHAPTER FOUR

THE TRIGGER AGENT

KEISER MOVIE THEATER

1923 REVOLUTION ST.

PAVEL'S CONTACT TOOK THE SEAT to the left of him, as previously arranged. He fidgeted in his place, laying a trayful of popcorn and two paper cups of Coca Cola in his lap. Even the United States' defeat in the war with Japan had failed to diminish the drink's popularity.

"H-h-hi," stuttering, he whispered without turning his head.

"Hi," Pavel replied. "Thanks for coming. Long time no see. This calls for a drink."

The other man studied the dark theater and grinned. They sat in the back row: the "kissing seats". The house was nearly empty. The feature hadn't yet started. Pre-trailers and commercials ran non-stop: predictably Japanese, like the one for Godzilla yogurt. The air conditioning wasn't working. The air smelled of dust and sweaty human bodies.

"W-h-hat would you l-l-like, a sch-sch-schnapps?"

"Oh, do me a favor. Bad enough that all these idiots drink coffee now instead of tea. As if that would turn them into Germans. Pour me some pepper vodka, would you? I know you always have some on you."

The other man bared his teeth in a grin. He set his tray onto the empty seat next to his and reached behind his jacket collar, feeling for a flask.

Pavel couldn't help thinking that this was the first time he was seeing his friend in plain clothes. Obersturmführer Jean-Pierre Carpe from the special Gestapo science division seemed never to shed his blue lab coat. Admittedly, a scientist's attire didn't suit him. Burly with a shaven head and huge fists, he rather resembled a comic-book monster out of the Universum Film flicks. What else could have been born out of a liaison between a Ukrainian peasant girl and an officer of the French SS division Charlemagne? The result was truly explosive.

Looking at him, Pavel couldn't help thinking of a banned book he'd read as a child:

about some guy called Gulliver, a clumsy but good-natured giant. Back at school, they used to read hand-written copies of it under their desks, choking with laughter, while the teacher was looking the other way. Not so long ago, the Ministry of Propaganda and Public Education had released a new version of the book and made it into a movie. The main character had received a new name: Arnold, after some guy called Arnold Schwarzenegger, an Austrian butcher who'd risen to fame having starred in three films by cult director Leni Riefenstahl, including her *Triumph of the Will: The Sequel.* Polls showed that 70% of the population wanted to see Arnold as the new Führer. The new motion picture *Arnold's Travels* became a mega box office hit the moment it had been released.

Pavel took a swig from the helpfully offered paper cup. The pepper vodka scorched his palate.

"W-w-what do you want t-to know?" Jean-Pierre hunched over the flask. "Thi-thi-this is weird. They p-pulled you out of Hong Kong w-w-without telling you anything. V-v-very st-range."

Pavel paused, waiting. The lights began to dim. The feature began.

"You think I don't know it's weird?" he said calmly. "I had an excellent deal going. I was about to meet the local yakuza boss. And just as I was going to give my contact a ring, I received a message to my e-funk. A minute later, I was emailed an economy class ticket for a Moscow flight. What was I supposed to do? I took a taxi and went directly to the airport. All I know is that the Gestapo want to show me a picture of some sort. Not a photo: a drawing. A portrait. They didn't even bother to say whether it was of a man or a woman. They want me to locate that person."

He took a large gulp of his drink. "To tell you the truth, I've never had such a ludicrous job in my life. But the money they offered... you can buy the Moon with it. Or the Sun. Or the Earth, even. Money's no object. And the main thing is, once I've completed the job, they've promised never to bother me again. You know what's funny about it? I still haven't seen the picture. Still waiting for my clearance. I haven't been back in the Reich for quite a while. Their bureaucracy has only gotten worse. The Gestapo is inundated by its paperwork. Very soon they'll make you fill in a form every time you want to take a dump."

Jean-Pierre took a large swig of his drink and began crunching on popcorn. "You kn-n-now, don't you, that we've n-n-never had th-th-this conversation."

"Absolutely. I've never seen you. I've no idea who you are. These seats have to be bugged. The office might have tabs on this place, anyway. But I don't think it's got anything to do with us. I'm pretty sure that the Gestapo are just as clueless about the person in the picture as I am. Otherwise they wouldn't have needed to get the Triumvirate to issue the order."

"The Tri-tri-triumvirate was only re-re-recently p-p-put in the picture," Jean-Pierre pointed out. "Our d-d-department received the research material two years ago f-f-from the Main Security Office. That was wh-wh-when the v-v-very first cases began to occur. But a month ago they conducted an ex... experiment near Novgorod. Wanna know what h-h-happened? Three lab workers ended up in a m-m-mental fa... facility. One more d-d-disappeared into th-th-thin air. I th-thought it just couldn't get any w-w-worse. But t-t-trust me, the w-w-worst is ye-ye-yet to come."

He stopped, then launched the remaining vodka down his throat. "That's better," he said in a clear voice without a trace of stuttering. "You can't imagine how many times I went to the speech therapist. But this is the only thing that helps. And you have to agree I can't drink vodka four times a day at work."

"Why not? Oh yeah, I see. Your French blood won't take it."

The Obersturmführer ignored the quip. They'd been friends long enough — ever since their Berlin days where both had been part of the MG Project — to indulge in occasional familiarity. It was during that experiment that Carpe had begun to stutter.

The theater's sound system assaulted their ears with rousing music.

"I'd venture a guess that the contamination

might have started earlier. Probably, right after the end of the Twenty-Year War," Jean-Pierre crunched on the last of his popcorn. "The Moskau office had no idea. The local Kommandaturs... they must have ignored the phenomenon at first. And once they couldn't do so any longer, they did their level best to keep it under wraps. You know what they're like in Russland: hoping that if you pretend there is no problem, it'll just sort of go away by itself. Well, it didn't. The phenomenon became more and more widespread. Concealing it became dangerous. The Main Security Office began receiving the first classified reports. They got the Gestapo involved who put together a secret research group to look into it. They enrolled me — as much as my clearance allowed. This was something, I tell you..."

"Wait," Pavel whispered. "What contamination are you talking about?"

"That's exactly what I'm going to tell you now. Point by point."

Groping couples in the darkness paid no attention to the two alcoholics boozing in the back row. Moskau's government encouraged a healthy lifestyle. The city was hung with *Aryans Don't Drink in the Morning* posters (featuring the omnipresent Schwarzenegger).

That only applied to hard alcohol, though. Beer had been proclaimed part of the national heritage and a symbol of the 1923 Revolution[3] and received the status of "Aryan nectar".

Smoking too had been banned.[4] SS patrols from the Health Service checked all *nacht clubs* and fined them a thousand reichsmarks for every cigarette they found.

They'd tried to ban alcohol too in the 1980s during the Twenty-Year War. Initially, the Triumvirate demanded a mandatory death sentence for both the sale and consumption of schnapps. Twenty-four hours later, the order had been revoked. Someone must have explained to them that they couldn't just sentence virtually all of the country's population to death.

The theater screen rattled with advancing tanks.

The Reich Union loved making war films: trench dramas, comedies like *The Good Soldier Ivan* and epic battle scenes. Nobody cared about their box office performance: patriotic propaganda was key. If one wanted to lay his or her greedy mitts on a wagonful of dough, all one had to do was submit a query to the Ministry of

---

[3] By "the 1923 Revolution" the narrator means the Beer Hall Putsch — a Nazi coup attempt in Bavaria in 1923.

[4] The Third Reich is considered the first country in the world that began a government-supported anti-smoking campaign.

Propaganda and Public Education and pitch to them their idea for yet another movie about the Great Battle.

Hundreds of such half-baked flicks had come out even though no one really bothered to watch them.

As an example, *The Sea Lion* — a film about the Wehrmacht's successful invasion of Britain on May 11 1942 — had been shot in two parts and cost fifty million yen. Its entire audience consisted of five hundred: the director, the acting crew and all their numerous relatives.

Filmmakers could get away with all sorts of goofs which were fobbed off as the "author's vision". And if one of the *Völkischer Beobachter* venom-spitting critics dared to question the merits of the dubious masterpiece, Shogunet trolls would start a rumor that the critic was in fact a *Mischling*: a half-breed unable to appreciate the Aryan film creator's artistic bent.

Pavel, however, wasn't interested in the movie in the slightest. He was too busy listening.

Very busy.

A couple of times the left corner of his mouth twitched. Those who'd known him for a long time might have realized he was quite agitated. He reached for a handkerchief and began to mechanically wipe the paper cup clean.

"Are you sure?" he touched Jean-Pierre's arm, stopping his soliloquy. An admittedly inane question, but he had no one else to ask.

Carpe gave a calm nod. “Absolutely. Otherwise they wouldn’t have summoned you. We’ve wasted a lot of time looking for the source of all the problems but now we think we’ve located it. We’ve set up a radioelectronic trap at the testing grounds near Novgorod. It registered an unclear reddish outline on their radars. Survivors offer confused accounts but they’ve managed to approach it within arm’s reach. This unidentified object seemed to exude inordinate amounts of energy. It was almost leaking radiation. Which leads our experts to conclude that this object must have triggered the contamination.”

He turned to Pavel. “That’s why the Triumvirate has summoned *you* to solve the problem. They don’t know what it is. Whether it’s a god, a ghost or a human being — we need to get to the root of this evil. I dread to think what might happen if this lasts for another six months or so. Are they going to show you the drawing? This is excellent. I’ve never seen it myself. I’m waiting already a month for the proper clearance, pushing pencils in the meantime. You’re right: the Gestapo has gone paper mad.”

Pavel produced his e-funk and marked something down in its Notebook.

“This is crazy,” he admitted. “For a moment I thought it might be the entire Gestapo staff gone loony, and not those three researcher idiots in the mental facility.”

Jean-Pierre grinned. “That’s what I thought at first. Before I saw it with my own eyes. You’ve no idea. N-n-never mi-mi-mind.”

His stutter was back just as abruptly as it had left him.

“If you say so,” Pavel agreed. “In any case, I’m going to talk to one of the eyewitnesses. Thankfully, my rank still allows me to do that. The drawing is all good and well but I’d like to hear the description of this so-called ghost straight from the horse’s mouth. And I want to do it before the Triumvirate and the Security chief approve my clearance. When I’m back at the hotel, I’ll email the Gestapo. Then I’ll sleep through the night. The gods know I need it.”

“Th-th-thanks for t-t-taking the precautions,” Jean-Pierre whispered. “There’s no one h-h-here who can re... recognize you.”

Without saying goodbye or waiting till the feature was over, he rose and walked out first, using his phone’s screen to light the way. The theater door slammed. Pavel cast a sad glance at his watch.

A CORPULENT UNTEROFFIZIER USHERESS — an old-age Russian babushka complete with floral headscarf — watched Jean-Pierre disinterestedly as he walked out. Normal, she thought. Not many moviegoers can sit through a war epic.

When Pavel followed, she turned pale and brought a hand to her mouth, unable to produce a sound. She felt a sudden urge to do something she hadn't done for many years — something she couldn't even remember how to do.

She wanted to make the sign of the cross.

CHAPTER FIVE

DAIFUKU

HINDENBURG LANE

NEXT TO THE BERLIN STORE

“YOU’RE PALE. Look at your face, it’s drawn. You’ve got dark circles around your eyes. Would you like a glass of wine?”

Oh no, lady, thank you very much. I don’t drink wine, anyway. Definitely not after what happened earlier today. My whole body is aching like hell. It’s as if they took me apart, limb by mechanical limb, then handed my body parts over to a drunken plumber to reassemble and wrangled some horses over me before throwing me into the path of an Eicher tractor. You wouldn’t want to feel what I’m feeling, girl, that’s for sure.

I blink. "Thanks. Odin's priests are obliged to celebrate a monthly Vegetarian Day to remember the Führer. So today it's cabbage patties and Karlsbad mineral water for me."

She sniffs, then makes a show of helping herself to a slice of turkey. The Schwarzkopfs zealously stick to their diet which is supposed to reflect their convictions. They avoid pork (without even considering the fact that we have Muslims serving in the Idel Ural Legion and the Croatian SS Kama Division), they don't drink beer (even though the production of Rhine vineyards isn't limited to grape juice) and ignore sausages, even veal ones. And in view of the Führer's vegetarian practices, some of the die-hard Schwarzkopfs even refuse vegetable foods. If they eat salad, they make sure it has meat in it: and not the sophisticated Alpine *wurstsalat*, but an obnoxious local dish which Russlanders call *Olivier* although the appellation *Titanic* might have been more apt: a pile of chopped veg and chicken hugging each other in terror as they drown in a sea of mayo.

The bubbles in the water tickle my tongue as I gulp it down. My tablemate has chosen a rather revealing dinner attire: a hugging purple dress with a deep décolleté exposing almost all of her braless cleavage. Her nipples are so stiff they almost pierce the fabric. She must be cold in this airconned room.

Poor girl. Hasn't she had enough of her

own games?

The Schwarzkopfs measure everything with their own yardstick. They think that every priest is dying to have sex, dreaming about it in his wet dreams, closing his hands around his... his blanket. Especially if the priest is a Catholic or an Orthodox monk. But I am one of the *Waidelottes*: the ruling caste of Viking priests (also known as the *Legend Keepers*). I can have a harem of twenty if I want to. Only Aryan women, unfortunately: the Moskau Priest Council has allowed the servants of Odin, Loki and Thor to take wives, provided they're natural blondes. Which is a problem to a degree, of course.

But marriage aside, a *Waidelotte* can sleep with who the hell he wants to.

"Some of humanity's most abominable murderers were known for their sentimentality," she says, sinking her teeth into the turkey as if it were the Führer himself. "Your darling leader was a vegetarian, he loved dogs and even doted on other people's children... while hating their parents. This is ridiculous! The whole of Europe is being governed by a ghost! While the authorities pretend this is exactly how it should be."

Aha, that's what she's driving at. Actually, I have to agree. At the end of the Twenty-Year War the Reichskommissariats unanimously decreed that the Führer was to remain the Reich's supreme leader despite his tragic death. Which meant that officially he was feasting with the fallen *Einherjar* in Valhalla instead of drinking blood in the underground caves of Hel's, the goddess of the dead. Which in turn also meant, according to the Priests Council memo, that its members could enter a state of trance in order to contact the Führer in Asgard and transmit his orders back to us. The Führer's decrees were then printed in Gothic font with a nice-looking facsimile signature.

This state of affairs suited every Reichskommisariat's Triumvirate perfectly: while presenting no threat to their own position in power, it provided them with a convenient front person whenever things went awry. And what better scapegoat than a nominal deadman ruler?

"What's wrong with that?" I reply in a deliberately bored voice, transporting a piece of a cabbage patty to my mouth. "The Führer's only been in Valhalla what, a few decades? Your Jesus has been absent for two thousand years and no one has seen him since, apart from a couple of nutters. This doesn't seem to baffle you, does it? You're quite happy to accept that he runs the Universe from atop his cloud, even though there's no documented evidence proving that Yeshua the Nazarene did exist, apart from Flavius' *Antiquities of the Jews*. And although he does mention him being sentenced to death, neither contemporary chronicles nor Pontius Pilate's personal diaries mention his execution, let alone his supposed resurrection. Besides, how sure are you we can trust Flavius in this sensitive matter? He was a Jew, wasn't he? Sorry for mentioning Jews at the table..."

I bite my tongue. Shit. I overdid it, didn't I?

The girl hurls her fork at the daifuku plate. The clinking of steel against bone china sounds like a funeral bell to my ears. Great gods, Odin and Thor, save me! Now all hell will break loose.

"Have you ever asked yourself what happened to the Jews and Roma? Where are they all gone?"

Aha, so that's what she's driving at. Predictably so. "Shipped to Africa on a Crystal Train," I reply impassively. "As if you don't know. Open any primary school textbook, and that's what it says. A perfectly legal deportation, voted unanimously by the Reichstag and supported by leading cultural figures. When Africa received the status of a self-governing colony, the whole of the "black continent", with the exception of Ethiopia, Morocco, Egypt and the South African Union, was fenced off by a concrete wall surrounded by mine fields and wound with barbed wire. All the government workers were evacuated and all troops withdrawn. From then on, the Africans had to fend for themselves. I don't think that the Crystal Train passengers had it easy. Africa has neither the Shogunet nor television. The streets of its ravaged cities are the theater of clan wars. Starvation, epidemics, all sorts of new viruses.

Still, deportation is more humane than extermination, isn't it?"

Her face breaks out in crimson spots. "They were killed," she enunciates. "The Jews. The Roma. The Yaoi. The drug addicts. Even the mentally ill. Why are there no mental hospitals anywhere? Why is psychiatry an illegal business, like tobacco dealing? When someone becomes schizophrenic, their families hide them from the authorities as they've been doing since the 1940s. Society has no place for the useless — or yes, this is one lesson we did learn from the Germans! The Yaoi, the Yuri[5], the schizophrenics — you're right, they're not executed openly anymore. You deport them to Africa through your control posts in the concrete wall. How's that different from execution? There're still some surviving eyewitnesses confirming the existence of wartime camps where millions of people were gassed and incinerated like rats. Ever heard about Auschwitz, Sachsenhausen, Buchenwald, Dachau? The monstrous factories that ground their way through tons of human bones every day? Here in Russland the Nazis used to burn people alive by the villageload; they had special

---

[5] The Yaoi and the Yuri: respectively gay males and females in the context of Manga and Anime. The popularity of all things Japanese in the Third Reich has apparently lead to the widespread use of these two terms.

gas wagons to dispose of hostages. Half of us were doomed to extermination, the other half were meant to become agricultural slaves for the Krauts' colonists."

"There's no evidence of this," I hurry to point out. "It's nothing but rumors."

The dinner is ruined. She has a tendency to do that.

"Yeah, sure," she says with a bitter chuckle. "It's bad form mentioning it these days. We may be a dictatorship but all dictators would like to appear hard on the outside and soft on the inside. A bit like a banana. The Triumvirate will never admit that the Führer was going to turn half the planet's population into garden fertilizer. Did you know that they performed a total archive purge already in the 1970s? Concentration camps paperwork as well as the SS and Gestapo archives were shredded in *papierwolfs*, camp ovens were converted into bakeries and gas chambers into shower rooms. When you stick to the same lie year after year, people start to believe you. That's what Dr. Goebbels used to say. Latvian researchers from the Reichskommissariat Ostland keep publishing those articles in the *Völkischer Beobachter* saying that all labor camp prisoners were paid for their work; that they had brothels and movie theaters, even football clubs, and that apparently Italian labor camp officials even organized free pizza deliveries for their prisoners! And how are you going to disprove it? All the ex-prisoners have been ordered to have their camp number tattoos removed. This is their formula of success, courtesy of the Triumvirate: you need to plunge people into the frenzy of consumption. Then you don't have to conquer them. Their mental abilities will atrophy naturally. Had the Führer been a bit smarter, instead of invading Russland he could have built a chain of Drakken Kaufhof malls complete with 3D theaters. When the human brain is only used for entertaining, it just goes to mush."

I appear to enthusiastically munch on tasteless cabbage. Oh Hel, the Lady of the Underworld! These Schwarzkopfs are such goody-two-shoes. So empathic and sensitive they make you sick. Yeah right, shopping malls and movie theaters, how awful, how brain-numbing. But had we still been living under martial-law National Socialism with its ration cards, margarine for butter and saccharine for sugar, they'd have been the first to scream their indignation about the terrible Triumvirate starving people to death.

"Listen, what's the point in dragging a bunch of seventy-year-old skeletons out of the closet?" I wash the cabbage down with some mineral water. "The Tatars in their time steam-rolled over medieval Russia too, pillaging cities, turning churches into stables and raping village women. You see any Russlanders losing any sleep itching to avenge *that* genocide? How about the French? Napoleon's army burned down the cities of Vilno, Smolensk and Moskau — and? The Russlanders absolutely love the French culture. Never mind that Paris has been under the SS Fashion Department since 1940 in the tender care of Oberführer Lagerfeld and his assistant Hugo Boss — still any lady worth her smelling salts will gladly spend a month in a Gestapo cooler for a bottle of French perfume. Even if you presumed, for the sake of argument, that by some fantastical miracle Russland defeated Germany in the war, we'd still have already been buddying up. We love our enemy and can't stand our neighbor. Take the Reichskommissariat Turkestan, for instance. Every time I see their legionnaires in the street, I can't help thinking, *Are these muttonheads Aryan too?*"

The girl is silent. She's too busy arm-wrestling her stomach into submission. On one hand, she's dying for a daifuku. On the other, this is a political discussion — as is our every dinner.

"Russland is under foreign occupation," she says, casting a sideways glance at the dessert. "You're not going to argue that, are you? We have a foreign state emblem, foreign laws... and foreign rulers."

There, she's already switched to the defensive. If I only could, I'd have smoked a cigarette the way some men do after good sex. Unfortunately, Odin's priests are obliged to lead a healthy lifestyle.

"That's an easy one," I finish off my cabbage patty. "As far as the emblem is concerned, Russland used the Greek double-headed eagle for the last five hundred years. It also had German laws for the last two hundred. The Royal court positions were also German: *Kammerherr, Frauleina, Hofmeister...* The names of Russian chancellors: Ostermann, Bühren, Nesselrode, Stürmer... Might that mean that this so-called occupation has never stopped? All right, so concentration camps did exist. But who might have guarded them? The Sobibor death camp in Poland was guarded by Ukrainians — their next-door neighbors. The burgermeisters, the auxiliary police, the journalists producing newspapers, SS volunteers, Gestapo interrogators — all of them were Russlanders wearing German uniforms. And you know what Russlanders are like: the moment a foreigner hires them, they're quite prepared to hang themselves with zeal. The ten biggest Russlandish cities now house Wehrmacht garrisons. Five hundred each! These aren't occupiers, these are toy soldiers. Ceremonial guards. True, we have plenty of German bureaucrats and brass hats everywhere: in the army as well as the police and civil ministries. But it was the same at the times of the Tsars! On the other hand, Russlandish businessmen have bought up some of Berlin's most prestigious real estate. In 1984, Russisch became one of the Reich's official languages. Who occupied whom, may I ask?"

Without saying a word, she springs to her feet. The daifuku remains untouched even though I can see it's still calling her name. I already know what's going to happen next. First she'll head for the bathroom to brush her teeth. Then she'll go back to bed. Her life is boring but rather safe, if I may say so.

The bathroom door slams. Finally I can relax.

When I had come round, lying sprawled on the floor back in the Temple of Odin, I immediately thought: what would have happened to *her* had I not come back? Every morning I replace her handcuffs for a couple of sturdy thin chains allowing her to get to the bathroom. Her bedroom has a small fridge containing everything she might need. But the bedroom door is locked. She can't escape. If I disappeared, she'd starve to death within a month.

I hadn't thought about that. My mistake. I'll have to consider installing a *Zeitschaltuhr* — a timer — on the lock and set it for like twenty-four hours. There are also other things I have to consider. I've been zoned out for two hours flat. I need to look into a couple of things.

Firstly, I need to find out where the goat is gone. And secondly, whatever has happened to the statue of Rübezahl.

Textbook No 1

World Geography

THE REICH UNION, or the Third Reich of Greater Germany.

Founded in 2004 after the end of the Twenty-Year War. Technically represents a confederation of several Reichskommissariats: Ostland (comprising Belorussia and the Baltics), Moskau (the European part of Russland), Deutschland (Austria, Germany and the Governorate of Poland), the Caucasus (Azerbaijan, Georgia, the Kuban and the sonderkommissariats of Chechnya and Dagestan), Turkestan (Tajikistan, Turkmenia, Uzbekistan and Kirghizia), the Ukraine (including the Russlandish cities of Kursk, Voronezh and Tsaritsyn (the former Stalingrad)); Norway and the Netherlands, and Britain (excluding the Republic of Scotland). Other "special territories" belonging to the Reich Union include: Lake Baikal, the Crimea (inhabited by German colonists) and the enclave of St. Petersburg.

The countries allied with the Third Reich:

Slovakia, the Italian Empire, the Independent State of Croatia, Finland (including Karelia and Murmansk), Transylhungary, the

Kingdom of Romania (including Odessa and Bessarabia), the Southern French Protectorate (with the capital in Vichy), The Federation of Spain and Portugal, and the Kingdom of Bulgaria (including Greece).

In 1951, Ataturk's Turkish Republic was ceremoniously returned its old French colonies of Lebanon and Syria. It was also gifted Armenia.

Restored in 1964, the Baghdad Caliphate was comprised of Iraq and the Maghreb sultanates, including Egypt and Morocco.

The Free State of India (also known as Azad Hind) is under the joint protection from the Reich Union and the Nippon koku.

Korea, the island of Formosa, Hawaii, Karafuto island, the Kamchatka peninsula, the Siberian cities of Khabarovsk and Vladivostok — now known under their Japanese names of Habarosito and Uradziosutoku — as well as Shanghai, Hong Kong and Singapore all make an integral part of Nippon koku.

Technically, the Siberian territories from Kamchatka to the Urals are also within the Japanese area of interest but in reality they are controlled by guerilla units of "forest brothers". The Republic of Far East (with its capital in the city of Chita) isn't independent, being a Japanese protectorate.

Japan's satellite states are: Manchukuo, China, Thailand, the Indonesian Emirate, the Vietnam Empire, Burma and the Philippines. The

Nippon koku also boasts a special territory of Australia which bears the special status of "holiday colony" where rich Japanese come to unwind on its seaside beaches. Australians have all been deported to Alaska.

The government of the United States of America signed their capitulation on April 18 1956 in Los Angeles after the 2nd SS Division Russland had battled their way into the city. In 1958, the USA was divided into the California Republic (a joint protectorate of the Reich and the Nippon koku), the colonies of Neuer York, Boston, Washington and Florida (with a Japanese governor), the Reichskommissariat of Texas and the "unclaimed territories of the Wild West": the anarchic uncontrolled ex-states of Alabama, Utah and Kansas. Alaska makes up part of the Republic of the Far East as an autonomy ruled by a Japanese daimyo.

Canada has been dissolved: Quebec has been given to Southern France, the north of the country is the property of Japan while the rest of it is used to deport the Chinese.

Argentina, Paraguay, Bolivia and Chile form the German Community of South America. Even before Wehrmacht troops entered these countries in 1983, their capitals had been taken by armed Landwehr colonists.

Africa received the status of an autonomy. All the racially inferior nations were deported there within the Chrystal Train campaign. African borders were turned into three-mile "security zones", its waters separated by a twelve-mile "anti-pirate zone".

Having been conquered by Italy in 1936, Abyssinia now has the status of an "overseas territory", as does Libya.

The 1984 coup in the South African Union led to the Afrikaners deposing corrupt pro-British politicians and recognizing the protection of Greater Germany. Six months later, joint Japanese and German troops landed in the Siberian city of Tyumen which is the official ending date for a world war that had lasted forty-five years.

A World Geography. Approved by the Moskau Ministry of Propaganda and Public Education

CHAPTER SIX

THE ANGEL

THE RICHARD WAGNER PEDESTRIAN ZONE

#22/7

THE GEHEIME STAATSPOLIZEI (Gestapo) Special Isolation Facility was situated at the very end of Wagner lane — or Arbat, as die-hard Moskauers still called the little pedestrian street. On the outside it was a two-story book shop. Its sign read Spirit's Delight — a name admittedly more befitting an alcohol store.

Inside its spacious premises flooded with light, sleepy and bored salesgirls helped the few shoppers to choose the Reich's newest literary masterpieces. In the shop windows, the latest bestsellers were gathering dust: the coloring book

The Childhood of the Führer and a how-to book from Leni Riefenstahl, *How to Make it as a Movie Star*. Few people bought books these days — most downloaded them for free from the Shogunet. *Mein Kampf* had been in the public domain since 1944 anyway. All other books had to pass a meticulous integrity check by the Ministry of Propaganda and Public Education.

The Gestapo's electronic department had their hands full with the Shogunet, blocking those of its sections which allowed users to upload illegal translations of banned authors like Jack London or Hemingway, and especially the dreaded Leo Tolstoy: an anti-war extremist whose books could earn you two months in the cooler. Not that it helped. The numbers of illegal download links to the works by the likes of Tolstoy and Margaret Mitchell mushroomed by the hour.

In order to make readers buy the book, you need to ban it first, Pavel thought, forcing open the glass door embossed with an emblematic eagle. *Prohibition is the best promotion.*

A salesgirl in an SS Bewerber uniform flashed him a professional smile. "Welcome to our shop, *mein Herr*. How can I help you?"

Pavel cast a wary look around. Actually, there was no need for it. The shop wasn't too popular: its prices of almost a thousand reichsmark per title would scare anyone off. Only a frail old man standing with his back to him shuffled from one foot to the other in the back next to a thriller stand, studying a volume of Stephanie Meyer. Pavel remembered the authoress' name: she'd recently been commended by the Neuer York Gauleiter himself for her series of spy thrillers *Abwehr vs. NKVD*.

Pavel leaned toward the Bewerber girl until he almost touched her lips. "My number is seven eight nine five double-two one six," he mouthed.

Still smiling (Pavel had the impression that the smile was painted on her face giving her the semblance of a shop window mannequin), the girl punched the number into her cash register. Its screen lit up, offering Pavel's number, Gestapo rank and clearance level. The girl clicked her heels softly as she pressed an electronic card into his hand.

"You can collect your books over there," she pointed at a door at the end of the corridor. "Please don't forget to give our worker your discount code. Thank you for shopping with us! *Danke schön*!"

He used the card to open the door, then locked it again behind him. Inside the narrow room was an elevator booth. Pavel pressed the single button on its control panel. The elevator moved downwards, heading toward the cellar.

They were already expecting him. A hungover overweight Volksdeutsche checked his ID, rearranged his own SS hat with an emblem of the medical corps, then made a phone call. A soldier in a black uniform took Pavel out of the room and along a concrete corridor dimly lit by a row of red light bulbs.

All the mental hospitals in Moskau had long been closed (as had they been in all other reichskommissariats); all the medical personnel had been dismissed. If someone happened to lose their marbles, they were sent directly to the isolation block. Once its doctors were finished with the patient, he was shipped to Africa.

The isolation block's commandant looked bored in his office. He was sitting under an emblem of the Reich with its swastika thoroughly blotted out, concealed under several coats of plaster at the center of an oak wreath.

The commandant nodded to Pavel. He didn't bother to rise, only flung a file across the desk toward him.

"All the paperwork and the pictures are inside. You wanna speak to him? No idea how you're gonna do it. Two of the researchers are basically vegetables. They don't react to anything. We use an IV drip to feed them. The third one is a bit better but... he won't speak to anyone. Sometimes at night he screams his head off. We have to inject him with downers by the bucketful."

"It's all right," Pavel said with a small smile. "He'll talk to me, don't you worry. I'm taking the file. Give me his cell number and don't bother with an escort. It's a personal conversation," he fell silent, peering at one of the pictures.

"I just hope you squeeze him for whatever you want to know," the commandant deftly swatted a fly on the table. "Go ahead, *bitte schön.* You have all the time you need."

The isolation cell lived up to his expectations. Twelve by twelve feet, it was padded with soft white felt to make sure the patient didn't break his head when having a fit. A light bulb and a surveillance camera under the ceiling completed the setting. The camera's red eye went out the moment Pavel entered the room. They weren't filming the visit.

The patient in the room paid no heed to him. He was small and disheveled, with tousled ginger hair. Good for him. Carrot tops didn't have to dye their hair to pass for Aryans.

The man was sitting on his cot mouthing something and rocking from side to side. Impressive. Well, let's do it.

"Hi there," Pavel said gently while cracking a folding chair open. He stood so that the light from the bulb fell onto his face.

The patient's gaze shifted toward him. He burst out coughing. "You... you... you... how is it possible... you're... you're-"

"Dead," Pavel finished the man's thought for him. "True, it happens sometimes. But, by Thor's hammer, it can't prevent us from talking, can it?"

Beads of sweat erupted over the man's

brow. He was shivering, feeling around himself blindly as if the padded wall could part and swallow him.

"I'll only be a minute," Pavel assured him. "And I'll leave straight away, I promise. You understand you have no choice, don't you? Tell me the truth... and it'll be over quickly."

The man gave a robotic nod. Pavel sat down.

"It was horrendous," the man whispered frantically.

"You managed to get a glimpse of it," Pavel reminded him. "Just tell me: *what did you see*?"

"I saw what can't be," the lunatic burst out coughing. "I thought I was hallucinating. But it was real! I touched *it... it...* was so real. The portal it came from is closed now, isn't it? You've locked us up to make sure we don't speak... but it won't be long before everybody knows... Don't you understand what's coming? We're all going to dissolve like melting snow. *It*'s coming for us."

The prisoner spoke hotly and feverishly. Pavel was calm: an observer might have thought that he was bored by the man's story. He even sighed a couple of times, glancing at his trendy Swiss watch: a limited-edition Apel with the picture of Horst Wessel on the lid.

"I got it," he finally said. "Did you manage to work out what had caused it?"

The lunatic fell silent for a while, mouthing something. "A fiery figure. A flash. I went blind in one eye. Blinding light. It's an angel."

Pavel wasn't surprised. What else did he expect a madman to discuss, quantum physics? The main thing was to keep him talking.

Pavel nodded, his whole body projecting his interest. "Keep going."

"The moment we entered the *impact zone*, it walked right past us. We saw it. Unbearably bright. The heat! Hermann's brains got cooked and leaked out through his nose. And then... *it* disappeared. I saw it clearly. *It*'s about to swallow us. We'll all be fragmented."

"Do you remember its face? The angel's? Think you can draw it for me?"

The prisoner snatched the notebook from him and began drawing in broad, sharp pencil strokes: a face framed by long hair, an aquiline nose, thin lips.

He can draw, that's for sure, Pavel thought. *That's life for you. Why do we have to push pencils in the office for a pittance instead of developing our God-given skills? Having said that, where did I see art in Moskau? The Reich needs minimalism and clear-cut lines, Schwarzenegger-type beefcake heroes — no unwanted subtleties. If you want fine art of ikebana and calligraphy, you need to go to Tokyo.*

The lunatic raised his head from the paper. His eyes were tearful. "It was so real that I could sense it breathe. It breathed fire."

Pavel adjusted his e-funk and took several

pictures of the drawing from different angles. He sent the images off, then asked a few more questions but didn't find out anything new. The madman's mind was going in circles: he kept seeing the flashes of fire going through the air, his dying colleagues, and the fiery angel.

Having wasted another ten minutes, Pavel rose from his chair. He knew exactly where it had happened. But now that he'd heard the story, he wasn't looking forward to seeing its horror for himself. He'd better concentrate on finding some protection from the trigger agent. It didn't seem to enjoy unwanted company.

He reached into his shirt pocket for the pill. "Here, take this. It might make you feel better."

The lunatic exploded in laughter. He knew. "Excellent! All this time I've been waiting for it... Finally! Valkyries, come to me!"

The folded chair in hand, Pavel walked back up the corridor while the walls of the isolation block shuddered with the lunatic's laughter.

Pavel's e-funk vibrated. He opened the message and chuckled.

Come now. I know who it is.

Behind his back, the laughter broke off.

THE JAPANESE BY THE BOOKSTAND watched Pavel leave, his gaze indifferent. He turned back to the shelves and resumed his perusing of Stephanie Meyer's new release.

CHAPTER SEVEN

BENITO PIZZA

THE TOP FLOOR OF VIKING TV

THE BUILDING WAS RATHER OLD, from 1957, with plaster peeling from its corners. Its entrance was barricaded by massive concrete blocks. Behind them, surrounded by piled-up sand bags, the German Phoenix Sonderkommando unit hunched up over their machine guns.

The motors of armored vehicles were growling in the back yard. Sniper teams kept watch on the roof: guerrilla units had repeatedly attacked the Ministry of Propaganda and Public Education.

The twenty floors of this concrete behemoth housed state television, radio stations, a dozen newspaper offices, a souvenir shop and the pretentious Thule restaurant. The corridors inside seemed to snake every which way. That and the eight elevators each leading to a particular department made losing one's way extremely easy.

The TV channel took up the five upper floors, the best and most sought-after ones. In order to get inside, any visitor had to show his or her *ausweis* to the security guards behind their bulletproof glass, then walk through a turnstile. From there, Viking TV workers were in charge of the visitors. To get in, you had to first press your hand to the scanner next to the sliding doors.

Opposite the elevators, a banner under the ceiling quoted Dr. Joseph Goebbels:

We always tell the truth. Well, almost.

In accordance with the Moskau Reichstag directive, the television received 20% of the budget: same as the army. And they were worth it. The Triumvirate leaders had had plenty of opportunity to convince themselves that television could be much more effective than tanks and missiles. Throughout human history, even the strongest of armies had had trouble suppressing mass uprisings. But the TV screen allowed a much harsher mind control than any amount of street patrols.

TV officers' ranks began at Scharführer; even their junior correspondents enjoyed the equivalent of Generals' salaries and free luxury food parcels. Their equipment made their colleagues squirm with envy: all those excellent cameras, expensive cars and high-speed Shogunet.

The marble lobby featured the bronze bust of Hans Ulrich Rudel with his illustrious bald patch: the first man in space who'd raised the Reich's flag on the Moon in 1952. His international fame, endless autograph-signing sessions and half-naked female fans who besieged the astronaut even on restroom trips had made quick work of Rudel's career. He'd drunk himself into an early retirement within a year and a half, a record time. He'd been grounded and transferred to a boring but cushy job as the head of Berlin TV.

Hans Ulrich had zealously attacked his new job which became a pleasant surprise for his superiors. He joined the Adolf Temperance Society and didn't sleep nights coming up with new ideas for talk shows, planning quiz games, and working on new stories for popular soap operas like *The Woman of My Dreams*. It was he who'd turned the entertainment TV into the proverbial kraken entangling the minds of billions of Aryans.

A 1965 law demanded that every citizen of the Reich swore an oath to watch at least three hours of TV daily. Factory workers began installing special timers on all new televisions they produced. A number of laws had been canceled since then... but this one was still in force.

"*Achtung!* Newstime in ten minutes! Everybody get ready!"

Sergei glanced at his watch. He still had time before rapping out the latest news, grinning inanely into the camera. That was peanuts. Now the briefing at the TV Direktor's office in half an hour, that was a different story.

All news broadcasts were pre-recorded in conveyor-belt fashion. The anchors had a list of prompts to choose from, lying in a special recess on their desk: "a temporary drawback", "decrease in radiation levels", "economic growth" and "the relative growth of the reichsmark against the yen". The list had a special set of phrases adapted to incidents of Schwarzkopf attacks: "needless cruelty", "civilian casualties" and "terrorism has no future".

The camera with a silhouette of Rudel on its side pointed at Sergei.

They may say what they want but Hans Ulrich is a genius, Sergei thought, mechanically touching his Versace tie. *Much smarter than Goebbels. The Nazis didn't sleep nights trying to come up with the very best ways to promote their propaganda but achieved only the opposite: everyone was sick and tired of politics. And this alcoholic astronaut has come up with the simplest thing: if you want to control the human brain, you need to soften it up first. When all you watch is a sequence of inane entertainment played out to mindless laugh tracks, you don't think. You don't have to choose, only to react, like Pavlov's dog. Give him a beer and switch the TV to* Tonight with Marlene Dietrich *— and you're free to press his buttons.*

Sergei wasn't afraid to admit (mentally at least) his dislike of the Triumvirate. He considered himself an intellectual; he used the Shogunet to read banned books online; he even left cautious anonymous comments supporting the Schwarzkopfs' activities. In all honesty, so did most of Viking TV workers. Passing a bottle of schnapps around after work, the journalists would curse the "invaders" political and economic dominance with the strongest of expressions. Once back in the office, however, they condemned "guerrilla terrorists" with a double zeal.

"I don't know what to do anymore," Sergei's fellow anchor Vasily Kolpakov, the Political Department's Sturmführer, had admitted to him ruefully once. "I think I've developed a reflex. I take my seat, I see the camera and my mouth just opens and starts to speak. I can't help it. The moment I see the Führer's portrait on the wall, I can't stop myself."

Every TV worker had a similar set of excuses comprised of clichés similar to those they had to use on air, "I need to feed my family", "Somebody else will take my place" and "At least we have some stability under the Krauts".

The sound of female laughter made him startle.

A manicured finger gave him a flick on the nose. "Serge darling, what's this for a beak? Did your parents lose a bet with God?"

Sergei forced a smile. Having swayed her hips one last time, Masha the makeup lady disappeared round the corner of the corridor. Wretched bitch! Saying something like that in front of everybody! Someone was bound to put two and two together. Then it would start all over again: visits from the SS Race and Settlement Office: 'How did you manage to get past us with that kind of schnozzle?' Again he'd have to submit his family tree, pass blood tests and undergo phrenological control. He'd have to grease their palms once again, too, because they were bound to discover that his maternal great-grandfather was half-Armenian. Being a non-Aryan wasn't just bad form: it was plain uncomfortable. To get any job these days, you needed a certificate from the Racial Department.

Sergei knew quite a few people who had sunk all the way to the gutter, living in one of the *Arbeitslagers* — barracks for forced migrant labor employed for the Reichskommissariat's needs. The statute of Moskau forbade all Aryans to do menial work like sewage cleaning, railtrack laying or even the selling of fruit at village markets. A special agreement with the Nippon koku allowed the importation of millions of Chinese slaves who didn't cost anything and worked 24/7 for a bowl of rice. This was the kind of life awaiting all non-Aryans.

Sergei shuddered.

Oh, no. He'd rather become a brothel supervisor. Anything but the arbeitslager.

He switched on the mike. The countdown had already begun on the plasma screen. Three, two, one...

"*Dear Damen und Herren*, welcome back to Viking TV! Let me begin with our headlines. The Reich's cities are being consumed by a wave of renaming. The citizens of Veliky Novgorod demand their metropolis be returned its 9th century Swedish name of Holmgard. This event is supposed to coincide with the building of the temple of Loki — the Scandinavian god of fire — in the city's main square. Yesterday the population of Krasnoyarsk sent a petition to the ruler of the Nippon koku, asking his official permission to be called City of Fragrant Chrysanthemums. A sushi festival held for the Reich tourists by the new Shichō — that's Mayor to the rest of us — of Uradziosutoku has been a resounding success. The guests received balls of rice topped with slices of grayling, dogfish and omul[6]. Abdullo von Zimmerblut, the Führer of the

[6] Grayling, dogfish and omul — types of fresh-water fish indigenous to Lake Baikal.

Reichskommissariat Turkestan, finished Friday prayers in the Ashgabat mosque by issuing a statement threatening the pig farms of the Reichskommissariat Ukraine with airstrikes. Meanwhile in the Crimea, Prussian colonists have celebrated the beginning of the holiday season with fireworks, simultaneously tripling their rent for the holiday makers. Apparently, this is how they start every summer season which is why last year tourists chose to ignore this traditional holiday destination. The new Oberkommandant of Moskau has pronounced traffic jams part of our national heritage, officially refusing to do anything about them. In Hollywood, Japanese producers have begun shooting Episode 57 of their blockbuster Godzilla. This time the giant sea monster is about to head off to Greenland to destroy an Eskimo village, the last place it hasn't yet been to. Stay with us! After the commercial break, my colleague Fräulein Irina Nosov will continue with tonight's news."

A commercial began, showing a very happy, very fat housewife in a frilly dress who looked like a native of Bavaria, Russland and Ukraine all rolled into one.

"When I make my wurstsalat," she chirped, "I always use Eva Braun, the only mayonnaise which lends my food the taste of the Reich's victories. Low radiation levels, only the best artificial coloring, and lots of safe anti-cholesterol additives. Eva Braun: the eggs that taste like those your Wehrmacht granddad stole from the poor old village lady!"

It was followed back-to-back by an ad for the Benito pizza chain. Its cooks had topped international rankings with their "Duce pizza": tomatoes, mozzarella and a cooked carrot fashioned as Pinocchio's nose. In Moskau, pizza and sushi were in close competition. The ad was nothing new: shots of steaming pastry and deliciously runny cheese followed by the promise of a twenty-minute delivery time.

The closing shot showed an actor impersonating Benito Mussolini, with bulging eyes and a tightly pursed mouth.

"Benito pizza!" he shook his fist at the camera. "Immortal like the Reich!"

Irina began reading the news, her voice ringing with enthusiasm. She'd only been working for a couple of months. Normally, new workers gave it their all.

Funny people, these Italians, Sergei thought. *They make even a dictatorship look like a circus show. While all we have is the labored drama and haughty airs. Why is our regime even trying to fight the Resistance when it's perfectly clear that the Forest Brotherhood can't be defeated? Why can't they admit that every empire needs an enemy, otherwise it reduces itself to a street sausage vendor? The kind of affairs happening in the 1940s! Those were the days! Bolshies, Semitic plutocrats, Wall Street tycoons...*

We consciously decided to stop blaming the Semites while they had always been humanity's perfect scape goat. As were the Bolshies — another dream trademark. So convenient to blame our problems on.

The news edition was over. Sergei scooped his papers up from the desk. The weather forecast began.

"Have you got your radiation meters on?" the slim, tall blonde weather girl asked cheerfully. "Well, you shouldn't have! Today we expect radiation levels to drop considerably. It might have something to do with the activation of two new sarcophagi around the nuclear power stations in Voronezh and Kostroma. The temperature is ninety degrees which is quite normal for December. Enjoy the sun!"

Between the global warming and radiation leaks, Sergei thought, *the inhabitants of Moskau wouldn't know what to do with snow if it jumped on them. What kinds of times are these? We wear shorts in December; air conditioners sell like hot cakes. The Reich's plant breeders promise everyone to start banana plantations. That would officially make us what we've been for quite some time: a run-of-the-mill banana republic.*

He heard footsteps and rose. Two officers in gray business suits were walking toward him, followed by the news Oberst, pale and buttoning up his suit jacket as he walked.

"Sergei Kolychev?" one of the strangers

asked, a seven-foot giant.

He nodded, feeling his insides turn to ice. *The Gestapo. Did that mean they already could read human thoughts?*

"We need to ask you a question concerning one of your ex-colleagues."

Sergei was confronted with a small picture. A pencil sketch.

CHAPTER EIGHT

TUMMO MEDITATION

YEBISU MASSAGE CENTER, TIBET LANE 7

"D-D-DID YOU SEE that g-g-g-guy by the front door? He l-l-looked the spitting i-im-im... image of you. Don't you th-th-think it's funny? D-d-did you borrow his ap-appearance?"

"Oh, Jean-Pierre, for Thor's sake," Pavel said, setting aside his tea bowl. "Don't you have something better to do? He looked like me, so what? Every human being has a lookalike. I've no idea who my parents were; neither can I remember where I got his appearance from. Can a man forget? But seeing as it's entered into the SS database... All right, all right. Do shut up, will you? I need a break."

Obersturmführer Carpe promptly did as he'd been told.

The masseuse's fingertips pressed down on the veins of Pavel's temples. A hot towel hugged his shoulders. A jasmine scent enveloped his nostrils. He could hear his own breathing, calm and level. The Yebisu massage parlor chain was the best in Moskau even though its employees weren't at all Japanese but Chinese and Kalmuck trying hard to impersonate young geishas.

The girl's touch became light and almost weightless. Pavel began mouthing his favorite mantra that he'd memorized in the special-training camp during his long internship in the Tibetan Tashilhunpo Monastery.

His eyelids closed of their own accord. He could hear the distant bubbling of a brook and the delicious singing of birds.

The sounds grew clearer. Stronger. More defined.

Pavel looked around him. He floated along a jungle path amid palm trees of deep burgundy color entangled by masses of green creepers. Parrots fluttered in the scarlet-red sky. Jets of hot steam escaped geysers, enveloping the ground underfoot.

Funny how acidic my subconscious is, Pavel thought. *It's probably the same with everyone prone to negativity.*

Whenever he needed to have a think, he liked to go on a meditation trip. His thoughts would roam in a strange world, dissolving in a riot of color amidst orange birds and red grass. Sometimes he wondered if this was what heaven looked like.

Tummo — which meant "the inner fire system" in Tibetan — was a very special school of meditation. It indeed burned the brain from the inside, heating it like coals. Experts didn't recommend doing it often but only on special and very important occasions.

Now was exactly such a case.

Pavel walked up the orchid-entwined steps to the top of a hill. A carved ivory throne awaited him there, surrounded by four red drums. Pavel hit the drums one by one and began rocking in place, imbibing their hum.

As soon as the last echo died away, he took his place on the throne. Immediately the vines entwined his bare feet; the sky overhead opened up, awash with lightning.

Pavel stared hard in front of himself. Now. It was coming.

He saw a penciled face. A delicate nose. Long hair. The black dots of pupils. Olga Sélina, a Viking TV presenter. She'd died two months ago. Who would have thought: a celebrity, a University graduate, a TV star with her own fan club — a guerrilla fighter? A leader of a Schwarzkopf terrorist cell?

Her group had attacked the cortege of Moskau's Oberkommandant von Travinsky by ambushing it on Aryan Street. The terrorist attack of the year. Armed with grenade launchers, the terrorists had set the front and rear cars on fire while their snipers opened up on them from the roofs of the München Shopping Center.

The Oberkommandant had been the first to be killed, followed by fifteen security staff and all eight of the attackers, eliminated by the arriving Vogel helicopters. Four of the terrorists' bodies had never been found: they'd been simply torn to shreds. They'd had to be identified using the DNA tests provided by Gestapo researchers.

According to Jean-Pierre, all the top brass, the Triumvirate included, had been in shock when they'd discovered that one of the terrorists was a Viking TV star. Street cameras had registered the beginning of the attack: Olga, in black leather, a Schmeisser slung over her shoulder, snapping commands to the terrorists.

None of which was mentioned in the media, of course. Celebrities suspected of having been in contact with guerrillas were sentenced to a very special punishment: oblivion. The names of the actors, TV presenters or singers who'd had the imprudence to commend the Forest Brotherhood on the Shogunet network were forever expelled from the media.

This was death. No interviews, no talk show appearances, nothing. Already a week later, the ostracized celebrity was willing to star in the cheapest of porn simply to draw attention back to him or herself.

It didn't help. The punishment erased their names, dooming them to oblivion — and no one was brave enough to challenge it.

Normally, such an ostracized actor or singer committed suicide within three months. Some proved to be of sturdier stock, but none lasted more than six months. Which was why Olga's disappearance hadn't really surprised anyone — neither the audience nor her ex co-workers. She must have done something, as simple as that.

The questioning of Kolychev — Olga's co-anchor — hadn't turned anything up. He seemed to have been Olga's only friend and clubmate. Apart from him, nothing: she had no family nor friends. They checked Kolychev's phone but found no calls from her made after the attack.

The creepers had entwined Pavel's entire body and closed in over his head. In places the vines had split, spewing out acid-red petals.

The body of the TV presenter had never been found. She, as well as three other terrorists, had been at the very epicenter of the explosion. A bunch of bone fragments, tissue and some blood had been the only material evidence available for DNA analysis.

But the unfortunate experiment that had resulted in the mental incapacitation of the three Gestapo researchers had only been conducted very recently. And at least one of the lunatics had recognized Olga as a fiery angel — the fact that had cost him his sanity.

That could mean at least two things. Either the afterworld indeed existed, revealing a winged fire-enveloped Olga to the Gestapo researchers. Alternatively, she was the "trigger agent" that the Triumvirate had ordered Pavel to locate. Olga Sélina was the spitting image of the fiery angel on the picture. He was almost sure of that.

But how was he supposed to find her if she was dead?

The sky crumbled, turning into knots of squirming snakes. Geysers spat out jets of blood. The air thickened. Unseeing, Pavel could sense panthers circling him, growling and swishing their tails.

She hadn't died. He could feel her heart beat.

The body hadn't been found. Olga would rather everybody considered her dead. Fingernails, bits of skin and the scraps of bloodied clothing that had served as DNA material weren't really proof of death.

But how had she managed to escape the city center cordoned off by the SS? Camera footage had been thoroughly studied but you couldn't really see that much: Aryan Street had been engulfed by smoke and stone dust. The special forces had searched everything within a two-mile diameter with a fine-tooth comb but found no one, either dead or wounded.

He squeezed his eyes shut. Blood seeped from under his eyelids. The jungle came to life, each leaf wailing, a tornado swirling the water into an enormous splattering twister. Words began typing in his head, letter by Gothic letter imprinted on the typewriter ribbon,

The Ministry of Public Education
München Shopping Center
Oberkommandant's Office
The Burgermeister's Residence

That seemed to be it. On top of that, the Shopping Center had been closed for renovation already a month. What else?

Oh yes, of course: the Temple of Odin. Neo Scandinavian style: a fake cave, a copy of the Islandic Viking temple. Well, well, well.

According to Jean-Pierre's report, immediately after the terrorist attack the SS Sonderkommando *Kalinka* had searched all the adjacent buildings. They were all listed on a separate sheet of paper, including their street numbers — those Gestapo bureaucrats wouldn't have had it any other way.

There was only one building missing from the list. The Temple of Odin. That's right. Who would come to a holy place with a search warrant? That would defy reason. The priests of the cult of Asgard were the cornerstones of the existing regime, just like television was. They had enormous wages, houses, medals, SS ranks, the lot.

Which meant that no one had checked the Temple.

And it was only fifty feet or so from the scene of the attack. The smoke cover could possibly have allowed someone to rescue the wounded girl and hide her on the Temple premises. The congregation's noticing the bloody trail wasn't even a problem: sacrifices were frequent in Viking temples, priests slaughtering rather large animals like sheep and goats. And even if the search group had paid the Temple a visit, what then? "Guten tag, Herr Priest, is everything all right?" — "Oh yes, sons of Odin, all is well."

He had to go there, now. He needed to know whether she'd been there.

The wailing in his ears stopped. The orange birds exploded like toy balloons. The palm trees shrank, crumbling into flakes of wheat cream. The throne melted into thin air.

Pavel opened his eyes.

He sprang to his feet, easing the masseuse girl aside. The towel slid to the floor.

"Wake up," he shook Jean-Pierre. "We need to get to the city center. Aryan Street."

They were walking through the door when Pavel saw the Japanese man. He recognized him straight away: this was the same wrinkly old boy who'd sat next to him on the flight in. He stood not far away, next to the guard who, according to Jean-Pierre, was Pavel's lookalike.

The realization pierced Pavel's brain. He knew.

He's here for a reason. He's come to get me.

Pavel stopped. He whipped out a Browning from his pocket but failed to get a round off in time.

The thunder of an explosion ripped through the air. Yellow flames seared Pavel's face.

Reichskommissariat Archives No 1

File ZL8: Politicians

"... ON OCTOBER 20 1941 Wehrmacht troops entered Moskau. After two more months of fierce street fighting they took control of the capital, including the Kremlin.

The search for Joseph Stalin garnered no results. According to the Main Security Office report, he was behind the terrorist attack Vengeance '42 at the Nibelung square that had wiped out the entire Reich elite.

According to Abwehr's intel, later Stalin used to hide in an underground bunker in Kuybyshev (now Führerburg) from where he coordinated the Resistance's actions. After the taking of Führerburg, he disappeared off the radar. The Ural and Siberian guerrilla groups still consider Stalin their spiritual leader.

Daniil, the patriarch of the Forest Church (the sect that had united those of the Orthodox clergy who hadn't recognized Russland's yielding to the battleaxes of the gods of Asgard) worked hard to support the legend. According to it, Stalin had become a hermit living in the thick of the Siberian taiga praying for victory. Between themselves, guerrilla fighters call Stalin "the holy man" — he's a bit of a religious icon for them.

His military commander Klim Voroshilov escaped to Iran and went into hiding in Kurd-controlled areas as "invited by Masoud Barzani". In 1948, he was apprehended during a razzia by SS paratroopers but blew himself up with a grenade during his arrest.

Russia's ex-Head of State Mikhail Kalinin publicly denounced his old masters. He produced paperwork proving his Aryan descent and got himself a job in the Reichskommissariat Moskau. Later he worked for the Ministry of Finances under Walter Funk.

Having retreated from Moskau, the Generals Georgy Zhukov and Konstantin Rokossovsky formed the "forest brigades" near Murmansk whose secret underground factories produced everything they needed, including tanks and howitzers.

The Prime Minister of the United Kingdom, Winston Churchill was captured during the taking of London and imprisoned in the Tower in the same cell as Rudolf Hess had been. Churchill committed suicide in 1949 by cutting his veins.

King George VI had managed to escape to Canada on a submarine; from there, his trail was lost. General Charles de Gaulle became the leader of the French resistance in Africa and died in 1955 in the Madagascan jungle during a Luftwaffe air raid.

The Emperor Hirohito, as tradition required, didn't leave his country during the entirety of his rule; he even refused to visit the first Japanese nuclear test in 1948 on one of the Indonesian islands.

Hirohito refused to grant Japanese citizenship to the residents of the occupied territories. Which is why, unlike the Japanese themselves with their white-bound passports, the Australians and Alaskans have to make do with a temporary yellow ID card.

Mixed marriages between Japanese and Europeans are forbidden. A similar "racial purity" law had been introduced in the Reich in 1935. Now the Nippon koku is ruled by Akihito who is indifferent to politics and spends his spare time writing hokku.

Both President Harry S. Truman and the US Commander in Chief Dwight Eisenhower were tried by a Neuer York Tribunal and publicly hanged at the Zeit Platz on December 11 1958. Both the Democratic and the Republican parties had been banned as "loathsome samples of plutocracy in politics".

The remains of President Roosevelt had been exhumed and thrown into the Hudson River to drum rolls.

Tens of thousands of Americans died during pogroms (the so-called 'D.C. massacre') started by Japanese released from relocation centers[7]. The Mikado's army didn't interfere, announcing the slaughter to be their 'rightful revenge'. The pogromists burned down the Capitol and the White House, causing many congressmen to choke to death in the fire.

Chinese communists have never stopped fighting the Nippon koku, their guerrilla units still going strong in most of the country's provinces. Their leader Mao Tse-Tung made it his goal to leave as many successors as he could, calling his project *The Hydra of a Billion Heads*. By the time of his death from cancer in 1982 in the rainforests of Yunnan Province, he'd fathered three hundred children from a hundred young female guerrilla fighters.

Other field commanders had adopted the same system, supplying Chinese communists with plenty of new cadre.

---

[7] Issued by President Roosevelt, the deportation order of February 19 1942 sent 110,000 Americans of Japanese descent to special "relocation centers".

MOSKAU

Stalin's deputy Nikita Khrushchev was arrested in Moskau in 1980. All that time, he'd been hiding in his own apartment but no one had thought of looking for him there.

Permitted for public release

Signed: Deputy Reichskommissar Paul von Breuwitz

CHAPTER NINE

URADZIOSUTOKU

MIKADO'S JOY STREET

NAGASAKI CAFÉ

BLOOD IS THROBBING in my temples. I feel even worse now than after I had fainted back in the Temple. I can't think straight. It's as if my head has been cut off — and still I can feel the rest of my body. A bit like sensing your own feet after they've been amputated. Phantom pain, it's called. My skin, my nails, my bones — everything seems to have peeled off. Actually, that's quite possible. To have survived *this* without losing any of your body just wouldn't be possible.

I can see myself as if from above. My priest's robes are gone. I'm wearing black boots, a black business suit and a bowler hat to match. Standard workday attire here in Uradziosutoku.

A paper parasol protects my face from the scorching sun. A waitress in traditional geisha costume clutters her geta sandals across the floor, then bends in a deep bow.

“Would you like something else, Sir?”

“Danke schön,” I say with a frail wave of my hand. “Only... this...”

She nods subserviently. “The yakitori is coming. It’s just as it should be, soy sauce and all. We’re heating your sake slowly: we’re doing our best. *Irasshai...* sorry for the wait. I have something else to offer you.”

The geisha leans toward my ear, enveloping me in a fresh aroma of morning chrysanthemums. “We have our own moonshine,” she whispers stealthily. “Clear as a crystal.”

“Good,” I agree, mimicking her. “Got some pickled cabbages to go with it?”

“We’ll find some, darling... we could dress it up as funchoza, I suppose... these Japanese heathens will never know.”

Her cheeks burning, the waitress walks back to a door marked in Japanese and disappears in the kitchen.

The mind boggles. The Japanese took Uradziosutoku on September 10 1941 — as soon as the Nippon koku had officially entered the war. Seventy years later, there’s very little left of this old Siberian megalopolis which used to be equal doses of Bolshevik and the Tsar. The first thing the Japs did, they restored the Amur Republic[8] and even summoned the Merkulov brothers, its one-time White Guard émigré ex-rulers. Still, it didn't last: in less than a year Japan must have realized it simply had to have a prime morsel like this all for itself.

Now Uradziosutoku was a typically Japanese city sliced into neat squares just like Karafuto Island and built with identical gray and white cottages, their curved roofs inviting swallows to nest inside, its streets drowning in cherry blossom — made of plastic, of course, because real wild cherries aren't that mad to blossom at this time of year in Siberia. Street shops flash their fancy Japanese neons, their owners laying squid tentacles out to dry. You can hear the screams of fishmongers at the pier market.

Disgusted, I stare at the wasabi on my plate. Where's my moonshine?

These cherry blossoms
Mess with my head;
I think I need some booze.

---

[8] The Amur Republic: an independent state that existed in the Russian Far East from May 26 1921 to October 25 1922. Recognized by both the US and Japan, the Amur Republic ceased to exist with the taking of Vladivostok by Bolshevik troops.

The hokku comes naturally. The *Nagasaki* café occupies several cozy Buddhist-style verandahs atop a hill. They offer an excellent view of the bay busy with adorable little boats strung with red paper sails. They're called junks in China.

I vaguely remember us going up Calm Dragon Street the other day. Kimonoed shop assistants looked out of their shops and smiled to us, bowing and saying "*Okaeri nasai!*" — "Welcome!"

The Japanese culture has taken over the city — although not entirely. The locals have preserved a few more exotic bits, like the Lutheran church, the Polish Cathedral of The Most Holy Mother of God and the Arch of Tsesarevich Nicholas. Hokkaido tourists love taking pictures with them. Uradziosutoku means Salt Bay in Japanese but Russlanders still use the city's old name, Vladivostok.

Closer to the Harbor of the Morning Calm (called so in honor of the neighboring Korean Province) towers the Amaterasu Arch dedicated to the goddess of the sun. Newlyweds hurry there after their shintoist wedding ceremonies to pay their respects and drink tea in the shade of the goddess' true wisdom.

The white and blue mansion of the Manchukuo consulate is only a ten-minute drive away: formerly the seat of the city council, it's surrounded by a colorful array of Chinese restaurants. From what I've gleaned from Viking News, recently the city was in a state of mourning. Geishas stopped receiving visitors as a sign of their grief. Apparently, the city's ex-Shichō — a Mayor — had performed a *seppuku*, leaving behind the following inscription on silk,

My Emperor!

I am forced to disembowel myself, unable to govern this territory where they smash their sake glasses on the ground every time they finish their drinks. I am sorry to have saddened your heart. I just cannot take it any longer.

True, Japanese nationals don't have it easy here. They're run off their feet trying to Japonize the Russian Far East — but to no avail. Things don't change. Shigemitsu Ivanovich still beats the holy crap out of Dzimmei Petrovich over the former's wife — the well-respected tea mistress Kumiko Sergeevna — who has been wearing a rather revealing kimono lately so that the latter just couldn't help himself and dipped a stealthy hand under the provocative silk.

No bowing, no apologies, no poems describing the remorse eating through the black heart of the bastard Dzimmei.

The rising sun has set.
The three drunk samurai
Bow to their sake barrel.

This was the hokku that the Shichō wrote with his own blood after he'd sliced his belly with a katana.

The Germanization of European Russia has been much more successful. Everyone there seemed to be pleased with becoming a "blond beast" whose Aryan ancestors had arrived from Mount Kailash, the one with the swastika on its slope.

It's true that in Moskau proper the Japanese culture is popular purely due to the distance separating it from exotic Tokyo. But here, the locals can't stand the sight of it. No matter how many times the police have raided underground samovar[9] tea parties, they mushroom by the day.

"This is your sake, Master. I beg of you, in the name of Amaterasu, *do pay attention*," bowing deeply, the waitress offers me a china flask on a tray.

I nod. My hand shakes as I pour the liquid into a tiny cup. I down it in one gulp. My chest burns like the fire in Loki's eyes. It feels too good.

The pickled cabbage is crunchy to bite.
Life is flooding back into me.
Time for a second drink.

---

[9] Samovar: a traditional 19-century water urn that became synonymous with Russian tea culture.

Here, one begins to think in hokkus. Who needs Aspirin when there's moonshine?

I don't expect Olga — but she's just appeared in front of me. At first, I take her for a waitress: she's wearing a kimono too. A black one embroidered with yellow dragons.

She flashes a sarcastic smile. "It didn't take you long to lose that Aryan veneer. So it's vodka now, is it? Where's your schnapps?"

I'm not embarrassed. After what happened, I can drink windscreen liquid.

"Schnapps is German for moonshine," I help myself to more cabbage. "Slightly more sophisticated, maybe. Do sit down. Have you got what I asked you to get?"

She nods and reaches under the table for an attache case. Inside is a portable Buch computer. A Sony, of course, the only type purebred Aryans would use. It's white and very pretty.

I lick a finger, then touch a button. The system IDs my DNA automatically. The computer begins to reboot.

Its screen lights up. The Sakura OS is slow and glitchy. Little bells begin to chime their sweet melody.

"I rented it," Olga answers my silent question. "Five hundred yen. I paid by card."

I type away, then open my personal Shogunet account where I have surveillance camera controls set up, allowing me to monitor them from any place on the globe. Three of the cameras are installed in the Temple of Odin and two more in my apartment. Password: *asgard*. Not very original, I know. I switch to real time and swivel one of the cameras.

The temple is absolutely packed with people. Some are wearing the camos and black uniforms of the SS special forces. Others are in plain clothes. They look around themselves as they walk, studying the interior. The camera is low-res but I can make out the puzzled expressions on their faces. I bet. I too was surprised when I'd come round after my fall.

The sacrificial altar is floating in the air, ghostlike, like a horror movie projection. It's translucent; you can see right through it. The grotto's walls quiver like sea waves, rippling.

One of the officers approaches the statue of Rübezahl, the king of dwarves. Yes, there he is, my stooping white-bearded old man, the work of a fine sculptor chiseled out of a whole chunk of cave granite.

Now the fun bit. The SS officer touches the statue. He is probably screaming with fear as his hand sinks inside. Rübezahl's body may look like stone but it now consists of a viscous jelly-like substance.

What he doesn't know is that there were four more stone deities lined up next to this one. They disappeared the moment I fainted. And not only them. The sacrificial goat is nowhere to be seen, either.

A man in a gray shirt and matching pants seems to be in command of the squad. He barks orders; they jump to attention. A big wig. I've never seen him before. I move the camera closer, just in case. He turns round. I take a snapshot of him. And another.

The picture disappears in a flash. What's happened?

"He shot at the camera," Olga explains. "They'll be over at your apartment at any moment. That's why we are here. I had a strong premonition that they might locate me soon. That they'd come for me... in the very near future. I was right."

I click the Buch's lid close and top up the bone china with more moonshine.

"*Sehr gut*," I take in the original aroma of good old home brew. "Let's try and reconstruct what happened. There isn't much to reconstruct, really. I came back home. You were still handcuffed to your bed. I walked over to you in order to remove them..."

I look over the bay. Seagulls squawk and squabble over the ocean. The waitress bows deeply to a new customer. I exhale sharply[10] and

---

[10] Russian drinking traditions prescribe to always exhale before downing a stiff drink in one draught; doing so prevents the drinker's breath from being seized.

down my drink, then hurry to pinch some cabbage with my chopsticks. "... and the next moment we were here. Seven thousand miles away from Moskau. What happened?"

She laughs softly and rearranges her black hair. She's unbearably beautiful. "I've no idea how it happens. It must be the danger that does it. I can't control these things. That's how I teleported into the temple where you later found me. You thought guerrillas had brought me there, remember? Even though the front doors were locked. You lay me under Rübezahl's statue to dress my wounds. It's the energy within my head... it works like teleportation. But I never know when it's going to happen."

"Why didn't you disappear earlier, then? Somehow I don't think my handcuffs would have stopped you."

She clicks her lighter. That's the Nippon koku: no one would arrest you here for smoking in a café. "Probably because I knew you weren't a threat."

Crashing noise. Howls of agony. Screaming.

As if in slow motion, I watch as Mikado's Joy Street caves in. A round crater appears in the middle of the pedestrian zone. The doll houses adorned with red lanterns begin to slide into the chasm; the St. Paul's Church crumbles, listing to one side, bell tower and all. Hundreds of human figures pour into the crater as it gapes like a huge, smiling lipless mouth. I hear the inhuman screams of dying people. Houses sink through the tarmac which is now fluid like sunflower oil.

The city dies before my very eyes but I can't do anything about it. People wail with horror, their bodies turning transparent as if made of fine glass. I can see their hearts, their livers, their brains, I watch their blood run through their veins. Crowds of glass people.

Uradziosutoku rapidly breaks out into a gossamer net of crevices. Trees snap like matchsticks. The ocean hisses, convulsing, spewing out dead fish. Instinctively I grab a knife from the table.

I sink it into my right palm already covered in scars.

Blood splatters onto the plate, mixing with the soy sauce. I look at the girl's face. Not a face: a skull. A grinning, scowling skull greedily drawing on a cigarette.

"What are you?" I croak. "What the hell are you?"

Her gaze alights on me. Her eyes have no pupils. They're filled with unfathomable darkness.

"What a strange question," she lets the smoke out. "Don't you know yet?"

PART TWO

The Black Sun

All are waiting for the light;
Fear it or fear it not.
The sun shines out of my eyes,
It will not go down tonight —
And the world counts down to 10.

Rammstein, *Sonne*

CHAPTER ONE

SEPPUKU

SAKURA HOTEL, SUITE 298

"I AM WRITING THIS LETTER in compos mentis. My name is Yamamura Onoda. I am a Major with the Nippon koku General Staff. I am also a Casio representative in the Reichskommissariat Moskau. I plead forgiveness from all those who have suffered as the result of my terrible mistakes that brought about the failure of Operation Yukio Seki[11].

Yes, it was none other than myself who had

[11] Yukio Seki: the twenty-three-year-old Japanese kamikaze pilot who on October 25 1944 rammed into a USS carrier in the Leyte Gulf. This became the first kamikaze attack in human history.

put forward Kiyoshi Itiro, the assistant military translator and my old Karafuto co-worker, as a potential tokko tai — a suicide bomber. I was badly misled, considering the retired geriatric Itiro the best candidate for the job. Suffering from brain cancer, he readily accepted the assignment on condition that his children receive a one-off payment of two million yen from the Mikado Bank.

His wife Sadako expressed her desire to die together with her husband. Highly appreciating her intention, I agreed: a family of Japanese tourists would arouse minimal suspicion from their target. Our best Tokyo experts built an explosive device to make it look like a clumsy amateurish job made to the anarchists' instructions supposedly downloaded from the Shogunet. Itiro-san made a recording of a video address, which he had previously rehearsed several times, in which he calmly admitted his support for the Schwarzkopf movement and the Bolshevik Party of Nippon.

On December 12 of the Heisei era 23[12] (may it last forever!) the Hong Kong Imperial Kommandatur arranged for the Itiro couple to board a Junkers 564 Moskau flight without a

---

[12] In the Japanese calendar, the ascension of a new emperor generally starts a new era. The current Heisei Era started with the ascension of Emperor Akihito in 1989.

security check. As usual, we had no description of the subject even though our secret services guaranteed his presence on board the plane. Following my instructions, Itiro's wife was going to activate the bomb as the airplane started its approach to Moskau airport. According to Sadako-san, she did switch on the detonator hidden in her purse which, for some reason, failed to activate.

The woman told the truth. Already after meeting her husband, I studied the detonator and came to the conclusion it had been intentionally disabled. I have no doubt that this had been Itiro-san saving his wife's life, unwilling to see her die together with him. This was regrettably stupid. By doing so, he missed his chance to complete his mission while his family lost the money.

Later, he expressed his regret at what he'd done.

Embittered by the aforementioned failure, I would like to point out that later Itiro-san did everything he could in order to restore his honor and rectify the disgusting consequences of his disabling the detonator. It is only thanks to him that we now have a detailed description of the target, as Itiro-san had watched the Sturmbannführer being escorted with honors down the steps and into a limousine.

Itiro-san rented an apartment and approached the mission with all seriousness as befits a samurai. He used the operative information I sent him to follow the subject through Moskau, attempting to approach him at a closer distance. On a tip from a Gestapo mole, Itiro-san arrived at the Spirit's Delight book store and spent the entire day in the shop waiting for the target to arrive.

Later that evening, he swore by the God Susanoo that the subject had never arrived. Another failure added to my account! Wary of a potential leak, I had never informed Itiro-san of Pavel Loktev's peculiar behavioral patterns.

This, in turn, influenced everything that followed.

Today an uncomplaining Itiro-san pressed the button on a new detonator and, praising the great Mikado, consequently transported himself to the feet of the Goddess Amaterasu. He activated the explosive device by the entrance to the Yebisu massage parlor standing next to the person who bore an uncanny resemblance to the target. Seven people died in the blast, including the bomber himself. I tend to believe that the growing tumor had stripped Itiro-san of his ability to think straight otherwise he'd have been bound to ask himself why Pavel Loktev was wearing an Obergefreiter's uniform posing as a parking lot security guard. Whatever the case, the target escaped either unharmed or with the slightest of injuries.

I accept the blame for the failure of my

strategy. Years of life in Russland must have corrupted my heart with the rot of irresponsible carelessness. I failed to consider the possibility of Itiro-san not blowing up the plane. By my meticulous planning of the operation, I got drunk on the sophistication of the petals of my ideas. The explosion on board the plane was intended to be a terrorist act performed by a terminally ill fanatic, an old-age loner who'd lapsed into the senility of the Bolshevik ideal. The video of his confession would have convinced the Gestapo that the death of their special agent in the blast was a tragic coincidence. We were quite prepared to plant other evidence aiming to divert attention from the Japanese secret services. The plan was perfect — which was its biggest weakness. I failed to plan for any eventualities.

A faithful agent prepared to die without hesitation. The enclosed space of the plane. A brilliant cover story and the video confession. What could be better? For the first time in years, my gaze alights on my samurai sword. I find it almost impossible to forgive myself.

...For the last ten years, I've been heading the Moskau intelligence station. I've been paid double for the emotional damage. Moskau is indeed a terrible place where one can never relax. Let me assure you that I work hard to earn every yen of that money while some of my colleagues lounge around somewhere on the Solomon Islands or laze away on Ngapali Beach sipping their plum whisky cocktails. I'd have loved to swap places with them: not only with those serving in Asia but also with my European colleagues.

Some of them might point out anxiously that Europe is a dangerous place. The Resistance is still active in countries like the Netherlands, Denmark and Norway. Yes, I'd say, but their so-called Resistance is a far cry from the 1940s. It's all a big theater show. A group of masked youngsters who, breathless with their own audaciousness, rip down the Reich's flag from the statue of the Little Mermaid or deface a monument to the Führer with spray paint. Every such escapade makes the headlines as TV dooms Europe to an era of terrorism.

Their Resistance is just a trend. Being a revolutionary and an activist is trendy in Europe. They love nothing better than to write songs of protest and upload banned books to the Net. And then what? The Gestapo apprehends them, they crack and sell all their friends down the river, then indulge in bouts of public repentance on TV, blaming their actions on the side effects of drugs.

All European Resistance is encapsulated within the Shogunet. Not many Aryans are willing to risk their creature comforts after the Twenty-Year War. Chinese slaves rebuilt European cities from the ruins; an economic boom followed, turning Europe into a land of milk, honey and Mercedes Benz.

Churchill once promised that if the Germans invaded Britain, his country would fight to the last man. And what do we see? All those weird little campaigns, the so-called flash mobs: young people, terribly proud of themselves, gathering at Das Gros Ben to form a huge phrase FUCK THE NAZIS with votive candles. Can a regime be overthrown with candles? Please. I want my European colleagues' job.

Still, it was here that the Nippon koku sent me, into the very heart of quagmires and gloomy towers: Moskau. Here, it's different. Some Russlanders hate the Germans as invaders while others welcome them as the guarantors of European civilization. But nobody likes Japan.

You don't need to believe me but here, everybody praises Japanese art, loves the Japanese cuisine, appreciates Japanese culture... and despises the Japanese. I habitually check my car three times a day to make sure no good-wisher has attached a magnetic bomb to the chassis. I only eat salmon in a few trusted restaurants to avoid food poisoning. I only indulge in late-evening poetry readings with young Kyoto geisha school graduates who've mastered the art of the tea ceremony.

Every day I walk a sword's edge between Scylla and Charybdis. Guerrillas hunt me for being an ally of Greater Germany. The Reich's supporters don't like Asians, either; they'd be more than happy to plant a slug between my eyes if I was imprudent enough to ride the nighttime subway. By Amaterasu, everything's so complicated here.

... There was a time when I used to write poetry, painstakingly drawing the symbols on rice paper. I've given it up now. I don't have the inspiration. Moskau eats right through you like a tapeworm, destroying you from the inside. You imbibe the local lifestyle and mentality without even realizing it. I've become a Russian. I can chase down a dish of fugu with pure laboratory alcohol with the best of them. It actually tastes better that way.

I know very well how you expect me to finish this letter.

I'm very sorry. But my experience of many years in Russland prevents me from performing seppuku — even though my samurai honor bemoans it and my katana is begging to be unsheathed. I understand perfectly well that locating Pavel Loktev isn't going to be easy, mainly because now he knows that he's being hunted.

I'm not looking for excuses but I assure you that I've taken all the necessary precautions. Sadako won't speak. She was taken care of half an hour after the bomb had exploded. Her body has been cremated and won't be found. We made a new video of Itiro-san before the blast, with all mention of the plane edited out. It's now being uploaded to the Shogunet. Our priority now is to do our best not to damage our relations with the Third Reich. Greater Germany and the Nippon Koku are the best of friends.

Not having enemies is awful. You're sadly forced to spy on your friends.

There's too much at stake: my Tokyo friends expect the mission to be a success. It's not the first time we tried to take Loktev out. There were other attempts, performed with surgical precision but equally unsuccessful. The air crash would have been a perfect scenario. Unfortunately, it failed due to Itiro-san's inopportune sentimentality. I'm going to do it myself now. Casio's Moskau office is closing. I'm going to find Loktev myself.

Signed: Yamamura Onoda
Major with the Nippon koku General Staff

CHAPTER TWO

THE PARADISE

MASTER RACE AVENUE

GELI RAUBAL HOTEL

THE FIRST THING EMERGING from the gloom of Pavel's memory was the cellar. Back in Paradise, this had been where they sent delinquents. It was a sterile room: no rats or cockroaches there. Still, it was very scary. You spent hours in the pitch black. Gradually, you couldn't help sensing there was somebody there after all. You wanted to reach out and touch them but you were too scared *they* might bite your fingers off.

Pavel too had been sent there on a couple of occasions: once for three hours, on another occasion five. During nap time, big kids told them scary stories, like the one about the boy left there forgotten for two days. He had gone blind and lost his mind. How could you forget it: the way your eyes hurt adapting to daylight when the Paradise's attendants unlocked the cellar door which bore the sign of two lightning bolts set in a black triangle.

That was Paradise's logo, the same as nurses wore on the lapels of their starched lab coats. Sterile girls they were, like incubated clones. They reminded him of dairy maids on a farm. Which was probably the most accurate description, for children were bred there like one would breed cattle. Neat ranks of obedient boys and girls: fair-haired, ginger, strawberry blond, dressed in brown shorts, shirts and pinafores with the ever-present triangle on the sleeve. Not a single smile nor laughter, nothing but the teachers' snapped orders.

They'd been told they weren't in captivity. This wasn't a prison. This was a place for the chosen, the best of the best. They hadn't been kidnapped: they'd been granted the great honor of joining the Paradise. Long after Pavel had left its heavenly pastures, he came across the black triangles on office doors in every European city. The biggest one, with its own apple orchard and swimming pool, was located in the center of Moskau within walking distance of the Greater Germany metro station. He had to hurry past it quite a few times while on business; he used to look into its windows, curious, but had never actually plucked up enough courage to go in. Pointless. Doubtful anything had changed within. Same nurses patrolling the corridors, same lookalike children, same watchful guards in black uniforms: the Paradise was curated by the SS.

They had indeed changed the rules, though. These days they needed the family's consent to remove a child; the parents had to provide blood test results and a certificate from the Race department confirming the purity of his Aryan provenance.

Who might his parents have been? Pavel hardly ever thought about it. The DNA test he'd taken in the Gestapo lab ten years ago had confirmed that he had Slavic blood running in his veins. Either Russlanders or Slovaks; possibly Czechs or Bulgarians even. He didn't know his real name: the children's names were changed upon arrival.

Afterwards, he'd changed names many times. He had about a hundred of them.

The Paradise was stifling in its orderliness; it stuffed your mouth like cotton wool, blinding you with the sterile white of its painted walls. Calorie-appropriate nutrition, classical music, *Let's Draw the Führer* art contests and lessons in Aryan comportment: a purebred person was obliged to know how exactly he differed from the *untermensch.*

They studied eight hours a day. The

Paradise's main task was to plant the required ideas into their heads. Nurse Berta Lüdinghausen was a gaunt Hessian woman (pronouncing her name used to be a torture) who took them out for walks along Moskau streets noisy with construction works: the now-deceased Oberkommandant pulled old buildings down by the hundred, erecting new ones which were "in keeping with the Teutonic spirit".

The Physical Education lessons were held in the giant Triumph sports center built in place of the Kolomenskoe Estate torn down in 1945. Berta, who had an answer to everything, explained to them in her barking tones that the estate had been considered a "garish abomination typical of Slavic architecture". Walking along the Moskau river embankment with children trailing after her, she never forgot to point her finger, informing them that back in 1931, the Bolsheviks had destroyed the snow-white Cathedral of Christ the Savior only to build another "garish abomination" in its place, namely the Palace of the Soviets.

What Berta forgot to mention was that in the very beginning of the war the Reich's leaders had had both the Assumption Cathedral in Kiev and the St. Sophia Cathedral in Novgorod razed to the ground. Today, Greater Germany and Russland may call each other brothers, but in those days the Slavs hadn't been supposed to have much of their history left.

Someone knocked on the door. Softly first, then louder.

"Pavel! P-Pavel, fu-fuck you! O-open the d-door! You asleep or wh-what?"

Pavel jumped to his feet, knocking the chair over. The unfinished tea cup softly dropped sideways onto the carpet. He must have fallen asleep. He'd been dreaming of the Paradise again. It had been years but he couldn't get it out of his head. He'd returned there almost every night, walking the white-walled corridors amid identical pallid faces.

Pavel draped the hotel dressing gown around himself and turned the key.

Obersturmführer Carpe froze in the doorway, black as thunder. His both cheeks and forehead were covered in bandages. The first-aid surgeons had counted twelve cuts on his face from the glass that had flown everywhere during the explosion. Pavel didn't look much better. Talk about idiot's luck. Had the Japanese suicide bomber activated his device a second later, the rescue team would have had to scrape their guts off the sidewalk.

"L-lucky b-ba-bastard," Jean-Pierre said, looking at him. "It didn't take you l-long to re-recover."

Pavel flashed him a cynical smile. His skin was perfectly intact. "What would you like, whisky or gin? Your pick. It's Japanese. I brought some from Hong Kong."

"Whi-whisky s-sounds good. Haven't had any p-p-plum spirit in quite a whi...while. I could dr-drink it all day l-long," he downed the glass, his teeth chattering.

"Go sit down," Pavel offered, wrapping the dressing gown tighter around himself. "Wanna order some chow?"

"*Kein problem*!" Jean-Pierre agreed. "My stomach thinks my throat's been cut."

Pavel dialed the restaurant and, ignoring the menu, ordered some *eisbein*. The law demanded pork to be permanently available in every Aryan Nutrition joint, so you could eat Bavarian anywhere, even in some God-forsaken Germanville somewhere in a Russian backwater.

Pavel replaced the receiver. "Have you found the old lady?" he asked without much hope.

"You're joking?" Jean-Pierre mumbled. "Our detectives even ripped out the floors and tapped the walls all over in the old Jap's rented apartment. Not a trace. Now, it could have been two things. Either she legged it — or, may the Iron-Forest witches take me, some smartass had been there before us. Someone uploaded a video to the Shogunet half an hour ago in which the old boy accepts responsibility for the terrorist attack and praises the Forest Brothers in broken Russian."

Pavel walked over to the window, clasped his hands behind his back and cracked the joints of his fingers. “No way he’s a Bolshevik. It has to be a stitch-up. It’s the Japs, I just know it. They’d love to serve my guts up in a hole in the ground with some concrete sauce on top. And they would, had it not been for my little secret ability. I’ve been to the Nippon koku God knows how many times doing Gestapo jobs. Last year, remember? Manila, the Solar Tower? I had to stab the Japanese General Staff’s courier and retrieve his briefcase. I just don’t know how they worked me out. They can’t have my description. Tracked some e-funk message? Whatever. They just knew I would be on board that plane and they were going to take care of me. You can’t take someone like me prisoner. You kill ‘em on the spot.”

“I just hope next time I’ll be somewhere else when it happens,” Jean-Pierre took a long swig of whisky. “Your wounds heal in a couple of hours while I had to have God knows how many stitches. And once I came round, I had to go to the old Jap’s apartment to take some DNA samples. I had no choice but to go by the wretched metro — I’m so fed up with our traffic jams. Shaking on the train like some fucking jelly. Can’t stand our subway, you know that? Never have done. It’s only five lines, but all those throngs of people! You can’t breathe on the trains: they have no air conditioning. I think the Reich’s public transportation is an extension of their concentration camp system.”

Pavel listened to him absent-mindedly while studying the yellow roof of a Mitsubishi bus by the hotel entrance below. They circulated all around Moskau, advertising the magical services of the Thule Society. Black magic was undoubtedly popular in the Third Reich: just as popular as the cults of Odin and Thor. Triumvirate-licensed wizards had the right to practice their lore. At the peak of its popularity in the 1940s, the Thule Society had made a name for itself by claiming that Aryans had arrived on Earth from the Aldebaran solar system. The society had attempted to set up a mass resurrection of dead soldiers; they imported Tibetan lamas and tried to master the art of thought reading. Over time, this facility which once had boasted the Reich's best mystics and visionaries had become a mundane fortune-telling show. These days, Thule's customers were mainly young unmarried girls wishing to know their future who'd sometimes buy protective charms which guarded their bearers against guerrilla attacks.

"Well, what do you want?" Pavel yawned. "They built five lines: four to form a swastika and one as a ring road encircling it. Ideologically very clever. But in reality, people are crammed down there like sardines in a can, cursing the wretched subway to hell and back."

Pavel walked to the table and took a file stamped *Confidential.*

"Olga Sélina stayed with the priest for two months," he said pensively, rustling the pages. "Not as a slave but rather as a privileged prisoner. She had dinners with him and received care and medical treatment even though she couldn't leave the premises. The DNA test has shown," more rustling of paper, "that the traces of blood on the sacrificial stone belong to the priest. She contaminated him like she contaminates everything around her, the temple included. You've seen what's going on in there: we had to lock the gate, cordon if off and post guards all around," he paused, leafing through the file. "There's one thing I don't understand... your people all lost their marbles when exposed to her. But the priest didn't. Wonder if his little blood-letting ritual prevents this from happening? Their meeting was an accident but now Olga Sélina won't let go of him. She needs him really badly. No idea why. That's what scares me. There's some sort of connection between the two of them."

The sound of clattering plates came from outside the door as security checked their order.

"We might have less time than you think," Jean-Pierre sighed. "We can't keep it under wraps for much longer. Our operatives back in the temple saw what contamination can do. Very soon Moskau will be plagued with the kind of rumors that would make the *Völkischer Beobachter* weep with envy."

A gray-haired waiter in the uniform of a kitchen service Hauptmann (with silver-ladle collar badges and a white peaked cap) rolled in a serving table crowded with plates. Smiling politely, he served out the side dishes and moved the mustard pots closer to them.

Jean-Pierre's e-funk rang. He apologized and walked out, only to return promptly. "I've got two bits of news for you. One is excellent. They've apprehended both. They used their card to rent a Buch computer. How stupid can you be? Later they withdrew one hell of a sum from a *Geldautomat*, then blocked their bank account. The second one is not so good. They're in Uradziosutoku now, and the Gestapo needs to get clearance from the Japanese police to work there. Thor almighty, how on earth did they get there? They were in Moskau today. Uradziosutoku is seven hours by plane."

Pavel lifted the cover off a dish. The room filled with eisbein's delicious aroma. "They didn't fly there," he licked his lips. "They teleported."

CHAPTER THREE

THE INVISIBLE

URADZIOSUTOKU

RYOKAN 'SWALLOW'

POLISHED WOODEN FLOORS. Sliding paper partitions depict long-legged cranes dancing amid groves of bamboo. These doors don't open normally: you have to slide them apart like those of a wardrobe. Thin tatami mats cover some of the floor. Steaming tea is waiting on a tray, next to the inevitable little bowl of soy sauce and some rice in bone china cups.

We've found refuge in one of the *ryokans*: small Japanese hotels styled as a traditional country cottage. These days there are hundreds of them all over Uradziosutoku, patronized mainly by secret lovers. *Ryokans* are perfect for their purpose. The receptionist can't even see you: part of her cubicle window is frosted so you can only see her hands as she accepts payment. No names asked, no IDs required. Just pay and go to bed.

Which suits us just fine.

It's getting dark. When I look through the window, I can make out the streetlights on the Mikado Peninsula, covered in Japanese characters.

She's sitting cross-legged on the tatami eating rice, deftly using her chopsticks.

"That was really stupid, renting a Buch with a card!" I say bleakly.

"Absolutely," she touches her hair, rearranging it. "Now the Gestapo know which city to search. They still need to get here, though. It might take them some time. We can at least spend the night and get some rest. We need to decide where to go and what to do next."

Good point. Back in Moscow I had a job, an SS rank, a status, a service car (unchauffeured) and holiday bonuses every Thorrablot and Disting[13] day. I used to be quite an important person any way you looked at it. Now I am a criminal on the run, sitting on the floor in this

---

[13] Thorrablot and Disting: Norse mid-winter and end-of-winter festivals still celebrated in Iceland

bug-ridden hole while my record must have already been added to the Weltgestapo database. Assisting Schwarzkopfs is very serious business. The best-case scenario: banishment to Africa. The worst, the Spitzbergen concentration camps where inmates die within the first two weeks.

"What to do next?" I say with a sarcastic smile. "Next, we go into hiding for the rest of our lives. Forest or cellar, take your pick. There're no neutral countries anymore. Even Switzerland has allied itself with the Reich. Its capital city has been moved from Bern to the German Canton of Zurich. *You* can always find shelter somewhere in the Ural Mountains controlled by the Schwarzkopfs. But me... it might probably be easier to just buy a Japanese passport, adopt a Japanese name and stay here. The Schwarzkopfs kill all Odin's priests, as the Forest Church demands. The Triumvirate will be looking for me, of course, but..."

She clicks her chopsticks in a most contemptuous way. "The Triumvirate?!" whenever she has to say the word, she always does it at the top of her voice. "We live in a country of ghosts. Our head of state is a schizophrenic who died seventy years ago. His will is executed by three men no one has ever seen. Don't you think it's funny? This secrecy, this holy mystery of power? Our people don't even know the names of those who rule them. We hear their speeches on the radio, we read their articles in newspapers but we have no idea what the Triumvirate members look like. They're ghost rulers devoured by the dark."

There she goes again. Her nightly dose of bleating. Yes, so the Moskau administration is anonymous. Nobody argues that. After the Führer's death in the Mausoleum blast of 1942, all of the Reich's top officials were ordered to abstain from public speaking. They stopped attending NSDAP congresses, couldn't go to the Reichstag or have beerhouse meetings.

Not that it helped though. The Schwarzkopfs went on a hunt for all remotely important National Socialist leaders. At different times, guerrilla fighters slew the Reichskommissar of Ukraine Erich Koch, the Finance Minister Funk and the chief honcho of all work camps Adolf Eichmann. Over the years, the city streets grew safer as the Schwarzkopfs moved into woods but still, the powers that be already knew they'd never cease to be a target.

So upon the ending of the Twenty-Year War, all the Reichskommissariats apart from Turkestan switched to the three-leader system: the Triumvirate. Now that guerrilla fighters didn't know which of the three was the Reichskommissariat's actual leader, they couldn't plan an assassination attempt. The leaders didn't ride cars, they didn't fly, they made no TV appearances: only radio addresses read by presenters with identical steely voices. Triumvirate leaders couldn't be killed, but most importantly, this system allowed them to be replaced at any given moment, swiftly and soundlessly.

Moskau rumors had it that ghost politicians were constantly being shuffled like a deck of cards: some lasted in the role of Reich leader for a month, another maybe a year. It didn't matter. The empire was being ruled by the dead Führer and any number of ghosts with blurred, mist-corroded outlines.

At least none of them had to worry for their lives.

But would I actually let her have the final say? I don't think so.

"Sorry, I'm afraid I'm not in the mood for a highbrow political discussion," I inform her with sarcastic courtesy. "Especially seeing as you never answered the big question."

She sighs and leans down to place the cup on the floor. I can see her chest. She's not wearing anything at all under her kimono: I'm sure she'll go to bed naked. What a shame I didn't think of renting a pair of handcuffs at the same time as the Buch.

"You still don't believe me?" she asks. "You simply fainted, I assure you, you just zoned out for a while. I have no doubt that you might have seen the collapsing Uradziosutoku and me as a perambulating zombie. Hallucinations are known to be a common byproduct of teleportation."

Oh, I've made her defensive! The gods

would have been proud of me. But I have to strike while the iron is hot. I have a splitting headache and can lose control of the situation at any moment. “Do you suggest I should calmly embrace the fact that once I discovered you lying in a pool of blood on the temple floor, my life has never been the same? Of course! It’s perfectly normal, isn’t it? I’s nothing. You’re staying at my place, and every night I have apocalyptic visions of Ragnarök: cannibalized horse carcasses, dying people, frozen cities lying in ruins. What’s so strange about the fact that objects around me begin to disappear and stone walls turn into sand dunes? Nothing weird about that, is there? It takes us two seconds to transport ourselves seven thousand miles away from my apartment: I find myself sitting in a café watching the earth open up, devouring Uradziosutoku. Don’t get me wrong, I have nothing against it. It just takes some getting used to. And now I’m sitting here talking nicely to you instead of trying to strangle you with my bare hands because I realize perfectly well: such things do happen. I’ve gone mad.”

She leans toward me. Her lips smell of rice. How unromantic. Or am I a hardened cynic?

“I’ll tell you everything about myself, I promise, whatever you want to know. The moment we get somewhere safe, I’ll do it. But I really don’t know why certain things happen to me. I can only guess. I’ll try to explain... I’ll show you why it's the way it is. But not here."

"Where, then?" I ask a logical question and promptly shut up, unwilling to hear something I might regret: the Schwarzkopfs aren't known for their lack of expletives. But admittedly, my intellectual approach sometimes does work to restrain her primeval lack of manners.

"There's this place to the north of Moskau... I'll take you there. It'll happen soon enough, I promise. Strange how tables turn, don't you think? Twenty-four hours ago, I was your prisoner. And now I'm free but... I don't want to leave you. We can't really tell now which one of us holds the other captive, can we?"

It's time I snatch the initiative before it's too late. "Back in the Temple, there was this guy in a gray suit, he was in control of the search," I say nonchalantly. "I took a picture of him with the surveillance camera and did a quick image search on the Shogunet. It didn't take long. You may laugh but apparently, he is the spitting image of somebody called Walter Shumeiko who was killed during the Kiev standoff between the SS and the Wehrmacht in 1986. Luckily, this is Russland not Berlin: those idiots forgot to cancel my access to the SS database. And there I found something very interesting. Shumeiko's personal ID number is still valid even though it belongs to somebody totally different."

Even in the dark I can see how pale she's become. "What do you suggest? That he's one of the walking dead like those Tibetan Ahnenerbe subjects?"

Had the situation not been so serious, I'd have laughed out loud. "Ahnenerbe! It's the ultimate in kitsch, one of those Universum fantasy movies for the masses. Even back in the 1940s, they were never a serious research institute. And now they're even worse! They're trying to keep up this phony image of dark mysticism while self-publishing all those book series about their work, like those murder mysteries featuring Marta the Professor's daughter."

I pause. "There's another office, though perfectly real. They did give their graduates the names of long-dead people complete with their personal SS numbers. I suppose you heard about that old project by Reichsführer Himmler? The Lebensborn?"

She flaps her eyelashes in confusion. I enjoy my moment of triumph.

"You mean the adoption society? Of course. There were so many orphaned children after the war."

"Not exactly. From the start, the Lebensborn saw its goal in creating an incubator for the Aryan race. Since 1935, they've graduated hundreds of thousands of children. A child's parents had to be of the Nordic type, healthy and have no criminal record. Initially, their orphanages harbored kids from Norwegian girls who slept with Wehrmacht soldiers. But that apparently wasn't enough. They needed to do things on a bigger scale. Standartenführer Max Sollmann, head of Lebensborn, became interested in the practice used by the Medieval Turkish janissary corps. The Turks had found a way to create lethal bands of cutthroat assassins in Serbia and Bulgaria by taking babies from Christian parents and raising them as bloodthirsty Islamist fanatics. Sollmann just loved it! He thought it was a brilliant idea. Lebensborn workers in Russland, Ukraine and Poland sought children aged two to five years old of picture-perfect Aryan appearance, kidnapped them and took them to their orphanages.[14] There a child would usually receive a new name and be explained at some later date that they're lucky enough to live in the Paradise. The Lebensborn was supposed to create the 'new man': an Aryan fully devoted to the ideas of his Führer, one who was an expert both in modern sciences and

---

[14] Lebensborn, meaning a "source of Life" in German. Controlled by the SS Reichsführer Himmler personally, the 38 Lebensborn centers in Europe dedicated themselves to the raising of "purebred Aryans". Their Norwegian orphanages alone contained 12,000 children. In Poland, Lebensborn workers forcefully removed young children from their parents in order to "Germanize" them. The Nuremberg trials, however, acquitted Sollmann as head of Lebensborn.

martial arts. Some sort of an intellectual military bomb. Many of the Paradise's ex-charges have lived on to make brilliant careers which was actually their tutors' purpose. So I'm not at all surprised that they put a Lebensborn graduate on our tail."

She says nothing. I can sense her breathing. The Schwarzkopfs really think they know everything about the inner workings of the Reichskommissariat's private life. Well, they don't know a fraction of what I do.

"How do you know all this?"

It's not a question even, rather a groan coming from deep within her heart.

I chuckle. "It's simple, really. I'm Lebensborn too."

The street has grown dark. Our room is pitch black. I can hear crickets — specially imported from Okinawa — chirping by the front porch. The siren of an ambulance wails at a distance. Someone must have eaten the wrong part of a fugu fish again... and now the meat wagon was hurrying his way, sporting the rising sun on its door.

The girl is astonished. She hasn't even heard all the truth yet. Not that she needs it. Only then will I open up to her when she does the same. This is what I'm waiting for.

ZOTOV

Vision Two
The Day of the Monsters

THIS TIME I'M NOT at all cold. On the contrary. The heat is suffocating. I feel like a chicken in the oven. The air is almost red-hot with the sun.

I wipe the sweat away. This looks like a village. Small cottages — but everything seems to be enveloped in a dark haze.

I look up in surprise. Large flakes of snow float onto my head. What, in this heat? I walk slowly, holding onto the stakes of a wooden fence. I can hear dogs barking. Someone bellows orders in a muffled deep-chested voice.

I catch a large snowflake in my hand and crush it between my fingers. It leaves a dirty off-gray smear across my palm.

Now I understand the reason for this summer snowstorm.

This is ash, not snow. The village is on fire. Flames crackle as they escape cottage windows, opening above their roofs like red blossoms.

My face turns black. Sweat streaks my skin, washing away the soot. The log cottages aren't the only ones on fire: the trees, the benches by the porches, children's swings — everything's enveloped by the flames.

An insane firestorm.

The air is mixed with smoke. You can

barely see. It's daytime but it feels like twilight.

A woman is running toward me, reaching out blindly in front of herself. She's young and disheveled. A submachine gun rattles. She drops face down, her flaxen hair sinking into the dirt. Three crimson spots on her back grow fast, merging.

I recoil and stumble over another corpse. This one is old, his bulging eyes filled with blood. Another one is crouched next to a birch tree: a young woman, her head listing to one side.

A monster looms out of the smoke.

It has a weird porcine snout with a flat spongy nose and huge round eyes. It has a large hump on its back and long fat fingers on its black front paws. The monster holds its proboscis in its paws and points it at the window of the nearest house, showering its walls with a jet of liquid fire. Bloodcurdling screams assault my ears.

"Doing okay? It's damn hard work," another monster appears next to the first one. Its face is equally scary.

"Yes, Sir! Too hot in this wretched gas suit."

"What do you want, it's not some toy carnival mask. I'd have given anything for a beer, and you? Unfortunately, we need to finish up here first. We have orders. The village and everyone in it should be exterminated."

They walk on: one holding a flamethrower, the other with a Schmeisser submachine gun at the ready. They're not alone. A whole platoon of soldiers fuss about in their field-gray uniforms, their black lapels glistening with runes, their faces concealed by gas masks. Flames dance in their round goggles. The loudspeakers mounted on their trucks spit out a triumphant march,

Es geht um Deutschlands Gloria,
Gloria, Gloria,
Sieg Heil! Sieg Heil! Viktoria!
Sieg Heil! Viktoria!

Rifles rattle non-stop, killing everything that breathes. Not just human beings: the soldiers fire at cats and dogs in the back yards. Their high boots are splattered with blood to the knees. An army of faceless killers are doing their job with the nonchalance of market butchers.

There's no escape from death. The flamethrowers scorch both cellars and attics, their fiery jets licking roofs.

Corpses are piled up on both sides of me. Lots of them: dozens, hundreds even. An old woman in a floral headscarf covers her face with her hand as if shielding it from bullets.

A machine gun rattles away at the edge of the village. People, burning alive, jump out of windows and drop to the ground, convulsing and screaming in agony.

The gunner (young, in rolled-up sleeves, a silver eagle topping his forage cap) has no gas mask on. He turns to his partner,

"Look how they dance!"

Both guffaw. Another couple of gun bursts, then everything's over. The human groaning dies away.

The chief monster is standing atop the hill, admiring the burning village engulfed in smoke. A handmade embroidered towel lies forgotten on the ground. It's smeared in blood: he's used it to wipe his boot clean. Another monster walks over to him and clicks his heels, jumping to attention.

"Sir, the mission's completed. My men have double-checked everything. No survivors. We've put all the children into the remaining house. Should I get a lorry to take them to town?"

The monster stares at him, then removes his gas mask. The lenses of its goggles are murky. "No need to. Pointless. Sort them out yourselves."

"But... Sir... these are children..."

"Lieutenant, you heard the order. Get on with it!"

The other monster walks down the hill. He stumbles through the row of blazing houses to the other end of the village where children are crying.

He makes a sign to his soldiers. They surround the cottage and reach for their grenades, then stand by the windows, awaiting orders.

Gas masks are great. No one can see what

you're feeling. Provided they *can* feel.

They're robots. Nothing more. Just killing machines.

"Get ready," the muffled voice says. The monster raises his hand.

He must be mad! What's he doing? Why can't the soldiers stop him?

His hand drops sharply. Grenades smash the windows in their flight.

There's no more crying. Silence fills the air.

CHAPTER FOUR

ETERNAL ICE

LHASA, THE REICHSKOMMISSARIAT SHAMBHALA

PAVEL'S FINGERS PULLED spasmodically at his collar, unbuttoning it. A crimson mark encircled his neck. Air, he needed air! His chest was collapsing. His heart was racing, thumping against his ribcage as if he were about to take the Olympic gold in five thousand meters.

Which Olympic Games? he thought sarcastically. *Since Jesse Owens amassed four gold medals in Berlin back in 1936, no untermensch has been allowed to participate. All the Olympic gold is evenly divided between the Reich Union and the Nippon koku. Silver goes to whoever gets to it first. There's no intrigue left.*

He stopped abruptly as his head began to spin. *One, two, three.* He only needed to cross the road but he couldn't walk fast for fear of hypoxia setting in. He had to take pills at the slightest signs of altitude sickness. Once your lungs filled with blood, you were gone in a few days.

The monument at the center of the avenue depicted two gold yaks. Flags flew at their sides: a red one with an eagle — symbol of the Reich Union — and the other one sporting the Tibetan Snow Lion.

The enormous brown and white Potala Palace seemed to be carved into the rock. This ancient abode of the Dalai Lamas counted a thousand rooms as each new Dalai Lama had to occupy his own.

The flat houses of the Old Quarter with their gold roofs and painted brickwork; the guttural singing of orange-clad monks; the sandal-stick smoke swirling over the altar — and crowds of unavoidable, unescapable pilgrims swarming everywhere.

Lhasa was the same to Tibet as Trondheim was to Norway.

But if Norway was the sacred birthplace of the Viking religion, Tibet was the cradle of the Aryan race. Only the best of the Lebensborn's best got sent here to study at the ancient monasteries, the likes of Tashilhunpo. When human history had still been in diapers, Aryan tribes had marched from the swastika-marked

Mount Kailash all the way to Europe: the race of handsome fair-skinned warriors, blond and blue-eyed. The master race, sent by the gods to govern Earth. Mount Kailash didn't look like itself anymore, dug inside out and covered in holes like a chunk of Swiss cheese after all the Ahnenerbe and Thule Society researchers were finished with it.

Now they charged two hundred reichsmarks for a guided tour of the digs. Ahnenerbe diggers had advanced almost four miles into the mountain as they were looking for evidence of Hanns Hörbiger's Eternal Ice theory. According to Hörbiger, there once used to be four moons traveling our skies until three of them dropped to the ground in the vicinity of Mount Kailash, their fragments triggering life on Earth. Every time the archaeologists had run out of money, the expedition leader Schäfer would send a telegram to Berlin:

Samples of lunar soil discovered bringing us ever closer to a breakthrough.

Immediately after that, his bank account would receive a new injection of reichsmarks. After decades of fruitless search, Schäfer had joined a local monastery, becoming a humble Lamaist monk in the hope of slipping into nirvana and discovering the route to the magic lands of Shambhala.

The Thule Society conducted their own research looking for the legendary underground land of Agartha: a round island amid an ocean of the sweetest nectar, inhabited by fluttering firebirds. Apart from the Himmler Fund, they also received their financing from large concerns like Krupp and Heinkel. Agartha was infinitely more important than some old ice deposits. Legend had it that at the center of the island was the Fountain of Youth whose water granted immortality.

Predictably, they had never found the fountain, either. Just like Ahnenerbe, Thule was just going through the motions, pretending it believed in legends: both organizations were staffed by seasoned cynics who knew how to spend the budget.

A Panther armored vehicle bearing the emblem of the local Buddha Shakyamuni SS legion froze at the entrance to the Potala Palace. Two Tibetans in black uniforms with orange sleeve badges stood watch next to them, looking utterly bored. Not waiting for their request, Pavel offered them his plastic ID card without a mug shot.

A brown-faced Obergefreiter slid the card into an electronic reader. It reacted with a long pleading ping and the flashing of a green light.

The SS man jumped to attention. "It's a pleasure, Herr Sturmbannführer!"

Pavel nonchalantly raised two fingers to his fedora hat in salute. He disliked all that *Heil!* stuff. He retrieved his card from the guard and slid it blindly into his gray plastic wallet. All visitors to the Reichskommissariat Shambhala were subjected to a thorough body search. No items made from animal or avian flesh, skin or bones were allowed here.

This was one of the local peculiarities. Back in 1937, the first Ahnenerbe expedition had only been allowed in on condition that they wouldn't squash a single cockroach nor swat a single mosquito. There was nothing you could do: reincarnation was part of the Tibetans' religion.

"Keep going straight on, then upstairs and turn to the left. Would you like me to show you there?"

"It's all right. I can find what I need."

He climbed to the third floor and squeezed his body into a narrow passage: a realm of tiny rooms smelling of dust, mold and mouse urine.

Pavel smiled. He'd forgotten what it was like here. His breathing took time to slow down. And back then, it had taken him no time at all to come to grips with the constant lack of oxygen, obnoxiously bitter-tasting food and austere furnishings.

As he walked, orange-clad monks bowed to him politely from their cells. Their walls were hung with portraits — but the weak glow of yak fat candles prevented him from getting a good look at the man's face with a scar running across one cheek, his hands put together in the traditional Tibetan greeting. The Ocean of

Wisdom, the 15th Dalai Lama, the great Ngawang Tashi.

Back in 1944 in Lhasa, the Abwehr had pulled off one of its most brilliant missions: the New Buddha. The previous Dalai Lama, the nine-year-old Tenzin received a shot of cyanide while the leader of the SS special forces, Hauptsturmführer Otto Skorzeny, was pronounced to be his reincarnation.

At the time, the Reich put a great deal of hope in Tibet as both Ahnenerbe and the Thule Society pointed at it as the future birthplace of a great new religion. Reich leaders planned to gradually destroy all pictures of the Führer, including all photos, drawings and statues. Then — say in three hundred years' time when the memory of his appearance would have sufficiently faded — they were going to declare the Führer to have been a blond, blue-eyed giant born of a block of Shambhalan ice: a god and arch father of the Aryan nation.

Skorzeny had quickly got used to his role as a living incarnation of the Bodhisattva of Compassion — even quicker than Berlin had expected him to. He'd so warmed to his role that he started his term by prohibiting any archeological digs outside of Mount Kailash because they "threatened the life of earthworms". Next, the 15th Dalai Lama proclaimed the Swastika's spiritual affinity with Dpalbe, the Knot of Eternity: the symbol of Tibetan Buddhism representing the Five Original Wisdoms.

Skorzeny began spending more and more time in the meditation cave, staying there for months and years at a time. He'd gotten so engrossed in Lamaism that he completely forgot all about his mission. The ex-Hauptsturmführer's lectures were especially popular in the universities of Neuer York: *How to Attain Inner Bliss While Practicing National Socialism.* Female students achieved nirvana right there while listening to the charismatic Dalai Lama (who incidentally also was Reichskommissar of Shambhala).

In any case, it was all in the past now. The ancient Ngawang Tashi (who'd recently celebrated his hundred-and-fourth birthday) had long ceased to control Tibet. His soul now permanently resided in the astral world while his emaciated body was sustained with mountain herbs alone. All religious and laic authority had been handed over to the Oracle — a person even more powerful than the Reichskommissar himself.

It was to his quarters Pavel was heading now.

The Oracle determined the Dalai Lama's schedule by prophesizing everything, including what the Divine Keiser was meant to eat for lunch. Skorzeny's illness allowed the Oracle to take power into his own hands — both literally and figuratively. To give you an example, he would tilt the Dalai Lama's head at moments when he was supposed to nod his approval.

Prophets have one hell of a life, Pavel thought, smiling back to the monks as he walked past. *Has anyone ever thought how hard they have it? Your wife comes home from work in the evening and you start a row because you know that in a year seven months and four days from now she would cheat on you in the toilet with a delivery man at the Führer's birthday party. You always know the outcome of a football game. You don't need to check the weather forecast. I'm surprised he hasn't lost his mind yet.*

The Regent's quarters were guarded by Germans: a special SD unit, equally orange-clad but gun-toting. Here, his Gestapo ID didn't cut it. Pavel was told to go to a separate small room for a full body search, then ordered to don the orange robes. He was already happy he didn't have to do a blood test. Every Third Reich official feared an assassination attempt — even here in Tibet where killing a living being was the greatest of all sins.

The room's wrought iron door opened.

Pavel removed his shoes and walked in, stepping over the straw mats. The Oracle sat with his back to him. He seemed to be deep in meditation. He must have sensed Pavel's presence. His eyes opened.

"I knew you would come today," his wasn't a voice but the rustle of the wind.

I bet you did, Pavel thought sarcastically. *You're not called a soothsayer for nothing!*

Obediently he crouched on the mat Tibetan style, knees tucked in. "Lansang, I need your help. Sorry, I can't think straight. I've come all the way from Moskau with a changeover in Delhi and you know how I hate flying. I have big problems."

"There's no such thing as a problem that can't be solved," the Oracle replied softly without turning to him. "It's that what you wanted to hear, isn't it? Admittedly, I'm surprised. Didn't I teach you everything already in Tashilhunpo? I showed you how to perceive, how to free your mind, how to feel. I was sure you'd never give me the chance to doubt your ability. What's changed?"

Pavel heaved a sigh. Every Lebensborn student was told he had to be the best. He couldn't commit the slightest error. Once he had witnessed a Lebensborn graduate fail a test and shoot himself in the university restroom.

"I really can't tell you," he said, studying a mandala on the wall. "It's very important that I tune into two particular people but... I don't seem to be able to do it. I just can't sense them. Neither their electricity nor their auras, nothing. Especially the woman. I'm not even sure whether she's alive. I feel her as something nebulous like a cloud which you can neither touch nor squeeze. And... it gives me some very unpleasant ideas. If I can't feel her at all, even when I meditate — what is she then? The man is different. I can tune into him... but not when she's around. She seems to siphon all of his energy."

The Oracle sprang from the mat. Turning round, he waddled toward Pavel. This old Lama always knew the deepest nooks and crannies of one's heart even when it was thousands of miles away from Lhasa, hidden in the depths of a forest overgrowing a different continent. The tiny room could barely accommodate all of his knowledge.

All those gray-bearded mentors in Japanese flicks loved brandishing their swords or breaking their opponents' bones with their bare hands. Lansang didn't need any of it. He could defeat his enemies with the power of his mind alone.

"We can rectify that," he said. "I'll try to guide you through the maze of the human mind."

"I have very little time," Pavel warned him. "I'm very sorry."

The Oracle shrugged. "Time is only a droplet in an ocean of thought. Very well, we'll only work with the man to let you sense his aura. It might be easier this way — and faster. It's quite possible that the woman is out of my reach too. But I'd appreciate you telling me why you want to locate them. I know you. Are you going to kill the man?"

Pavel shook his head. "No. I'm just doing everything I can to... to separate him from her."

CHAPTER FIVE

THE BLACK SUN

MOSKAU. THE CITY CENTER

WEWELSBURG CASTLE

THE TRIUMVIRATE BUNKER

THE CLOUDS HUNG SO LOW they enveloped the towers of the Kremlin, submerging its scarlet red brickwork into their snowy depths. The Writers Union Brigadenführer Kurt Vonnegut once said a great thing about those towers: "These pillars are the epitome of Buddhism: at first, frequent changes annoy you. Then you get angry. Finally, you get used to the constant shakeups and you start to view regime changes philosophically: *This too shall pass.*"

Initially topped with the double-headed

eagles of the Russian Empire, the towers had briefly sported the ruby stars of the Soviets, later knocked down by the swastika-clenching eagles of the Third Reich. The swastikas hadn't lasted, either: once the Twenty-Year War was over, riggers had scaled the towers to promptly take them down.

As almost every evening, the main Nibelung Square was absolutely packed. Crowds of Japanese tourists flashed their cameras at its buildings. Street kiosks manned by ample-breasted young women were busy pouring out a poor excuse for Bavarian beer. Wrapped in filthy trench coats, veterans of the SS Turkic Division — alcoholic despite all the healthy lifestyle propaganda — posed for the Japanese for a couple of yen.

Next to the Lobnoye Mesto where the monument to Minin and Pozharsky used to stand, the gloomy bulk of Ernst Johann von Bühren — the bewigged abomination of the 18th century — glowed bronze on its pedestal. The Germans had erected it in 1944, complete with a little plaque that quoted this much-hated favorite of the Russian Empress Anna Ioannovna,

The only way to govern Russians is by the lash and the axe.

In the 1950s, however, they'd removed the plaque for reasons of political correctness. About the same time, they'd torn down St Basil's Cathedral with its fancy colored domes: they needed the space to build a copy of the Wewelsburg Castle, the highest academy for the ideological training for SS officer cadets. They'd completed the build in record time. The first initial meetings — "consiliums" — of the Triumvirate had been held in its Obergruppenführer Hall, a large room in the castle's north tower with twelve columns and the sign of the Black Sun laid out in its mosaic floor.

The Black Sun was the official seal of the Moskau Triumvirate: the invisible center of the Universe, the source of life on Earth casting its phantom light onto our planet. Theosophist Helena Blavatsky had in her time proclaimed it the symbol of the extinct "ice people" that once had lived beyond the Arctic Circle, while Reichsführer Himmler considered it the image of Farbauti, the deity of lightning.

The acoustics of the Obergruppenführer Hall were astonishing. They lent any voice, no matter how dry or high-pitched, the timbre of a nightingale singing. The center of the Black Sun exuded the flames of the eternal fire which had supposedly given birth to the Aryan race.

As late as in the 1970s, SS top ranks used to meditate there together, seeing their skin acquire a tan-like hue cast by the dark star's ominous glow. Their hearts had harbored the hope that one day the Black Sun would reveal itself to everyone and not only to a chosen few, granting happiness to Aryans and blinding all inferior races. At least that's what the philosopher Rudolf Mund used to say.

Wewelsburg had actually fitted quite nicely into the Nibelung Square, housing several Reichskommissariat offices. In 1945 Obergruppenführer Hans Kammler, the prominent "wonder weapon" expert, had his laboratories moved there. His secret research had led to the creation of portable nuclear devices, anti-aircraft lasers, invisible tanks and even planetary rovers designed to obtain alien soil samples and battle aliens themselves if necessary.

Everything had seemed hunky dory. Still, Wewelsburg had been destined for other things.

Nine years later, during the visit of the then-Reichschancellor Albert Speer from Berlin to Moskau, the Varangians SS volunteer division had mutinied, demanding their backpay be honored. The SS mutineers took over Wewelsburg, burning it down and fatally wounding Speer in the resulting shootout. The castle had barely been rebuilt when a new tragedy struck the Reichskommissariat: someone had poisoned Hans Kammler's wine during an official dinner. The government blamed the assassination on the Schwarzkopf Resistance but the fact remained that no one had really found out who was behind it: the Japanese secret service or just some jealous workmates.

All this had resulted in moving the

Triumvirate offices into an underground armored bunker complete with an exact copy of the Obergruppenführer Hall with its Black Sun mosaic on the floor. The bunker was equipped with a complex defense system including gun turrets and a highly evolved security system.

Twilight fell over the Nibelung Square.

The city dissolved into the darkness. Occasional streetlamps exuded a weak glow: the economy of all and sundry was one of the Empire's base principles. The government liked to call it a "blackout" in case of guerrilla attacks.

Even the street signs of the insanely popular night clubs like Death's Head and Das Reich barely glowed. Both boasted only two types of gigs: boring symphony orchestras playing The Ride of the Valkyries, and Alpine yodelers in their Tyrolean hats.

The first black-market cigarette dealers sneaked out of the dark onto the sidewalks. Hiding their eyes under tinted glasses, these pale vampire-like creatures lurked in the unlit side lanes, offering Japanese tobacco, black and resinous, or sometimes also homegrown stuff. They would stealthily mete out some fragrant strands into a scrap of paper while shoving a handful of reichsmarks into their pockets.

In all Moskau houses, TVs switched on automatically, beginning the obligatory nightly entertainment. One of the presenters, Rüdiger Storm — a sleazy guy with bottle-blond hair —

stole toward the microphone,

"Anyone know the meaning of this phrase, 'Ten dead untermenschen swimming in the sea'? I'll tell you! It means a good start to the day!"

The Moskau denizens stared at the screens, preparing to laugh their heads off. Hundreds of professional comedians of every caliber — from seasoned Brigadenführer heavyweights to Oberschütze newbies — showered them with their gags and jokes on just about everything, excluding politics. In the "black" districts behind the ring road officially known as the Ring of the Nibelung, brothels opened their discreet doors. Some far-off locations like the Goering industrial zone were absolutely packed with them. Their state-employed staff worked themselves stiff: as civil officers of the Auxiliary Corps, they were guaranteed the right to retirement food parcels and the honorary rank of Forhelferin. The unending chain of wars had resulted in Moskau's female population being twice its male counterpart, which had caused prostitute's rates to plummet, reducing their clients' payment to a symbolic sum barely enough to buy a sandwich.

Saturday night oozed weariness. Reich workers had only one day off: Sunday. Exhausted factory *arbeiters* left the underground tunnels of the metro (The Holy Roman Station at the very end of Aryan Street and the Nuremberg Station near Henry the Fowler Square, the former

Lubianka) and stopped by beer kiosks to down a *stein* or two of the ersatz Bavarian brew.

Girls winked at them, pouting their lips: in Moskau, initiating sex was a woman's prerogative while men could afford to pick and choose at their leisure. If you had a *mann*, you had to grab and bed him while you could, sister, otherwise you'd stay on your own. You had to enjoy life while you could: if a new war started, your *mann* would have to go fight the Forest Brothers up in the Ural Mountains with a next-to-zero chance of ever coming back. All male citizens of Moskau above fifteen years of age were subject to conscription and could be drafted at any given moment.

Still, girls shouldn't worry that much. They didn't know every detail of a man's so-called "military service" which more often than not was a fake. All you needed to do was slide a wad of Reichsmarks into the draft doctor's hand and he'd immediately proclaim you handicapped and unfit for duty. Luckily for Moskau's population, there were no statistics of such dismissals, otherwise it would have emerged that half the male Moskau population had missing limbs or suffered from spinal fractures plus a whole number of terminal conditions. Local officials did their best to combat corruption — at least until they themselves were arrested for the same.

Night gradually snuck up on the city, the TV laughter replaced by groans and the creaking of bed springs. The TVs themselves fell silent only to switch back on simultaneously at 7 a.m.

...Jean-Pierre raised his head. He couldn't see anything. A special lightproof blindfold covered his eyes, obligatory for all Triumvirate bunker visitors. He'd been urgently summoned from work without as much as a chance to shave. He'd been sitting in an empty room for an hour already, awaiting the country's leaders who apparently wished to talk to him. Why on earth would the Triumvirate want the information about Pavel's research? They knew very well who they'd hired, didn't they?

Jean-Pierre could have sworn he was sitting on the very edge of the Black Sun. He couldn't have left even had he wanted to: his hands were tied behind his back, his legs cuffed to the legs of the chair. Standard security measures. They trusted no one here.

Footsteps shuffled.

"Good evening," "Good evening," "Good evening," the three voices greeted him almost in synch.

Female voices.

MOSKAU

Reichskommissariat Archives #2

File FD75 : Authors

THE VICTORIOUS THIRD REICH needed to create a very special literature, free from the dubious heritage of the Bolsheviks, Semitic plutocrats and British imperialists. The old literary system had crumbled, burying false writers under its debris.

Upon the fall of Moskau, the leaders of the Russian Writers Union Sergei Mikhalkov and Alexander Fadeev fled behind the Urals where they published the clandestine *Forest Daily*. The author of the sci fi utopia classic *Aelita*, Alexey Tolstoi had disappeared: according to a few Gestapo informers, he'd changed his appearance, becoming one of the priests of Loki.

Sharp-tongued satirists Ilya Ilf and Evgeny Petrov escaped to Uradziosutoku in the Nippon koku where they had written the third novel of their Ostap Bender series, *The Chrysanthemum Marmot*, in which the indefatigable smooth operator arrives in Tokyo setting his sights on a Daimyo title. The acclaimed author of another sci fi classic *Professor Dowell's Head* Alexander Belyaev had been arrested by the Gestapo on charges of spreading Bolshevik propaganda; his books had been banned. It took the children's poet Kornei Chukovsky four civil processes to successfully prove in court that the character of his evil pirate captain Barmalei hadn't been based on the Führer.

In the US, surviving relatives of Margaret Mitchell had been sentenced to public repentance while *Gone With the Wind* was declared "an abominable sample of pro-Negro pulp fiction" and publicly burned.

The young author Ray Bradbury who in 1953, three years before the capitulation of Los Angeles, had published his first novel *Fahrenheit 451*, was arrested, tried and deported to Africa while the Third Reich supporters arranged his book burnings in squares all over California.

British mystery authoress Agatha Christie turned coat, joining the new regime and even writing a series of books about Siegfried Braun: a fat Gestapo officer with a Führer-like mustache who successfully solved Bolshevik conspiracies from one book to the next.

In 1955, all of the Reich's libraries and book stores had been subjected to one ultimate purge which resulted in the creation of the *Guidelines and Recommendations for Literary Work*. Every aspiring writer had to prove that he was at least an Untersturmführer, loyal to the Reich and could recite several chapters from *Mein Kampf* from memory. Those who could attest to all of the above, received a special "writing clearance".

The list of the subjects approved for publication:

Science fiction. State-commissioned works on scientific subjects:

What would the Earth be like in a thousand years after the complete triumph of National Socialism?

Mars occupation, to save the Red Planet from the Bolshevik ideas brought there by Stalin who'd escaped the Earth in a starship;

A society of immortal Aryans;

Colonization of other planets with their consequent accession to the Reich, etc.

Military science fiction. The bestselling *W.E.H.R.M.A.C.H.T.* series featured stories about the seizure of a nuclear power station by a Semitic terrorist group, followed by the leaking of radiation and the special forces' incessant combat with mutant Bolsheviks and lonely looters[15]. The 40,000 titles of the series were hugely popular with its young readership.

Romance. It had to feature emotional

---

[15] *W.E.H.R.M.A.C.H.T.*: a satirical allusion to *S.T.A.L.K.E.R.*, the bestselling Russian science fiction series based on the computer game of the same name (which in turn was loosely based on the classic of Russian science fiction, *Roadside Picnic* by Arcady and Boris Strugatsky). Featuring dozens of novels from both leading and upcoming Russian sci fi authors, the series is set in a post-apocalyptic Chernobyl inhabited by aggressive mutants and ruthless mercenaries.

relationships between purebred Aryans. Any such relationship should lead to marriage and polygamy, as the Reich Union officially promoted multi-partner marriages. Novels had to have a happy ending where the handsome hulk of a protagonist and all six of his wives rode off happily into the sunset.

Cozy mystery. The protagonist had to be female, divorced and middle-aged, a housewife or an old-age pensioner, occasionally also an SD investigator who boasted rare crime-solving talents. The most typical examples of such works were *The Mysterious Affair of Mein Kampf* and *Death of the Scharführer* which topped the Reich Union's bestseller lists. "The main task of this type of fiction," said the Ministry of Public Education's Pressführer Victor Pilulin in an interview to the *Völkischer Beobachter*, "is to entertain our women. When they read more, they're easier to guide."

Prohibited Philosophies. Those were books for the "intellectual elite" which possessed all the forbidden-fruit charm of underground literature. They were mainly penned by a special literary department under the control of Victor Pilulin himself or his deputy Major von Nachtigall. With a naivety typical of them, the Schwarzkopfs considered these types of books semi-legal for the sole reason that they criticized the regime. Never mind it had been the regime itself that had invented this sort of book to help the more intellectual readership vent safely.

Starting 1971, more and more series and standalone books were published without the author's name on the cover, written by teams of unknown ghostwriters — like *W.E.H.R.M.A.C.H.T.*, for instance. Star authors are dangerous: they can capture their readers' minds, leading them into all sorts of unwanted directions. Naturally, Moskau still had its share of acclaimed wordsmiths — not many, about a dozen: those who'd proven their loyalty to the regime and always submitted their manuscripts to the censor on time.

And that's all we need from them.

Speaker: the Literary Einsatzgruppe Hauptmann Sergei Semyonov.

Confidential. Requires clearance from the Reichsminister of Propaganda and Public Education.

CHAPTER SIX

HELHEIM

THE OUTSKIRTS OF URADZIOSUTOKU

SPRING ABUNDANCE LANE

WE'VE CHANGED HOTELS twice in as many days. According to Olga, you can't spend two nights in one place in a row. She must have read this in some spy thriller or other. What's the problem if no one here sees our faces anyway? But you can't explain it to her. She's away with the fairies, that one, playing their Schwarzkopf games with abandon.

The funny thing is, she believes I'm on her side. I think not. I might be unhappy to make up part of this weird society where everyone is classified, from managers to writers to Krupp executives. But it doesn't mean I approve of the

Schwarzkopf route. Oh no, thank you very much. All those constant haughty phrases about regime-fighting are just a buzz, nothing more.

The dislike for our government is a trend, especially among young people. Even Führerjugend members draw satirical cartoons of the SS and the Triumvirate. Guerilla fighters may be united all they want but they're still unable to gain control of our cities. They seem to be quite happy having control over forests and villages. Why? That's one question the Schwarzkopfs don't seem to be asking.

We lie on the floor. Our bodies are almost touching.

She's predictably naked even though she's wrapped herself in a sheet, merely for appearances' sake, revealing one small breast. Admittedly, she isn't trying to jump my bones. She's so full of herself she must be thinking I'm bound to lose my guard lying inebriated next to a naked woman. Very well. Let her indulge in her fruitless hopes. All Schwarzkopfs do.

I'm drinking Kirin beer. She's sipping her plum wine. Ideology separates us even here as we lie on a straw mat in the heat of the night.

The room is pitch black. This cheap *ryokan* has no windows at all.

"This regime is only held together by shopping malls," she whispers. "No one likes it. Look, they keep sending the best Wehrmacht units to the Urals, and what happens? Within a few years, they either desert or become so morally corrupt they defect to the guerrillas! Everything's rotten to the bone. To bring this regime down, all you need to do is poke it with your little finger. They only remain afloat because they've unplugged people's brains, submerging them into the quicksand of TV, sex and money making."

I gulp my beer directly from the bottle. An Aryan should never do that. But I'm a Russlandish Aryan.

"Still, the Triumvirate hasn't been toppled yet," I grin, savoring the taste of malt. "Lots of talking, zero effect. True, you couldn't make anyone join the Wehrmacht at gunpoint anymore. No one wants to soak to the skin in forest patrols anymore. They'd much rather munch on popcorn in front of their TVs or download porn on the Shogunet. That's why we have to hire Chinese mercenaries to defend parts of the Ural front under the command of our officers. Even if they get smoked one on a hundred, they still manage to contain the Forest Brothers. Cannon fodder is costly, which is why the Reich is obliged to turn to the Nippon koku for new loans. We get deeper and deeper into debt; we've no idea where to get the money from, but still, our peace of mind is worth it. We don't want any more tanks to shell the Reichstag like they did in the Twenty-Year War."

Olga raises herself on the mat and reaches

for me. The sheet slides down to her belly. The smell of wine comes from her lips.

"So what if they shell it," she snickers. "As long as this stagnant swamp begins to bubble. The Reichstag! They're but a hundred faceless slaves, the passive biomass that has been granted the right to press buttons. The only reason the Triumvirate still keeps them is because that's where your Führer started his journey. Otherwise the Reichstag would have been recycled a long time ago. Now that the NSDAP is dissolved, we don't have a single political party left. Great, eh? A country that's deficient in every respect. We don't have leaders, only ghost front figures. We don't have a culture, only cheap television laughs. We don't have love, only brothels. Everybody's grown so uncaring it's as if their hearts are being amputated at birth. The rich prefer to splurge bundles of Reichsmarks on Das Reich Club strippers while Schwarzkopfs blow up armored convoys in the suburbs of their own city. *Marlo* and entertainment, these are the only two things that maintain the occupiers' power. And I'm pretty sure that the Triumvirate know what they're doing, pretending to be fleeting shadows. In order to hate something, you need to have this something first. But how can you hate thin air?

Marlo. That's a local slang for Reichsmarks. Well, what can I say? All I can do is beg with Hel, the Goddess, to take me down to her world of the dead. It's true that Garm, her four-eyed dog, might never let me back out, forcing me to re-enter the black waters of the river Gjöll brimming with skulls and maggots... I'd have to shiver in the freezing cold of the Iron Forest, listening to the wailing of witches and running for my life, escaping trolls into the bush.

Still, all this ridiculous number of cons was outweighed by a single plus. There, I wouldn't have to lie on a straw mat listening to a Schwarzkopf supporter busy messing with my head. It's been two months already. I saved her life, for crissakes! Never again. It's all finished: no more helping old ladies across the road or saving kittens from trees. No good deed goes unpunished.

I grope through the dark for another bottle and open it. That's the only thing that can save me now. The beer hisses like a squashed snake — apparently protesting too.

"Why would the Third Reich need a parliament?" I ask. "Has it ever done any good to anyone? A parliament is a boring slapstick show for third-rate clowns. The Emperor Nicholas II used to have the State Duma — did you know it was off limits for women, by the way? The air there was apparently blue with cussing, Duma deputies too busy throwing punches to discuss politics. Talking about Stalin, he turned the inhabitants of the Kremlin into a similar kind of biomass — and still the Schwarzkopfs dote on him, and you don't seem to be too upset by the fact. Here in Russland, a single bottle of vodka can replace an entire parliament. You drink, you yell, you punch someone's lights out — just like they did in the Duma."

She's silent. She must be busy thinking of counterarguments like she does every time. I stealthily stroke the bag hidden to my right. Two Walter handguns and four full clips to go: I bought them earlier today at the black market. You never know what kind of surprise the streets of Uradziosutoku might have in store for you. No wonder the Resistance have plenty of ammunition! You can buy what the hell you want here, provided you're prepared to pay triple. Rifles, handguns, submachine guns — brand new, still in the grease, with factory numbers. I wouldn't be surprised if the Forest Brothers receive weapons and gear deliveries directly from the factory.

That's why this war will never end. These "Forest Knights" combat the nasty "capitalist Nazis" while charging manufacturers the "tax on people's war". The Wehrmacht is solemnly prepared to die defending the *Vaterland* from the horrors of Bolshevism while their supply officers sell state-of-the-art weapons to guerrillas through the warehouse back door. What goes round, comes around. Especially *marlo*.

"You don't by any chance approve of the slave trade, may I ask?"

Oh gods! Come, I pray, and transport me to the gold bridge Gjallarbrú so I can cross it through the perilous mists of Helheim and fall into the arms of the Goddess of the dead. It has to be better than here.

Her sheet slides down to her knees.

Normally, I have excellent self-control. But this room is tiny. Too cramped. Not only can I hear her breathing, I can also hear her heart race. She's not handcuffed anymore. Yes, yes, I'm a priest; a philosopher. Unfortunately, all philosophy turns to putty when you're sitting on the floor next to a woman wrapped in a sheet. We're not Christian priests. We haven't been taught to switch off our libidos. Oh but to grab, to pin to the floor, to dominate... where was I?

I take a gulp of beer. That might help me to channel my thoughts in the right direction. "I have nothing against work camps," I say, cool as a cucumber. "I'd say they're truly necessary. Any citizen of Moskau can arrive at a foreign workers depot — like the one at the Sleipnir metro station — and sign a work contract. Only purebred Aryans can use hired labor. You rent them from the state. You choose the workers you need and you sign a paper obliging you to feed them a certain number of calories a day. You call it slave driving? Somewhere in Ancient Rome, a slave owner could do anything he wanted to his slave. Could kill him even. Here, arbeiters are the property of the state. You have no right to harm them. Old-age pensioners are happy: every springtime when they need someone to dig up their garden allotments, Sleipnir offers 'two for the price of one' discounts. What's wrong with that?"

Had her plum wine been decanted in a water pail, I'm pretty sure she'd have already poured it over my head. The Schwarzkopfs are notorious for their Shogunet forum protests against the "invaders' dictatorship" — but God save you from offering an opinion different from theirs. The forum's Systemführer would activate *Verboten*, banning you from the discussion. In Russland, everybody loves the sound of their own voice. If tomorrow the Schwarzkopfs somehow came to power, my body would dangle from the nearest lamppost, and not just mine. A revolution may look like cute romantic drivel only while it's still brewing. But once it wins, it turns into the dragon's jaws.

"I would so love to make people finally come to their senses," there's no anger in her voice, only bitterness and disappointment. "At least national socialism was an enemy. But this is a dummy, a clone that's not worth a single *pfennig*, a cheap imitation of the Third Reich. You only argue with me to defend the Triumvirate out of principle because you'd hate to see Moskau taken by the Forest Brothers. But in fact... what kind of *Vaterland* is this, if you have the Chinese defending it? Why would all the senior officials keep their money in Tokyo banks? Why is the yen more popular here than the reichsmark? The SS and the Gestapo may be the regime's backbone, but even they are tired, serving out of habit simply because that's the way things are! Our thinking is as thick as two short planks: 'We're already used to the Krauts, but what are the Forest Brothers going to be like? No one can tell. At least now we have marlo and plenty of brothels, restaurants and night clubs.'"

She takes a sip of her wine. "When you brought me to your place, they were about to launch a new reality TV series: *Africa*. In it, they planned to attach a mini camera to the forehead of a convicted untermensch and drop him off in the thick of the African jungle. He is hunted simultaneously by a Wehrmacht infantry division in helicopters and by a local warrior tribe to see who can kill him faster. The Viking TV's Direktor has promised that if the game takes off, the Reisebüro Travel Agency will arrange safari trips for wealthy tourists. To join in the fun, you understand. Can't you see what they're doing to us? We watch popcorn movies, read disposable books and laugh at conveyor-belt jokes. The Reich has devoured our brains like some real-life Cthulhu. My brothers honestly believe they're going to bring this regime down. I'll say, not without some help from lobotomists."

Did she just say *Cthulhu*? Then again, why not? Lovecraft has never been banned.

I take her in my arms, unexpectedly for myself.

She shuts up mid-word. Glory be to Asgard! I should have done it earlier. Silence is a bliss: a silent woman is so much better than the one that preaches her politics to you.

My fingers burn against her cool skin. My mouth turns dry, my lips erupting in a web of cracks. Suddenly I sense this light coming from her. Yes, her body is exuding light, her eyes glowing like embers. If Uradziosutoku collapses again... let it do so, I don't care.

Olga throws the sheet away. She's completely naked. Oh Gods... she's *awesome.*

"I'm sorry," I croak like a schoolboy who's just had his teacher flash her tits at him. "Your arrogance is outrageous-"

How could I explain to you what I feel? Every time she touches me, it's like being electrocuted. She bogs me down, deeper and deeper, until all I can see is a whirlpool overhead and some frogs and algae caught in it.

"Why did you save me?" she thunders. "I need to know."

I'm too weak to resist. Her energy consumes me, enveloping me like honey. Very well, I'll tell her. I know I'm gonna regret it. If that's what she wants...

Our lips are close, almost touching.

I hear a rustle. Barely audible but one produced by a rather voluminous body. This is another forte of these ryokan places: their doors are but sheets of paper. The sound carries far, making your eardrums explode with the groans of other lovesick couples.

I duck to my right and whip a Walther out. Its carriage thunders shut in the silence of the room.

“Stay where you are,” I snap. “What is it they say in the movies? Move and you’re dead.”

I least expect to hear the sound emitting from the screen. A soft giggle.

CHAPTER SEVEN

THE TATTOO

MOSKAU, HORST WESSEL ST

THE GESTAPO LABS

THE MOMENT JEAN-PIERRE CARPE reached his lab, he got down to the pressing business of opening his desk drawer. As he produced the precious flask, he half-turned to cast a glance at the Führer's portrait as if it could reproach him for such an immoral act. The Führer (whom the artist had depicted against the backdrop of the Reichstag, holding a hysterically grinning little girl in his arms) remained predictably silent, so Jean-Pierre tilted his head and took an impressive gulp of pepper vodka. As he tried to replace the top, it dropped to the floor where it bounced away, ringing against the tiles.

Jean-Pierre still couldn't get over it.

Apparently, he'd been wrong. The shit was going to hit the fan much sooner than he'd told Pavel it would. The Triumvirate had just released a classified memo. The contamination had reached a new level. Oh, yes. Just like that. They had expected it to happen, of course, but not so soon.

Yesterday morning an entire SS base staff had disappeared from the forest not far from the town of Johannesburg (the former Ivanovo) where they used to train commandos for anti-guerrilla missions. The building itself, the rooms, even platefuls of soup in the mess hall were still there. The personnel, however, had disappeared. One of the SS men had managed to leave an inscription on the wall, made in blood: *Not me.* Riddles, riddles.

He took a third swig. He couldn't taste the pepper at all.

He immediately thought of all the files he'd recently perused in the Main Security Office.

The Maya Indians. In the 10th century A.D., the population of several Yucatan cities had disappeared into thin air. The surviving tribes had fled north believing this to be divine punishment.

Then there was the Roanoke Colony in 1590: all 118 of its inhabitants had similarly disappeared without a trace. They too had left laid tables behind as they had been about to have dinner when they disappeared. And in 1930, all 200 inhabitants of the Eskimo village Anjikuni had been transported to God knows where. Arriving police had seen lights still burning in the houses — but no people.

In December 1945, a trainful of passengers traveling from Canton to Shanghai had disappeared, several hundreds of them. It had never arrived at its destination, as simple as that. Despite prolonged searches for the train, not one of those who had boarded it had ever been found either dead or alive. No satisfactory scientific explanation of these cases had ever been offered.

Which only provided for one possible explanation, however unsettling.

The contamination had happened before. It had the tendency to reappear with remarkable regularity. Before, it had always disappeared by itself — or people had somehow managed to eliminate it. So it had never lasted for very long. Now, however, it seemed to be growing: expanding. This was the biggest epidemic of its kind in the history of humanity, and it was considerably stronger than those before it.

He'd already seen the consequences of this in a few White Sea villages near the city of Archangel in the very north of Russland. Oh yes: there it had already been unfolding — in the area where night was traditionally longer than day. What had he seen there? Same shit as in the Temple of Odin, Aryan St., the other day. The peasants' meager kitchen utensils, earthenware and even the ovens themselves were floating in the air, translucent, until they disappeared completely as if through some hole in space. You could put your hand through a log wall as if it were quicksand.

The number of contaminated locations had been growing every month. It was a chain reaction. They were too many to be contained, whether by placing concrete sarcophagi over them or by posting roadblocks and SS guards all around. Not only houses but entire areas of forest had turned into ghost locations — next to St. Petersburg as well as near Moskau. The most amazing thing about it was, you'd walk through the woods knowing there used to be some pine trees there but they weren't there anymore! You'd make your way through thickets and you'd hear this strange rustling noise as if you're forcing your body through a sand dune. In some places, entire collective farms[16] had disappeared in less than sixty seconds. Their panic-stricken inhabitants had to be taken to special camps to make sure they didn't tell anyone about what they'd witnessed.

Jean-Pierre took another quality swig from

---

[16] Collective farms: when occupying the USSR in 1941-1943, the German administration decided against disbanding collective farms, believing them to be "the best way of controlling farmers".

the flask.

Still, before it had been only buildings that disappeared. Things like hills, kitchenware and potted plants. But all the while, both the Gestapo and the Triumvirate had known it was only the beginning.

Soon it would be the people's turn.

They'd expected it to happen. And now it had. A hundred well-chosen men — commandos, trained killers — had disappeared into thin air. Wherever had they gone? Whatever had happened to them? Actually... this wasn't even the worst thing about it all. Those in Roanoke and on the Shanghai train had disappeared too, so the Gestapo researchers had expected this turn of events to come. There was something much more sinister than this.

A delicate knock on the door disrupted his thoughts.

"Come in," in one fast practiced motion, Jean-Pierre slid the flask back into the desk drawer.

The lock clicked, revealing the blue wheel of the janitor's trolley in the doorway. No one in the Gestapo knew the name of this puny but agile old man. Lab workers had nicknamed him Uncle Adolf. The old man wasn't a corporate climber type: he seemed quite happy with his current Beschlagmeister rank in the Cleaning Department.

"Heiley heil, Sir," he greeted Jean-Pierre

unceremoniously. "Mind if I give it a quick clean?"

"Heiley, Father," Jean-Pierre heaved a sigh. "Oh well, go ahead, then."

"I won't be long," Uncle Adolf nodded, pulling in his rattling trolleyful of mops and zinc buckets. "As quick as a greased A-bomb," he cackled.

He rolled up his sleeves and leaned over the bucket to wring the mop.

Jean-Pierre doubled up, choked by a bout of coughing.

A blurred tattoo materialized on the janitor's wrist: a sequence of digits listing slightly to the left, the numbers 6 and 2 darker than the others. It looked like a phone number jotted down by a drunk girl in a night club.

Uncle Adolf followed his stare. Mechanically he glanced at his own wrist and dropped the mop. "I'm s-sorry," he managed. "It's... I was still a child... I was in Ravensbrück camp with my Mom... that's where I got it... I d-don't remember much, I was only fi-five at the time. But I had it re...moved in the seventies! What is it now? I- I don't understand..."

Despite the pepper vodka, Jean-Pierre sensed that he too was about to stutter. He motioned the janitor toward the door.

The old man backed out of the room crab-like, pulling his trolley behind him. The expression of fearful amazement froze on his face.

He twisted his hand awkwardly, trying to hide it behind his back.

The door slammed close behind him. Oh. That was unexpected. Jean-Pierre had just received the latest classified data from the Triumvirate bunker. He'd barely had time to digest it. And there it was, a living proof.

The contamination kept mutating. The present was dematerializing. The past was taking its place.

Last night it had happened in Auschwitz in the Governorate of Poland. The place had long been cleaned up and sown with flowers. And last night everyone could see a faint but clear image of the crematoria ovens hover in the air. And on the roll-call square, the glittering outline of a Christmas tree had appeared out of nowhere. Yes, exactly. The thing was, back in 1940, Auschwitz commandant Karl Fritzsch had set up a Christmas tree in Auschwitz and laid the frozen bodies of prisoners under it, referring to them as "Christmas gifts".

Crematoriums were coming back. Camp number tattoos were coming back. What next?

Jean-Pierre finished off the flask in one gulp. No need to chase it down. He finally felt in control. Oh, well. They'd managed to cover up the fact of the contamination for years — and quite successfully, too. But now people would start asking questions. *Is all that information posted by the Forest Brothers on their Shogunet forums really true? Did Nazi troops really burn, rape and kill millions of people? Did they really consider the Slavs and many others inferior races?*

Doubtless, some smartass might lay his hands on the very first (yet unedited) edition of *Mein Kampf* and ask the inevitable question: *Were we designated to be the Aryans' slave force?*

Then the fun would begin.

The Reich would be consumed by rioting. The Forest Brothers would jump at their chance. And they just might use it better than they had during the Twenty-Year War when their summer offensive on all the big cities had been successfully repelled by both the Wehrmacht and the SS who'd united to stand up to them. But now, Jean-Pierre just could see it coming, the Reich Union would crumble like a broken milk jar. No matter how much he despised the Triumvirate, he knew perfectly well that the taking of cities would end up in the mass executions of all SS and Gestapo workers. Guerrillas had never made a secret of their intentions.

Could he flee while he still could? Sure. He knew a few places. But what would he do there? Become a Tokyo street sweeper? Or a cabbie like the noble-born Russian post-revolution emigres in Paris, sleeping on a heap of rags in some underground hovel?

He shook the flask, squeezing out the remaining drops of liquor.

His friend Pavel seemed to think they still had loads of time. Well, they didn't. If they failed to stop the trigger agent, the Reich would melt like a snowman in springtime. Both SS divisions, the Viking and the Death's Head, would melt like a puddle of slush under the scorching sunrays. The edifices of the Ministry of Propaganda and Public Education, the Gestapo, the Wewelsburg Castle would sag to the ground in a spongy mass of melting snow, complete with their staff. Cities would dissolve into nothing, reducing the Reich Union to a handful of ashes torn apart by the warm wind. The Forest Brothers would march right through the phantom walls with no one to oppose them. And where would Pavel spend his marlo then, amid the desolation of ghostlike wastelands?

Jean-Pierre opened the file. The seal on the title page sported a large black eagle.

He reached for it, pinching it with two fingers like a pickpocket, and checked it against the light the way one checks watermarks on bank bills. Unbelievable. When they'd been running the DNA tests of the Schwarzkopf terrorists killed during the von Travinsky assassination attempt, no one had thought of checking Olga Sélina's blood sample. They'd searched her house, hacked her email and questioned her neighbors: the file included a complete report of it all. One thing they'd omitted was that any successful job applicant in Moskau, whatever the position, was obliged to submit his or her DNA sample to a classified depository. Jean-Pierre had contacted them and requested it: a small vial containing Olga Sélina's blood.

Before his meeting with the Triumvirate, he'd run a thorough check, paying special attention to her DNA's polynuclear chains. And then... oh, yes. Why was he so nervous? It had to be expected after the Novgorod experiment with its show of flames and mass psychosis.

He'd give himself another minute, then call Pavel on his e-funk. He had to know what he was about to deal with. He also needed to understand that his talents might not even be needed.

Olga Sélina wasn't a human being. No idea where she'd come from.

Tourist Guide #1
The Cities of the Reich Union
and Their Cultural Differences

...SOON AFTER THE TRIUMPH of National Socialist ideas, the capital cities of the leading reichskommissariats, primarily Moskau, Amsterdam, London, Dallas, Oslo, etc, enjoyed a major overhaul. Most streets received new names; quite a few buildings were torn down and replaced by new edifices in the Teutonic style.

As an example, the Novodevichy Monastery in Moskau was destroyed in 1964 after having turned into one of the secret Resistance symbols: back in the 18th century, the monastery had served as a prison for Princess Sophia the Stupid, the sister of the Emperor Peter the Great who was a passionate opponent of the German culture. In its place, architect Alex Obergau had erected a new Gestapo building complete with a complex network of underground floors.

The road leading to the Bismarck Airport received the new name of Hindenburg Autobahn while the widest Moskau street became Mein Kampf Avenue. The Reichsleiter Bormann Metro now included stations like Friedrich the Great, Prussia, Hohenzollern Road and Brandenburg Gate (the former Red Gate). The Recreation Park Station became the Triumph of Will and the Smolensk Station built during Stalin's rule became June 22nd.

The Kiev Station had its name changed in 2004 soon after the end of the Twenty-Year War, due to the falling out with the Reichskommissariat Ukraine. Its name had been changed to Ostermann Station[17]. That had been the period of naming streets and landmarks to

---

[17] Ostermann: a dynasty of major Russian 18th and 19th century statesmen of German origin.

commemorate those Germans who used to serve the old Russlandish Empire. In 2005-2010, Moskau had received a Minister von Kleinmichel Lane[18], a Prime Minister Boris Stürmer Boulevard[19] and any number of parks named after the Emperor Peter III: the ex-Duke of Holstein who could barely speak any Russian but boasted the rank of a Prussian Colonel.

Everywhere you turned, new monuments to the two Katharinas were being erected, with the emphasis on the fact that both Empresses boasted pure Aryan blood[20].The ex-Bolotnaya Square had been renamed Michelson Square after the Estonian German Major General who'd in 1774 successfully suppressed the peasant

---

[18] Minister von Kleinmichel (1793-1869): one of the favorites of the Emperor Nicholas I who took the post of the Russian Minister of Transport in 1842–1855.

[19] Boris Stürmer held the post of the Russian Prime minister from January 10 to November 20 1916. Was arrested by the Bolsheviks after the revolution of 1917 and died in prison.

[20] Two Katharinas: the Empress Catherine I (1684-1727), the lowborn Lithuanian wife of Peter the Great who ruled Russia briefly after his death, and Catherine II "the Great" (1729-1796), the German wife of Peter the Great's grandson Emperor Peter III, who deposed her own husband and went on to rule Russia in 1762-1796.

revolution led by the Cossack Yemelyan Pugachev while the finest of the Kremlin towers, the Spasskaya clock tower, had been given the name of Field Marshal von Münnich, the military leader at the court of the Empress Anna Ioannovna.

They hadn't renamed the Moskau district of Lefortovo, though, as it had already been named after the Swiss General Franz Lefort, a close friend of Peter the Great. But the Preobrazhenskaya Square became Anna Mons Square after Peter the Great's disgraced lowborn German lover.

The village of Kholmogory in the North of Russland, previously famous for being the birthplace of the great 18th-century scientist and polymath Mikhail Lomonosov, was renamed Braunschweig-Lüneburg after the family of the hapless German Regent Anna Leopoldovna[21].

In 1944, the legendary Solovki Monastery had been handed over to the Metropolitan Sergius Voskresensky, the founder of the Aryan Orthodox Church, who preserved its status as a cloister. After the death of the Reichskommissar

---

[21] Anna Leopoldovna: the half-Russian Duchess of Mecklenburg-Schwerin by her German husband Anthony Ulrich. In 1740, she became the regent of their baby son, the new Russian Emperor Ivan VI. In 1741, the baby Emperor was deposed by Peter the Great's daughter Elizabeth Petrovna who exiled the entire family to the village of Kholmogory.

of Ukraine Gauleiter Erich Koch in 1986, the Senate Square in St. Petersburg had been renamed Koch Square which prompted the witty Petersburgers to call the memorial column opposite the Temple of Ullr the "Koch rod".

Still, due to the constant assassination attempts on the Third Reich officials, it had soon become pretty clear there wouldn't be enough streets to go around. Many major avenues were named after the official religion, like Thor Street, Loki Boulevard and Odin Thoroughfare. The Neskuchny Garden, the oldest park in Moskau, had become the Valkyrie Woods. The Fontanka River in St. Petersburg had become the Hvergelmir, the poisonous stream running through Niflheim — the world of gloom.

Kiev's main thoroughfare Kreshchatik was renamed after Nidhogg the Black Dragon while a whole plethora of new builds had been added to the League of Nations' list of world heritage sites.

The best artists of the Third Reich had created the mosaics and frescoes of the Bormann Metro. The Ostermann Station still boasted the rare fresco depicting the Führer entering Kiev on a white charger to the enthusiastic greeting of local women offering him cabbage patties and mineral water.

The lobby of the Triumph of Will station was lined with the busts of Aryan athletes who'd earned 33 gold medals during the 1936 Olympics in Berlin. The exit of the Bauer Station (what used to be the Agricultural Exhibition Station) was graced by a monument to Hans Ulrich Rudel, the first man in space. Clad in his spacesuit, the hero astronaut was sitting in a chariot holding the reins of Hrimfaxi — the Norse horse of the Moon.

The old Myasnitskaya, or Butchers' Lane, became Sausage Street, now housing some of the best beerhouses in Moskau including the Aryan Meal, the Princess of Hesse Darmstadt and the Bürgerbräukeller — an exact copy of the one in Munich where Hitler had launched his Beer Hall Putsch back in 1923. The latter place used to be called Leo Tolstoy but was renamed after a scandalous article in the Völkischer Beobachter which proved that Leo was in fact a Semitic name.

The Reichskommissariat Ostland, previously known as the Baltics, now remained the only place in the Reich Union where they still worshipped Hitler as a holy martyr. In Riga, they had his monument erected topping the Schwarzkopf House in gratitude for liberating Latvia from the horrors of Bolshevism. And in Tallinn, a hundred-foot statue of the Führer had been put up next to the Tall Thomas Tower: raising the torch of Liberty in one hand, Hitler was clutching a little Estonian girl to his chest, symbolizing protection from the Red hordes.

In 1971, the old capital of Belorussia the city of Minsk had been renamed Sleipnir after

Odin's eight-legged horse. The city's Oberkommandant (who'd been running the city for the last 70 years, having survived about fifty guerrilla attacks which had left him deaf and blind) was still active, building new stables and upgrading the horse race course, regularly staging the Sleipnir Cup races which attracted a lot of Japanese tourists.

Endorsement: "Remove the above guide from publication and send it to the Gestapo's classified depository. Arrest the author, charge him with blasphemy and slander of martyrs' names.

Signed: SS GruppenFührer Georg von Travinsky, Oberkommandant of Moskau

CHAPTER EIGHT

DARKNESS AWAKENS

THE OUTSKIRTS OF URADZIOSUTOKU

RYOKAN 'KYUSHU.'

THE GRIN SLIDES OFF my face. I change my grip on the Walther's butt, grabbing it with both hands. "I'll count to three. If you don't come out..."

"Go on," the voice says, soft and polite. "If I don't come out, then what?"

The air fills with dry crackling. The painted cranes on the partitions explode in a confetti of ripped paper. The room fills with Japanese soldiers: five on one side and five on the other. They look identical in their green tunics that make them resemble toy crocodiles. All are holding Arisaka automatic rifles. The red dots of their infrared sights converge on my forehead.

A man ducks slightly to enter the room. He's wearing a three-piece suit and a bowler hat.

How touching. The Japanese can be so old-fashioned.

"Lay your gun down," he says in an excellent Russlandish. "Right now."

No accent, wow! He got his "l"s and "r"s right! He must have spent some quality time working in Russland to speak the language like that.

Olga has wrapped the sheet around herself. With her face unnaturally white in the torchlight, she resembles an ancient Greek statue. The soldiers are impassive. They don't smile at all, just hold their weapons: a set of plastic dolls, human machines waiting for you to press the button to set them into motion.

"'xcuse me," I say to her shyly. "You aren't going to dematerialize, by any chance?"

"I would've if I could," she snaps back. "I told you I can't control these things. They just happen. And right now, they don't."

Oh great. There isn't even a window here to escape through. This is a perfectly confined space.

I open my hand. The Walther drops to the floor. The soldiers indifferently move their sights away from me.

"Good decision," the besuited Japanese

nods his approval. “You’re a wise man, Priest.”

He steps forward and bows to us. I don’t think I’d be able to describe him at a later date. I can never tell the difference — it feels as if all Japanese are produced at some classified clone factory.

“Who gave you the right-” I know it sounds pointless but I need to say something.

He dissolves into a smile. “What are you talking about? What right? In a totalitarian regime dealing with citizens of yet another one? If I understand it correctly, you’re here illegally. Don’t worry, no one’s going to extradite you. Allow me to introduce myself. I’m Major Onoda of His Majesty’s intelligence service. I can offer you help and protection. Do me the favor of coming with us to my office. It’s not far from here. I have some excellent green tea there.”

He makes it sound as if we’re exchanging niceties at some tea party, not stuck in a cheap brothel with a bunch of soldiers pointing their bayonets at us. Still, it doesn’t look as if they intend to kill us. They had plenty of time to do so. That’s why Olga’s defense instincts haven’t kicked in.

You just can’t rely on her, can you?

“How did you find us?” I ask. Not very original, but you’re not supposed to be. Not in this kind of situation.

“I assure you it wasn’t difficult,” he bows gallantly again. “First of all, the Moskau

Triumvirate has put you on a classified Wanted list. We have enough informers among the Gestapo staff. Secondly, you used your card to withdraw some yen from a cash machine in Uradziosutoku. You can't believe how happy you made me by doing so. It was like winning the lottery. I asked our police to add your pictures to their database. So the moment you showed up on a street camera next to the ryokan in Spring Abundance Lane, those images were automatically forwarded to the police. All I had to do was arrange for some backup at the risk of disrupting the course of your undoubtedly important date."

At this point I regret dropping the gun. Not because of the Jap: I'll kill him anyway simply to repay his mocking courtesy. But the second bullet is going into Olga. What did I tell her? Isn't she supposed to be a freakin' Resistance member? The leader of a hit squad? How can one be so negligent? Using a bank card, in this day and age, like a scatterbrain schoolgirl! No wonder none of her group survived — they wouldn't, would they?

"Mind waiting behind the door while the lady gets dressed?" I say.

He bows. "Absolutely. But I beg you to accompany us. We'll all wait behind the screen to give Madame some privacy. Hope Madame won't mind my soldiers taking her purse along... I dread to think what might be inside... could be another gun, you never know."

Olga stares at him, silent. She's beautiful. I could forgive her everything, even her dumbass ways. She didn't even apologize for her blunder. Not that I'd expect it from a Schwarzkopf. The Forest Brothers don't seem to be able to realize that they too can make mistakes. I still have a faint hope she might escape while we're waiting for her. Unfortunately, there're no escape routes out of here.

She dons her kimono. We walk out into the street, past the hotel's owner at the reception studying a thousand-yen bill against the light. A Lexus is parked next to the streetcar stop, apparently meant for us. A Nissan truck next to it is supposed to take the soldiers.

It's dark. The men's faces are tinged red from the round street lamps covered in Japanese lettering. A ruffled black pigeon lands onto the ryokan's upturned roof. The air brings a whiff of oyster sauce from the ryokan kitchen. Clumps of flowers are swaying in the wind. Far out in the bay, a group of samurai is getting drunk on sake. I can hear the sounds of a Japanese folk song,

Kalinka, kalinka, kalinka mayaaaa!
Ah malinka, malinka, kalinka mayaaaaa! Yeeh!

I gulp the warm air. The night is so beautiful. Still, there's only one question on my mind. "Mind telling us what you need us for?"

'It's for your own safety," Major Onoda isn't smiling anymore. "You're in big trouble, I assure you. I'll tell you everything, I'm not going to keep anything from you. I'm your friend. Do get in the car, please. I'm asking you nicely but I don't have to. You understand that, don't you?"

I cast Olga a meaningful look but she just won't dematerialize. Oh, well. Back in the Lebensborn we had excellent PT classes. All would-be priests had to practice close combat. Even between the two of us, we don't have much chance against eleven Japs. But at least we're out in the open — plenty of places in this street to take cover in.

I cast a look around, taking in the scene. Now...

An ear-shattering buzz rips through the air.

A soldier by the Lexus turns in surprise, unsuccessfully trying to pull a short throwing knife out of his neck. Blood gushes to the ground. He collapses onto the cobblestones. His Arisaka rifle clatters down next to him.

With more buzzing noise, two more knives land into a second soldier's chest. Major Onoda disappears behind the Lexus with remarkable agility. The remaining "toy crocs" throw their rifles in the air, peering desperately through the dark. Pointless.

The night fills with the buzzing of more steel bees. In less than a minute, the Major's men cease to exist. The sidewalk is lined with dead bodies. Finally, the last soldier makes a squelching sound with his throat and falls silent.

I'm calm and reserved. I've seen too much in these last three days.

"Onoda-san," a voice calls out of the dark. "Where are you? I'd love to say hello to you."

Now I'm next to hysterics. They're always so polite!

Not a sound emerges from behind the Lexus. It's perfectly possible that Major Onoda too has received a steely blade as a welcome gift, rendering him somewhat indisposed to reply. It takes me some time to realize that the darkness shifts, moving, rippling, losing parts of itself which float toward us. Unmoving, I watch this psychedelic scene. How is it...

Ah. Now I know. I couldn't see it at first.

These are men: special forces, clad in black uniforms, their faces concealed by masks. They scale down the buildings' walls like human spiders. No idea who they are but they're probably Asian: short and agile. There're only four of them. They've done a nice job on ten opponents without even getting close. I might find them a problem.

"Oh well," the voice mocks regret in the dark. "If you're not coming, I might just as well come to you myself."

I have a funny feeling I already know who that might be. It just has to be that Lebensborn guy.

The owner of the voice walks out into the light of the round red streetlamp. He's wrapped in a gray cloak. A matching hat sits on his head.

My reserve is shattered. I bring my hands to my face and rub my eyes. Impossible. *It can't be.*

I cast a look at the girl. She looks at him, then at me. Her lips shake. "What is this?"

That is something I'd like to know too!

He walks over to me. I freeze like a rabbit under a python's stare.

Great gods, Thor, Odin and Loki!

The man has *my face.*

CHAPTER NINE

CHANGE OF FACE

SPRING ABUNDANCE LANE

NEXT TO RYOKAN 'KYUSHU'

HE STARES AT ME, impassive. We're twins. Deep inside, he's probably enjoying my reaction. But... how did he do it? Plastic surgery? So quickly? I could swear by Odin's guts, this is the man from the video tape.

"I expected Major Onoda to have come to greet me," he says, looking at me with my eyes. "I made sure to get caught on CCTV next to another ryokan in the city center. But apparently, once the system determined your address, it didn't bother to dig any deeper and simply switched off. Which is why I had to come back here ASAP.

Sorry I was late."

"But you... Sir... eh..." I shut up. How do you talk to yourself? On one hand, the guy is a perfect stranger. On the other, calling yourself "Sir" is the ultimate in snobbery, isn't it? Who the hell is he — my custom-made clone from some secret Gestapo lab?

He snickers. "No, I'm not a clone. I can't read your thoughts, either. It's just that I'm used to this being the first thing people think when they see me. Don't worry about Olga. She'll be all right. I need *you.*"

Suddenly I understand. He's right: he's not a clone in any shape or form. This man simply has my face on, the way a Druid wears a wolf skull during the Samhain carnival. A clone would have had my voice — but the man speaks in a cracked, weary baritone. Which means he can't copy sounds.

"Come with me," he reaches out his hand. "It's better if you stay with me, I assure you."

The midgets in black fatigues surround me, apparently to influence my decision.

"Thanks," I barely refrain from making a Major Onoda-style bow. "It's the second such offer I've received this evening. My reasoning urges me to wait and see if any more are forthcoming. You understand, don't you? I need to compare the price."

He doesn't smile. He just stands there studying me. There's a certain dose of curiosity in his stare. "This isn't an offer, Priest," he says roughly. "This is an order."

He shouldn't have said that. Now I'll turn violent, I can see that. What kind of day is this? Everyone wants a piece of me!

Shots ring through the air, one after another. Four in total.

Four crimson spots spread over the gray fabric of his cloak. Still, the stranger doesn't collapse. Smirking, he touches the brim of his hat like some old-fashioned British colonialist from an old movie. His mouth curves; he struggles to stay on his feet. Still, he's not dying even though the blood on his chest is evidence he's not wearing a bulletproof vest.

The midgets leave me alone and hurry to pull Major Onoda from under the car. He doesn't look surprised. Apparently, he knows the stranger.

My lookalike gives his henchmen a nod, "Search him."

They promptly turn out Onoda's pockets, shaking him like a tree. A wallet drops to the ground, followed by a fountain pen. A handful of loose change also clatters to the tarmac.

"Did you plant the old boy on that plane, Major?" the stranger asks. "In which case you've lost me. You know bullets can't kill me. I'll be as right as rain in an hour."

Major Onoda looks up at him. There's a certain sympathy in his gaze. "Of course I do. My objectives are slightly different, Mr. Loktev. My job is to bide time."

I have the impression that even if someone sliced his belly open and ripped out his guts, Major Onoda would continue speaking nicely, bowing and apologizing. Crazy nation. At least, thanks to his niceties, now I knew my lookalike's name.

My legs sense vibrations underfoot.

The sky overhead fills with the rattling and screaming of helicopter motors. Their blades slice the air. At a distance, army vehicles rev their engines. Major Onoda must have called for reinforcements. The noise is such you'd think half the Japanese army is descending upon us.

Did I say there would be more offers forthcoming?

Olga finds my hand in the dark and squeezes it tight. From the moment she saw my lookalike's face, she hasn't said one word. Her nails dig into my skin — but I don't feel the pain.

My lookalike kicks Major Onoda in the face, sending blood flying as he knocks out at least half a dozen teeth. Can't say I'm upset.

Two of the midgets grab at my shirt sleeves, preventing me from making any effort to move.

"Priest, none of this is your business," my gray lookalike raises his voice. "She is bad news!"

Olga wakes up. "You monster," she drops impassively. "Go fuck yourself! He saved my life!"

My clone stares at her. His eyes are dead.

His hand froze in the air halfway to me. "*You* are a monster. Go ahead, tell him who you *really* are. I'm quite curious too. It's time to quit your game, Olga. He's going with me whether you like it or not."

The air around me explodes with unbearable heat. Have I just dropped onto the Sun? Or have some Forest Brothers thrown me into a giant furnace?

The air turns red with a smattering of black dots laced with orange flashes. Olga's hair stands on end, hovering around her head like that of a drowned woman. Her eyes are two glowing coals. She parts her lips, disgorging jets of fire like some mythical dragon. Everything and everyone screams. I watch as the Sony Hayes choppers break apart in mid-air, enveloped in flames. Police armored vehicles burn like cardboard toys.

The roaring wall of fire crumples my lookalike and hurls him through the air together with a dozen Japanese policemen in their neat white little tunics. The copters' charred cabs drop into the ocean and sink with an unpleasant hissing sound.

The fire has ripped the sky apart. The clouds are tinged with blood. As I soar above Uradziosutoku, I can see a pale rose glow creep over the city.

The twister swirls us, pressing us tight to each other. We break into gazillions of particles which mix, uniting us. My inert body is ripping at the seams, baring my bones. She too slides out of her skin, flirtatiously as if shedding a swimsuit. I can see her heart beating, splashing blood everywhere. She and I, we're both burning. We are fire, we're part of its flames, we breathe it like we used to breathe air. It feels so good... too good.

The fire expires as if snuffed out by a TV remote.

I don't exist. I'm gone. Evaporated. I'm nowhere. I'm nothing. I can't see.

...PAVEL OPENED HIS EYES. His skin was still smoking. This amazing sensation of the first seconds after: you've survived; you're reborn. An explosion of this magnitude would have pulverized a normal human being. He'd been lucky with the shock wave. Had he stayed put, he'd have melted away like an ice-cream.

He listened closely. Nothing. Not a single scream or groan. This kind of silence is normally called *deadly*. The Tibetan ninjas that Lansang had kindly rented out to him must have turned to ashes. This time it had been even more impressive than back in Novgorod. They might not be able to hush-hush the event this time. Naturally, the city's Mayor would make sure he kept TV crews out, but by the morning the Shogunet would be completely flooded by all sorts of pics and videos.

Pavel slid his tongue around his mouth,

feeling for a left-side crown, and crunched hard.

The bitter medication made his tongue numb. Never mind. He'd feel better soon. The pain was mind-boggling. If he only could, he'd be rolling and squirming on the tarmac now, convulsing in agony.

Problem was, there was no tarmac to squirm on.

A vitrified pavement was littered with the fragments of boulders split by the heat. Trees had exploded, disintegrating. Square black spots on the ground marked places where houses had previously stood.

His burned skin had been carbonized in the corners of his cheeks. Was this what they called a fourth-degree burn?

The medication was about to work. He tried to move and screamed out in agony. What was the name of that old Japanese movie? *The Samurai*, yes. In it, some Bolshevik terrorists invented a time machine and used it to send a robot back to 1889, to the Austrian town of Braunau with orders to kill Klara Pölzl who was pregnant with the Führer. He'd remembered the catchphrase uttered by the protagonist, an SS officer born of a German (naturally) father and a Japanese mother,

"Come with me if you want to live."

Well, in the Priest's case the good old phrase apparently hadn't worked.

Next time Pavel would just pull him out

unannounced. Failing that, there were also other ways. An ambush, a trap, a tranquilizing shot. Still, this scenario would imply engaging Olga in combat. The girl was tough.

Then again, so was he.

His e-funk rang loud and clear, dissolving in the tinny old-fashioned melody of *Oh du lieber Augustin.* Unbelievable. It was still in one piece and without signs of fire damage. This was a Wehrmacht HQ frontline model protected by wafer-thin layers of tank armor. A Tiger e-funk. No wonder they cost two thousand yen in luxury stores on Aryan Street.

Crying out in pain, he strained his every muscle to pull the e-funk closer to his ear.

"Hi man," Jean-Pierre's voice reached through the crackling and hissing of interference, "How's it going?"

"Fine," Pavel said cheerfully. "Whassup?"

"Bad news," the receiver crackled. "I want you to listen very carefully..."

Pavel fell silent. As he lay there staring up into the night sky ablaze with fires, his face started to change. His skin fibers began twisting and braiding together like strips of dough in the hands of a deft patissier. His cheeks grew swollen, turning into a thick and viscous mass. Then the "dough" began to melt his charred flesh, devouring it, while new tissues emerged in its place, pink as a baby's bum. An onlooker might have thought that Pavel's face was crawling with little snakes.

His eyes stretched into slits. His gaze grew dark, changing color from blue to dark brown. His scalp was rapidly covering with a new growth of jet-black hair.

He had a totally different face now.

PART THREE

Gjallarhorn Thunders

Moscow,
Your golden towers glow
Even through ice and snow,
Sparkling their shine.
Moscow,
There is a burning fire
That never will expire
Deep in your soul.

Genghis Khan, *Moskau*

CHAPTER ONE

Brain Revolution

LOS ANGELES, LIBERATION BOULEVARD
FROM A CLASSIFIED AUDIO TRANSCRIPT

[The sounds of an aircon working, drinks being poured out and the clinking of glasses.]

"HERE, HERR POLIZEIFÜHRER. This is Jack Daniels, pre-war vintage. My father saved it in the cellar of his Kentucky home. Go ahead, swill it around for a bit. The bouquet is something else, isn't it? I wish I could breathe it instead of air. These days people get killed for whiskey like this."

"This is excellent, Herr Gauleiter," the other man smacked his lips. "I'm speechless. It's only thanks to the old cellars like your father's that we can still remember what real American whiskey used to be like. Now that Tennessee distilleries have been burned down and their equipment looted... Do you remember that story on TV about the Nashville unrest over two kegs of Jack Daniels? Street fights, forty dead! The robbers even managed to engage anti-aircraft defenses. Please don't get me wrong. It's just that I was born too late. I find sake too weak and schnapps too basic."

"You mustn't forget, Herr Polizeiführer, that this is the price we have to pay for our liberation from Bolshevism," the other voice said weightily. "Politicians were too soft in the old days. I'd rather we do without whiskey than worship a clique of Negroes and Semitic sorcerers. Putting it bluntly, Negroes are the much more dangerous of the two. Had it not been for Liberation, we might have had a black President one day... Before I forget, what about that Liberation monument cleanup? The Moskau ambassador arrived yesterday; he laid some flowers on the Remembrance Wall for the SS Division Russland. And we have all this shit to contend with! Did you manage to find out who'd poured black paint over the monument?"

The other voice sighed. "Not yet, Sir, unfortunately. We're now busy studying the CCTV footage."

More sounds of whiskey being poured out, followed by the rustling of roasted peanuts.

“I see. If the truth were known, we don’t really need it, do we? It’s only there to humor our German allies. A Liberation monument in Los Angeles, of all places! When it’s been proven historically that it was America – or rather, California – that won the war on Bolshevism to begin with. While Wehrmacht soldiers drank vodka and courted Russlandish girls, the American Resistance had to single-handedly fight against British plutocracy and Semitic moneybags. Have you been to Professor Brzezinski’s recent lecture?”

The other man heaved a sigh. “No. I decided against it. I was a bit concerned about his non-Aryan origin.”

“Unfortunately, you’re right,” the other man sounded somewhat regretfully. “The Governorate of Poland has submitted forty applications to the Reich’s Racial Department but they still refuse to recognize the Poles as an Aryan nation. Still, as a freed slave, Professor Brzezinski enjoys the *Hiwi* status of a volunteer collaborator. And being a personal ex-slave of Dictator McCain’s, he’s been granted freedom of movement within California. Naturally, he can’t appear in high society or eat in Aryan-only restaurants, but the Dictator has a very high opinion of his published works. Professor Brzezinski managed to prove that 80% of the whole American population did their utmost best to resist the joint dictatorship of Negroes and Semites as well as their puppet rulers Roosevelt and Truman. It was their powerful albeit silent protests, dubbed as “the brain revolution” by our schoolteachers, which ensured the Great Battle victory of the allied forces of Japan and Greater Germany. Don’t get me wrong, I’m not questioning the role Russland played in that victory, insignificant as their input was. Don’t forget that the SS Division Russland only took Los Angeles at the very end of the war by drowning the US army’s defenses in their own blood. But was the storming of the city really that necessary? It resulted in uncalled-for losses. And now we’re obliged to visit their monument to hold boring ceremonies, lay wreaths and generally maintain it. It’s as if we owe them, you know.”

The other man chuckled. “May Odin shower you with his mercies, Herr Gauleiter. It’s been a long time... luckily. You won’t find many babies in this country who still believe that either Russland or Moskau made any significant contribution to V-Day.”

“May the gods in their eternal kindness send you a sacrificial goat! Unfortunately, we’re obliged to shake hands with the Slavs and call them our allies. Don’t forget that the Third Reich described them as an inferior race only some seventy years ago. But no one seems to remember it now! There are forty doctored editions of *Mein Kampf*, one for each nation. Did you read the Ukrainian edition? I suggest you look it up on the Shogunet. It says in as many words that racially, the Ukrainians are the second purest nation after the Germans."

The other man sipped his whiskey. "It's nothing new, unfortunately. That's exactly what *Mein Kampf* says about the Finns and the Spanish in their respective versions. And you know what I think, Sir? I think it was the right decision. When I last was in Chinatown, I saw there stacks of the Führer's portraits they'd just had delivered from China. The portraits weren't exactly slant-eyed, but... going in that direction."

Both laughed. "A slant-eyed Führer! That's a first. Right, what are we going to do about the monument?"

"Just buy a shedload of all-purpose cleaner. Should be good enough for our bronze Untermensch."

"Okay. You can't imagine how busy I am. Dictator McCain is in Tokyo for a briefing while the Japanese ambassador in California is here on vacation, enjoying Cuban beaches. You shouldn't wince. It's true that not many in Los Angeles like it, but our young republic wouldn't have lasted long without the support offered by the Nippon koku. Who else can we stick with? The Japanese are infinitely smarter than the Third Reich's leaders who have gone loopy with their idea of world domination. Japan's reasons for joining in the war were perfectly normal. They wanted to make some money. Do you remember Emperor Hirohito's first address *To the Population of the*

Former United States of America? They closed car making plants and TV factories, they banned American filmmakers from Hollywood. And what do we see now? Everybody's driving Nissans and Mazdas, buying Panasonic televisions, eating sushi and watching Godzilla movies. Political occupation is nothing compared to the economic one."

The other man flicked his lighter. "I'm not saying anything, Herr Gauleiter, Sir. Even though Dictator McCain can't control all of California, this is still a true independence from inferior races. I love seeing Los Angeles streets filling with white people. We did the right thing shipping Negroes back to Africa. So what if there is lack of workforce? Any farmer can go to an arbeiter market and hire himself a few Chinese. Still, people complain. As in, this Independence isn't worth a hair off Odin's sacrificial goat; it would be so much better to just surrender to the Mikado, becoming a Japanese province. True, it would require taking Japanese names and complying with Japanese traditions, like wearing kimonos and such. But at least they offer political stability and high wages – as well as low crime rates. Which would allow us to finally get rid of neighborhood militia units."

The other man drew on his cigar. "You're absolutely right. But I'd rather put all the Independence critics on a cattle train and send them directly to Kansas. Let's see how their

Semitic reasoning helps them against wild tribes. The Far West is worse than Africa, did you know that? When the US was broken apart in the sixties many cities found themselves outside of official state limits. They're completely cut off. No hot water, no electricity, no Geiger counters. Their only argument is an StG-44 automatic. Poor bastards hunt possums and feral cats for food. Here, it could have been the same! At least California is safe in the daytime. Ah, that's something I meant to ask you. Do you know what happened in Chinatown last night? The Shogunet is flooded with videos of a huge flash in the sky. It looked like a powerful bomb explosion. What do you think it was, terrorists?"

"I wish I knew, Sir," the other voice betrayed regret. "The special services arrived at the site within twenty minutes. No signs of any explosives have been found despite the fact that the buildings' walls at the epicenter were covered in soot and part of the tarmac had melted. We tend to think it might be a meteorite impact, something like that."

"What about the CCTV?" the other man sounded surprised.

"With due respect, Sir, we have no cameras installed in that particular neighborhood. It's pointless."

More sounds of drinks being poured out were followed by a pause and a knowing meaningful clink of glasses.

CHAPTER TWO

Coca Cola

LOS ANGELES
NORTH OF THE HAUPTBAHNHOF
(CENTRAL STATION)

THE SUN'S BLINDING MY EYES. It feels almost like home from home: 105 degrees at least. We walk down a street thoughtfully lined with palm trees. At any other time, I'd have admired their grace and had my fill of camera shots like any normal tourist should. Still, I'm not in the mood at the moment. The city reminds me of Moskau with its charred skeletons of burned-out cars lying everywhere. The only difference is, they've only been burned very recently – not eight or ten years ago like they had been in Moskau.

Shop windows are protected with steel shutters. The shops are all closed, every last one of them. A large banner stretches across the road from one row of palms to the other, fluttering in the wind. Upon it, a blond Californian in a black uniform shakes hands with a Japanese soldier.

A slogan below says, *The Führer's ideas guide us toward the rising sun!* Its red lettering has faded in the heat.

I'm thirsty as hell but you can't get water anywhere here.

I look in front of me. A white skyscraper looms right ahead. It resembles one of those towers that top wedding cakes. Unbelievable. I never thought I'd ever see it with my own eyes. The 1933 *King Kong* movie, black and white, made by Merian Cooper and Ernest Schoedsack. The one in which the giant gorilla climbs this very tower and battles the biplanes attacking it[22].

The film was banned already fifty years ago: both directors turned out to be of Semitic origin, but you could still download it from one of the Shogunet pirate sites.

"I'm admittedly a bit tired of our constant relocations," I croak, addressing Olga.

She shrugs. Even now, in her charred

---

[22] The Priest makes a mistake here: the first King Kong movie was set in New York.

kimono and sooty geta sandals she's still capable of attracting half the stares in Los Angeles. Admittedly, their stares aren't particularly admiring. You can tell that the locals don't like foreigners. A teenager in a Stetson hat points his finger at us in a gun-like gesture. What a sweet kid. In moments like these you realize you should actually have bought a gun. You can never be too careful in a strange city.

I've plenty of yen in my pockets, but both my Walthers have been confiscated by the late Major Onoda.

I stop in my tracks. I'm thoroughly fed up.

"You're going to tell me everything," I inform her in as many words. "Today. Otherwise, I'm not following you anymore. You're very welcome to stay here and enjoy palm tree views for the rest of eternity. Me, I'm going to ask how to get to the Moskau consulate in LA so I can go there and surrender myself to the Weltgestapo. It can't be worse than knowing that I must have taken some LSD cut with cocaine and washed it down with some trippy mushroom brew. After the abolition of capital punishment, I don't think anyone would bother strangling me in my cell. They might ship me to Africa – well, I don't mind. I'd rather eat wild rice and sleep in the jungle listening to the monkeys' screaming than turn to ashes on one side of the globe only to immediately resurrect on the other. So I'm sorry, Fräulein, but this is my last question to you..."

She stares down at the battered tarmac. Roads here leave a lot to be desired.

I heave a sigh and look up into the blue sky. "Just what I thought. Have a nice day. Only..."

Who said that drama effects don't work anymore?

"Give it a break," she interrupts my soliloquy. Her voice is sad and lifeless. "I'll tell you everything today, I promise. You of all people deserve to know the truth. One word of warning, though. If you decide you don't like my story or if you as much as claim that I'm out of my mind..."

Excellent. She said it herself. Now I can give her a piece of my mind. "Why would I want to do that?" I shift my gaze to the rows of whitewashed, steel-shuttered little houses in the old Spanish style. "I was there when you burned half the Uradziosutoku garrison to a crisp, then soared up into the clouds only to disintegrate into nothing. Do you think you can still surprise me? Even if you turn out to be Garuda, the God of birds, or Buddha's latest reincarnation – go ahead. I have no problem with that."

She hears me out, then gives me an indifferent nod and kicks off her getas. As in, *information received loud and clear.* She patters on barefoot, wincing from the scorching hot tarmac. She looks exhausted. Still, she keeps looking around herself with interest.

Three blocks later, she tut-tuts. "That's not

how I imagined America to be," her dilated pupils make her look like an owl. "Not what they say on Shogunet forums: like, California is the safe haven of democracy, they have *two political parties* there, nothing like our Nazi dictatorship. And what do I see? Scorched earth piled up with garbage. The shops are all shut. The roads are empty. Not even a cab in sight. Did you see that billboard over there? It's advertising the Last Survivor TV show where a Chinese is being hunted by farmers' dogs. Is this what a democracy is supposed to be?"

I can't control myself any more. I double up, guffawing, choking and gasping with my own laughter. Black spots dance before my eyes. Had this been Moskau, they'd have already diagnosed me as a mental case and sent me to the SS psychiatric isolation block.

"I just love it!" I struggle to speak. "Two political parties, the pinnacle of democracy! The sheer idea would blow up any totalitarian brain trying to embrace it! You're worse than a child, really. Two Californian parties that normally keep rotating every election, the National Socialists being relieved by the Social Nationalists and vice versa. One party has a logo with a swastika facing right, the other with a swastika facing left. But what difference does it make if the whole political game of this puppet theatre takes place backstage? The Japanese ambassador moves the local politicians like chess pieces. That's exactly why they got rid of the NSDAP in Russland. Every election this party – do you know that it was nicknamed the Stiffs and Cats Party by Shogunet users? That's because it often included dead politicians and even animals in its election lists to make sure that every election it garnered 100% of all votes. What's the point voting, then?"

She grabs her head with both her hands. A painful groan escapes her lips. "My God, what is it with this horrible world? There's nothing good about it at all!"

Big day for her today. An eye-opening day. "I might agree with you for a change," my parched sandpapery tongue scrapes against my palate. "Apart from the God part, that is. There is no God. Admittedly, our world is a failure. Why? Because every time you start dreaming of conquering it, you should ask yourself: is Papua New Guinea part of the package too? How about the Congolese malarial swamps? Or Haiti with its yellow fever that made short work of the Napoleonic troops? It's a bit like a toddler trying to swallow a watermelon whole. The ultimate carve-up of the globe between its two superpowers failed to include the world in its entirety. You can't station a garrison in every backwater. Now California is different: the Japanese need to retain their control of Hollywood. Movies are more important than oil rigs. If denied entertainment, the masses will riot. The Führer too should have limited himself to

Europe and the Western part of Russland up to the Volga River. Extra conquests breed extra problems."

She seems shocked by my words. All her painful distress is gone. "You speak like a Forest Brother," she chuckles. "Is this the effect I have on you?"

"In your dreams," I hurry to add. "I'm just a level-headed patriot of the Reich. Allow me to use mythology to explain. If some dragon unthinkingly swallows a fat princess whose body exceeds the size of his stomach, he'll suffer from heartburn and indigestion. But he can't do anything about it: firstly, because there is no medication that could help him and secondly, because any attempt to disgorge the said princess would cause his stomach to burst. In which case-"

I stop mid-word. Great Odin, have you really heard my promise of a sacrifice? That's right! The steel door of a shop opposite is ajar!

Not waiting to be invited in, I push the door handle and barge inside.

A shotgun's muzzle is pressed to my forehead. A large lady with her hair in rollers spits heartily at my feet,

"Freeze, motherfucker! What the hell you doing here?"

"Sorry, lady, er, Frau!" I don't understand a word of their wretched Anglo-Saxon tongue so I switch to German, "I just saw a gun on your shop sign. I'd like to buy a gun and something to drink. Or maybe a drink first and then a gun. It's up to you."

"You two Aryans?" she asks in German with a thick American accent without lowering the shotgun.

"Have been for quite a while," I assure her.

"Show me your racial IDs," she demands half-heartedly. "Or piss off back to Africa."

Unhurriedly I reach into my jacket's inner pocket and produce a plastic *ausweis* sporting the holographic logo of the Racial Department. The card confirms my Aryan descent back into antiquity, including my blood group and results of the DNA test. All normal people (as opposed to Lebensborn graduates) also have the names of their parents and grandparents listed on theirs.

The woman shoves the card into a reading slot on her cash register, then silently mouths the data. You can tell she used to skip her German classes back at school, probably getting drunk with other girls in some seedy cellar instead. Or they could have even smoked, seeing as smoking isn't illegal here.

Finally, Lady Rollers cracks a listless smile and lowers her gun. "Odin's priest! Sorry, Sir, been a bit too quick on the draw. Your broad, is she Aryan too? Arright. You never know, you see. Racial laws are strict here. You sell a gun to a non-Aryan, you spend the night at the station. At the *polizeirevier*, I mean. What kind of money you got? Californian dollars, Russisch marlo or yen? New models can't be bought with dollars. They're not popular here anyway."

"I've got yen," I say matter-of-factly.

The woman's face turns crimson with pleasure. "Excellent, Sir!" she presses a button. The steel shutter behind her back slides up, revealing a large display of weapons. "What would you prefer? An StG, a Panzerfaust... or how about an MG 42?"

An MG 42 is a machine gun from the times of the Great Battle. A 250-round belt, fires up to 1,500 rounds per minute. It can take out this whole block, easy. Oh no, thank you very much. I don't need a beast like that. Now an StG, that wouldn't be so bad. It will fit into my bag quite nicely, too.

The woman takes it from the display and offers it to me. I take this fine creation of Hugo Schmeisser and check the action. The weapon smells of cordite. The gun is second-hand which means it's already been zeroed.

The woman meets my sideways glance. "Five grand," she grumbles. "I can make it four for you."

I don't think so. Gun trade is legal in California. Sooner or later we're bound to find what we need. The shop owner is brazenly trying to rip off the Aryan tourists who have chanced to walk through her door.

I haggle mercilessly. After I make a motion

toward the door, she drops the price to two grand.

I thumb through the bills sporting the portrait of the Emperor Akihito. Just think that only before the Great Battle the American dollar was considered a currency to be reckoned with! Now it's worth less than the paper it's printed on. Here in California, three cities print their own dollars with a variable exchange rate. The San Francisco dollar is slightly more expensive than its LA counterpart. All vendors are also obliged to accept reichsmarks because of the law which forces them to recognize the Third Reich's currency.

"I also need three Cokes... make it four," I say cheerily as I lay the StG into a duffel bag (included in the price). "Chilled, please. Head-numbingly cold."

The woman opens the rusty door of a dilapidated post-apocalyptic fridge. Inside, bottles are lined up in serried soldier-like ranks. Her fat fingers scoop up four Cokes.

"This is original stuff, none of those fakes you can buy at other places," she proudly informs me. "See this red rising sun on the cap? Made at the Nagasaki factory in Japan."

I just love how the Japs did it. Having won the war, they simply confiscated the trademark and moved production to the Nippon koku. Taking Coke out of America is a bit like ripping its heart out. No wonder the country has gone to the dogs.

I empty a bottle in one swig. She's right: it's the same familiar tang. You can't confuse this chemical taste with anything.

"Many thanks," I say in English, using a phrase I still remember from school. "Can I make a phone call?"

"The lines are down," she scratches her oily head. "Ain't had no phone for a month. The power comes and goes. I have a generator to power the fridge. Had to scrap the TV. No point keeping it."

Judging by the smell coming from her house coat, they haven't had hot water for the last two hundred years, either.

I turn to Olga. "Is this how you'd like to live?" I ask her in Russlandish. "This is democracy in all its beauty, so praised by the pro-Western Schwarzkopf faction. And that's if we forget that two thirds of the guerrilla fighters are Bolsheviks. I'd love to see you transported to Stalin's era. If the *Völkischer Beobachter* is anything to go by, this so-called "holy man" used to have his meals made with children's flesh. Apparently he was into black magic and fashioned voodoo dolls out of human skin. How I envy you. You're in for quite a few revelations still. The Schwarzkopfs love to idolize their own fantasies."

She preserves a sullen silence. We walk out of the shop, choking on the hot dry air.

“Where to now?” she pretends she hasn’t heard my last words.

“To the city center,” I sling the bag over my shoulder. “Meiji Hotel. I have this old Lebensborn mentor of mine who lives there. Dr. Sorokin, from my orphanage days. About five years ago he contacted me over the Shogunet and left his address. He said I was always welcome. I had no idea then I’d ever come here. He works for Dictator McCain now, studying the anti-aging serum. He has access to all of the Lebensborn’s electronic archives. So now I’m gonna ask him who the hell this Herr Loktev is and how he manages to shapeshift into me. Plus I’m gonna ask him what makes this man so impervious that even four slugs can’t send him on a trip to Valhalla. I suggest we look for a cab or at least a bus. We can’t walk all the way to the center in this heat. Besides-”

Pain floods over me, ripping my brain apart.

“Stab me, quick,” I croak as I slide down the wall. “Into my right hand.”

Darkness opens its jaws, devouring the street.

ZOTOV

Vision Three

The City of Skeletons

THIS TIME I'M BROUGHT to a different place. There's no snow here. Nor summer heat. Wind sings in my ears. A thick layer of rotting leaves underfoot sinks into the splattering mud. Judging by my childhood memories, this has to be late October. Slapdash plank barracks line the large square yard, their wood dark from the rain. They're absolutely packed but still there isn't enough place for everyone inside: thousands of people live and die outdoors. Emaciated skeletons, their ragged clothes rotten with the damp, they swarm in the mud like maggots. The trunks of the silver birches growing next to the barbed-wire fence are not silver anymore: they're black, stripped of their bark within human reach. The trees still bear the traces of human teeth.

On a watchtower at the center of the yard, four gunners wrap their trench coats tighter around themselves as they watch the dying people impassively through their gun sights. The prisoners of the death camp receive next to no food. In an attempt to survive, they eat leaves, insects, worms and what wilted grass there still is. They don't speak to each other. Food is the only thing on their minds. Starvation has stripped them of their humanity. Who cares what they used to be before? Who cares whom they loved, what children they raised, what jobs they did? They're reduced to a herd of starving crazy animals.

A bolt of lightning rips through the gray clouds. A clap of thunder follows. The first raindrops hit the ground.

The sky opens, pelting the city of skeletons. Incredibly, instead of seeking shelter from the freezing rain, the people crawling in the mud turn to their backs all at once, catching the thick streams of water with their mouths and choking on it as they swallow greedily. Two of them die almost instantly. Water fills their open mouths, overflowing their glazed eyes. Those lying next to them are envious. The dead have already come to the end of their ordeal while the living still have to struggle to survive. For how long? They know that winter is coming. Those who haven't found a place in the barracks will freeze into the mud. Having said that, those in the barracks die just the same: both from the cold and diseases. Typhus, cholera, dysentery... Welcome to hell on Earth.

Hell should be better, actually. At least it's warm there.

An athletic man in field-gray fatigues walks out of a house next to the entrance. The wind is tattering the flag of the Aryan-cross on its roof. Two angular lightning bolts and three silvery diamond-shaped pips glisten on his collar.

He is followed by another officer. He wears a black tunic. Solicitous, he opens an umbrella over the senior officer's head. "How many do you need?" he inquires.

The rain beats against the fabric of his umbrella.

"I can't really tell you, Oberscharführer," the one in gray replies. "Fifteen men might do it. We need to demine the entire field. We can't cross otherwise. It's probably better if we send them in in serried ranks. Don't worry: if a few survive we'll bring them back to you."

"Please," the one in black says with a weary wave of his hand. "It's raining cats and dogs. Why would you want to come back here and fill in the paperwork? You might just as well dispose of them there. I'll think of something to tell the Commandant. I might say they tried to disarm the guards. Or whatever."

The one in gray walks over to the gnawed birch trees. Shaking his head, he studies the muddy mess of bones and the rags of trench coats. The Oberscharführer closely watches the expression in his eyes.

"This is all dead meat," his voice rings with disgust. "I was told so many good things about your camp. Admittedly, I expected something better. They can barely walk. Who do you expect me to take? Half of these animals will die on the way."

His voice is calm and matter-of-fact, as if he actually means animals.

"I'm sorry," the Oberscharführer hurries to explain. "The camp is small. Reichskommissariat Ostland gives us a life expectancy deadline of three to four months. For this reason we only feed those who work in the quarry. If you would be so kind as to wait here at the gate... I'll go and handpick some of the fitter ones for you myself."

The one in gray nods, impassive. Shielding himself with the umbrella, he lights up a cigarette as he walks toward the gate.

Accompanied by two dog handlers, the Oberscharführer walks to the center of the yard. The dogs' hateful barking echoes throughout the camp.

Squirming, prisoners try to crawl away as far as they can. Camp guards like to set a dog on a prisoner, betting on how long he would last. The dog handlers generously deal out blows. Their dogs pull on their leashes.

It doesn't take long.

The guards take a group of prisoners to the gate. They're fifteen, the strongest the Oberscharführer could find. They can barely walk but they know that falling is not an option. Whoever lags behind will be shot on the spot.

The one in gray is still waiting next to a truck and a group of accompanying soldiers. He studies the prisoners, feeling their muscles like a slave trader, then nods his approval.

“Excellent. I’ll take them. All but these three cadavers. I don’t need them. Thank you, Oberscharführer. I’ll mention your cooperation in my report.”

The one in black shoots his right arm up in a salute. The soldiers hustle the prisoners into the truck with gun butts. The other three stand stooping under the rain. Water streams down their faces. The Oberscharführer seems to be contemplating whether taking them back is worth the trouble. He unbuttons his holster.

The guards force the men to their knees. They comply in weary obedience. The Oberscharführer draws his gun and takes three well-calculated, tidy shots, stepping back every time to avoid being splattered with blood.

Then he walks back, whistling a cheerful tune.

CHAPTER THREE

Sworn Friends

MOSKAU, SAUSAGE STREET

THE BÜRGERBRÄUKELLER BEER HALL.

DESPITE HIS EXPLOSIVE MIX of German and Gallic blood, the Alsatian Jean-Pierre wasn't a big lover of fine French cuisine. He was quite happy with a couple of pints of white beer with a pinch of caraway seed and a serving of *eisbein*: a hearty two-pound ham hock.

The marble beer hall crammed with massive tables and benches was a copy of the one in Munich where in 1923 the Führer together with Rudolf Hess had attempted what was now known as the Beer Hall Putsch. Munich was now considered a holy city and the cradle of National Socialism – the title that even the dissolution of the party had failed to affect.

In 2004, Munich had been made a territorial district all of its own under the direct jurisdiction of the Priests Council. Next to Marienplatz in the very heart of the city, crews of untermensch slaves had built a Lower Valhalla: a number of boat-shaped tombs holding the ashes of the Third Reich's defunct leaders. The Führer's tomb had turned out the most impressive of all: a twelve-room boat temple cut in black granite.

Every room had a tunnel leading to the pantheon of the other Reich leaders where the tombs of Goering, Goebbels, Hess, Himmler and other founding fathers of Hitler's empire rested in eternal peace. No visitors were allowed in Munich apart from once a year when a thousand people, hand-picked by the Priests Council, were granted pilgrim visas to come and pay their respects to the Führer's ashes. The numbers of pilgrims remained high: worshipping the Führer's tomb had even become trendy among the young while seasoned Great Battle veterans believed that touching the tomb could heal cataracts, gout and piles.

When Jean-Pierre had been young, he was dying to visit Munich. Over the years, however, his yearning had gradually subsided. It was true that he didn't have piles yet.

A stout waitress hovered past, her uniform sporting battered Hauptfeldwebel insignia.

"Ex-c-c-cuse me, Fräulein!" Jean-Pierre

called, annoyed. “M-mind tak-king my or-rder?”

Her starched pinafore screeched to a halt. “I’m awful sorry, Herr Customer! We’re serving a group of Japanese tourists. Too many orders: everyone’s run off their feet. What can I get you? Strudel is excellent today.”

Having heard his order of two pints and a ham, she shuffled her downtrodden shoes back to the kitchen. As he awaited his lunch, Jean-Pierre opened his Buch computer and connected to the Shogunet WiFi.

The benches all around him were packed with people gulping down barrelfuls of beer and tons of ham and sauerkraut.

Jean-Pierre winced. The economy was going to the dogs, the reichsmark kept dropping against the yen, the country had been in a state of guerrilla war for the last seventy years. They couldn’t even rebuild the city ruins! And posh restaurants were packed like sardine cans. Great Gods of Northland, would it ever stop?

Jean-Pierre frowned. It had taken the Abwehr and the Gestapo mere hours to identify the man who’d planted an old-age pensioner stuffed with explosives onto the Hong Kong flight to Moskau. The name of the Japanese resident spy was no secret to anyone. It was Yamamura Onoda, the head of Casio HQ and incidentally also an Abwehr Major. The search in his house and work office had produced zero results. The man himself had predictably disappeared.

Before leaving for Lhasa, Pavel had received a printout listing Onoda's movements in Moskau. He must have had directions from the top – either from the head of the Japanese secret service Marquis Mayamoto or even the Minister of War in Tokyo. Their interests were obvious: they didn't want Pavel to get to the trigger agent which had caused the destruction of whole villages and military bases. But why?

Jean-Pierre could see several potential scenarios here.

First: for some reason of their own, the Japanese were interested in having this planet destroyed. Why? No one could tell. Which allowed us to disregard this particular theory for the time being. Secondly. Let's presume that the Japs had somehow found out about the trigger agent and were trying to destroy it themselves simply to present themselves as the saviors of the Universe. The Orient's love for drama was just as strong as it was here in Russland which made this version rather credible.

There was also a third version – which to Jean-Pierre seemed the most realistic of the three. The Reich Union and Japan had indeed been allies. Together they'd liberated the planet from the yoke of Semitic plutocracy, colonialism and Bolshevism. Still, sooner or later they were bound to part ways. Even two house-sharing brothers would part company one day. Two good friends would eventually became jealous of each other's successes. Two loving spouses could start throwing kitchenware at each other. And these were two alpha dogs competing for dominance.

Every country dreams of single-handedly conquering the world. This was the reason behind the great Mexican standoff of June 22 1941 when Adolf Hitler and Joseph Stalin hadn't slept nights shunting their respective armies to the border, afraid of their friendly neighbor dealing the first blow.

Now it was the same. The moment you turned lax enough to allow yourself a few minutes of undisturbed sleep, your friend and ally would bury a knife in your back. Why, might you ask? Not to get some new territories – your ally still didn't know what to do with his earlier acquisitions. But while their war ministers traded smiles and handshakes in front of Viking TV and Mikado Channel cameras, both the Reich Union and Nippon koku spent restless nights dreaming up a new war.

The Reich Union was disjointed, weakened considerably by the constant guerrilla war, but it wasn't going to skimp on the latest military technologies. Krupp's factories never stopped working for one second. The Japanese army had the best electronic equipment but it was tied down fighting off the children of Mao Tse-Tung.

Last but not least, in 1984 the Third Reich and the Nippon koku had signed a non-nuclear pact. They simply had no more enemy territories to bomb and they weren't stupid enough to use them against themselves: poisoning their own lands would defy logic, even if the said lands were controlled by guerrilla fighters. So once the Twenty-Year War was over, both superpowers had buried their nuclear arsenals at the bottom of the Atlantic Ocean.

Had that led to mutual trust? Yeah, right. They'd only become more paranoid. The two countries' secret services were trying to outsmart each other, both suspecting some crazy allied general of having stashed away a couple of warheads awaiting their hour.

The flavors of roast pork coming from the Bürgerbräukeller kitchen continued to assault Jean-Pierre's stomach. Blood pulsated in his temples. His head went round. He felt sick. Was he just hungry – or was it something else?

He pulled open the Velcro flap securing a Geiger counter in his computer case. The other customers paid no heed to his actions. He was right. The radiation was slightly higher today. No wonder he had a splitting headache!

He reached for a carafe and poured some water into a glass, then added four tablets of activated charcoal and two soluble aspirins (German-made, naturally). He would feel better in a minute.

The radiation was killing the Reich slowly from the inside, but the Triumvirate had neither the money nor the resources to tear down the damaged nuclear power stations. Cancer had become the most common disease, with life expectancy barely attaining 70 years. And because 70 was the new retirement age, there were very few old-age pensioners in Moskau, most of them hardened veterans of pre-war vintage who didn't give a damn about radiation. Pavel had been lucky to sit it out in Hong Kong: the Hong Kong nuclear power stations had never been bombed.

But back to the third scenario.

The Japanese secret services were considerably superior to their German counterparts. Not because they were more professional, practiced ju-jitsu or could read their opponents' thoughts. They simply had more money, period. In the old pre-1941 era, Bolsheviks could corrupt an unsuspecting foreigner by ideas of the working class' common good; in return, the Abwehr would recruit a Volksdeutsche Muscovite by urging him to help his Aryan brothers. But here and now, ideologies had long gone out the window. Money worked, always. Three-quarters of all Abwehr officers could be bought for a wad of cut paper featuring the portrait of the Mikado on one side. The remaining quarter simply valued their services as two wads.

If you had yen rustling in your pocket, you could quit your day job and move to Uradziosutoku or Habarosito. Considerably lower radiation levels, no bearded guerrilla terrorists staging car explosions in those clean, neat streets. Also, the Mikado could grant meritable citizenship to an especially successful spy. Which was why you couldn't trust anyone – neither in the Gestapo nor in the Abwehr.

Let's presume that a conveniently posted agent had leaked the Novgorod incident file to the Japs. All of a sudden they discovered that the once-powerful Reich was now being eroded to the hilt. Whether it was a bacterium, a natural phenomenon or a side effect of some new secret weapon was irrelevant. The fact remained that entire areas of the German Empire seemed to be transforming, turning into some mysterious sandy substance and disembodying only to disappear without a trace.

At first, Tokyo must have made themselves comfortable, passed some popcorn around and watched the unfolding events like some reality horror show, curious to find out what would happen next. But the moment the Triumvirate had summoned their main troubleshooter from Hong Kong, the Japanese must have realized they might lose the chance of winning the competition and scooping up all the gold medals without even entering it.

All they had to do was make sure the trigger agent did its job. The Third Reich would disappear from the face of the earth and the Nippon koku would win its world dominance combat without as much as a single gunshot or human casualty.

One casualty, to be precise. Pavel's. But who was going to miss him?

The Triumvirate had no antidote to the plague. The moment whole cities began to disappear, the Reich's structures would collapse. Refugees would flood toward its borders while the Japs would simply close the frontier, leaving everyone inside to boil to death like crayfish in a soup. At least then the Nippon koku would be able to sleep at night knowing that their good German friend wasn't stealing toward them knife between teeth to stab them in the dark.

So this must have been the reason the Japanese were trying to stop Pavel. He had simply happened to stand in their way to global domination. Admittedly, now that they'd lost the element of surprise it wasn't going to be that easy.

The Buch computer whirred softly. The email icon blinked at the top right corner of the screen. Finally! This was the Abwehr's coded message with the Tokyo file attached.

Blessed be Odin and Thor, Jean-Pierre thought. *I really should get a dozen chickens tomorrow and offer their sacrificial blood to the gods' altars. Modern technologies make it so easy. A spy doesn't need to walk through a snowstorm into the woods anymore lugging a bulky radio transmitter on his back, then shiver with cold and apprehension as he taps out a coded message, expecting to be discovered any moment, triangulated and then put up against a wall.*

When Jean-Pierre had been little, he used to devour Max von Sydow spy thrillers depicting the brave Gestapo hero's adventures in Bolshevik Moskau under the alias of Major Christophorov. In the books, he'd very nearly killed Stalin (unfortunately, the bomb planted in a bathroom had failed to go off) and attempted to poison his bosom buddy Kaganovich[23]. Breathtaking stuff. These days, a spy didn't need to risk his or her life. All you had to do was create an email account and send a letter. You could even attach a virus that could destroy the message once it was read.

So what was inside this Abwehr email?

Jean-Pierre read the message, then smiled and shook his large head. How good was that? Not only was he, Obersturmführer Carpe, a good scientist – he was also an excellent analyst. The Gestapo's best.

His scenario #3 had just proven to be true.

He was about to close the Buch when he realized that the food hadn't been brought yet. Had the Schwarzkopfs kidnapped the fat Hauptfeldwebel waitress? The richer the

---

[23] Lazar Kaganovich (1893-1991): a Soviet statesman, Stalin's close supporter and associate.

population, the worse the service. Never mind. He had plenty of things to do to while away the time.

For the last three days, Jean-Pierre couldn't stop thinking that he definitely knew one of the three Triumvirate voices. He'd definitely heard it somewhere before, albeit fleetingly. Back in the bunker, he'd been interviewed by three ladies. One of them, judging by her heavy gait (he had a good ear for these things) was bigger than the others. The other two, although not exactly slim, were of rather average weight. So while his ham and beer were still languishing in the kitchen, Jean-Pierre might kill some time seeing if he could find a match for that particular voice pattern. There was a little piece of voice-matching software available on the Shogunet...

An hour later, the Hauptfeldwebel waitress cast him a puzzled look as she walked past his table. His ham was long cold, his beer mug untouched, its froth sagging sadly. Instead of enjoying his meal, her customer stared at the Buch screen, mouthing something in surprise.

Beads of sweat covered his forehead.

CHAPTER FOUR

Ragnarök

LOS ANGELES

DISTRICT 5, SIEG SIEG FREEWAY

ONE'S MAIN PROBLEM ABROAD is narrowmindedness, believing that this new place is just like home, only better. Yeah, right. After half an hour of trying to flag down a cab I realized it must have been wishful thinking on my part. The streets remained deserted like during a curfew. Abandoned houses gaped their broken windows. I only saw one bus, its charred carcass lying on its side next to the collapsed bus shelter. Whatever rust buckets happened to rattle past weren't in a hurry to offer a ride to a man dressed like a Jap and a barefoot girl in a kimono.

Oh, great. The Coke had been drunk to the last drop. I was thirsty as hell but there was not an open shop in sight. So much for all those travel-agency posters advertising the Californian beach-and-palm-tree Paradise. I had no doubt it did exist: somewhere in Hollywood, next to all those villas bought up by Japanese film producers. I was surprised no one had tried to mug us yet.

"How far is it?" the girl spits out. Her hair is disheveled, her feet sunburnt. She's sweating like a pig. All her posh finesse is gone.

"Twenty miles?" I offer sweetly. "Why worry, anyway? We're only here thanks to you. Next time you decide to transport us somewhere, do make sure you reserve a room first, complete with a restaurant and a swimming pool."

She'd love to talk back but she can't. Her mouth can only produce hissing sounds. No, it's not the proof that all women are snakes. She's simply parched.

Me too, I'm on my last legs. Like some porter slave, I haul the hefty StG-44 bag, ammo and all, over my shoulder. But deep within me, there's a celebration going on, complete with fireworks. Our conversation has only just started and she's too weak to argue! And that's only the beginning. The moment we got to some decent shade, I'm going to bug her with arguments. Right ahead, I can already see a twin-tower building looming out of the haze.

I can't believe my eyes. No way! This miserable excuse for a city actually has a Loki temple!

The building stands by the roadside, its appearance in stark contrast with the squalid row of plywood shacks with barred windows. They look like shops – or mini jail barracks. The temple, just like mine back in Moskau, is built to the Icelandic standard, shaped as a mountain with a cave inside. Fake hills flank its front doors, complete with imitation Norwegian firs buried in banks of artificial snow.

I grab Olga's hand and pull her toward it. She opens her eyes wide but refrains from asking questions. The doorbell is broken. I pound on the iron-clad door and yell in Old Norse,

"Glory be to Loki, the God of Fire, may he outlive Eternity itself!"

This is a dead dialect no one speaks anymore. It's only used for church services. But all priests are obliged to study it in the Higher Theological College.

A bolt screeches on the inside. The door's halves swing open. A priest stands in the doorway, a fat guy with a sleep-bloated face. Oh. The city may seem destitute but they definitely don't starve here. His disheveled curly hair hangs halfway down his back; his black wolf-skin vest reveals perfectly toned biceps. His deerskin pants are part of our work attire. He too is suffering from the heat: the inside exudes the cool freshness of an aircon.

"You a priest?" he asks me in the same butchered German as the woman shop vendor. Apparently, they don't know any better. "Sorry, I need to see your passport first."

The formalities only take a minute. Having checked my *ausweis*, he invites us into the Banquet Hall.

O Gods of Asgard, what a bliss! It feels almost like home. The sacrificial altar covered in blood and scraps of meat, the fire pits, the walls of dark rock, the sword rack... It's all so wonderful, so dear to me that I feel tears well in my eyes.

"Eric Adams," the priest introduces himself as he shakes my left hand. "Don't look," he nods at the sword rack, "this is disposable crap. I just got it from the depot. I can see you've performed quite a few funerals. Even if a guy dies choking on a hamburger, his widow will rip you apart if you don't lay a sword in his hand and pronounce that he died in battle."

A ten-foot statue of Heimdallr towers by the altar. The guard of the rainbow bridge between Asgard and Midgard, he has the eye of a falcon, capable of seeing a drop of dew at a hundred miles, his ears so perfect he can hear the grass grow. Heimdallr is the son of nine sea virgins, the daughters of Aegir the sea demon. He is the only human being who has nine mothers. I'm not sure if this is supposed to make him happy. On one hand, during the Sun festival he can stuff himself silly on nine celebratory meals. On the other, even one mother can be enough to drive you nuts.

The statue was of Greek marble, hand-painted. Not some cheap factory cast.

"What's with the gold teeth?" Olga snickers, studying the statue. "Did he use to serve in the Azeri Legion?"

Adams stares daggers at her.

"Not in his case, sweetheart. He's not one of those who made a fortune selling rotten fruit and veg in Moskau markets," I say weightily as Adams' face turns crimson. "The Gods of Asgard nicknamed him Gold Fang because his teeth were tinted yellow, like a beaver's."

"I see," she gives a bored nod and moves to the mural on the next wall depicting Ragnarök, the Vikings' Apocalypse. The painting is excellent.

"The girl's got a heat stroke," I calmly inform Adams in Old Norse. "Plus the nervous breakdown over a makeup bag she's lost. Besides, she belongs to a very rare cult – I don't even think you know about it. Ever heard about Christ?"

He scratches his head. "Ah, I know," he finally croaks. "The guy who cut his mentor's body into tiny pieces and ate them every day, washing them down with blood? You be careful. Cult members can be dangerous. But enough of that. Have some beer, brother, and tell me what I can do for you."

Good gods, who in their right mind would say no to a beer? As Adams pours out some Bavarian Life Brew, he complains about the intricacies of a priest's life in LA. He has to order disposable swords in Mexico and single-use burial boats in Argentina. He answers to the Priests Council of NYC but the subsidies are not forthcoming. Adams is forced to breed skunk pigs in the temple's backyard, otherwise he'd have nothing to sacrifice. The city is almost dead. The only place you can buy food from is Paradise City near Hollywood, the abode of Japanese traders, the local moneybags, and Dictator McCain's Secretaries of State.

The posh Meiji Hotel is there too. Excellent.

I shake my right hand. A sharp pain pierces my mind.

She did manage to slice through my right palm with the knife just in time, bringing me back from the nightmare of my vision.

There's no way I'll admit it to her, but every time I dread being stuck there for good. Blood seeps through the bandage. And you know what? I may be mild-mannered and all, but I have a strong desire to grab Olga's throat and bash her against the wall. Which I just might do tonight if she continues playing the silent game.

In the meantime, I need to find out everything I can about this Loktev guy. I swear by the eight legs of Sleipnir, he'll show up again soon enough. You think he's dead? Yeah, dream on. As old men say, he who's survived four gun bullets won't burn.

Now where's Olga? Ah, she's still busy studying the Ragnarök mural.

It is a feast for one's eyes indeed. On the left there's Fenrir the wolf holding the sun in his jaws. On the right, Jormungand the serpent rises from the sea depths. The artist especially excelled in depicting the moment Jormungand sinks his venomous teeth into Thor while the god buries his sword in the serpent's neck: according to the prophesy, they're doomed to kill each other in this combat. The fire giant Surt is busy scorching the earth with his sword of flames while Hel, the goddess of the dead, grins with her rotting mouth. Behind her back, Naglfar, the ship made entirely of dead people's nails, resurfaces from the depths. A bearded Odin fearlessly swings his sword at Fenrir, not knowing that soon the monster wolf's jaws will rip his heart out of his chest. On top of the mural, Heimdallr complete with gold teeth blows his Gjallarhorn whose thunderous sounds will announce the beginning of Ragnarök to Asgard.

"Monsters getting killed by monsters," Olga says softly. "Is this how you think your regime will end?"

Adams and I exchange quick glances.

"Absolutely, Fräulein," Adams mumbles.

"Only this isn't the end but the beginning. Odin's sons will survive as will the sons of Thor. And in the woods of Hoddmímis Holt, a man and a woman will take refuge from the disaster. Their names are Lif and Lifthrasir. They will beget children, giving rise to a new Nordic race. Which is why-"

"No," she interrupts him. "This isn't how it's going to end."

She turns round and heads for the front door. Priest Adams heaves a strained sigh like a wounded buffalo. I can see he's got a lot to tell me. Unfortunately, now we don't have the time.

"Please, brother," I lay my hand on his shoulder. "Do take us to Paradise City."

"I only have a motorbike," he informs me, grim. "Gas costs a fortune in California. Can't afford it. You need a shitload of yen to run a car here. But I can help a brother priest and his nutcase lady. You wait a couple of minutes. I need to offer Heimdallr a sacrifice so he grants us a safe trip, fuck it."

He leaves. Soon he reappears, carrying a squealing skunk pig by the scruff of its neck.

"Savages," Olga says with disgust.

"Go and eat your own god, girl," Adams replies indifferently.

He throws the pig onto the altar and slices its throat in one practiced motion.

Archive # [...]

Blood ID-ing (the Racial Department memo)

The physical characteristics of the Nordic race:

Hair type: straight or slightly wavy
Hair color: blond to brown
Eye color: blue/gray/green
Lips: thin
Chin: narrow, angular, pugnacious
Skin: fair, white with a pink undertone
Constitution: Normosthenic
Lower jaw: deep

IT IS THE DUTY of the Moskau SS Racial Department of the Main Security Office to ensure that no Aryan certificates (the so-called "Blood IDs") are issued to persons of inferior races. We all remember the scandal over SS Gruppenführer Reinhard Heydrich, Chief of the Reich Security Office. This man who used to occupy one of the Third Reich's highest posts, had concealed the fact that his grandfather, a violinist with the Vienna Opera, was of Semitic origin. It wasn't until 1959 when new hemotests allowed the science to expose his crime. Heydrich committed suicide by taking a lethal dose of poison.

Racial Department workers should never

hesitate to demand new DNA tests from people who have already passed them. Vigilance is the key. Untermenschen cannot take up positions in government, they cannot own shops, banks or any form of real estate. As of the recent 1984 amendment to the Nuremberg Law, even the owner of a street sausage stall should be of Nordic race. Non-Aryans are allowed to receive primary school education but are banned from colleges. All applicants for positions in public administration must prove the purity of their blood and submit their DNA samples to a dedicated depository.

The concept of the untermensch embraces a much wider range of inferior races than the more commonly-known Semitic and Roma. Polish blood is considered non-Aryan while Iranians who are direct descendants of Aryans have the right to work freely beyond the confines of work camps. The 1935 Blood Defilement law forbids mixed marriages between Germans and untermenschen. Any sexual relationship or even a kiss between the two is punishable by prison. Persons of Semitic origin are forbidden to employ Aryan women under 45 years of age. Within this last year alone, the Moskau Racial Vice Squad have arrested and sent 140 Aryan girls to work camps for kissing an untermensch (usually a Pole). Times have changed: these days, all schools and colleges should include the Concept of Racial Hygiene in their curriculums.

What is that, exactly?

The Concept of Racial Hygiene secures the purity of the superior nation. We all know that in 1935-1945, the Reich conducted the forced sterilization of all persons suffering from chronic diseases including blindness, deafness, epilepsy, as well as mental patients and those suffering from alcohol addiction. Prior to 1956, all terminally ill persons were euthanized; now they're deported to Africa.

All these actions have resulted in a significant improvement to our gene pool. Nowadays, in order to sterilize a person in the Third Reich you need to acquire the permission from the next of kin – which normally isn't hard to do. The risk of meeting a handicapped beggar, an old-age invalid or a mentally unstable individual in the streets of Moskau has been greatly reduced, especially considering that the majority of such society misfits are foreign crooks faking disability. All of the genuinely handicapped have by now been locked up in appropriate classified facilities away from big cities.

The SS medical service conducts regular checks of all citizens, obliging them to report themselves to special health exams. The country can't afford those who overstrain its resources by taking frequent sick leaves.

Over time, the Reich's racial policy has proven a success. Unfortunately, the rapid progress of copying equipment as well as the easiness of the anonymity of the Shogunet network offer vast possibilities for the frauds manufacturing fake “Blood IDs”. In over 20,000 unrelated incidents, persons in possession of an Aryan certificate proved to be what the Third Reich qualifies as half-blood – or Mischling as they’re also known.

The Wannsee status adopted on January 20 1942 qualifies an Aryan as a Mischling if he’s proven to have an ancestor of either Semitic or Roma origin going back 300 years. The SS conducts ‘Spot a Jew’ game sessions in Moskau schools. Overall, the levels of the Kommissariat’s racial commitments are high.

Signed: Curator of the Ministry of Propaganda and Public Education SS Oberführer Ivan Petrov.

CHAPTER FIVE

Lab Rats

PARADISE CITY

MEIJI HOTEL

DR. SOROKIN OF LEBENSBORN FAME didn't look at all like a doctor. He didn't have that old-fashioned Chekhovian goatee-and-pince-nez look of an Aryan intellectual about him at all.

A fit old man with a gray crew cut opened the hotel room door to us. He wore a T-shirt with an elephant print and a pair of long baggy shorts. On seeing me, he pushed his shades to the tip of his nose and opened his arms to me.

"Well, well, well. What a sight for sore eyes! Consider yourself at home, my boy."

The fact that "his boy" had arrived with a

girl in tow didn't seem to baffle him.

Paradise City lives up to its name. The hotel suite is decorated in shades of orange: all three rooms of it, including the bedroom and the lounge, every poof and easy chair. Even the glass bar in the corner is orange. The room has electricity and running water.

Once done with all the hugging and back-slapping, Sorokin promptly called the Il Duce restaurant and ordered us a pizza and a shedload of local corn whiskey. Ignoring Olga's objections (finally someone brave enough to confront her), he dialed another number, contacting a Chinese tailor who took our measurements and promised to deliver her a new dress by the morning to replace her tattered kimono.

Three hours later, the whiskey jug empty and nothing but crumbs left in the pizza box, I cautiously move to business. I tell him what brought us here.

His face darkens. No wonder: this is what any man would feel if his son came to visit him, only to ask for a favor. He gives us a curt nod and leaves the room.

"You sure he won't call the Gestapo?" Olga whispers.

"I am," I mumble through the last mouthful of pepperoni. "He's like a father to me. Of course I'm only one of probably five hundred children he used to tutor but he's always been different from other Lebensborn *kinderführers*. He never followed the rules to the letter; instead, he tried to guide us on the way to our own vocations. He noticed my interest in Scandinavian mythology and encouraged it, sending me to Norway to Young Priests' Summer Camps. He introduced me to sword fencing and Japanese martial arts; he sent me to Mein Kampf courses and taught me the history of National Socialism – and it's been a while since it was removed from school curriculums."

She nods, drawing on a cigarette. The California republic may formally be a third Reich lookalike with a dash of Japanese exotics but at least here they failed to enforce the tobacco ban.

"They kidnapped you from your parents," the girl points out. "How can you love someone who took everything from you? You're just used to him. He's not your father."

I shake my head. "I don't even know my biological parents. Who do you think they were? Were they really a picture-perfect loving couple? That's what everyone seems to think: that the Mom and Dad you never knew would lavish their love on you. Even the Führer's biography is classified. We know nothing about his father Alois, apart from the fact that he used to be an *'honest man and a patriot of our Fatherland'*. Never mind this honest man used to batter both his wife and the future Führer black and blue. You cannot say these sorts of things in public, it's considered antigovernmental propaganda.

Who knows how I might have turned out had I stayed with my parents? Lots of people brought their children to the Lebensborn because they were paid compensation and received better rations and discounted bus passes. Sorokin treated me like his own son. You've seen it yourself: he's still happy to see me. Yes, he was an SS officer. But I assure you he was never interested in their ideology."

Before she can reply, Dr. Sorokin walks back into the room holding a small flat black box. An external disk. A logo is attached to its side. I'd recognize it anywhere: two lightning bolts against a black triangle and a Gothic inscription below,

LEBENSBORN

"You're right," Dr. Sorokin says in a hollow voice as he powers up a Buch computer sitting on an orange desk. "I've known Loktev's name for quite a while. They brought him to Moskau about the same time as you, only they sent him to a different home. He was six months old. Soon he began showing signs of some extraordinary abilities. Everybody loves prodigy children even though they are in fact quite commonplace. Now Pavel Loktev, he was *unique.* They constantly spoke about him at Lebensborn conferences. The Main Security Office kept tabs on all children of his kind."

He paused. "When Pavel was ten years old, the Moskau Lebensborn branch received a visit from a man who was to be addressed as Professor. He was very old, stooping and emaciated. He brought us a secret Triumvirate memo, authorizing him to choose children for the so-called MG Project. He inspected about a hundred potential candidates from ten homes and chose but two: Loktev and another boy, the son of a French officer and a dying Ukrainian girl with leukemia. He had such a funny name, that other one... was it Cod? Or Trout... French names can be most funny. Our staff had liked the name so much they'd decided not to change it. He took both boys to Berlin."

He turns the computer screen so that I can see. An old man stares back at me: his hair gray, his face furrowed.

Olga reacts first. "Jesus Christ almighty! This is Hauptsturmführer Josef Mengele!"

At this point I very nearly drop off my chair. "I'm sorry Doc," I say. "How is it possible? Mengele died in the 1960s. You told me that his Birkenau experiments on Jewish children in Auschwitz were only Bolshevik propaganda, a horror story they invented to discredit National Socialism."

He sighs and lays his hand on my shoulder. "The main disappointment of this life, my boy is that every man wishes he could forget his past. This is true about political regimes as well. Mengele was pronounced dead in 1961. You weren't born yet. According to the news story on Viking TV, his Opel was destroyed by an anti-tank mine planted on the Professor's route on the Anhalterstrasse in Berlin. A lavish funeral followed, complete with the Professor's tomb and monument. This was in fact a ruse to cover up his disappearance. A lot of people were unhappy about him. The unsavory details of his rumored experiments were too much even for our Japanese allies to stomach. So the Chancellor decided to bring him undercover. Officially dead, he in fact continued his experiments in the Gestapo lab."

My breathing seizes. I used to discuss Mengele with Olga. Hatred filled her voice every time she spoke about him, telling me the most incredible things. Apparently, the Shogunet was packed with eyewitness stories of his Auschwitz exploits when he was still on the SS medical team. According to Olga, he injected chemicals directly into a person's iris trying to change their eye color. He harvested children's organs. He sewed identical twins together. Of the three thousand twins he'd claimed for his experiments, only three hundred survived.

If you listened to her, he performed surgery without anesthetics on three-month-old babies, he sterilized nuns and castrated young boys. Mengele had a special interest in midgets, submerging them in snow to find out how long it takes a man to die of exposure.

I remember my telling her that this was a bunch of lies. Nothing but blood-curdling gothic horror stories. A creature born of a human mother cannot be a monster who in cold blood tortured thousands of people to a slow death. This must have been just another Shogunet fake. The informational war is much crueler than trench warfare. The Schwarzkopfs would stop at nothing to spin a scary tale. Then again, don't our schools teach that Joseph Stalin used to eat babies for breakfast, that the Red Army leader Klim Voroshilov was a homosexual who shared his bed with Stalin's best friend Kaganovich while the Soviet minister of foreign affairs Molotov suffered from schizophrenia? Whoever wins the war gets the right to rewrite history.

So Olga was right, then. It was all true.

What else do I not know?

Sorokin opens a classified directory and leaves the computer for us. Silently he rises from his seat and goes back to the bedroom, shutting the door behind himself. Olga and I brush shoulders as we peruse the dry wording of an official report in front of us.

Mengele spent eleven years working on Loktev. The French boy with a funny name proved a disappointment. Three years after the experimentation had started, Mengele sent him back to Lebensborn. The way the French boy's body began to transform as the result of the experiments didn't answer his expectations. Besides, the boy's constant stuttering was driving Mengele mad.

With Loktev, however, everything worked out just fine.

Ever since the late 1940s, Hauptsturmführer Mengele had been possessed by an idea quite popular among the Reich's leaders.

He wanted to create a super human.

His classified research was dubbed MG: "Mengele's Project". By trying to change prisoners' eye color back in Auschwitz, the Professor had in fact sought to create a being which was capable of instantly changing its appearance.

Mengele plied Pavel with injections, he transplanted other people's stem cells and tissues into him, operated on his brain to change its structure and changed his DNA. Twice Loktev died on the operating table, and each time he was brought back to life.

Finally, Mengele succeeded. The boy's face had turned into a malleable biomass similar to water in its structure. Pavel now could turn into anyone he wanted. It was enough for him to glance at a person's picture to soak in every detail of their appearance the way a sponge soaks up water.

Basically, Mengele built a shapeshifter. A

werewolf.

And that wasn't all.

Loktev could regenerate. Slowly, but still. His cuts and bruises heal faster. He's very difficult to kill unless you hit him in the eye with a large caliber or blow him up with a quantity of explosives. Minor injuries like burns, frostbite or concussions don't hinder his function. Having completed a three-year meditation course in Tibet, Pavel now can connect to the brain of a person he needs – just like a computer connects to the Shogunet – in order to determine his or her whereabouts. This was how he located me in Uradziosutoku.

He's not exactly a super human yet, but definitely a good working model. Mengele died before he could fine-tune him.

The list of Loktev's abilities makes my brain swim. It's a miracle the guy can't fly.

I turn to Olga. "Why is he looking for you?"

"I already told you I don't know. I mean it. I have a theory, of course. I'm not even sure if it's me he's hunting down. You saw him yourself over there in front of the hotel, didn't you? He wasn't trying to arrest me, was he? I had the impression he was after *you.*"

The bedroom door creaks softly.

Dr. Sorokin reappears behind me and eases me away from the computer, gently but decidedly. He unplugs the external disk from the computer. The screen turns black. He closes the computer. End of the show. Not that I was dying to see more.

He shakes a Banzai cigarette out of the pack: the best you can get here.

“Mengele became Pavel’s first assignment,” he says, nipping the filter. “The Professor had a stroke. He became superfluous. So the Gestapo decided to get rid of him. Although he couldn’t conduct any more research, he was very dangerous by sheer token of his still being alive. Mengele was convalescing in a classified Gestapo hospital. The only person he accepted medication from was his son Rolf. Loktev arrived at the hospital posing as Rolf and kindly fed Mengele a cyanide pill. After that, he became the Gestapo’s most prized agent.”

Sorokin draws on his cigarette. “This assignment was followed by a great many missions of every possible caliber. A person capable of shapeshifting can glean all sorts of secrets. He can spend a night with someone’s unsuspecting wife. He can pay a visit to someone posing as their long-dead father so that the dumbfounded person mechanically answers whatever questions Loktev poses them. You shouldn’t think he’s a run-of-the-mill hired killer.”

How typical. As usual, the kindly Doctor is trying to justify his patient’s idiosyncrasies. “Who is he, then?”

“A problem solver. I only told you what I

know about him. I'm sure he has other abilities. Loktev is the Gestapo's secret weapon. And if they're using him to track you down it means your number's up, my boy. It doesn't mean he's gonna kill you. He might need you for something else. Think about it."

He turns to the door. "I'm going to the lab now. I'm a night owl. I'll be working all night so the room is yours till morning. Enjoy."

I can't even thank him. Neither do I turn to the slamming sound of the front door.

CHAPTER SIX

The Son of God

MOSKAU

DAS REICH SHOPPING MALL

THE TRANSPARENT GLASS ESCALATOR glided upstairs, its steps filled with happy, laughing people loaded with brand-name shopping bags.

Sexy girls in cropped tops and field-gray cargo pants and cute young men in T-shirts and Dassler sneakers[24], they were all carried up

---

[24] Dassler sneakers: the Dassler brothers were prominent German shoemakers specializing in sports footwear. Both were passionate Hitler's supporters

under a large fluttering banner sporting a black eagle.

A red sign overhead sported a cigarette ban with an inscription,

NICHT RAUCHEN!

If you smoke, you're a Bolshevik!

Pavel smiled. What sweet idiocy. Considering how many Moskauers supported the Schwarzkopfs, the Moskau administration must have doubled the tobacco profiteers' yearly turnover with this announcement. These days, lots of people had stopped letting strangers into their kitchens for fear of them spotting any tobacco plants. Having said that, no copywriter with any amount of brain cells would willingly work for the Ministry of Propaganda and Public Education.

Aimlessly Pavel paced the wall, whiling away the time by studying the shoppers. On weekends the *kaufcenter* was packed, women crowding the sales areas, men drinking beer.

---

since 1920. After their factory was confiscated in 1945, one of the two brothers, Adolf (Adi) went on to create Adidas while the other, Rudolf, became the founder of Puma.

Should he buy something too, maybe? He was only human, after all.

Every lad on the escalator had at least two girls clinging on to him. No one found it unacceptable: the long war had decimated Moskau's male population. Polygamy was the order of the day. As an old joke went, *"What's three sultanas and a raisin?" — "Three wives of a Turkic Scharführer." "What about the raisin?" — "They're raisin' his kids, aren't they?"* When Pavel had been a child, the joke was constantly on the radio recruiting new volunteers for the SS Turkic Brigade. It felt like ages ago.

Pavel remembered his childhood well. Still, he tried to block out the memories.

This time he'd borrowed the inconspicuous identity of a twenty-year-old Uradziosutoku guy. Pavel had spotted him drinking tea in a street café as he walked past. It had taken Pavel twenty seconds to memorize his face: he had a passport with a similar photo.

Mengele had always told him to get rid of the original whose identity he'd used. Still, Pavel rarely followed his advice. He only killed when he absolutely had to. He never enjoyed killing people: this was an emotion reserved for sick people whose place was in the African camps. Having said that, he always carried out Security Office assignments without hesitation. An order was an order. When they'd told him to administer poison to that ginger nutcase researcher in the

Gestapo's isolation block under the book store, Loktev had done exactly that. To a degree, it was an act of mercy: the guy must have gone completely nuts when he'd seen his dead brother in the flesh.

Pavel couldn't copy voices but he didn't need to. When you meet your family member who's been dead for the last ten years, your brain goes into a coma. You don't ask yourself why he speaks in a low baritone instead of his old falsetto. Loktev sometimes used his ability just for fun (even though it was admittedly childish), like back in the movie theater when he'd absorbed Jean-Pierre's face. The usheress had very nearly had a fit seeing two identical men leaving the theater the one after the other.

Borrowing the face of the guy in the café was the same game Pavel kept playing. He didn't need to copy strangers' identities: he had a whole array of stock characters at his fingertips. Those were bland inconspicuous faces that don't stand out in the crowd. They could be anyone. You donned one of those, and no one would be able to identify you later. Their originals were long dead, some even during wartime.

Pavel always carried a boxful of passports in his suitcase. Those were his spare faces, issued by the Third Reich, Nippon koku, Manchuria and the California Republic. He very often did the same thing he'd done in the Gestapo's isolation block: he would enter a place as one person and leave it as someone different. All you had to do to activate the process was crack an ampule buried in a tooth. The substance inside triggered the facial biomass, setting it in motion. Not particularly pleasant despite the addition of a pain killer to the formula.

For a while Pavel had carried his frayed childhood photo in his wallet, just to remember who he used to be. Recently he'd disposed of it. His past was now irrelevant.

Because the only things that exist are in the here and now.

Mengele had told him about werewolves: savage monsters in human shape who used to turn into wolves during the full moon. Still, the Professor denied his MG Project had anything to do with them.

Turn into a wolf... that would be fun but nothing more. Wolves belonged in the zoo. His abilities made him more like the son of one of those Nibelung gods. The Security Office turned a blind eye to the bit of freelancing he did on the side: on orders from the Sicilian mafia or Hong Kong criminal triads. They paid well while the Gestapo's accountants were stingy with every reichsmark. Which was why he'd had to fly back to Moskau economy class in that Junkers rust bucket and had to subsist on a Sturmbannführer's wage.

Not that money mattered to him anymore.

He was into a much much bigger game.

This time he'd come back to Moskau from Uradziosutoku in secret. None of his co-workers, even his best friend Carpe, knew about it. He needed some time alone to have a good think.

"Friend, I've got something for you," a wheezy whisper came from behind him. "Looking for some tobacco?"

Pavel turned round. A school kid looked expectantly at him, dressed in Führerjugend uniform: gray shorts and a diamond-shaped red and white sleeve patch.

That he'd live to see this! Children profiteers offering bootleg tobacco in broad daylight! This was the Gestapo not doing their job properly.

"How much?" Pavel whispered back, trying on this new role.

The kid cast a cautious look around. "Half a grand. Cool stuff, man, you won't regret it."

Pavel did a mental check of his finances. He seemed to have enough. Reaching into his pocket, he produced two brand-new bills. One of them was a five hundred. He shoved the bill into the young vendor's hand and received a small plastic bag.

Why not, Pavel thought as he shook the bag (it seemed the kid had ripped him off for at least ten grams). *Everybody will look for a non-smoker. Definitely not for someone who smokes like a chimney.*

The other bill lay slightly crumpled in his hand. He brought it to his eyes.

A thousand Reichsmarks, bearing the hologram of the Reichskommissariat Moskau. A pale-blue bill, covered in Gothic script with a smattering of some Cyrillic letters on top.

Before, all money used to bear the portrait of the Führer. The Twenty-Year War had introduced some changes, though. First they'd tried to print new money with portraits of famous philosophers, writers and actors on them. But after the first scandal (when DNA tests of the exhumed remains of one such philosopher had proved his Semitic origins) they'd been forced to change the system. Now all money bore the images of various animals: deer, rearing horses, rampant bears (which made up part of many town emblems, Berlin as well as quite a few Russlandish ones) and even a proud spread-winged eagle. The repeated idea of depicting a wild boar was equally repeatedly rejected as no one in Turkestan would accept Reichsmarks bearing it.

Pavel raised the bill in his hand. The black sun watermarks glistened against the light. Every Reichskommissariat had the right to print its own money. The Reichsmark wasn't as good as the yen but there was no other choice, really. Even Americans themselves didn't accept the dollars of either California or Neuer York (a non-descript gray excuse for money) anymore. The

British pound had been discontinued in 1971 when the Brits had been forced to accept the Reichsmark. What else was there left? The Thai baht? The Manchurian yuan? The rupees of Azad Hind? All of them were worthless wads of paper.

Whenever Pavel freelanced for the mafia, their bookkeepers never paid him in bills. Only diamonds. They would never depreciate.

Pavel looked around himself. The mall's eateries were packed with dozens of people huddled in lines, casting impatient glances at their watches as they waited for a free table. The local crowd always liked to pretend there was no war going on in the Urals.

And what if they were right? It was after all the Chinese dressed up as Wehrmacht who were doing all the fighting. The legless underground beggars in fake uniforms were Romanian crooks. Moskauers' philosophy was to *seize the day*; their modus operandi was to drink themselves silly in posh clubs, drive the coolest Japanese cars and generally burn their money... whoever didn't, was an untermensch.

Here, time had frozen, congealed like stale honey. Life stood still, unchanging. How had the Russlanders overthrown their last Emperor? Nicholas II was at the frontline of the Fratricidal War between Russland and Greater Germany — while in Moskau and St. Petersburg soldiers' wives fought in queues over the rations of rotten herring as there'd been no bread deliveries for two weeks. At the same time, the Yar, the gaudiest restaurant in Moskau, had been serving desserts of naked girls – smeared in cream and decorated with fresh fruit — to stinking rich war suppliers.

Feasting at a time of plague was Moskauers' signature character trait. The Triumvirate knew how to distract them from their discontent. Recently, Viking TV's presenters had planted a new idea in their viewers' minds: of Moskau proclaiming its independence from the Reich Union. The commotion it had created! All the online hoo-hah! Shogunet forums had exploded with ecstatic discussions complete with references to the prosperous lifestyles of Manchuria and the California Republic — the two other independent states – and how cool would it be to have one's own money, laws and beer brands. Forum tittle-tattlers had chosen to ignore the fact that it was the Japanese Ambassador calling the shots in California while the Manchurians obeyed orders from the Head of the Kwantung Army[25].

The moment the Reich Union collapsed, Moskau would tumble like a house of cards. The

[25] The Head of the Kwantung Army: the Japanese general in charge of this part of the Imperial Japanese Army in 1932-1945 in Manchuria, he had the right to cancel any decision made by the Manchurian Emperor Pu Yi.

Triumvirate was up to their eyeballs in debt to the Nippon koku; without Japanese money injections, they would soon be forced to declare Moskau insolvent. Then the true owners of the city would crawl out of the woodwork and restructure Moskau life like they'd already done in South-West Asia. The entire country would turn into the Nippon koku's resource colony. The whole of Moskau would become one large work camp until the Japs squeezed it dry.

Pavel had spent enough time in the Nippon koku to know its population's opinion of the citizens of the Reich. Basically, they viewed the latter as a useless pile of shit.

Blood trickled from his left nostril. Pavel pulled out a handkerchief and wiped it away.

Radiation. Was this why Moskauers were in such a hurry to seize the day? They knew they would die soon anyway, their lungs exploding in bouts of coughing. Ever since he'd been a child, he'd always wanted to live abroad. Funny his dream had come true.

The Japs were really stupid. Twice they'd tried to stop him thinking that the trigger agent would corrode the Third Reich from the inside in less than twenty years, ridding the Nippon koku of its sole competition. They hadn't even bothered to ask themselves where the said trigger agent had come from.

How totally naïve. Had the contamination affected the Reich alone, dissolving it bit by bit to nothing, Pavel wouldn't have been so anxious. Cynical but true. If your shack has been destroyed by a tornado, you can always move to another one. This wouldn't fill your heart with a mind-chilling horror, making you toss and turn through the night while staring sleeplessly at the ceiling. Everything was much worse than the Japanese thought.

This wasn't the end of the Reich. This was the end of the world. The end of planet Earth.

The world was about to crumble, turning into a sand-like substance, then dissolving into thin air. Tokyo's turn might come later but it would come nevertheless. The contamination ignored territorial borders. The Japanese curved-roofed houses, their dazzling city towers and even Mount Fuji itself would evaporate just as the Kremlin or Unter den Linden would. But until it started, the Japs wouldn't lift a finger.

Not that he cared, really. He'd been warned of the Japanese looking for him. The Reich Security office didn't even know he was in Moskau which meant that the Japs' mole wouldn't be able to warn his employers of his arrival. As for Pavel, he knew where the trigger agent was going to strike next.

He peeled himself off the wall and headed for the bathroom. He had to try this homegrown Führerjugend weed. He'd lock himself in the cubicle, roll a cigarette and take a deep draw. It had been a while since he'd done that, hiding from his Lebensborn teachers.

No, he hadn't followed the priest and Olga to their destination. After a three-hour meditation session, he could sense them both now on some other continent – possibly, in California. As he'd meditated, he'd clearly seen tall buildings topped with fancy towers and a sunlit street lined with palm trees.

Luckily, he'd also sensed something else. Something that now filled his heart with calm expectancy.

He didn't need to follow them. They were coming back soon.

Textbook #3

A History of the Reichskommissariat Moskau

THE FAKE SCHOLARS of days past, all those Kabbalist plutocrats, concealed Russland's true past from its people. Finally, using the declassified chronicles and first-person accounts that they had kept under wraps all this time, the Ministry of Public Education could compile new history books, free of Bolshevik fabrications.

1. **The rulers of Kievan Rus** were Scandinavian Aryans who founded the Rurik dynasty. Research conducted by Professor Friedrich Königshof of Heidelberg University has proven that

the population of Kiev between 862 and 988 AD spoke Old German and worshipped Norse gods. Only later, bribed by the Greeks, did the Aryan princes betray their people by adopting Christianity.

2. **The 1242 Battle on the Ice**[26] was a terrible act of fratricide. False accusations cooked up by the local Semitic community and Lithuanian plutocrats forced the Russlanders and the Germans to turn their swords on each other. Contrary to earlier fabricated evidence, the Germans won the battle, decimating the Russlanders' army led by Prince Alexander Nevsky. The Prince himself fled to Novgorod, promising never to fight Aryans again.

[26] The Battle on the Ice: the 1242 winter battle on Lake Chudskoe (a.k.a. Lake Peipus) in the medieval Russian Novgorod Republic between the invading Crusader troops of the Teutonic Order and the Novgorod army led by 20-year-old Prince Alexander Nevsky. The battle ended in the Germans' defeat; many of the Teutonic knights drowned as the ice broke and the German warriors' suits of armor dragged them underwater. Alexander returned victorious to Novgorod, allegedly uttering the Biblical phrase, "All they that take the sword against us shall perish with the sword!"

The Teutonic army left the battlefield and received Alexander's capitulation in writing.

3. **The 1380 Battle of Kulikovo** when Moskau's Prince Dmitry Donskoi defeated the Mongol hordes led by Khan Mamai is another prime example of such fabrication. Prior to the battle, on an initiative from Lidwig Archbishop of Hamburg, all the churches of the Holy Roman Empire held a service to pray for the success of Russland's army and to inspire Aryan warriors to battle. Unfortunately, the manuscript containing the full text of the service was later destroyed by Hamburg's Semitic shopkeepers assisted by some unidentified plutocrats. The latest DNA tests show, however, that the Russian champion monk Peresvet who slew the Tatar champion Chelubey in personal combat before the battle was in fact a purebred Aryan.
(When teaching Russland's history to Tatar students, it is strongly advised to use *A History of the Reichskommissariat of Turkestan* textbook which states, in part, "Archbishop Ludwig prayed for Khan Mamai's victory" and "the Tatar champion Chelubey who slew Peresvet was in fact a purebred Aryan".)

4. **The Time of Trouble of 1604-1612.**[27] It has finally come to light that Tsar Michael Romanov could only ascend to the Moskau throne thanks to an army of German mercenaries who defeated the Polish invaders. The story of "Russland's liberators Minin and Pozharsky" was a propaganda myth spread by the untermenschen striving to bury the evidence of the military solidarity of Aryan nations.

5. **Russland's Golden Age** under the rule of German monarchs. The reign of Peter the Great had started an era of prosperity even though no one at the time dared to admit that it was Germany

---

[27] The Time of Troubles 1604-1612 – the interregnum period in the history of Russia when the old Royal dynasty of the Rurikids (descendants of Rurik) had already discontinued with the death of Tsar Feodor I in 1598, allowing for numerous impostors supported by foreign (mainly Polish) troops to take their chance at seizing the Russian throne. Finally in 1612, the 16-year-old Michael Romanov — the late Feodor I's closest eligible male relative — was elected by the National Assembly to become the new tsar while a nationwide war on foreign invaders, led by Prince Dmitry Pozharsky and merchant Kosma Minin, liberated the country from the Polish and mercenary troops.

and its best minds that had become Russland's greatest acquisition. Peter the Great, the orchestrator of the Great Aryan Revolution, turned Russland into an exemplary German princedom complete with pipe smoking and coffee drinking. He was so eager to be German that in 2004, the Moskau Triumvirate decided to grant Peter's biggest dream by issuing him a posthumous Blood ID. His reign, followed by the regency of Duke Ernst von Bühren[28] and the wise rule of Empress Katharina the Great turned Russland into the richest country in the whole of Europe. The latest research conducted by the Reich's historians has proven that Katharina the Great never killed her Emperor husband Peter III in order to usurp the throne: the unfortunate Emperor fell victim to a Semitic conspiracy which used his blood for their Kabbalistic rituals.

---

[28] Duke Ernst Johann von Bühren (1690-1771) – the favorite of Russian Empress Anna Ioannovna and later regent of the baby Emperor Ivan VI, known for his sadistic cruelty and ruthless anti-Russian sentiment. His control of the Russian state manifested itself through unlimited torture and execution of any potential undesirables. Common Russian people hated von Bühren, nicknaming his unofficial rule "the German yoke".

6. **The 1812 war on Napoleon.** It was in fact Napoleon's Prussian troops who turned their arms against the fabled French Emperor, thus saving Russland from being occupied by foreign heretics. To celebrate this joint victory over France, a monument has been erected in the Third Reich Square depicting a Viking handing a spear to an Aryan warrior clad in medieval Russlandish armor.

7. **The Great Fratricide of 1914-1918.** A terrible disaster which brought about the collision of the million-strong armies of Russland and Greater Germany. Betrayed by Rasputin's Semitic lobby, our Aryan brothers were dying for the profits of British industrialists, Wall Street traders and French black marketeers. In 1917, Russland's progressive forces stopped the bloodshed by making a separate peace with Greater Germany and handing over the Baltic and the Ukraine. By doing so, they saved thousands of lives. Unfortunately, the Bolshevik cannibals took a rapid and treacherous advantage of the truce.

8. **The Liberation War of 1941-1984.** Finally Russland's centuries-old dream came true as all Aryan nations united

into a federation of Reichskommissariats, prosperous under Greater Germany's guidance. The Führer and his followers broke the back of Bolshevism, freeing the world from the danger of the Red Plague and liberating the Slavs from the combined yoke of Semitic capitalists and British colonialists. The day of July 25 1984 celebrating the fall of the Bolsheviks' last stronghold in the Urals has been made an official public holiday.

Approved for publication by the Ministry of Propaganda and Public Education, the Reichskommissariat of Moskau.

CHAPTER SEVEN

Isonomy

LOS ANGELES

MEIJI HOTEL, FLOOR 9

I CAN'T SAY I'M SHATTERED by what I've just learned. Shocked, yes. But not swallowing-sedative-by-the-handful shocked. Not shocked enough to faint with the news. As I've already said, there've been too many inexplicable things happening around me just lately, most of them of the most nightmarish or, should I say, mind-fucking kind. Normally I don't use this sort of language: the priests of my rank take pride in their truly Scandinavian reserve. But I just can't put it any other way. This brain-searing information fits the crazy sequence of recent events stretching from Moskau to Uradziosutoku and on to LA perfectly.

Olga has a point: I have several potential courses of action:

1. To blindly believe everything she says.
2. To admit she's a schizophrenic in remission.
3. To visit a psychiatrist to have us both diagnosed with the same.

Ignoring the orderliness of the place, we lie on top of the fancy orange bedspread in Doc's bedroom. We haven't slept all night, too busy talking until we've poured our respective hearts out.

I don't even know what to ask her next. "Haven't you ever felt this wasn't normal?"

"Of course I have. When it first happened I thought I was losing my mind. The easiest explanation I could find was that I was hallucinating. I thought it was caused by too much work and not enough sleep. Or just simply having a mental disorder. I read at least a ton of psychiatry books, I think. Did you know you can have tactile hallucinations? Because that's what I had. I could sense everything. I could shake a ghost's hand. I could run my hand against a phantom wall and feel its roughness. I could smell burning. After it happened five or six times, I realized I wasn't hallucinating. What I saw *was* real. And I couldn't even talk to anyone. Even Sergei, my best friend, would have thought I was losing my marbles. They'd simply fire me and ship me to Africa."

She was dead right there. Personally, I'd have her shipped to Africa right away. "Do you still remember anything... from *that period*?"

"Very little. I feel I'm a child... about three years old, probably. I had a rag doll, Nana. Her hair was made of straw. I also had some painted wooden tablets I used as toys. I can vaguely remember a woman who picked me up in her arms... probably, my mom. I remember stroking a kitten... hiding under some large leaves in the garden... I remember eating raspberries. My cheeks were red with their juice. I hated red for a long time afterwards. The sight of it made me panic. I found it disturbing, frustrating even. For years afterward I saw the same scene every time I closed my eyes: a soldier in a field-gray uniform emptying his gun into my mother. Red spots on her chest. Raspberry color. As if she'd pressed a handful of berries to her dress."

I knew what she meant. I'd have found it disturbing too. "And that's when it happened?"

"Yes. I saw a flash. A blinding light. And a terrible roaring sound. I thought my ears would explode. Screams. Everything around me blurred, disappearing in a wall of flames. I fainted. When I came round, I was somewhere else. I didn't recognize the place. It looked weird. I kept crying and screaming until I was blue in the face. Then I fell asleep."

She paused, staring in front of her. "Later my adoptive parents told me what a shock it had been. In the morning they'd left for work as usual, and when later that evening they'd come back, they discovered a three-year-old girl sleeping on their lounge rug! They were religious. I mean, they were Christians. Nothing to do with your Valhalla thing. So they thought it was a miracle. They didn't have children of their own, you see. All foundlings had to be surrendered to Lebensborn but my parents were well-connected enough to keep me. Mom was a TV makeup artist and my Dad designed uniforms for the Ministry of Propaganda and Public Education. The DNA test proved I was Aryan, the rest was paperwork. They might have greased a few palms or called in a few favors... no amount of Third Reich laws can wipe out the Russlandish 'scratch my back and I'll scratch yours' mentality."

She took a drag on her cigarette. "For years afterwards I would wake up in the middle of the night, screaming and in tears because I'd been dreaming about that soldier and other creatures in field-gray uniforms. My parents didn't want to take me to a psychiatrist. Had he confirmed this to be schizophrenia, no amount of connections would have saved me. My parents loved me too much. They spoiled me rotten. Like many Moskauers at the time, they both died from leukemia when I was twenty."

She reaches for another cigarette. The

ashtray is already overflowing.

"Do you remember your real name?" I ask her.

"No. When I turned fourteen, that's when my teleportations got really out of hand. I kept finding myself in different time periods and spoke to different people who always told me the same thing: the village of Alexeyevskoe had been burned to ashes. No survivors left. Apparently, it had been an SS punitive operation as retribution for partisan attacks on their patrols. They shot all the adults, then locked the children in the only remaining house at the edge of the village and threw grenades into the windows. All the children died. Well, almost."

My heart clenches into an icy-cold fist. "I saw it, too. Soldiers wearing gas masks. They were shooting at everything that moved. There was rousing music playing... a march of sorts... The gunner was laughing. But I thought I was sick and hallucinating."

She shakes her head, then lets out a few smoke rings. "You weren't. You saw what really happened. Through my eyes. This was another war raging in another world, simultaneously. Gosh, it was scary. I'd sit at home reading a book and then I'd be pulled out into a different time and place. And you'd never know whether they'd bring you back or if you're supposed to perish in there. I tried to find out what it was that was happening to me. I looked for books to read up on it. It was Democritus — the Greek philosopher — who finally opened my eyes. You see, the Ministry of Public Education still isn't sure whether Greeks can be considered Aryans. At least they don't ban their books in the meantime. So it was Democritus who first suggested that there were other worlds co-existing with ours in the void of universal chaos. Some of them may be similar to ours, others totally different, but they all co-exist, this is the main principle of the Democritean universe. Isonomy in its initial sense means equal opportunity. In other words, the very existence of our world means there's bound to be another one out there somewhere which looks just like ours — but whose history might have run a different course."

She cast me a sideways glance. "Sometimes I stayed there for a few days. A week in one case. As I wandered through space, I had to do something with myself so I started looking for their books, especially schoolbooks. And I'll tell you something. Their Germany *lost the war.* The allied forces of Russland, Britain, France and the US accepted the Germans' capitulation in Berlin. They besieged the Führer in his bunker where he shot himself."

I still have the impression she's rambling, delirious. "Listen, Olga. This, of all things, couldn't have happened. At the time, Germany possessed by far the best army in all Europe. Its troops had trampled the soldiers of France,

Poland, Yugoslavia and Greece into the ground. Operation Typhoon which saw the storming of Russland's capital had been conceived by top German generals trained and hardened under von Moltke the Younger! Moskau was doomed from the start."

She flicks off the ash and shakes her head, insistent. "No. It wasn't like that at all. Germany was defeated. It didn't start any more wars after that. President Truman dropped two A-bombs on Japan, forcing Emperor Hirohito to surrender to the US. Mussolini was executed by Italian partisans who then hung his corpse upside down for everyone to see. The Reich's entire leadership was tried in Nuremberg. Most of them were hanged, apart from Himmler and Goering who killed themselves with cyanide. In that other world, the Nippon koku is the land of tourism and electronic revolution while Germany is forced to buy gas from Russland."

On this I beg to differ! Germans dependent on our resources? Yeah right. Still, it's not the right moment to argue with her.

"Very well," I interrupt her. "Then how do you explain your coming to our world?"

She throws her hands behind her back and shifts her body, making herself comfortable on the orange pillow. "I wish I knew! I thought my brain would explode. Having done all the research I could on psychiatry and Democritus, I turned to physics. I tried to understand why this was happening to me. I might have accepted my being constantly pulled out of one world and thrown into another, but why those two? Why wasn't I teleported somewhere else? There must have been hundreds of parallel worlds, according to the theory!"

Her face darkened. "I got my answer when I first came to the village of Alexeyevskoe. You can *feel* there's something wrong there. Some anomaly. All metallic objects tend to clump together. The sky there can turn pitch black at midday. Every summer there's one day when it gets really cold. Then the wind brings snowstorms whirling through the village at the exact hour when the SS murdered those children. Apparently, the grenades' combined explosion inside the house was so powerful it opened a tunnel between the two worlds. No idea what triggered my ability to teleport. It could have been the explosion itself or it could have been the children's tearful angst, the sheer horror of it all. So basically, I was sucked into your world a split second before I died."

Staggering, I head for a side table and pour myself some whiskey. I don't give a shit about being patriotic at the moment. "If I understand it rightly, my visions and all those weird things that were happening at the temple, including the disappearance of the sacrificial goat... were they also the result of your, ahem, travels to a parallel world?"

An expiring cigarette sizzles in the ashtray. "You and your goat! I think I'm gonna reimburse you for it when we're back in Moskau. Yes, you and I seem to be connected somehow. I can't really tell you how it works. You seem to be transported there too and are capable of seeing the same things as I do. But as you weren't born there, you can watch the events without influencing them. You're a visitor. And when you cut your hand to let blood, it sort of brings you back here, preventing you from merging with that world. Mind telling me how you worked out the blood-letting bit?"

I shrug. "Easy. I thought you were hypnotizing me. It looks very similar to hypnosis, anyway. And one of the first things you learn in Higher Theological College is that a priest should let his own blood whenever the gloom of the demonic morass tries to enshroud you with its magic. I tried, and it worked. But it's of no consequence. I'd love to know what happened to the Temple walls."

She heaves a sigh and gropes for a new cigarette. "If I'm right, my travels have somehow affected your world," she exhales the smoke. "It's beginning to corrode, growing almost cancer-like metastases. Your Temple walls are only a fraction of the oncoming Apocalypse. I saw whole mountain ranges disappear, rivers evaporate, forests vanish. No idea what I've brought with me to your universe but it doesn't look good. It's as if

I've infected it with some sort of virus, so now it's dying. And you know what? I don't feel sorry for it at all."

What can you say to that? I know it's stupid but I have to ask. "Why?"

"Because a world ruled by a victorious army of children-burning scumbags has no right to exist. It doesn't make sense. It's a fault in the makeup of the universe. There's always been plenty of shit around throughout human history, but until now, no one had thought of killing human beings in their millions by gassing and cremating them in camp ovens. The Third Reich is a sick joke, don't you understand? Just look at the crazy surreal world you have to live in. That's their victory backfiring."

Here, I'm obliged to butt in. "Women come in two kinds: they're either heartless or naïve. You somehow manage to combine the two. Do you mean that your world is the best thing since sliced bread? Does is flow with milk and honey? You have no diseases, no smug plutocrats, no trigger-happy generals, is that right? In your world, the poor don't beg on street corners? No one gets slaughtered simply because they belong to the wrong race or religion? Your powerful countries don't rob the weak ones — they don't bomb their cities nor confiscate their museums? In your world, SS squads don't burn villagers alive in their homes? Well, in that case let me tell you: you haven't come from another world, no.

You've simply died and gone to heaven."

She gets out of bed and walks over to face me. "You're right. My world is everything you've just said. Life seems to be cursed in the universe. I'm sure other parallel worlds have rotted alive with corruption, too. Their politicians must be the same bunch of treacherous douchebags. Whatever regime they have there, it's inevitably evil. But I'd rather the lesser evil wins. My world sucks, I agree. But it was so drenched in blood that even now, seventy years later, it's still wary of waging any large-scale wars. Yes, I do hate National Socialism. I was so keen to fight this regime which lost there but was victorious here. I didn't give a damn about your beauty parlors, travel tours and shopping sprees. The Schwarzkopfs welcomed me with open arms."

How sweet. You can't begin to imagine how fed up I am with these spoiled diamond-laden bitches and their attitudes. They're constantly on TV, they get the best in cancer treatment, they swill champagne by the bottle and spend fortunes in spas. And if you listen to them, they just can't wait to topple the regime: oh, the revolution, the holy right of the poor and needy; oh they'd love nothing better than to hurl a grenade at some policeman, then post the video on the Shogunet.

But if the truth were known... what would I have done in her place? Honestly, no bullshit? If someone burned children alive in front of me? If I knew for sure what kind of macabre experiments that nutcase Mengele conducted, vivisecting his screaming victims? Or if I'd had any idea that the Führer's entourage was made up of first-class butchers? Would I, knowing all this, still be able to drink my morning coffee, pretending it was none of my business? Would I be able to distance myself from it all and live as if nothing had happened? Or would their constant lies make me sick?

I really don't know.

The likes of Loktev are bound to realize what kind of masters they serve. Not that they seem to care.

My head is splitting. I don't want to decide! My faith in the Reich is falling apart, but... I just can't bear the Schwarzkopfs.

A red haze begins to fill my field of vision. Can't they all do me a favor and go take a running jump?

"Can I ask you something?" I say. "Logically speaking, wouldn't it have been easier to tell me everything from the start?"

"Oh really? You reckon you'd have believed me?"

I have nothing to say to this. Of course I wouldn't have.

She lays her hands on my shoulders. Her palms are scorching hot even through my shirt.

"What do you need me for?" I ask. "It's about time you tell me."

She whispers in my ear, her voice breaking

all the time. She doesn't make sense. Her lips keep touching my earlobe. I find it arousing. Very. She's rambling, trying to explain. Oh. What an unorthodox explanation.

Having said that, how much of what has happened to us *is* normal?

I have no desire to object.

"Very well," I heave a sigh. "That's not a problem. I do remember your promise. But if I do what you're asking me to, will it stop the contamination? Or let's put it this way, will we still have a chance?"

She nods. "Sorry about all the theory. You shouldn't think I don't give a fuck about what's gonna happen to you. Yes, everything will get back to normal. I tried to take a different route but it doesn't seem to work. So we'll have to do it another way. We need to catch a plane. It's getting a bit urgent."

I very nearly choke on my whiskey. "A plane!" I can't believe my ears. "What, just like that? You suggest we go to the airport like two idiots and book a Junkers flight back? Not transport ourselves through time and space, leaving LA behind to be consumed by flames? Boring."

She doesn't get angry. She explodes. "I'm fed up with your sardonic bullshit! I told you before: in order to teleport, our lives must be in mortal danger. So what do you want me to do? Go out and dial the Luftwaffe, tell them to send a few bombers over here? I can do that! Question is, where will we end up? In Australia? On some desert island in the middle of the ocean? Or in Africa? You don't make it easy, do you?"

I just love her bouts of temper. I can't help wondering what she's like in bed.

Actually, why am I so afraid of thinking about that? Why do I always have to quit at the most interesting bit?

I seem to be prejudiced against any potential relationship with her. For several reasons. True, as an SS officer I don't want to be pushed about by a Schwarzkopf activist, even if only in bed. For several weeks I've been playing hard to get, I've been really good at it, suffering her nightly masturbations (and that wasn't easy, I assure you). I really don't want to give her the impression she's finally got one up on me.

But now... I don't really give a flying fuck. It's ten in the morning. We've talked through the night. She's so close, drawing me like a magnet. I don't want to let her go. Our time has come.

We hear a screech. A key is turning in the door.

That's Doc back. Shit! Your timing is seriously wrong, Teacher!

CHAPTER EIGHT
Harun al-Rashid

MOSKAU

THOR'S HAMMER LANE

IT TOOK JEAN-PIERRE SOME TIME to arrive at the only possible solution. Ever since his Bürgerbräukeller epiphany, he'd looked at hundreds of possible scenarios, from even remotely logical to the most improbable.

First he'd done it using his home computer. Then he'd visited a friend at the Gestapo audio surveillance department and played the recordings on his professional Japanese equipment. His friends had agreed with him. The voices *were* identical.

Stubbornly Jean-Pierre had done everything he could to disprove his own findings, looking for every possible error, inconsistency or technical glitch. The facts, however, seemed to grin back at him as if to say, *Sorry man, you're dead right here.*

The day before, he'd skipped work for the first time in his life without telling anyone. He'd locked himself in his apartment and stayed put. He hadn't eaten anything for twenty-four hours, only drinking icy cold water as he listened hard into his headphones, replaying the words he'd so meticulously matched.

He was trying to understand. His head was sore with all the theories. The main one of which was, *What the hell did they need this shit for?*

The most loyalist theory was, this was simply a security measure to make sure the Schwarzkopfs didn't get to the Triumvirate leaders. It was no secret that the Resistance had its moles entrenched in all of the Reich's offices, including some Wehrmacht officers. They very easily could have planted a few amid the Triumvirate's staff too. In this case, such secrecy was understandable but... how far could it realistically stretch? The Moskau Reichskommissariat leaders never appeared on TV. Their radio addresses were read by radio hosts. Moskau's citizens never heard their leaders' actual voices nor had they seen their actual signatures under published decrees, only the Black Sun seal. Even on Freia's Birthday — which symbolized the end of the Icelandic

Vikings' lunar cycle between the two full moons — it was Helen Stein, the smiley blonde and the Reich's most popular actress, who read the Triumvirate's celebratory address on TV.

So in this case, such security measures would border on paranoia. Were the Triumvirate leaders afraid someone might work out their real names? As if! If anyone ever learned the terrible truth, their reaction would more than likely be a relieved *'That's exactly what I've been thinking!'* They'd claim they'd worked out the truth by themselves already, putting two and two together through occasional slips of the tongue, dropped hints and other things they'd never really paid attention to but which must have registered subconsciously, finally falling into a pattern.

Restless with anxiety, Jean-Pierre couldn't believe his own deductions. Could it really be *so simple*? Was it really what he'd always secretly suspected deep within?

He'd forgotten all about his lab and the trigger agent. He tried not to think about Pavel still not contacting him. He just didn't care. This was mind-boggling.

The glow of the Buch screen cast a weak light on the inside of a small room.

Jean-Pierre had been living on his own for quite a while. His was an average apartment in a standard ten-story block the Gestapo rented for its workers, complete with a steel apartment door, video surveillance and a gunner manning the front desk. No female presence: Mengele's experiments had rendered Jean-Pierre useless in that particular department. All his male potential, as Pavel used to quip, had been channeled into his muscles.

Cheeky bastard! He'd been lucky enough to escape this fate.

Jean-Pierre preferred living alone, anyway. He was obsessively clean; he wiped the phone receiver every time he finished talking; he had his dinners delivered; he had his TV soaps and comedians as well as a steady supply of pepper vodka for whenever he had to speak without stuttering. That was the extent of his life.

The office hadn't called him yet. That was weird. Especially considering he'd been working long hours just lately, ever since they'd been involved in the trigger agent investigation.

Despite their own paranoid secrecy, the Triumvirate leaders in fact tended to summon quite a few visitors. Not just Wehrmacht generals or SS Oberführers: the three Triumvirate leaders were quite happy to meet heroic soldiers, exemplary farmers, prominent scientists and Reichstag deputies. Naturally, all visitors were blindfolded before the leaders meted out their medals and awards, followed by the mentioning of all the boring details of every such event on radio and TV. The Triumvirate was perfectly accessible but still unattainable; it kept a watchful eye on everything in the country while remaining intangible.

One of the Viking TV hosts had compared the Triumvirate with Harun al-Rashid, the Caliph of Baghdad, who used to walk the city streets in disguise pretending to be a commoner. "Imagine riding the underground from Horst Wessel Station to Torch Parade Square," he'd said, "telling a Reich joke. And the guy sitting opposite you is in fact one of the Triumvirate. You'd be naïve to think they know nothing about the mood in the country."

On one hand, the regime had done everything to deny its own existence, redirecting the population's anger to more convenient targets. On the other, it was now well and truly ubiquitous. TV statements like these would render everyone paranoid, imagining the pale face of one of the Triumvirate hovering behind his or her back.

Jean-Pierre had been scratching his head for another twenty-four hours, thinking what to do with his discovery. Should he tell Pavel about it over a beer and pick his brains about it? That was one solution. Still, Pavel was away — and Jean-Pierre had no idea when he might be back in Moskau.

Or should he maybe upload the news to some Schwarzkopf forum? Then again, Jean-Pierre had been wearing a blue SS lab coat for far too long to turn it at a moment's notice. Having to choose between those you dislike and those you hate isn't an easy thing to do. Yes, so the Lebensborn had turned him into a mental wreck, making him into one of the thousands of walking robots who could harbor disagreements with the system but still had to do what it told them to. The system that had first snatched him from his parents, castrated him like a young pig, then forced him to do the kind of work it wanted him for. Why should he even contemplate it? It was much safer thinking old comfortable thoughts like most Moskauers did, rerunning stale dreams of being promoted first to Hauptsturmführer, then to Sturmbannführer until you could finally retire sporting the proper Standartenführer insignia.

That's provided cancer hadn't carried you off earlier.

The Schwarzkopfs? Oh, he'd read their mission statements on the Shogunet. Their guerrilla groups spent more time fighting each other than challenging the Reichskommissariat's armies. They only joined forces once a year during the Wehrmacht's Great Offensive: then indeed no one could defeat them. The Schwarzkopfs' ranks were patched like a Chinese quilt: Bolsheviks, anarchists, Imperial White Guards, polizei deserters[29] and village militia. If

[29] Polizei: members of the Hilfspolizei, the local collaborators' Auxiliary Police force set up by the Nazis in the occupied territories to help keep the

this motley crew ever seized power, it would mean a new Twenty-Year War over city control! Jean-Pierre had no illusions about his own fate among others like him: the victors would simply line them up along a freshly-dug trench and gun them down, end of story.

So no, he wasn't so eager to play into the Schwarzkopfs' hands. But he couldn't stay silent about what he'd just found out, either. This had been the last straw. This freakin' Triumvirate really took them all for *untermensch* idiots. They were probably laughing in the safety of their bunker knowing that Moskauers had no other choice but to pull their weight for the regime, cheering the Reich's decisions. The moment they stopped doing that, the big bad Schwarzkopfs would fall on them like a ton of bricks.

What a bunch of lowlifes. Never mind. Jean-Pierre knew what he was going to do.

He would withdraw all the yen he'd saved for his vacation and book a flight to Hong Kong. He had enough to last a couple of months there. In the meantime, Pavel (complete with a new face and new identity) was bound to pay a visit to the

---

population in check. Often more brutal than the SS and the Gestapo themselves, the polizei were usually rectruited from the dregs of the local society seeking to wreak revenge on their neighbors. In Russian, the word *polizei* became synonymous with a murderous Nazi collaborator.

safe house in the Springtime of the Glorious Tiger district, the one with all the high-rise towers by the port. And that's where they'd finally talk: in a bug-free environment devoid of Gestapo agents. He would put Pavel into the picture and they'd decide what to do with the data. Jean-Pierre would have uploaded the audio file and all the comparative analysis to... not to his own email box, oh no. It was too easy to hack. If the truth were known, he wasn't a hundred percent sure he wasn't being watched: most (although not all) staff computers were routinely bugged.

Never mind. He knew of a place where they'd never look for it.

It took him an hour to upload the massive file. Immediately he felt better. That was basically it. He would catch a few winks, then go to the office. He still had a few hours of sleep left.

Jean-Pierre walked over to the window and screwed his eyes tight against the blazing sun. He lay both his hands onto the black curtains, parting them.

The window pane popped. A spider's web of cracks ran from a tiny hole at its center.

The bullet hit the top of his head, razing the upper half of the skull level with his eyes. Blood and bits of brain showered the ceiling and the wall behind him, tinting the gray wallpaper even darker.

Jean-Pierre's body collapsed to the floor, knocking over the little table and the Buch computer on it.

In the People's Apartments tower opposite, an SS sniper gingerly lifted his Mosin rifle off its stand. The modern optic sights looked out of place on the battered ancient weapon. Normally he'd have used a Mannlicher for the job but this time he'd been obliged to lug this five-shot bolt-action behemoth on his back.

His orders had been to eliminate the target using this old Stalin-era weapon still in service with some of Forest Brothers groups. The orders had been issued by the *Einsatzgruppe-A* — the Security Office Electronic Department — after the checks had been conducted on the target's office computer following a fellow worker's report of the target's filing a suspicious inquiry.

The sniper didn't care who'd issued the order. Normally, it was the Triumvirate who sanctioned these kinds of missions.

The sniper was dressed in non-descript shorts, a T-shirt and a tatty pair of Dassler sneakers. He lay the rifle on the floor, peeled off the gloves and dropped them next to the weapon. The person who was to clean up after him was going to arrange for the required set of fingerprints.

He pulled a Mannerheim Nokia phone out of his pocket and dialed a number. This was a special Gestapo line used for mission completion confirmation.

One of those stupid bureaucratic tricks.

He'd followed the instructions to a T. He'd had both incendiary and armor-piercing ammo on him. The latter was a necessity: all Gestapo workers had bulletproof windows installed in their apartments.

What was taking them so long?

Finally, the telephone dinged.

Then it exploded in a flash of orange flame, disintegrating. The mere ounce of explosives stashed inside was plenty enough to take him out.

In Thor's Hammer Lane, the few passersby froze, open-mouthed. Some reached for their mobile phones to film what they were seeing while most had turned into pillars of salt from the spectacle. The walls of the tower block began to ripple. Its front doors evaporated into thin air, revealing limpid glasslike stairwells.

PART FOUR

The Carnival of Phantoms

Outside the barracks, by the corner light
I'll always stand and wait for you at night.
We will create a world for two,
I'll wait for you the whole night through,
For you, Lili Marlene.

Hans Leip, Norbert Schultze. *Lili Marlene*

CHAPTER ONE

The Tea Ceremony

TOKYO, SHŌWA ERA STREET
RED SUN TEA HOUSE.

FROM A CLASSIFIED AUDIO TRANSCRIPT

THE SOUND OF POURING WATER and the clutter of bone china breaks the silence.

"With all due respect, Minister," a voice says adamantly, "my lowly position in the light of your presence makes me unworthy of the slightest show of your mercy. What I've committed isn't a mistake. It is a catastrophe. If you be so kind as to allow me to use your presence in order to-"

"In order to do what?" the other voice asks curiously. "Do you purport to wipe away the stain of your mistake by committing hara-kiri?"

"How did you know? It's true that I've already drawn the symbol of honor on the palm of my hand. But-"

"Had you been a Cabinet Minister for as long as I have, dear Marquis, you too would have learned to tell your visitor's intentions the moment he or she enters the room. The Nippon koku may have imbibed quite a few foreign influences but it still sticks to its traditions. Look at this pretty bamboo tea house we're in. Do you know it's quite popular for all sorts of secret encounters? Celebrities from all around Tokyo come here and pay five thousand yen for the pleasure of discussing art and politics with its geishas. I can't deny the fact that the girls have the scent of chrysanthemums about them; they pour tea with the long-forgotten grace of the Fujiwara period, they will expertly arrange an ikebana or play their shamisens for you. It's considered classy — and you're supposed to derive a truly artistic pleasure from their company. And if one of these girls gives you goosebumps, you're free to offer her a sum of money large enough to make her forget the geishas' code of ethics and subject you to her more intimate attentions. Am I right? If I am, do me a favor and offer me an ounce of logic from the shop of your reasoning. You pay a woman for drinking her tea and listening to her playing music (which can be quite a painful experience, I assure you) and then some extra for the luxury of her love, provided you manage to impress her enough to talk her into it? Oh, the joys of an orgasm. In Europe, Marquis, you offer a girl fifty yen and she'll be more than willing to please you any way you want. It's primitive, I agree, but it works. And if you ask her for some shamisen playing or for a parlor game of *tora tora tora*, you'll have to pay extra as if it's some rare and perverse pleasure."

"If you'll excuse me, Your Excellency," the other voice offers with a hint of indignation, "there's no art in it!"

"Do me a favor. If you shell out fifty yen for a love-making session, at least you get exactly what you pay for. But if you offer five grand for a tea ceremony, you're obliged to derive some sort of perverted secret pleasure from her actions whether you like it or not. You might even write a poem praising the sexy grip of her little fingers on the teapot handle. You'll tell your friends about this incredible feeling of experiencing sakura blossoms touch the bottom of your heart as you gulp your tea. In other words, you'll be looking for any excuse to justify your ridiculous expense without feeling like a total idiot. That's the whole explanation of the geisha phenomenon for you..."

The voice paused. "So what was I talking about? Yes, to err is human. Every other agent I meet in here thinks his mistakes are his fault. So what does he do? He wants to follow the ancient honor code by ripping open his own belly. Had I agreed to every such request, this nice little tea house would have long turned into a butcher's shop and we'd have had no one left willing to work in the civil service. Which is why I'm asking you now: what would make you change your mind, Marquis?"

"Minister," the other man pauses to sip his tea. "It's been twenty years that I've been in charge of the Mikado's intelligence service... even though this last unforgivable failure is enough evidence of my ineptitude to occupy such a high post. If you'll excuse my being so blunt, what else do you expect me to do? My unforgivable error has caused the impending Apocalypse. I haven't slept for forty-eight hours. I know I should die."

"I assure you," there's a smile in the Minister's voice as he watches a geisha bow, "your wish may well come true in the next few days. Instead of beating yourself up, I dare you to do something crazy. Something that's always been lurking in the deep recesses of your mind but you were too scared of facing up to its dark challenge. Eat the heart of a sixteen-year-old virgin, or take a skinny dip in a public fountain, or just drink yourself blind on sake. Who would have the heart to blame you? Here in Tokyo, population doesn't panic which is excellent. We've always had this ability to hope for the best even if our world is being devoured by a ravenous demon. Having said that... what about the late, what's his name, Yamamura Onoda?"

The other man sighs. "Only a few finger fragments and a charred skull were located at the scene. A DNA analysis allowed us to identify them as belonging to Onoda. He was posthumously promoted to Colonel and awarded the Supreme Order of the Chrysanthemum. Still, his death weighs heavily on my conscience. This sole failure is enough to describe myself as a *hara-no-kuroi-hito*, a man with a black soul[30]. It's only through cutting my belly open that I can expose the entire extent of my remorse."

"I'm afraid, the only thing it would expose is your gut," the Minister's voice rings with a subtle smile. "You shouldn't get so upset about the late Colonel Onoda. Events of the last three days show that we're all about to die anyway. You, like many others, have been misinformed. Having studied the contamination's effects, I too tended to believe it would only affect the Third

---

30 *Hara-no-kuroi-hito*: "literally, "a man with a black stomach", a Japanese expression used to describe a despicable traitor. In Japan, a man's stomach is considered the vessel of his vital force; in this respect it's the equivalent of the European "heart". The idea behind the ritual of *seppuku* (or *hara-kiri*) is to expose one's stomach by slicing it open to show that it's pure with no black thoughts harbored inside.

Reich. Which was why I thought it imperative to eliminate Pavel Loktev. None of us thought at the time that if the contamination symptoms indeed only manifested themselves within the area of Moskau, we should have assisted him in his mission, not tried to stop him. Unfortunately, now both Loktev and the trigger agent have gone missing. And I have a funny feeling that there's nothing we can do to stop this catastrophe."

A china cup clinks softly. "Your Excellency, your usual insight colors my face crimson with shame. In these last three days, the contamination has been spreading faster than 'flu. I saw satellite images of Moskau. Aryan Street is gone, razed to the ground! Same has happened to half of Mein Kampf Avenue. The Eiffel Tower has vanished into thin air, and so has Tower Bridge in London. The Shogunet is seething with rumors that all this is the result of Schwarzkopf scientists testing their latest secret weapon. Still, the Schwarzkopfs seem to be just as confused as the Third Reich supporters. The Earth has begun to collapse, whole areas of the globe imploding. The ocean is riddled with vortexes sucking in entire islands. The day before yesterday, the contamination finally reached the Nippon koku, dissolving some wooden houses in Kyoto. And today..."

Calm shamisen music begins to sound as a geisha runs her expert fingers over the instrument. The Minister sighs. "Yes, I know. I made the mistake of turning the car radio on as I headed for our meeting. Mount Fuji, the ancient symbol of the Nippon koku, is gone too. The TV is playing for time, offering believable explanations such as scientific experiments or even testing new camouflage methods in case of a new war. That's the only reason the population isn't panicking yet. This is good news. Our dear Viking TV colleagues in Moskau, however, weren't as prudent. I won't badmouth my friends but their enemies might say that they spent too much time in contemplation without putting their brains in gear. At first Viking maintained a reserved silence as Moskau buildings began to disappear into thin air. And now they describe the contamination as a — imagine! — a mass hallucination triggered by abnormal weather conditions. Gestapo agents dress up in lab coats and impersonate bespectacled professors on television, befuddling the audience with scientific mumbo jumbo. In the meantime, the phantoms of wartime death camps materialize out of nowhere and ghostly gallows begin to rise in city squares. Did you hear that the Jewish mass graves of Babi Yar ravine near Kiev have opened up, revealing the pale faces of the dead? The Forest Brothers' recon battalions have already entered the outskirts of Moskau, Yekaterinodar and St. Petersburg — apparently, meeting no resistance. The Chinese mercenaries have fled. The Wehrmacht is demoralized; some of its barracks are already contaminated. The

Patriarch of the Forest Church has served a mass which was streamed by the Shogunet, praying to 'grant victory to the army of the righteous over the murderous enemy'. The Reichskommissariat Moskau lives on borrowed time."

The other man sets the tea cup onto the tray offered by a kneeling geisha. "Isn't that what we wanted, Minister? Even if the world survives by some miracle, my descendants will be doomed to lay face down in the dust before the Mikado's throne, begging to forgive their unworthy ancestor. Today's reports from the borders of the Nippon koku are like acid to my ears. The dematerialization of the commandant's office building in Uradziosutoku and the disappearance of the city's entire garrison have triggered unrest. Crowds of plunderers strip off their kimonos and, clad in crude embroidered Slavic shirts, go on the rampage, destroying rock gardens, burning Imperial flags and looting the city's cultural centers. The beautiful Amaterasu Temple on Bronze Mirror Street has been pillaged and is burning as we speak. The chopstick museum has been reduced to ashes. The crowd has razed the Geisha College to the ground, calling this excellent institution a whore factory! I didn't tell any of this to my revered father — who's spent fifty years in honorable service under the Mikado's banners — for fear of seeing him reduced to tears. So is this the Russlanders' gratitude for everything we've done for them?

After the Mikado, in his eternal grace, was kind enough to grant them citizenship status allowing them to take Japanese names and worship Amaterasu — is this what they're giving us back?"

"I understand your indignation, Marquis," the Minister's voice is filled with the benign smile he casts at the bowing geisha. "But you really shouldn't pay so much heed to all this nonsense. Here's my advice to you: let go of your inhibitions. Set your instincts free and storm your way into the jungle of desire, roaring like a tiger. What a shame I'm eighty-four, otherwise I too would have indulged in a tireless orgy with this house's entire staff. Unfortunately, all I can do is hold this tea cup and wait for the contamination to crumble this world into dust and scatter its gray ashes, mine included. What difference does it make whether we were right or not? It's irrelevant. So let's live these few days the way we've always wanted to."

"Well said, Your Excellency," the other's voice rings with hidden anticipation.

"Would you like some more tea, Marquis?"

"Yes, please. It tastes especially good when you know your moments in this world are already numbered."

CHAPTER TWO

The Occupation

GRÜNBURG

A SATELLITE TOWN IN THE VICINITY OF MOSKAU

I'M BEGINNING TO GET A TASTE of my new life. My fake American passport — courtesy of Doc — is of the highest quality, stashed under a shirt with a loud print known as an "explosion in a pigeon house". I haven't looked inside yet. I have this funny aversion to seeing my own passport pictures — like most people, I suppose. A false Blood ID is sitting in the back pocket of my stovepipe pants. A wig and a pair of shades complete the look of a crazy Californian tourist.

I probably look quite a sight. Sometimes I wonder what I actually look like. I never seem to be able to remember my own face. It must be some kind of condition I have.

We arrived in Moskau on an LA flight. The passport check went without a glitch. We left the airport in a taxi. Apparently, the Gestapo had their hands full without us. The city of Moskau is an unrecognizable wreck. The streets are mangled in places, half-dissolved into nothing like rock salt in soup. I can't believe how fast the contamination is progressing. You could walk past a building and when you go back an hour later, it's already gone! Well, almost: you can still make out the barely visible outlines of its phantom walls.

It's as if someone has flown in on a magic carpet and dropped an enchanted bomb on the city. The Kremlin is reduced to two remaining towers. The Wewelsburg Castle, however, is still in one piece: even Goddess Hel herself might not be strong enough to tackle that monstrosity.

On our way from the airport, Olga contacted some of her Schwarzkopf friends (who were apparently overjoyed to hear of her return from the dead). They took us to their Grünburg safe house on the outskirts of Moskau.

Naturally, Olga knew better than to tell them I was Odin's priest and an SS Standartenführer to boot. That could have complicated matters unnecessarily in all sorts of petty little ways, creating useless squabbles and a smattering of dead bodies in our wake. So she wisely recommended me to them as a Thule

Society Archmage, thus putting their minds at rest: who in their right mind would be afraid of a government-hired fortune teller?

Their “safe house” isn’t much to write home about: a minimalist Speer-style studio with a kitchenette just big enough to cook a canary. The bathroom is a capsule-style affair where the toilet bowl is fitted inside the bathtub. We’re staying there only until next morning, anyway. The Moskau Resistance made an arrangement with the Forest Brothers to give our car safe passage: all main roads out of Moskau are controlled by their guerrilla groups.

Moskau is under military curfew. All ceremonial Wehrmacht garrisons have been rushed from Greater Germany to Russland. At Prussian Station earlier that morning, I saw a truckful of sullen German soldiers wearing helmets and field-gray uniforms. Good decision on the Triumvirate’s part. You can never rely on the Russlander Wehrmacht forces. Now Germans, they’ll stand to the last even in the face of a global disaster.

Olga has got her wish, then. The unfolding situation can safely be called a new occupation. I can see the fear and resentment in the eyes of old people who still remember the Führer’s victorious entrance into Moskau back in 1941. And now when you’d think everything has long been forgotten, the field-gray uniforms flood the streets again, filling the air with the rattling of weapons and the guttural sounds of their barking language.

Younger-generation Moskauers don't seem to care much, though. They walk the streets zombie-like, their smiles frozen, their eyes glazed over. Mechanically they keep going to work without really being sure their office will still be there when they come back from lunch break.

You can't flee the city. Concrete barbed-wire checkpoints have risen overnight, blocking all of Moskau's access roads. Checkpoint guards turn everyone back. It doesn't apply to us: Doc's paperwork opens a secret passage unavailable to anybody else.

The city is rife with rumors about a new secret weapon, an upcoming change of power and the impending street fighting. You can't scare a Moskauer with anarchy. In the turbulent days of the Twenty-Year War, the city's inhabitants grew too used to constant changes of power. One day Moskau would be governed by a tank battalion commander promptly replaced by an SS Oberführer who'd be ousted by a Labor Front leader: a bespectacled nerd in a business suit.

The townspeople seem to be too immersed in virtual reality. Those of the Schwarzkopfs Olga spoke to, mentioned that when their militia groups entered towns, local population seemed to be unable to peel themselves away from the TV screens.

Actually, I too tend to watch the TV

whenever obligatory transmissions are on. What else is there to do? I stare at scientists offering explanations for abnormal weather conditions, rod-backed generals alluding to their troops' loyalty to the Triumvirate, famous actors and authors engaging in unhurried haughty discussions about the regime's invincibility and the consequent dangers of rocking the boat. For some reason, I envision their audiences filling dark theaters where they sit in the screen's faint glow, shoulder to shoulder, jaws clenched, nodding at every new statement they hear. You don't think so?

The Triumvirate maintains its silence.

This isn't the kind of reaction I expected. I used to think that people would make a beeline for the temples *en masse*. In such moments of uncertainty and civil unrest, religion becomes a straw to clutch: a hope for a higher force that will decide everything for you, turning the circumstances to your benefit and advantage.

Nothing of the kind. Odin's temples are empty while shopping malls are packed with people, restaurants are booked solid and gold dealers have sold out in the first twenty-four hours of unrest. Little wonder: if Bolsheviks enter Moskau, the first thing they'll do is abolish private property, replace Reichsmarks with rubles and introduce ration books. If you can't escape hell, at least you can try and buy it up.

The Shogunet is still up but bound to be

taken down soon under the pretext of maintenance. Or whatever.

The car drive takes me down Aryan Street. There's nothing left of my temple, apart from a single scruffy fir tree. You can't seriously call it ruins. The temple has vanished into nothing.

On every street corner, freshly-installed loudspeakers bark their messages,

"People of Moskau! We urge you to stay calm! The situation is under control! It's nothing serious!"

The speaker's German-accented voice is a clever idea. Here, Germans have the reputation of being overzealous control freaks. They won't allow the situation to careen out of control. That's why the city is wallowing in sleepy nonchalance. Television and the field-gray uniforms: a perfect formula. The Triumvirate knows what it's doing. Shogunet forums are plastered with pictures from other parts of the Reich. Strangely enough, they too show little reaction to the events. Buildings keep disappearing, phantoms of gallows loom up through the air — and nobody's saying anything! As some Dresden online user said, "What's the point in panicking? Beer hasn't evaporated yet!"

The only area showing some anxiety is the Reichskommissariat of Ukraine. Their Triumvirate has announced the anomalies the result of "the Moskau Gestapo and their tricks". Mind you, that's their favorite excuse for whatever happens.

I'm really not happy that I've been instrumental in causing the end of the world. I've contributed to it; without me, it wouldn't have worked. I feel like some sort of Victor von Frankenstein breathing life into a monster only to watch it devour our planet, grinning, while I languish in frustration, unable to stop him.

The Schwarzkopfs seem to have problems, too. From what I've managed to glean from snippets of their conversations, whole guerrilla camps disappear complete with hundreds of fighters. In their place, ghostly mass graves appear out of thin air. The Schwarzkopfs don't like it! Nobody wants to know the truth about themselves.

In these last couple of days, we've had dozens of visits from all sorts of dissidents: from Shogunet nerds to Wehrmacht officers and from spoiled nutcase bitches — the type I can't stand anyway — to school teachers unhappy with their wages. It's amazing how the Schwarzkopfs have managed to permeate the Reich's entire system, like termites permeate an old house.

Olga is up to her eyeballs in Resistance affairs. She seems to have forgotten all about me. Her time has come. She's a heroine, the uprising's living banner: the epitome of Delacroix's *Liberty Leading the People* if you remember the painting. She just told me she had to check her email (she's been away from the

Shogunet for a good couple of months), opened her Buch and planted herself in the kitchen. It's night already but she's not done yet. Shogunet addiction, is that what they call it?

We still share the bed, by the way. It's becoming a tradition.

OLGA ENTERS THE ROOM just as the mandatory TV kicks in. She seems out of sorts. She's pale as a sheet, her lips pursed, her eyes dead and irresponsive. She slaps blindly around the coffee table for a pack of bootleg Japanese cigarettes. Apparently, Comrades Schwarzkopfs are in some serious shit.

I'm just about to offer a sarcastic comment about her freedom of choosing her own death — radiation or lung cancer — but she beats me to it,

"Fancy a coffee? We need to talk."

Oh, no. What's that now? A coffee. She must be really desperate to get on my good side. Before, she wouldn't touch the stuff with a barge pole. All good Schwarzkopfs only drink tea, dismissing coffee as "Kraut brew".

"Absolutely," I lean back on the couch. "With a splash of cream, please."

She goes back into the kitchen and soon returns with a trayful of Japanese china cups, a coffee pot, some biscuits and sugar lumps in a bowl. Like an exemplary Reich's housewife. Aww... the coffee smells awesome.

"I'm all ears," the coffee cup burns my fingers. "What is it?"

She falters. The sugar bowl shakes in her hands. I take a sip of my coffee, enjoying the taste.

"It's about... the Reichskommissars."

I take another sip and heave a sigh. Meeting her brothers in arms has pulled the girl back into the boundless sea of Revolution. Now she'll say that the denunciation of the Nazi regime obliges me to take their side. Very well, I'm ready to stand my ground no matter how much it's gonna hurt. Unlike Olga's interactions with the rest of the world which normally result in its disappearance, her effect on me produces the mother of all splitting headaches.

I open my mouth to speak — and can't.

Her face blurs. It turns cotton-wool white... or cloud-white, rather. Uncomprehending, I reach out to her, consumed by a swirl of snowflakes.

I choke on the white, drowning. I-

OLGA SPENT A FEW MORE MINUTES, finishing her cigarette and watching the sleeping priest. The sedative was indeed good. It had worked instantly, just as she'd been told.

She walked back into the kitchen. She washed the cups mechanically while thinking her own thoughts.

The phone rang an hour later just as she began to think their plan had failed.

“How did you do it?” a dry voice inquired in the receiver.

“Does it really matter?” she said wearily. “I need to see you. It’s that what you want, isn’t it? I have something that might surprise you. Really surprise you. And I suggest you refrain from calling your Gestapo friends. Trust me. You know what I’m capable of, don’t you?”

The voice sighed in the affirmative. “Right. What’s the best place we can meet?”

“I’ll grab a taxi and come to your place. Just tell me how to find it.”

She jotted the address down on a scrap of paper and switched off her phone.

At the other end of Moskau, Pavel Loktev did the same.

Vision Four

The White Haze

I CAN SEE FUCK ALL. The whirling storm is thick as a brick wall. You can’t even punch through it. No idea what I’m supposed to do here. Where can I go? Why is everything so white?

I can barely breathe. I struggle to gulp some air but there’s just not enough of it. I’m floating inside a weird world made of a viscous white substance which envelops me, soft and hugging. I feel like the proverbial frog that fell in the bucket of cream: I want to kick and struggle until it turns into butter.

The white mass pours down my lungs; I swallow it as it forces its way down my throat, filling my mouth. Still, I'm alive. It doesn't kill me. I keep floundering in it, looking around me.

How am I supposed to react? Where do I move to?

For want of a better solution, I try to struggle my way forward. The mass is devoid of any taste or odor. It's something sterile. Other smells abound though: they're strong, some bitter, others sweet. I seem to be surrounded by the tiniest specks of light. Like lightbugs they float around me as I push my way toward them, trying to work out what they are. The longer I walk, the farther away they seem. I'm exhausted.

A soft clinking sound approaches, a light *clink clank* of a wind charm.

Clink clank. Clinkety-clink. The white mass enveloping me seems to be alive. It's some sort of biological substance, like a sea of sentient plankton that somehow sucked me in. Now it bubbles and hums as if trying to talk to me. I can't make out the words though. My goal is to keep moving forward defeating this viscous goo until I get to the glowing little lights.

I soldier on, stubborn like a snowmobile plowing through a snowstorm, even though every next step is harder than the one before it. I set one foot down and pull the other one toward it, gasping with the effort.

A sharp pain pierces my left hand — *the* hand! Blood begins to seep from the palm, forming fancy spiral patterns in the creamlike environment, then dissolves in dancing motions. The clinkety-clanking. The humming in my ears. Wait a sec. How on earth have I ended up here?

According to Olga, her world occasionally sucks me in.

Still, this is different. Normally, I can see everything that happens in her world. I see it through her eyes, I can hear and feel it. And this is something *foreign.* Her world may be different from ours in the sheer scope of its military disaster but it's similar to us in many other ways, with similar people, weapons and methods. And this looks like a different planet entirely.

What's especially scary is that this thick goo is sentient. It governs this world; it knows right from wrong, it metes out punishment and acquittal, it can grant life or take it.

I can't move anymore. I give up. I stand with my arms sprawled, surrendering to the substance's judgment. It creeps into my nose and mouth, still tasteless. The clinking sound grows stronger, not so cute anymore. It begins to hurt my ears.

Olga could never understand why she only ever got transported between our two parallel realities while there must be hundreds more. I seem to have found the answer. She probably gets sucked into other worlds as well, only she doesn't remember it. Alternatively, she might believe it to be a dream. I can't blame her. Imagine me telling someone I was transported to a world ruled by sentient cream!

My mind fades. I try to remember what I was about to think of — but I can't. My brain is being brought under control, slowly occupied by an unrelenting exterior force. The white space thickens. I can't see the little lights anymore: nothing, not a glimpse. Only the screaming, ear-shattering wail filled with either fear or agony, I can't tell which.

A screeching noise rips the air right over my ear. I'm too weak to even turn my head. I close my eyes; I can't see anything anyway. Whether I like it or not, I've lost my battle against the substance. It controls me.

Great Gods of Asgard, why can't you cut my hand for me?

CHAPTER THREE

The Carnival of Phantoms

HEINKEL STREET
IN THE NORTH OF MOSKAU

THE TWO STAYED SILENT for a long time. He was mulling over what he'd just heard, replaying the voices in his head while suppressing the desire to go back to the computer and double-check. She was on her tenth cigarette, drawing deeply as she studied his profile. Now she knew everything about him. He, however, knew nothing about her.

Half an hour later, she tentatively broke the silence. "I take it you knew each other?"

"We did," Pavel replied in a stiff monotone. "He was my friend. We knew each other since childhood. We were at Lebensborn together. He died three days ago. As I was told in the Office, he was shot by a Schwarzkopf terrorist using a Mosin rifle. The assassin used armor-piercing bullets. I saw my friend's body in the Gestapo morgue."

"So you see," Olga said, impassive. "Proves I was right then, does it? What more do you need? You should be able to understand now who killed him. And most importantly, why."

Pavel nodded, silent. He had nothing to say to that. Soon after his phone call, Olga had brought him the encrypted file with Jean-Pierre's research. She'd discovered it in her old inbox while checking the emails.

Actually, that had been a clever move on Jean-Pierre's part. He'd uploaded the data where no one would have thought of looking for it. Olga's old inbox had long been hacked by the Gestapo. Why would they bother keeping tabs on an already-compromised address they'd checked a million times? Olga would never risk using it again, would she? Wouldn't she just create a new email address, rightfully believing they must have changed the access code or bugged the inbox with an IP tracker capable of detecting her current location?

Wrong, wrong and wrong. A highly intelligent woman makes few mistakes. But when she does... So yes, she had unthinkingly opened her old inbox. Or should he say Pandora's box?

Decrypting the file hadn't been a problem

with a little help from Schwarzkopf Gestapo moles. If you think about it, planning doesn't really work in this world. It's ruled by chance. If you took Klara, the Great Führer's Blessed Mother, all her newborn children had died in rapid succession one after the other. But the one destined to suck the blood of millions, he'd been the one who'd survived. Crazy. As if by some voodoo magic.

Enough to knock the guy off his trolley.

By using some simple voice recognition freeware, Jean-Pierre had stumbled across something truly incredible. He'd run the Triumvirate leaders' voices through the program until he had 100% matches. His discovery had rendered him speechless. The Triumvirate leaders spoke to their visitors in the meticulously re-engineered voices of long dead 1940s German movie stars: the likes of Marika Rökk, Lil Dagover and Anny Ondra.

Now that definitely was overkill. As Jean-Pierre had suspected from the start, this had nothing to do with the leaders' anonymity. No hardened paranoiac could be that deluded.

It had to be something else.

Jean-Pierre had located the online memoirs of those who'd met the Triumvirate leaders in Wewelsburg's bunkers. Equally ecstatic, they all had something else in common. Each Wewelsburg visitor remembered something that struck a familiar chord. Some voices were male, velvety and laidback, others female, sweet and melodious. The male voices too belonged to the 1940s film stars, the likes of Werner Krauss. The speaker addressed his or her visitors through a voice synthesizer, adding the lilt of long-dead sex symbols to the script.

His findings allowed Jean-Pierre to conclude,

No amount of Resistance agents and Schwarzkopf moles, not even the current martial law would have justified such complex multi-level security. Even the most cautious and paranoid dictators of their time, the likes of Stalin and Mussolini whose lives had been under daily threat from thousands of enemies, had never done anything like this. Yes, they'd been protected by a human shield of bodyguards; yes, they'd traveled in corteges of identical cars and had special food testers to make sure no one had messed with their meals. But if you summed it all up — the absolute anonymity, the blindfolds, the visual non-exposure, the synthesized voices — it all suggested one possible answer. You only did things like that when you had to conceal from the population that *there was no Triumvirate.*

Had probably never been. Who needed it, anyway? If the boss fails to show up at the office, it doesn't mean his staff will do the same. They'll keep pushing pencils and stare at computer screens — at least as long as they're getting paid. That's the way these things are done. They really couldn't care less about what happened to their boss. As far as they're concerned, he might be on sick leave or a business trip, unless he's gone off on an Alpine holiday. No one really gives a shit.

Now, what works for one office should theoretically work for an entire country. What a brilliant idea: the Reich, ruled by a bunch of non-existent dictators who are however perfectly real as long as the population believes they exist. A veritable carnival of phantoms: the Wehrmacht, the Gestapo, the Reichstag, all the Ober Kommandaturs and the Labor Front still working, convinced they're being run by someone else. By whom? — doesn't matter, really, as long as they exist, those mysterious righteous rulers.

What now, then? The Triumvirate was but a sterile imitation, a dummy to keep the population happy, a fake movie-like version of a non-existent regime. All this was so fucking sick. It was true that Pavel used to sneer at the system; both he and Jean-Pierre had made fun of the Triumvirate, but still they'd *served* it, honestly and loyally.

Served what, a bunch of ghostly fakes?

The main question remained, whose idea had it been?

Who was the puppeteer lurking in the wings and pulling the strings? Jean-Pierre had found the answer to this one too. He'd saved it on a separate file but Pavel hadn't gotten to it yet. He was trying to digest the news, oblivious of his surroundings.

"Did you do expose yourself on purpose?" he asked Olga.

She nodded. "I did. I knew you practiced Tummo meditation. So I opened my mind to you. I kept repeating the phone number, digit after digit, hoping you'd hear me. I wasn't sure though. But now it's over. I've won our little joust. The priest is mine. I'm afraid you've lost. You probably realize it yourself."

Pavel's mouth twitched. "You're right. I can see what's happening. I don't think I can change anything even if I take him away from you. Too late. The world seems to be ending. I've spent my whole life working on the system and now it turns out it didn't even exist? You can't imagine how pissed off I am. I knew my bosses were scumbags... but I had no idea they were a figment of my imagination."

Gracefully Olga alighted from her chair. She had nothing left to do here. She'd squashed her arch enemy and sucked him dry, leaving him weak and impotent. His life force was hers now.

"I need to go," she said, avoiding his eyes. "You know both you and your world are dying, don't you? I suggest you do the right thing for a change. Not for money. Not for the regime. Just make your own choice, provided they haven't fucked you up completely in Lebensborn. The fact that you've been lied to is irrelevant. It's up to you to decide whether you're a man or a waste of space."

She stubbed out her cigarette and turned to the door. Pavel's lifeless stare focused on her. He was biting his lips. His hands shook. He didn't look superhuman at all now.

"Before you go... tell me... who the hell are you?"

She brought her lips to his ear. When she stood back up, Pavel's hair was gray.

She curved her mouth in a grin. How funny. A young man, his head gray and shaky with old age. And she was the one who'd done it.

"I should have guessed," Pavel whispered. "The moment Jean-Pierre sent me the DNA results. He couldn't work out where you were from. But this explains everything. After our researchers died in the Novgorod incident... The mind boggles. I might just think I've gone mad. Okay? Much easier this way."

She shrugged. "Be my guest. Sorry about your hair. You can always change it, anyway, when you grow yourself a new face."

Pavel didn't try to stop her. The door slammed shut.

An hour later he opened the last file. He spent some time staring at the words and numbers. Reluctantly he rose and reached for the desk drawer.

He took out both his Browning handguns: generous 13-rounders. After some thought, he added two extra magazines, then tilted his head to one side, staring curiously at the remaining thermal grenade at the bottom of the drawer.

He already knew what he was going to do.

CHAPTER FOUR

The Semitic Hamster's Wheel

MEISTERSINGER FOREST

THE NEXT MORNING

I PRIZE OPEN MY UNYIELDING EYELIDS, seemingly stuck together with Henkel super glue. I can't see anything. A layer of murky white substance clings to my skin. Demons of Helheim, am I still here?

I grab at my face. I'm blindfolded. I pull the fabric off... glory be to Asgard! I'm home!

A woman laughs.

"I'm sorry!" Olga manages through her laughter, tightening her grip on the steering wheel. "I took the liberty of tying a towel over your face to protect it from the sun. It's so hot today, you can't imagine."

Her black hair flaps in the breeze like a pirate flag. I look around me. We're speeding along an *autobahn* in an old brown Horch cabriolet, the forgotten child of the German car industry. The Horch rattles its parts, spews clouds of black smoke but soldiers on.

I yawn. My joints crack as I stretch. "I really hope it's gonna end soon. I'm fed up with going in and out of your world like a yo-yo."

She keeps her eyes on the road, ignoring both mine and the car's complaints. "I hope so too. I frankly can't wait."

I don't get the chance to ask her what she means by this. Olga slows up as we approach a pile of concrete blocks: a makeshift security checkpoint. A scrap of red fabric flies over the barricade. It actually looks like part of the flag of the Reichskommissariat Moskau with the eagle cut out (or ripped out?) of it.

I can see the outlines of armed people in civilian clothes. All of them sport conspicuous red ribbons they wear either on their breast pockets or on their faded Wehrmach caps.

They're Schwarzkopfs.

It's the first time I see guerrilla fighters so close. There're about six or seven of them, each armed with either a Mauser rifle or a Sturmgewehr. The gunner behind the barricade swings his MG 42 machine gun, training its sights on us. The gun's blunt snout points at my forehead.

Olga brakes smoothly. One of the fighters walks leisurely toward the car, his hand resting on his gun. He's a young guy with a gorgeous raven-black head of hair and a beard that covers most of his face, leaving only his eyes exposed.

Olga offers him her *ausweis*. He lowers his head, reading it. The roots of his hair are strawberry-white.

How funny. The kid is actually blond. Still, he'd rather dye it black just to show his protest against the regime. They and their ideology!

"Comrade Sélina?" the disguised blond asks.

She smiles. "That's me. You should have received word of our arrival. I have a free pass to Novgorod. Did the Committee for People's Liberation contact you? Our clearance mandate was signed by Father Eleutherius of the Forest Church himself."

"Yes, yes, of course," the blond wakes up. "They emailed us yesterday."

He produces a shiny e-funk phone (definitely a trophy he's taken off a captured officer) and switches it on. The letter's icon lights up: a crucifix entwined with a hammer and sickle.

"We are to offer you our full cooperation," the bearded youth remarks deferentially. "Can you wait ten minutes? We'll contact the other checkpoints and tell them to flag you through. Fancy a cup of tea? We've just made some."

Tea! Yeah right. No hope of *them* drinking coffee.

In all the cities they take, guerrillas burn coffee stocks first thing. As if something's gonna change from the sheer fact that they will now drink a proper cuppa and not the hated "Kraut brew". Then again, Russlanders have always preferred destroying to actually rebuilding. They'd demolish the old, but instead of building something new in its place they'll just sit down for a smoke at the demolished site. True, I couldn't call myself a regime supporter anymore but just seeing Schwarzkopfs filled my heart with apprehension. These people have spent the last seventy years in the woods, fighting. They can't do much else. How are they going to run Moskau?

They take us to an impromptu guardhouse next to the barricade. It must have been a local café once. The Führer's portrait lies broken on the floor. The Schwarzkopfs walk right over it in their muddy boots, trying to step on his mustache. I don't feel sorry for him at all.

The blond picks up a filthy teapot from the table and pours tea into glass mugs. Two more fighters sit at the table. One is an old man wearing a tattered shirt and a pair of pants probably as ancient as himself. The other is young, in a smart black business suit and holding the latest computer tablet. Oh, well. These guys are so cartoonishly defiant of all things German but still they can't resist Japanese technology.

I have a funny feeling they won't be in a hurry to fight the Japs.

I take a gulp of tea. It's hot and bitterly tart with none of coffee's aroma at all. How can anyone drink this?

"How are things in Moskau, Comrade?" the young one asks me. "Are they expecting us?"

I'm dying to tell him who his comrades are and where he can shove them. Still, I can't afford to expose myself: even Olga won't be able to save me then.

She stares at me anxiously with a light squeeze of my hand as if signaling, *please don't.*

I'm not going to. Not on this empty road in the thick of Meistersinger Forest with only trees, birds and armed guerrillas for company. If anything happened to me here, no one will ever find whatever's left of me.

"Well, what can I say... *Comrade,*" I take vindictive pleasure in stressing the word ever so slightly. "Some are, others aren't. Most really don't give a shit. They watch their TVs and go shopping, that's the extent of it. Moskauers, what do you want? That's the way they are now. They couldn't care less about who's in power."

The young guy glares at me as he sullenly sips his tea. "That's exactly how the Nazis wanted them to be," he grumbles. "Their goal was to distract people and zombify them. You wait till we get Moskau back, Comrade! All the shopping malls will be abolished as detrimental influence. It's so much better to distribute limited amounts of goods to everyone. Say, a pair of pants per person. Otherwise it's not fair, is it? Some motherfucker might stash away ten good suits for his own consumption while another guy has to walk around naked! The owners of these shopping malls, we're gonna sort them all out. They shouldn't have brainwashed good people, should they? Offering them all those duds to wear! They'll be among the first to be court-martialed."

"Who else, then?" I ask, curious.

"All them fucking collaborators," the old boy joins the conversation, ancient pants and all. "Still, offering them fair trial is too good for them, heh. Just line them all up, one bullet to the head each, end of story."

I'd dearly love to wrap his teapot around his head. Still, I can't.

"You know many who didn't collaborate?" I ask him. "You just couldn't afford not to. Take tram conductors – they're all subalterns in Keselring's conductor regiment. Are they war criminals too? A regular janitor who works at the Department of Cleanliness – is he a Triumvirate's champion? And how about a candy maker from the Pastry Cooks Union – does he deserve a bullet or will ten years' hard labor do? If you think like that, guys, I'm afraid you'll have to put all of

Moskau up against the wall."

Olga keeps digging her nails into my hand but my brakes are off already.

"Why not?" the old boy says, oblivious of my sarcasm. "They deserve it. We've been fighting the enemy since childhood in these here woods while those motherfuckers lounged about in their hot tubs drinking their pagan coffees! Let them go and work at building sites now! Let them atone for their crimes with hard labor! They should have known better than to whore for the Krauts!"

This I don't even doubt. What a wonderful bunch of understanding and highly tolerant people. "But how about your *comrades* from the St Michael the Archangel troops? What are you going to do about those walking pro-tsarist anachronisms? They support the monarchy, they advocate capitalism – I don't think they'll be all that against shopping malls, brothels and work camps! They can always use cheap labor to tend their summer gardens for them. What if they disagree with your decisions? I'm pretty sure they have their own agendas."

The kettle boils again, spouting a cloud of vapor.

"Let us sort them out," the blond guy says. "They've been fighting Krauts too, no doubt about it. Still, they have these wrong ideas about the world. If they raise their objections, I'm afraid we'll have some explaining to do. And if it comes to that, we're more numerous and our weapons are better."

Olga sits there white as a sheet. Deep in my heart, I celebrate. It's one thing to hurl a grenade at the Oberkommandant and quite another to meet all these forest people who actually make the revolution happen. First the members of this mad tea party will hang everyone who's ever offered a helping hand to the regime (which were bound to be numerous if selling an ice-cream to an SS officer qualified you as a collaborator), after which they'll start mopping up their own ranks. This is bound to end in another Twenty-Year War as their victories will trigger yet another race for power just like the Wehrmacht's triumphs did.

Why oh why is Russland always in the same shit? Every hundred years or so starts all over again! Here, the wheel of history is more like some manic hamster's wheel.

Without waiting for me to answer, the blond pulls out his e-funk and walks out.

A heavy-set man walks over to our table, breaking the lingering silence. I look up. Oh.

He's wearing the cassock of a Forest Church priest.

"Are you enjoying your tea, brothers and sisters?" he asks, gasping from all his extra weight. "My blessing be with you. May the Lord grant us strength to defeat those German pagans."

Olga's inconspicuous squeeze very nearly breaks every finger in my hand. Oh no, fuck it. You wait.

"Did you say German, holy father?" I ask, staring pensively at the ceiling. "You know very well there're virtually no Germans left in the barracks. You'll have to fight your own, I'm afraid. What was Christ rumored to have said about not killing thy neighbor? From what I heard, no one had ever seen him blessing any armies to storm cities. You sure you're serving the right god? Never tried on a green turban, by any chance? It sounds like the Prophet Muhammad would suit you more."

The priest gasps soundlessly like a fish out of water.

Cussing under her breath, Olga pulls me out of the café. "Are you nuts?" she hisses. "You wanna see your brains smashed against the wall?"

We've almost reached our car when the bearded Schwarzkopf appears from behind the concrete blocks, heading straight for us. I slide my hand into my pocket and close my fingers around the Parabellum.

"It's all right," the fighter grins. "Here's your pass," he offers us a scrap of red paper. "Stick it in your windscreen and all the other checkpoints will flag you through. No worry. Something else?"

Olga takes — no, rather snatches — the paper from him and climbs back into the car without saying goodbye. I make myself comfortable next to her and flash a demonic grin at this motley Schwarzkopf crew.

An hour later, Olga finally slows down. All this time she's been speeding as if the Führer himself had risen from the dead and was after her.

She bites her lip, her eyes like two daggers.

"I'm sorry," I say meekly. "Couldn't keep my tongue in check."

She nods, demonstratively disappointed in my foul behavior.

We drive past a road sign that reads in Gothic lettering, *Novgorod, 140 km.*

I have a funny premonition. The closer we get, the harder it is to breathe.

Reichskommissariat Archives #3

File F299. Musicians

...AS THE VICTORIOUS WEHRMACHT TROOPS continued their liberation of Europe, the Ministry of Propaganda and Public Education completed their examination of literature and turned their attention to the reform of another highly important area: popular music.

Already in 1949, eager to meet the population's expectations, the Ministry banned jazz as "a product of an inferior race", removing all jazz records from distribution. The Untermensch musicians Louis Armstrong and Leonid Utyosov[31] were sentenced by the People's Tribunal chaired by Roland Freisler and deported to Africa.

In 1959, a new decree obliged musicians to record all new songs in German alone, aiming to increase the role of Greater Germany in the new society.

Unfortunately, not all the artists appreciated the importance of this measure. The French singer Edith Piaf refused to sing in Hochdeutsch and committed suicide by poisoning herself.

The Glenn Miller Orchestra was disbanded while Miller himself escaped to Nevada where he was forced to play bars for food.

Still, forbidden waters are sweet. Very soon, underground jazz bands were mushrooming everywhere (don't we all know the tendency of forbidden things to turn trendy overnight).

That included the Beatles: a British band singing in their local language. Bootleg copies of the band's records became widely popular all over the world while the group itself lived in hiding in

---

[31] Leonid Utyosov — the stage name of a leading Russian Jewish jazz singer and band leader Lazar Weissbein (1895-1982) who stood at the origins of Russian jazz and popular music.

their fans' houses, constantly moving town. Finally in 1971, the band members were arrested in Manchester by a special Gestapo unit.

The band's founders John Lennon and Paul McCartney were sentenced to ten years in work camps while George Harrison and Ringo Starr got away with a televised act of public repentance.

In 1964, another widely publicized scandal involved the sentencing of a certain Elvis Presley who, as the prosecution insisted, "sang in a Negro's voice". Having served his one-year sentence, the singer mended his ways by recording the song Alles in ordnung, Vater dedicated to the "Great Father" Alois Schicklgruber.

The Ministry of Public Education spared no effort in popularizing classical music. All primary school students were obliged to spend three hours a week listening to the creations of Richard Wagner who used to be the Führer's favorite composer. Symphonic orchestras competed to perform his masterpieces while pop groups offered various adaptations of his works.

Russland, however, was destined to go one step further and invent its own musical style.

Its Triumvirate issued the famous Decree #22 of May 15 2005, forbidding anyone to write their own lyrics. A week later, the Reich's Minister of Public Education sanctioned the following state-approved lyrics,

I very much love you,
You also love me,
That is so beautiful,
It is our love.
If you will leave me
I still shall love you,
I pine without you.
Flowers too pine without you
Love is very special
That is cool, that is delicious.
Love burns a fire inside me,
My adorable Fräulein.

Soon after the performances of the poem began, the Schwarzkopfs started a rumor that it had been authored by the five-year-old retarded grandson of the Minister of Public Education. The Ministry denied the rumor on the grounds that all mentally incapacitated persons were to be deported to Africa. In the following years, all musicians in the Reichskommissariats of both Moskau and Ukraine performed these lyrics with slight alterations. Their audiences didn't seem to mind, apparently not realizing that the lyrics remained the same, seeing as the music and the performers' appearance were equally identical. Pop music stages were filled with young people of both genders virtually indistinguishable from each other who dressed in the same way and sang in very similar voices. Such depersonalization was necessary if we didn't want our youth to be attracted to false idols.

Those who tried to write their own songs automatically fell under the Involvement in Illegal Musical Activities Act which was punished by three months incarceration and up to five years in labor camps. The profession of lyricists had become obsolete.

All and any elements of the Semitic and Roma cultures had been banned.

Previously, Roma performances had been highly popular in Russland, especially as wedding music. Which was why the Gestapo was forced to start raiding wedding parties in search of clandestinely played Gypsy music. As for actual Russlandish folklore performed by groups of cheerful babushkas, it was gradually replaced by yodeling Alpine singers and march-playing military bands.

The audience accepted the new entertainment choices rather easily, soon forgetting the likes of Armstrong and Edith Piaf. For most of them, simpler was indeed better. I'm pleased to inform you that the music reform has been successful.

(From the report made by Brigadier Klaus Meine of the Music Broadcasting Service at the request of the Ministry of Propaganda and Public Education analytic group)

CHAPTER FIVE

Lili Marlene

VIKING TV

THE MAIN BROADCASTING CENTER

WITHOUT TAKING EYES FROM his visitor, the TV Direktor pressed a button on his desk.

The man wore a Wehrmacht Major's uniform. He looked typically German with blond hair, thin nose and jug ears.

The automatic lock clicked, securing the door. Oh well. If the TV security Phoenix Sonderkommando leader had arrived at his office unannounced, it meant nothing good.

Unsmiling and impassive, the German studied the office: the brown paint of its walls, the fawn-colored chairs for visitors, the remote control on the desk and even the fruit bowl on a separate stand.

They still consider themselves a master race. What a stupidly arrogant, colonialist behavior. Unfortunately, we can't manage without their help.

The TV Direktor beamed. "What can I do for you? Would you like a-" he promptly shut up, staring at a Browning gun pointed at his forehead.

"To prevent any unnecessary questions, my name won't tell you anything," Pavel said calmly. "I'm a Gestapo agent and yes, I can promptly change my appearance. It's a long story. I saw your security chief from a distance as he exited the building. That was enough for me. He's just left for Wewelsburg which is why I took the liberty of coming to see you here. Your TV workers seem to really trust Germans. They didn't even think of asking for my electronic pass."

The Herr Direktor ground his teeth. His service gun was hidden under the desk. If he leaned forward ever so slightly... but no. This flabby, ageing man in a brown suit that matched his office walls was clearly not willing to play the hero.

"You must be a Schwarzkopf," he ran a nervous hand over his balding temples.

Pavel raised his eyebrows, then laughed wholeheartedly. The barrel of the gun shifted slightly lower. "Please. I'm not even affiliated to them. I hate them just as much as you do. The reason I've come to see you is completely different. An old friend of mine who's now partaking of Valhalla's festive viands committed the indiscretion of having conducted some highly interesting research. His involved computer experiments led him to an epiphany of sorts. Apparently, the Triumvirate members don't use their own voices when speaking in public. They do so using the voices of long dead movie stars. Understandably stricken by what he'd found, he submitted a classified inquiry in order to locate the person responsible for the voiceover process. No need to turn so pale. But you're right: apparently, the actors' archived sound files are the property of Viking TV. Even more interestingly, the files have been reclassified for no apparent reason. You, Herr Direktor, seem to be the only person who has clearance to access them. But there's more. A professional voice engineering studio seems to be renting premises in the Viking building. Its owner is unknown. Its legal address turned out to be a private apartment of some half-deaf old lady."

He paused. "I suggest you save my time and yours. I'm not interested in your expressions of surprise, shock or other appropriate emotions. And what's more: if you try to lie to me, I'll kill you. Agreed?"

It took the TV boss five seconds to assess the situation. "Agreed," he said through clenched teeth. "What do you want me to do?"

"Everything," Pavel said simply, playing with his gun. "But first I'd like to know... The Triumvirate has never existed, has it? It's just a smoke screen for the masses who love the idea of a strong-hand at the top, right? Gorgeous concept. Mind telling me who it was who came up with it?"

If he'd expected the other man to lose his composure, he was sadly mistaken.

"I did," the Direktor said. "And I still don't see anything wrong with it. The Twenty-Year War had bled the country dry. The Reich was in ruins. Our cities lay smoldering. All the known war leaders were dead. And those who'd survived were too scared to admit they were sick and tired of the constant fighting and just wanted a bit of a quiet life for themselves. By creating the TV as we know it, Hans Ulrich Rudel basically changed the world. This was an empire capable of controlling people's minds. The Führer's golden dream. With the press of a button, hundreds of millions obediently took their places in front of TV sets to watch, zombie-like, the constant flow of entertainment, action movies and soap operas. He didn't invent anything new. Already in Rome, the mob had been kept in check using the *Bread and Circuses!* system. Are gladiatorial games so different from TV shows of today? There's less blood, right, but we're working on it. The audience loves a touch of gore. People have grown to believe everything they're being told and sold on TV. They consider it part of themselves; they've merged together like conjoined twins."

He paused, staring at the gun in front of him. "So it wasn't that hard. We went on air with an official release which we'd previously cleared with other TV channels in other Reichskommissariats: *This morning the control of the Vaterland has been passed on to a Triumvirate comprised of honest sons and daughters of the Reich.* We didn't even need to convince anyone. The military were too tired of dying; civilians were just happy they didn't have to run to bomb shelters every night like headless chickens anymore. They believed it wholeheartedly because they wanted to believe in it. Are you angry the Triumvirate was a lie? Please. All these years you knew very well the Führer was dead and still you didn't bat an eyelid reading newspapers with all those decrees signed by him. That didn't surprise you, did it? And what's more, the individuals presiding in the Priest Council are just as virtual. Probably, not only there. This is the twenty-first century, my boy. This world is one media space wound with cables... servient to the every touch of remote controls."

Pavel rocked his head like a Chinese doll. "So it's all one big lie, is it?" he demanded, his eyes red. "Television passes new laws, creates new cookie-cutter ministers, sends the Wehrmacht behind the Urals to fight

Schwarzkopfs while none of it really exists? We're obeying an empty space? We're controlled by thin air; it creates new jobs and wages and all such happiness for the people, is that right? Un-fucking-believable. I should have known. Russlanders really don't give a shit about who rules them, to the point that they didn't even notice when their rulers are gone! Now, if television disappeared... that would be totally different."

"Absolutely," the TV Direktor cast a cautious smile. "TV channels are true incubators of the soul. Can you imagine what's gonna happen if tomorrow it disappears? The world will be plunged into a new Stone Age. We spoon-feed them everything: how to cook, how to brush their teeth, how to date a girl; we raise entire new generations; we are the illusion builders and the dream makers. So what if our dream is ephemeral? Do you see anyone unhappy with our rule? Apart from the Schwarzkopfs, that is. Shopping malls, restaurants, movie theaters — they're constantly packed. People love this kind of lifestyle. They don't need to worry about tomorrow. Much better than the cold, the rations and makeshift wick lamps of the long-winded Civil war. All you need to do is unplug human brains. And we're perfectly up to that. Don't you think?"

The TV boss was desperately trying to bide for time. Once the real Phoenix Major was back (and he might have been back already), they'll make quick work of this nutcase. How had he managed to change his appearance? Not that it mattered. This was a terrible blunder on the part of security which testified to their lack of order and discipline. He might have to fire a good half of them. They just had to lick German backsides!

"What's gonna happen if there's no television?" Pavel repeated his question in a dull voice. "Now that would be interesting... mind if we try it just now? As far as I remember, the red button disabling all TV channels in case of a Schwarzkopf attack is here in this office. Am I right? Well, in this case, press it."

The man froze and stared at Pavel, his pupils dilated. Still, he didn't attempt to move.

Pavel shrugged. He pointed his Browning at the ceiling and squeezed the trigger. White dust noiselessly showered over the TV Direktor. He looked like a baker covered in flour.

"Next time it's your arm," Pavel said. "Then a kneecap. I know how to kill a man slowly. Trust me."

The man rose and staggered over to a built-in closet, clutching the remote control. He walked as slowly as he could, dragging a leg, suddenly a good twenty years older as if he could change anything by procrastinating.

A light flashed on the remote's black surface. The closet's doors parted like those of a wardrobe, revealing an electronic control panel within. The TV Direktor approached the scanner next to it, pressing first his eye and then his hand up to the screen. Finally, he reached for the button in the middle of the panel.

He paused.

Pavel sighed. "Please don't let me do it. I have no qualms about killing people but I hate having to torture them. I only do it when absolutely necessary."

The man's shaking finger poked the button. Pavel closed his eyes.

Contrary to his expectations, nothing happened. No thundering roar, no nuclear explosion, no earthquake. The world hadn't split in two. The screens of two plasma TVs slung under the office ceiling had grown dark. That was the extent of it. A comic show choked on a joke mid-word.

Grazing his forehead against the closet door, the TV Direktor slumped to the floor. "What have you done... You've no idea what has just happened."

"I don't give a shit," Pavel replied sweetly. "This isn't the right moment to indulge in philosophy. The Reich has twenty-four hours left to live. Possibly, forty-eight. No amount of TV can save it now. The world is dying because-"

He was about to tell the man what he alone knew but reconsidered.

"Why did I have to do it," the Direktor shivered, slouched on the carpet. "You'll kill me anyway, won't you?"

"What a commendable insight. You're dead right there."

Pavel walked around the man and shot him in the back of the head. Then, taking a good aim at the control panel, he opened fire with both guns, trying to avoid the cascade of plastic fragments until all the little lights on it had gone out.

Television was dead and it wasn't going to recover any time soon.

Pavel heaved a sigh. For the first time in years he felt free and elated.

He unblocked the office door and walked out into the studio. The rattle of hobnail boots came from everywhere as Phoenix Sonderkommandos hurried to respond to the security breach.

He'd never killed Germans before.

Two guys hurried to the front, too young and too eager. One was tall and red-haired. The other had dark hair and fair skin. The first bullet hit the tall one in his head; he spun on the spot, then collapsed. The second bullet ripped the other one's throat out; he slid down the wall, spattering it with blood.

"*Outside the barracks, by the corner light*," Pavel hummed.

He remembered the song too well. Back in Lebensborn, Sturmbannführer Sollmann used to hum it every time he'd taken Pavel to the punishment cellar, digging his sharp fingers into his ear.

Pavel forced the studio table on its side and took cover behind it.

He'd been trained not to waste a single round. Ammo cost money, and the entire Third Reich had been built on penny-pinching. They even reused work camp prisoners' hair to fill sleeping bags for the homeless.

He fired. Yet another German in a field-gray uniform cried out, collapsing to the floor.

"*I'll always stand and wait for you at night...*"

Throwing the false economy to the wind, the enemy hosed him with automatic fire. His face was sliced by sharp computer fragments and chips from the broken table. Four or five rounds hit him in the chest and leg. He winced, shooting non-stop. Luckily, the Germans didn't seem to have any grenades otherwise the fight wouldn't have lasted that long. Pavel knew it, too. Only small arms were allowed into the building.

"*We will create a world for two...*"

Over the gunfire he could make out an officer's voice snapping orders as well as the replies of his soldiers. Alien language. Incredible how foreign it sounded now. Why hadn't he noticed it before?

Pavel snapped in his last clip, then downed two more attackers, calm as if it were a training exercise. This was something he was good at.

"I'll wait for you the whole night through..."

The studio floor was littered with people swimming in pools of blood and broken glass. He didn't count how many they were but there had to be twenty at least. None of them groaned: they were all dead.

Pavel had one round left. Not that he was worried about it. He fired at a field-gray shadow that had charged at him. The *Schütze* — marksman — tumbled down, his body hanging listessly off the edge of the table, convulsing.

"Surrender!" a hoarse voice shouted in Russian.

"Please wait," he replied in German. "Just a minute."

The thermal grenade fit snugly into his left sleeve, its elongated body resembling a fat pencil. Its charge was enough to disintegrate a tank. He set the timer for one minute, raised his hands and stood up in his blood-soaked major's uniform.

A shot rang out, adding another blood spot to his chest: one of the soldiers had freaked out. Pavel staggered but remained standing. Survivors in khaki uniforms surrounded him, their hands tight around their StGs.

A Major walked out through their ranks, his glare filled with hatred and confusion. He had the typical German looks: blond hair, a thin nose and jug ears.

He walked over to the prisoner and gave

him a powerful slap on the face.

The grenade blinked its red light through the fabric of Pavel's sleeve.

"*For you, Lili Marlene,*" Pavel said to the officer, grinning his bleeding mouth.

Smoke from the explosion filled the studio.

CHAPTER SIX

The Blackout

EVERY CITY AND STREET IN THE
REICHSKOMMISSARIAT MOSKAU

AT FIRST, NO ONE REALIZED what had just happened.

When a TV screen goes black, one thinks their box has broken down. Television works 24/7. It can't just go off, can it?

All around Moskau, people walked over to their televisions. They punched them. They tried to remove the back cover and fiddle with the parts. They checked the power and the plugs. None of it helped.

Their televisions remained dead, their screens blank and devoid of all the jokes, colorful settings, sitcoms, action thrillers and weather forecasts. They were stubbornly silent.

Soon the mobile network collapsed too as panicking people started calling each other trying to find out what was going on, asking desperate questions to which no one had answers. Authorities couldn't explain the situation simply because they hadn't been instructed on what to say.

The Triumvirate used to reassure everyone that their job was to obey orders. Thinking was a privilege reserved for the top brass. Now that the said top brass was nowhere to be found, everyone sat on their backsides awaiting orders. No one was able to think independently.

Gradually people took to the streets.

Instinctively they gathered at the city center, expecting a press officer with an explanation. A ten-thousand-strong crowd had gathered by the Ministry of Propaganda in the naïve hope that its workers who could undo any tricky knot with their tongues were sure to shed some light on the situation.

But the building's front doors were blocked; fire and smoke billowing from its top floor occupied by Viking TV only added to their anxiety. You'd think someone would come out to tell them that due to the unusually high radiation levels everyone was advised to go home; still, Ministry workers weren't willing to accept the responsibility. They just shrank deeper into their desk chairs and kept going on about their work, hoping it would sort itself out somehow.

It didn't.

By six in the evening, the first Schwarzkopf groups entered Moskau from the Khimki direction, only challenged by the German Wehrmacht checkpoints. The elite SS Russland division surrendered simply because the Triumvirate, never expecting the Schwarzkopfs to actually storm the city, hadn't left them any instructions in such a case. The attackers promptly solved the checkpoint problem by bringing in tanks and heavy artillery. They took no German prisoners but gunned them all down right there next to the concrete roadblocks.

Tiger tanks — some flying red flags, others the Russian tricolor — entered the city, their tracks ploughing through the tarmac. Street cops raised their hands in the air slowly as if sleepwalking. The Schwarzkopfs stormed the Gestapo office at the Novodevichy Monastery but found it deserted: all the workers had left the building and made themselves scarce.

Strips of red fabric began changing hands in the crowd as people — furtively at first and openly later — started tying them onto their chests. Some of the more forethoughtful ones popped into beauty stores, asking in whispers for some dark hair dye, then hurried home to dye their hair.

Fierce fighting unfolded on King Gaiseric Street next to the Greater Germany Cultural

Center — a 1930s-style red brick that had housed the first Ober Kommandatur in freshly-occupied Moskau. Surrounded and choking on smoke from fires, the Bavarian SS defended it to the last as they desperately radioed for help.

There was no one to answer their plea. The telephones were dead in the Polizei, the Main Security Office and Wewelsburg guardhouse. As for the military, they were only too happy to raise their hands and fraternize with the Schwarzkopfs.

The television still didn't work.

It was getting dark. The roof of the Cultural Center of Greater Germany caved in, enveloped in flames. Single shots continued banging in side lanes, the Germans' disjointed resistance a pointless act of desperation. Young Schwarzkopfs, with cigarettes hanging defiantly from their mouths, showed remarkable knack in hanging SS prisoners on Wagner Street lampposts while passersby filmed the execution with their phones. Few realized they were witnessing a change of regime: all they were interested in was getting some entertainment instead of the shows they'd missed. When you watch people kill each other in soap operas and action movies day in, day out, real death seems just as harmless and virtual.

Shopping centers and restaurants went up in flames, followed by Norse temples and government offices. As Moskau lay shrouded in darkness, it was consumed by looting as even the most respectable-looking people began stealing everything in sight, prompting mass fights with the stores' security guards.

A crowd of looters surrounded Wewelsburg expecting rich bounty, then recoiled in fear when the building's walls began quivering like a sand dune. They watched as the dark castle turned into a pale phantom of itself, then dissolved into thin air with all its contents, the Triumvirate's bunker included.

The Black Sun mosaic disappeared into the darkness it had come from, never to be seen again.

"No reason why we shouldn't loot," the more conscientious intellectuals apologized guiltily, scooping up computers, cratefuls of beer and bagfuls of food and lugging them home. "This stuff belongs to no one, and we've no idea who might claim it tomorrow." No one seemed to wonder about the buildings' disappearance. Hadn't the TV said it was something to do with the abnormal weather? They were the experts. They wouldn't have said it just for the sake of it.

Flashing red ribbons on their jacket chests, the Ministry of Propaganda workers greeted the first Schwarzkopfs to have stormed the building with flowers and symbolic bread and salt[32]. They

[32] Bread and salt: the ancient Slavic tradition of greeting respected guests by offering them a lavishly

clapped their hands, shouting "Hurrah to the liberators!" The Führer's portraits disappeared from the walls in a flash, replaced by icons of St. Stalin, bad photos of the Forest Church Patriarch and pictures of Emperor Nicholas II. The black-eagled flag was hastily lowered from the roof where a red banner promptly flapped in the wind in its stead.

The Ministry curator ex-Oberführer Ivan Frolov (his SS identity papers being promptly shredded to confetti together with all of the Ministry workers' IDs) invited guerrilla commanders into his office and began pitching to them his advertisement campaign promoting Bolshevist ideas in Moskau. Other propaganda officers too showed their impatience to swear their allegiance to Bolshevism, offering every

---

decorated loaf of bread topped with a salt cellar. The guests are supposed to break off some of the bread, dip it into the salt and eat it to show their acceptance of the hosts' hospitality. Here, however, this tradition is used as a sarcastic allusion to the Germans' initial advance into the Russian territory where some local communities, embittered with the Soviet regime, greeted the Nazi invaders as "liberators" with flowers and cheers, offering them bread and salt. As the German troops began their retreat later in the war, quite a few of those communities were gunned down or burned alive by SS squads mopping up whole areas of Western Russia.

support in replacing Reich ideology with that of Republican Socialism.

"Our main forte is that we're honest, loyal and competent," Frolov assured the guerrilla representatives.

In the overall confusion, no one seemed to have noticed the disappearance of the bodies of Phoenix Sonderkommandos from the ground-floor first-aid room. The soldiers had apparently been slain by some lone Schwarzkopf who'd gone on a rampage in the Viking TV studio upstairs.

By midnight, Moskau lay in ashes. The fires which had initially started in shopping malls, the brothels of the Goering industrial zone and the beerhouses of Sausage Street had quickly spread to residential areas. There was no one to put them out as the firefighters' Loki Division had deserted already in the morning, ripping off their black elbow patches and other insignia featuring the face of the Scandinavian god of fire. Crowds fought over heaps of loot in city squares, their faces bronze masks in the reflected flames.

More shooting started: having sorted the Germans out, Schwarzkopf squads began fighting each other over their respective patches for influence: the city center, the airport and the St Petersburg *autobahn*.

The Shogunet was seething with news. The Reichskommissariats Ukraine, Ostland and Turkestan had apparently surrendered without firing a single round. In Norway and the Netherlands, Oberkommandatur buildings had gone up in flames. Street fighting had begun in London and Neuer York. The regime which had only yesterday seemed rock solid had collapsed like a house of cards.

The warm night had passed quickly. The first rays of sunshine dawned upon the lampposts hung with swaying bodies. The skeletons of gutted buildings still smoldered. Now that tobacco smoking was officially permitted, sidewalks were strewn with cigarette butts. The remaining sidewalks, that is. Half of Moskau had disappeared overnight, including the Ministry of Propaganda building still flying its red flag.

This was a phantom city. Deep inside their surviving apartments, bloodshot-eyed people desperately pressed every button on their remote controls.

Still, their TVs wouldn't work.

Abwehr report #844

The Twenty-Year War: Outcomes and Deliberations

ACCORDING TO THE LAST POLLS, about 75% of the Moskau population are unhappy with the Triumvirate. Surprisingly, at the same time no one wants the current regime to change. How can two such mutually incompatible ideas coexist in the population's minds? Easy.

People still remember vividly the horrors of the Twenty-Year War when they had no heating or lighting in winter and freezing families had to warm themselves by breaking furniture for fuel in makeshift wood heaters. Inflation went through the roof: a loaf of bread that cost thirty billion reichsmarks in the morning would rise in price by the evening. Even cities lucky enough to escape the street fighting still shudder when they think about those terrible times.

SS divisions were in control of Moskau and Kiev, the Wehrmacht had been given Yekaterinodar and St Petersburg, the Gestapo wreaked havoc in Kursk while the Southern cities of Sochi, Tbilisi and Yerevan were plunged into the chaos of clashes between the Turkic legions. The Reichstag was destroyed in 1998, followed by the Reichsbank building in 2002. Damaged by Luftwaffe bombings, nuclear power stations leaked a constant stream of radiation.

Italy as well as the Reich's other satellites promptly adopted neutrality, keeping a safe distance from the collisions of the new Civil war. "Greater Germany is our beloved big brother," Romano Mussolini said openly. "And if our brother has an itch to scratch, we'll wait respectfully aside even if he draws blood in the process."

Soon after that, Italy completely distanced itself from Germany. Having started with Japanese loans and investments, Mussolini ended up becoming completely dependent on the Nippon koku. These days, Japanese is Italy's second official language. Everything in the country is owned by the Japanese, pizzerias included. The Sicilian mafia has been wiped out by the yakuza newcomers. The Mafia's unwritten omerta law was abandoned so that even in the old Palermo villages a guilty thug would offer the gang's oyabun leader his severed pinkie as a sign of his repentance. Both the tower of Pisa and the Piazza San Marco in Venice were leased out to the Japanese for 99 years.

Basically, we've lost all of our allies. The satellite states tend to support those with real power. We have nothing left to our name apart from overly aggressive statements.

Neither the Schwarzkopfs nor the Forest Brothers movement are likely to present any threat in the nearest future. Moskau's population isn't interested in the goings-on in backwater provinces. They may be badmouthing the Triumvirate and laughing at the lies spread by the state-owned TV and the stagnant system, but they will still support them, however reluctantly, as well as any actions aimed at preserving their piece of mind.

In their heart of hearts, they're wary of having to face the truth (because they know they shouldn't be thinking these kinds of thoughts). They're too afraid of a change of power because that's what it's like in Russland: every new regime is worse than its predecessor.

Having spent decades in the woods as hunters and gatherers, the Schwarzkopfs can't conceive any other lifestyle for themselves as one of struggle against the regime. The ideas of economy, food deliveries and even street cleaning are alien to them. All they can do is fight and brainwash others. This is a road to nowhere. This is exactly why the Third Reich (the one before the Twenty-Year War) failed: it had invested too much time into ideology.

If a law-abiding person has to support his family on ration cards year in, year out, he is bound to start questioning the regime's integrity. He will start wondering why his enemies have a better lifestyle than he and the likes of him who are the creators of the ideal Aryan state.

Any good empire is founded on two principles: ideology and economic successes. The exact methods of achieving the latter were irrelevant. Even the Nippon koku's loans were good enough. As soon as a previously impoverished citizen of the Reich got access to the world's pleasures, all you had to do was point out the enemies supposedly scheming to strip him of his freshly-acquired abundance. Make him fear his enemies: the rest he'd do himself. Fear is a tremendous force. Its power is behind many things in this world.

The Reichskommissariat Moskau seems to be living from day to day. The country is up to its ears in debt and to the best of my knowledge, we can't pay it back. If Japan asks for it, we'll have no other way but to start a war with them. The Nippon koku understands this too which is why the Japanese are forced to throw even more loans at the problem.

For the same reason, it wouldn't be wise to completely eradicate the Schwarzkopf movement. They seem to be one of the Reich's most important resources on a par with arms production, the timber industry and peat extraction. They could be made responsible for all kinds of economic or security blunders, allowing the Reich to enforce draconian measures on its population and blame them for having to fight the enemy within.

Until the country is self-sufficient and abounds with its own gold and money, it will always need an enemy: to stay in shape, to explain away the inexplicable and to always be at the ready. The Schwarzkopfs should be kept sufficiently weak to not be able to take over cities but strong enough to carry the blame for our failures. Luckily for us, the situation remains stable. But even the Schwarzkopf leaders have no idea who finances their military operations, buys their weapons and equips their field hospitals.

(From the Classified Archives of the Moskau Triumvirate)

Endorsement:

We need them like we need oxygen. Without them, we can't exist.

Top Secret

Unique clearance: Viking TV Direktor

CHAPTER SEVEN

The Revelation

THE VILLAGE OF ALEXEYEVSKOYE

NEAR NOVGOROD

MY EYES STING. I don't feel my legs. For the first time in years I'm scared.

My heart flutters with panic. This is probably what a deer feels when he hears the sound of hunters' bugles and the barking of dogs.

I stand at a deserted clearing amid the forest: a bodeful bare patch devoid of grass. The air ripples, sending waves of heat into my face. I'd love to run away but my legs refuse to obey me.

As I stagger uphill, the phantom outlines of cottages rise on both sides of me, gaining shape and color with my every step.

Olga has already told me: as the Reich disintegrates, the signs of their long-forgotten crimes bleed through the fabric of reality, becoming visible again.

I can see the houses well now, rising up amid the trees. Some miss a roof, others a wall or two. They are all charred.

Does that mean that this village existed in our world too?

It must have. I can see the ghostlike outlines of bodies doubled up on the ground: villagers gunned down by the soldiers.

Little by little, we reach the top of the hill.

Ravens croak overhead. The air is crystal clear but still I can't breathe. My lungs are packing up. I choke on the taste of bitter smoke in my mouth.

Olga turns round, staring into my eyes long and hard. She bites her lips with anxiety, apparently expecting something from me.

I too expect a lot from her. I made that much clear. She gave me her word — so now I want her to keep it and stop contaminating our world. I want her to go back to where she belongs and leave our planet alone. She promised me to do so if I came here with her. In that case, why do I feel so sick?

"So... here we are," I struggle to speak. My tongue is coated with ash as if someone has used it to put out the fires. "Happy now? What else do you... want... from me? I think I'm gonna faint..."

She touches my cheek, her red nails grazing against my skin. "You don't remember, do you? I shouldn't have hoped you would. What are you feeling now, my boy?"

My boy? Who does she think she is? Still, I'm too weak to indulge in sarcasms. I'm too busy thinking about her question. Admittedly it has thrown me.

The taste of smoke in my mouth keeps getting stronger, unbearably bitter. Ash grates against my teeth. I think I'm about to throw up. I can barely think straight.

Why is this happening to me?

Olga doesn't look as if she expected an answer. She walks over to the edge of the hill. The breeze ripples her hair. She points down, at the phantom silhouettes of the burned-out houses. The scene of the anomaly. Olga's portal; the wormhole that has triggered the disintegration of our universe.

The meatgrinder chewing through time. *My* time.

"Have you ever asked yourself why you don't know what you look like?" her voice assaults my eardrums, loud and clear. "Do you know why you don't have mirrors in your house? Or why you've never looked into your own ID papers? D'you know why none of your co-workers ever called you by name? You don't, do you? Otherwise you would have wondered if you really existed. You can't see yourself, can you? I brought you here hoping you might remember. But it looks like I'll have to help you."

She reaches into her purse and produces a pocket mirror. "Here. Take a look. Then tell me who you really are."

I take the mirror from her the way one might accept a venomous toad. My hands shake violently. I wouldn't have been able to hold a cup of tea without spilling it all over myself. Icy horror rips through my heart. I'm scared like a child in the dark.

My reflection stares unblinkingly at me.

A gaunt man of about thirty-five, his face covered with blond stubble. A filthy blood-stained bandage is wrapped around his forehead. A semicircular shrapnel scar on his left cheek. Blue eyes. I know that I know him.

I do. By Fenrir and all the gods of Valhalla, I do know him!

This is the guy from my visions. The Oberleutnant who shot that panicking deserter in the ruins of the dead city. The one who told his soldiers to throw grenades into the cottage with the children. The one who sent the prisoners of war to the minefield.

His field-gray tunic is half-rotten, covered in snow. Fat lice crawl over its lapels. A braided epaulette on his left shoulder; an eagle clutching a swastika above his breast pocket. The two SS lightning bolts are mounted on his one lapel, three silver diamonds on the other.

My eye begins to twitch. My reflection winks back at me. This is... He is...

I stagger and drop the mirror. It smashes to smithereens.

"Name?" the girl demands with military curtness.

"Erich Tannenbaum," I say mechanically. "Obersturmführer Tannenbaum, Waffen SS. I served in Riga, then in Novgorod. Decorated with the Iron Cross for my role in punitive raids. Was dispatched to Stalingrad on August 28 1942."

She nods. With a satisfied smile, she reaches into her purse for some cigarettes.

"Nice meeting you, Erich," she says as she lights up. "Here as you know, I go by the name of Olga Sélina. I don't know my real one. Neither do you. But it was me who burned alive in this village when I was three years old — in the house you told your soldiers to destroy. I told you about me, remember? I loved raspberries, I would eat them till both my little cheeks were red with juice. I loved playing with Nana, my rag doll. I learned to say "mama" early; I'd reach my little hands out to her and she would throw me up in the air and kiss me. I'd love to know what would have become of me. An actress or a painter, maybe. Or a famous physicist. Or a school teacher. Or even a housewife, why not, who might divorce her husband and start receiving lovers at home behind her children's backs. Doesn't matter now. I'll never know," she pauses as she always does, letting out the smoke. "*Because you killed me.*"

Panic-stricken, I shrink back to the edge. She smiles — again. Once again, like back in that Uradziosutoku café, I stare into the empty eye sockets of a grinning, scowling skull.

CHAPTER EIGHT

The Kiss

NOW I HAVE NO DOUBTS about what I suspected all along. Finally, it all makes sense. She's crazy. Oh yes she is, and it explains really a lot. The temple's disappearing walls back in Moskau, the charred cottages here... Her madness must be contagious. It's probably some kind of brain-destroying virus. Like in those documentaries when people go mad after being bitten by a rabid monkey.

I can't have killed children. I still cringe and recoil whenever I remember that vision. I might not be the most charitable person on earth but I've never raised my hand to a child, let alone burn one alive.

Time to put an end to all this. Time to shake off her witchery.

I'm trying to remain calm but I can't. My usual cool fails me. I dissolve into a fit of hysterics.

"It can't be!" for the first time in my life, I yell at someone. "You told me, remember? You came from a parallel world! How could I have gotten there? I couldn't have done it! It wasn't me! *It wasn't me*!"

As I scream, I taste the smoke again, mixed with something different, something salty. Blood? It seems to be. My every word brings it all back to me. Me, receiving my orders from Oberst Neumann and descending the trail back to the village, then walking amid the burning houses in my gas mask. I walk over to one of the cottages. A child is crying her head off inside. The girl who is about three years old looks out of the window, her face bloated with tears. She climbs the window sill and bangs on the glass. I can see her so clearly. Even now Olga still looks very much like her.

The soldiers look at me expectantly, awaiting my orders. I know them all by name. That one over there is Hans from Hannover; next to him is Heinz who loves to tell dirty jokes; and this one is young Wolff from Heidelberg. He's not as devoted to the Reich as I am and has only joined the SS on his Nazi parents' insistence.

I raise my hand, then drop it sharply, signaling them to begin.

Tears pour down my cheeks, burning my

face. “I can’t have... why... what’s wrong with me? Tell me... please...”

Her gaze fills with sisterly kindness. Gently she strokes my head. “You’re dying, Erich,” she says, her voice sad but calm. “Remember your vision? The one where the Oberleutnant killed the soldier in the dead city? He was then shot in the head by the Russian sniper, remember? Well... it *was* you. The bullet’s stuck in your brain. You’re in hospital, Erich. We’re in Stalingrad. They can’t remove the bullet: you’re gonna die if they do. But even so you don’t have long.”

A faint smile crosses her lips. “All this month you’ve been hallucinating about Moskau and your life there. You see, the bullet hit the part of your brain responsible for altering reality. Did you ask me about parallel worlds? I’m sorry, Erich. They don’t exist. Moskau, the California Republic, the Nippon Koku owning half the world... it’s all in your head. It’s only your mind playing up. Sorry.”

She stares past me into space. “Even unconscious, you can’t forget the little girl. The one you let be burned alive. Which is why I’m always here with you. You can’t stop thinking about me. The world around you fades, disappearing, turning into a phantom of itself. You’ll leave with it. The moment you breathe your last breath, your universe will die. I heard what the doctor said. You won’t see the end of this day.”

I raise my head to the sky.

That weird vision I had earlier. The viscous white mass, the clangor of steely objects, the little lights shining through the haze. But of course. Field hospital. The clatter of extracted bullets against surgery bowls. The flickering of dozens of candles in the dark because they have no electricity.

We're besieged by the Russians. We survive gnawing on horse meat and frozen bread. Schnapps is the only thing readily available. I've been drinking it nonstop trying to forget the little girl in the cottage window. It didn't work though.

All of a sudden I feel exhausted. That's it. That's the end.

I don't need anything anymore. I just want to die.

My fingers close around the swastika-clutching eagle on my pocket. I rip it off, followed by my SS insignia, stomping the braided epaulette into the ashes covering the ground. My legs give way under me. I collapse, kneeling before Olga. She's beautiful.

"I'm so sorry," I sob. "How can you ever forgive me... please..."

I want to tell her so much but I'm out of words. I keep repeating myself. My last seconds dwindle, the world around me shrinking like the snow in springtime.

The forest crumbles into ashes. A large crack runs across the glass-like sky, revealing flames behind.

She crouches next to me and takes my hands in hers. “Tell me,” she whispers, “what you always wanted to tell me. Tell me now.”

“I love you,” I’m surprised with the ease the words fall from my lips.

Our mouths touch.

The kiss is brief and innocent. None of that French tongue nonsense (from what I heard at least). Her lips are soft, warm and inviting. I waited for this a long time.

A clap of thunder booms overhead. My ears don’t feel the impact.

The world disintegrates. The universe is no more. Moskau, London, Neuer York and the Reichskommissariat Turkestan — they all turn to ashes. The Führer’s monuments blur into nothing; the eagle on Moskau’s emblem fades as if painted with invisible ink. No Odin’s Temples; no Security office, no tanks in the streets. No Schwarzkopf guerrillas taking over the city.

They’re all gone. Evaporated. Born of my fantasy, the world of Moskau dies an agonyless death. Pitch darkness envelops us. We float in a space devoid of top and bottom.

I let go of her lips. Now I can see I’ve been kissing a skull. Strangely, I don’t feel scared.

I know who she is.

“I know who you are,” I whisper in the place where her ear should be, “You’re my death, right?”

"I am," she says. "All people realize it sooner or later even though not necessarily consciously. Pavel believed me, though, as soon as I explained my nature to him. He was intelligent enough to understand he couldn't fight the supernatural."

"But why did you look... like *her*? Strange choice."

The skull grins. "Standard option. I always assume the appearance of the victim to visit the killer. And this kiss... had the Russian sniper killed you, it would have been different. But you're lying here comatose instead. It just shows the graveness of your crimes. Your soul can't enter oblivion. You're stuck between heaven and earth. In order to leave this world, you need to really crave death. In order for it to come, you need to fall in love with it. Which was why I came to you a long time ago; I knew you loved me. Still, in order for you to complete your life on earth you had to kiss me. So many times we were close but every time something happened. That's why I asked you to come here. I thought it might work. It did."

Holding hands, we scramble back to our feet.

I can see her face again: the young woman, the most beautiful one in the world. I'm completely smitten. I've never loved anyone the way I love her. She can take me, for all eternity.

"What normally happens next?" I ask.

She shrugs. "Dunno. My job is to take a soul into the darkness. No one ever told me what happens next. You still have two minutes. Would you like to wait?"

I close my eyes. Dozens of people stand before my eyes, all dead. Killed by me. I can see everything I've done. POW bodies blown to pieces. Burned cottages. Unburied bodies. Souls restless in eternal darkness.

The dead stare at me, silent and indifferent. A little Russian girl stands in front, hugging her rag doll.

"I don't need to," I say. "High time I burn in hell."

We walk off, cuddling each other like two lovers. I have a funny feeling... then again, it's probably just another illusion.

Thunder rolls, announcing the end.

EPILOGUE

GRETA BLEW ON HER FROZEN HANDS.

Jesus Christ almighty, this place was cold. She'd have willingly given herself to anyone at all for a hot bath. Doubtful there'd be many takers, though.

Good job Mom couldn't hear her.

They'd already cut all the available trees for cooking fires. Venturing any further under Russian sniper fire was pretty pointless. No one had ever come back from these forage missions.

The hospital was dark: they'd burned the last candles the night before.

The groans of the wounded behind the makeshift "wall" had subsided since morning. Not that it mattered: the nurse was too used to them to notice. Her mind had stopped registering them about the same time that she'd stopped wondering what the hell she was doing here, in this icebound city, its shattered streets piled up with hundreds of thousands of dead bodies.

She was already used to the thought she'd follow them soon.

She didn't give a shit it was February 2 1943. Her birthday. She'd seen enough death to know that a painless death was the only thing that really mattered in life.

That might have been the best birthday gift for her.

She lay her hand on the patient's forehead and promptly snatched it back: it was scorching hot. Erich Tannenbaum had a high fever but they'd run out of meds. Dr. Paul had warned her the man's condition might become critical tonight. His agony could begin at any moment.

She took a mug filled with icy water and brought it to the man's lips. He didn't swallow. The water trickled from his lips down his neck.

In all this time nursing him Greta had studied his face so well she'd be able to draw it from memory. He might have been quite handsome once you'd shave him and remove the ugly shrapnel scar from his cheek. It didn't belong there.

The girl shivered, wrapping the tattered blanket tighter around her trench coat. Dr. Paul hadn't done his morning rounds. He couldn't have, could he?

Dr. Paul, the cheerful bastard whose crooked smile had turned every nurse's head in the hospital! His appearance was quite ordinary with gaunt cheeks, balding temples and an aquiline nose — but the man was an unquenchable fount of optimism and had his own unique strain of humor.

Dr. Paul seemed to have had a soft spot for Erich, investing a lot of his time and expertise in the wounded obersturmführer. He'd had some reason to believe that he would bring the man back to life, turning his case into a medical sensation.

Any person with this sort of wound should have been dead a long time ago. But Erich was still alive. Did that mean he might have a chance?

Many a time Dr. Erich had arrived at work in defiance of military protocol, either wearing a clown's wig with his uniform or a big red rubber nose. Both items had ended in his possession thanks to his little daughter who'd planted her favorite toys in his suitcase before his dispatch to the Eastern Front. Not to even mention his mustache! Time after time Doc would start growing it only to shave it off after a week.

"I'm trying to deceive death," he'd laugh. "It already knows all my tricks. So when it comes next morning, still groggy from its slumber, it just won't recognize me. It might think I'm some new doctor on the team! A new face to look into!"

The way he behaved, you'd think he was on a pleasure cruise, not in a field hospital.

He was probably right. Humor must have been the only thing that could save you in this madness, under the non-stop cacophony of roaring bombers and wailing missiles.

But even Dr. Paul, this incorrigible optimist, had come to the end of his tether. As Erich's wound failed to improve, Doc had grown somber. Lately he'd be seen helping himself from the hospital's alcohol flask.

"He's gonna die," Doc would admit to Greta. "I don't think I can do much there anymore."

And still Erich, this comatose vegetable, continued to breathe.

From a medical point of view, his case was extraordinary: a man living with a bullet buried deep in his brain. He reacted to touch and even to light exposure, moving the stumps of his right hand (his index finger and pinkie had been septic and had had to be amputated) and even twitching his eyelashes. Things had seemed to be looking up.

Still, whenever Dr. Paul had decided to prepare him for surgery to remove the bullet, his condition would rapidly deteriorate.

Greta would often speak to Erich in his "private room" staked out with sheets of frozen cardboard. She'd told him about her life and work in the League of German Girls, about her home city of Düsseldorf which every spring lay smothered with lilac blossoms. An occasional smile would cross Erich's lips.

Could he hear her?

All last week, Erich had been getting worse. He'd developed mouth and nose bleeds, black blood escaping his brain which was being killed slowly by the bullet.

Dr. Paul had grown depressed. He'd forgotten all about his wigs and clown noses, emptying the alcohol flask before lunchtime. The other day, hospital director Major Storch (who looked eerily identical to Paul to the point where the two could pass for identical twins) had found him in the surgical theater drunk as a skunk and sent him to the cooler for three days.

"And?" Doc had laughed drunkenly. "When the Russians come, I'll be their hero! We're done for, anyway!"

This was enough to put him up against the wall for treason but Storch had chosen to turn a deaf ear to his ramblings.

His good deed didn't go unpunished: half an hour later, Doc had beaten the cooler guard to pulp and arrived at the hospital with his rifle. He'd whistled *Lili Marlene* as he opened fire, killing Major Storch and one of the patients with his first two rounds. Then his rifle got jammed and Doc was gunned down.

Greta had seen his frozen body in the hospital corridor, his face a gory mess of crimson. The clown's red nose lay on the floor next to it.

He must have gone off his head, she

thought, impassive. *He couldn't take it anymore, as simple as that.*

Nothing could baffle her anymore. Nutcases weren't something extraordinary. The week before, they'd discharged Unteroffizier Kurt Priebke; having checked out of the hospital, he walked into the duty doctor's office, said "Heil Hitler!", then shoved the butt of his handgun into his mouth and squeezed the trigger. They'd never managed to clean his brains off the wall as it had already frozen solid.

Human life wasn't worth a dime anymore. There were no sane people left in Stalingrad. They were all raving mad here.

The curtain parted. Greta jumped to her feet.

Johann Peter, the patient's old friend, stomped into the makeshift room: a burly man nearly seven foot tall in a Captain's uniform, with huge arms and a square head. Apparently, he used to be a school physics and chemistry teacher. She wasn't sure if it was true or a joke: the Captain looked more like a stevedore than an intellectual.

Without looking at her, Johann Peter shook the snow off his cap. A woman's woolen shawl clung to his cheeks. Greta didn't laugh: a soldier had to do everything necessary to prevent septic frostbite.

"Did you hear the news?" the Hauptsturmführer asked without raising his eyes.

"Sure," she said. "Field Marshal Paulus has signed the capitulation order. He and his HQ have surrendered. The front has collapsed. Those of the patients who could walk, all the nurses, the guards and the hospital direction have already surrendered to the Russians. But I can't leave Erich. The Russians will come here anyway, won't they? They are checking every building in Stalingrad."

The Captain studied Erich's pallid face. "Still nothing?" he wheezed.

"Paul said he wouldn't survive till the third," she shrugged the chill from her shoulders. "It certainly looks that way. The bleeding has intensified. His brain is literally floating in blood. He's got a high fever. My experience tells me he's in his death throes."

The Captain heaved a sigh. He rubbed his forehead, thinking about something.

The dying man opened his eyes, staring nonsensically at the ceiling. A smile fluttered on his lips.

"I always wondered," the Captain said. "Why is he always smiling? Is he happy?"

"According to Paul, the bullet hit the brain area responsible for lucid dreaming," Greta replied, her voice hollow. "Amazing what incredible fantasies such a tiny piece of lead can trigger. Erich believes them to be true. He's probably dreaming about something really good."

"I hope so," the Captain grumbled. "A victory in this war would be nice."

Outside, motors roared.

"Soldiers of Germany!" a voice came. "Field Marshal Paulus has signed your capitulation. Any resistance is pointless. Drop your weapons and walk out of the building with your hands raised over your heads. The Soviet Army guarantees your lives will be spared."

The voice enunciated the German words awkwardly, like a good school student. The loudspeaker mounted on the truck distorted the sound while the wailing of the wind added a diabolical note to the speech.

Greta covered her face, suppressing a sob.

"You should go," the Captain wheezed, choking on a cough. "You'll freeze to death in here. You can't help Erich anymore. I don't think the Russians will even take him. Why should they bother? They'll just leave him here to die on his own. Once you go out of the building, continue straight ahead. There's a POW collection point they made in the silo building. You go. Happy birthday, sweetheart. Twenty-five is a great age. I'll take care of Erich, don't worry," his frozen fingers scraped blindly against his holster.

Greta sobbed. She struggled to wrap the trench coat around herself; twisting her blonde hair in a knot, she used a scrap of blanket to cover her head, then fastened the helmet's strap under her chin.

The room swam before her eyes. Without saying goodbye to Johann Peter, she staggered along the corridor. Her feet in combat boots padded with rags for warmth skated on the icy floor.

She'd almost reached the front door when a shot rang out.

Greta slowed down, listening in. After a brief interval, the gun banged again, choking on its own sound. She heard something heavy crash to the floor behind her.

She scrambled to the entrance and froze in the doorway, numb with the scene.

A column of German POWs walked past the building: all that was left of the 6th Army of Field Marshal Paulus. Their limbs black with gangrenous frostbite, they staggered past wrapped in stolen shawls over their flimsy uniforms, their noses red with cold. They were a far cry from those cheerful bronzed soldiers in rolled-up sleeves who'd been so impatient to taste the water of the Volga. This wasn't an army but a maddened bunch of cripples, a ragged band of pillagers eager to die for a warm coat and a slice of roast.

One of the Russian guards turned around and looked at Greta. He was a young guy in white winter camos, with a red star on his hat and a round-clipped submachine gun slung over his shoulder.

He grinned and made a clumsy bow to her,

saying something she couldn't understand. His friends laughed. The only word she'd made out was *Fräulein*.

Slowly Greta raised her hands in the air and stepped down from the porch.

About the Author

GEORGY ZOTOV WAS BORN on March 1 1971 in Moscow.

The future bestselling author was a very bad student. His teachers struggled to push him up through the classes. He hated studying and barely finished high school. Looking back, he now wishes he never did. Working turned out to be much harder.

He found college a whole lot easier though, mainly because they taught him what he enjoyed learning: the history of the Byzantine and Roman Empires. But by the time he graduated as an archivist historian specializing in ancient civilizations, the fall of the Soviet Union had rendered his new job pretty useless. "You couldn't have fed a cat on my wage, let alone a big sonovabitch like myself," the future author admitted.

So he did a straight swap for journalism. At least journalists had fun, or so he thought. Zotov interviewed the dictator of Pakistan as well as Presidents of Moldova and Latvia (the latter interview proving so scandalous it even earned its own Wikipedia mention). He reported from war-torn Abkhazia and Tajikistan, then visited the fronts of Iraq, Afghanistan and even Syria –

where he was arrested and spent three days in prison without food or water. He still remembers it fondly. He was deported from both Syria and Iran in his capacity as a journalist and still enjoys his *persona non grata* status there.

This was his third arrest abroad which makes Zotov the only modern wordsmith who under the unwritten code of prisoners qualifies as an incorrigible felon. He received a shrapnel wound as well as a prestigious national journalism award for his investigative report on the Nazi Lebensborn project.

Zotov has published fifteen books whose combined print run exceeds half a million copies. He prides himself on a reader's review he saw on the Net,

"The guy is a total nutcase. He's completely off his head. Still, the book is very funny."

Thank you for reading *Moskau!*
If you like what you've read, check out other LitRPG, sci fi and fantasy novels published by Magic Dome Books:

***An NPC's Path* LitRPG series by Pavel Kornev:**
The Dead Rogue

***Reality Benders* LitRPG series by Michael Atamanov:**
Countdown

***Dark Paladin* LitRPG series by Vasily Mahanenko:**
The Beginning
The Quest
Restart

***The Dark Herbalist* LitRPG series by Michael Atamanov:**
Video Game Plotline Tester
Stay on the Wing
A Trap for the Potentate

***The Neuro* LitRPG series by Andrei Livadny:**
The Crystal Sphere
The Curse of Rion Castle
The Reapers

***The Way of the Shaman* LitRPG series by Vasily Mahanenko:**
Survival Quest
The Kartoss Gambit
The Secret of the Dark Forest
The Phantom Castle
The Karmadont Chess Set
Shaman's Revenge
Clans War
The Hour of Pain (a bonus short story)

***Galactogon* LitRPG series by Vasily Mahanenko:**
Start the Game!

***Phantom Server* LitRPG series by Andrei Livadny:**
Edge of Reality
The Outlaw
Black Sun

***Perimeter Defense* LitRPG series by Michael Atamanov:**
Sector Eight
Beyond Death
New Contract
A Game with No Rules

***Mirror World* LitRPG series by Alexey Osadchuk:**
Project Daily Grind
The Citadel
The Way of the Outcast
The Twilight Obelisk

***AlterGame* LitRPG series by Andrew Novak:**
The First Player
On the Lost Continent
God Mode

***The Expansion (The History of the Galaxy)* series by A. Livadny:**
Blind Punch
The Shadow of Earth

***Citadel World* series by Kir Lukovkin:**
The URANUS Code
The Secret of Atlantis

***The Game Master* series by A. Bobl and A. Levitsky:**
The Lag

***The Sublime Electricity* series by Pavel Kornev**
The Illustrious
The Heartless
The Fallen
The Dormant
Leopold Orso and the Case of the Bloody Tree

***Point Apocalypse* by Alex Bobl**
(a near-future action thriller)

***You're in Game!* (LitRPG Stories from Bestselling Authors)**

***The Naked Demon* by Sherrie L.**
(a paranormal romance)

More books and series are coming out soon!

In order to have new books of the series translated faster, we need your help and support! Please consider leaving a review or spread the word by recommending *Moskau* to your friends and posting the link on social media. The more people buy the book, the sooner we'll be able to make new translations available. Thank you!

Till next time!

www.ingramcontent.com/pod-product-compliance
Lightning Source LLC
Chambersburg PA
CBHW071640260626
47170CB00001B/171

* 9 7 8 8 0 8 8 2 3 1 7 1 4 *